THE MAN IN THE STREET

Also by Martin Howe

White Linen

About the Author

Martin Howe is a journalist who has worked for the BBC, Channel 4 and a news agency in Washington DC. Writing literary fiction is his escape from the constraints of factual news. The Man in the Street is his second novel.

mbhowe.com
Facebook.com/MartinHoweAuthor
Twitter: @_MartinHowe
Instagram: @martin.howe.925

THE MAN IN THE STREET

MARTIN HOWE

Copyright © 2019 Martin Howe

The moral right of the author has been asserted.

Apart from any fair dealing for the purposes of research or private study, or criticism or review, as permitted under the Copyright, Designs and Patents Act 1988, this publication may only be reproduced, stored or transmitted, in any form or by any means, with the prior permission in writing of the publishers, or in the case of reprographic reproduction in accordance with the terms of licences issued by the Copyright Licensing Agency. Enquiries concerning reproduction outside those terms should be sent to the publishers.

Matador
9 Priory Business Park,
Wistow Road, Kibworth Beauchamp,
Leicestershire. LE8 0RX
Tel: 0116 279 2299
Email: books@troubador.co.uk
Web: www.troubador.co.uk/matador
Twitter: @matadorbooks

ISBN 978 1789018 165

British Library Cataloguing in Publication Data.
A catalogue record for this book is available from the British Library.

Printed and bound in Great Britain by 4edge Limited
Typeset in 11pt Minion Pro by Troubador Publishing Ltd, Leicester, UK

Matador is an imprint of Troubador Publishing Ltd

In memory of my sister Jane

1959-2019

"SWIFTLY THE DAY ADVANCES."

* * * *

I had waited long enough.
I turned to Fascism.
Why?
Because, although democracy appeals to me, it has proved itself in practice, a perpetuated lie.
Because I am sick of muddling through.
Because I am tired of drifting along in the wake of garrulous statesmen.
Because I want to be positive rather than negative.
Because I realize that England is being left behind in the race for supremacy in a New Era.
Because I see no need for some 900,000 men, women and children to starve in a civilized country.
Because I want to be a citizen of an A.1 nation.
Because the Old Gang have failed disastrously.
Because I must bow to the demands of the Future.
Because I cannot help myself.

* * * *

I am the Man in the Street.

The Blackshirt, No. 26. Oct 21st-Oct 27th, 1933

Chapter 1

THREE FUNERALS – ALMOST

"This is the life, a proper funeral – it's all cremations these days – the church ceremony a flight of fancy, the interment a grounding in nature, the rites a time to grieve. If you want to, that is."

It was bitterly cold. David hoped he wasn't smiling. Some of the mourners looked distressed – they must be the family; but most – those he knew from work – appeared dutiful. The detective sergeant and his two constables standing conspicuously under the large oak nearby didn't leaven the atmosphere – even if they were out of uniform – reminding people, as they did, why they were there. The police officers had interviewed almost everyone here, some on more than one occasion, and David wondered why they had bothered to turn up. He gazed listlessly over the heads of the bereaved – there was scarcely a cloud in the sky. Something was concerning him and it was a surprise when he grasped what it was. He did want to grieve along with the others he realized, not for the deceased like they were, but for his own loss of virtue. He had changed.

An insatiable curiosity about the dead man had brought David early to the village, prowling the sleepy winding streets as the locals gradually emerged, their progress marked by cheery greetings on the briskness of the morning, on the chances of a flurry of snow. He had climbed the steep tree-lined incline to the late-Saxon parish church his mind vivid with images of his late employer and had been startled by the bent figure of the verger, who appeared suddenly in front of him in the road. The old man had just finished sluicing out the church's eleventh century thatched porch, steam still rising from the sodden flagstones, and was preparing to sweep up the leaves and other rubbish that had gathered beneath the timbered Wych Gate.

"It's always the same," he had complained to David as he leaned on his broom, "the vicar's given up and the police do nothing. There's no local bobby like there used to be. I'm left to clean up the mess." He'd pointed over to the gable end of St Peter's, "Look at the graffiti. On a church, for God's sake. It never used to happen. When I was a lad the locals would have given the layabouts a good hiding."

The stonework to the right of the ornate doorway, bordered with the sculpted heads of the twelve disciples, was covered in a host of elaborate tags and slogans, executed mainly in black spray paint. Slashes of colour adorned crude re-workings of the name "Bozo". Pink acrylic spelled out declarations of love, of who had had who, or who wanted to have who. There was a rash of "Kurts" around the edge of the free-form mural, the lettering fresh and distinct. Politics crept in here and there. "Thatcher is a cow" was daubed in large faded block capitals across the middle of the wall.

"You here for the funeral?" The verger asked. David nodded.

"You know we don't get many of them anymore, the place is full up. Today's lot go back years in the village. Got their own plot. Although I don't remember ever seeing what's his name … the one being buried today – certainly never in church. Lived in London didn't he?"

The churchyard wasn't large, but cluttered. Headstones were stacked, two-deep, against a new brick wall that separated the graves from the neatly trimmed gardens of three modern bungalows. David heard a baby crying as he wandered past searching for evidence of fresh excavation. The burial site should have been easy to find but it was in the corner hard against the wall, hidden by a large rectangular Victorian brick memorial topped with a heavy flagstone and overhung by the branches of a spreading Yew tree. The last resting place of the Beckinsale family had only just escaped being swallowed up in a recent parish property speculation boom.

"Lucky right to the end," thought David, "Bloody typical, Larry Beckinsale always got his own way, even in death. Anybody else and they'd have been scattering their ashes over next door's herbaceous border."

The hole was covered with wooden boards and the dark earth piled against the neighbouring tomb was encrusted with frost. There was a dank smell. The rimy brickwork was icy to the touch as David steadied himself. He noticed it was not a Beckinsale that was buried there but an Emily Fitzwilliam, spinster of the parish, who died after a long illness at the age of eighty-five in 1868. The large capstone had been pushed off-centre and rocked slightly when nudged. David could peer inside. It was empty. Suddenly the friable soil began to shift beneath his feet and a fall of frozen earth clattered on wood. He jumped back to avoid pitching onto the planks. Unsettled he glanced round then went to sit on a pile of neatly stacked granite slabs that had once been a memorial-cross and wiped the mud from his shoes. Looking down the hill David could see over the roofs of the village to the mist-shrouded fields beyond. The sun was breaking through. A crisp, immaculate, light-drenched, winter day had been forecast and he knew that would help him get through the next few hours.

The funeral was almost over. Handfuls of heavy clay were about to shower down on the glistering coffin, breaking the observance spell. The mourners would start talking, moving away, many looking forward to a drink in front of a roaring fire. In the lull between the fading words of the vicar and the first patter of the smothering earth that would finally bury the bastard, David understood that he was glad to have come this far, to have given nothing away.

The grieving widow, the weeping daughter, the son who couldn't face coming to the church; there were always victims. David had never met any of them so why should he care? The only connection was that he'd worked with a relation of theirs and that didn't warrant making a special effort to offer his commiserations. His signature in the office condolences card was enough. He moved off and joined his work colleagues, Chris and Paul.

"Let's have a pint, this has been thirsty work," he said.

"Too bloody right, I'm fucking frozen."

"I shouldn't have come, I've already got a cold and this'll finish me off," Paul coughed into his open hands, then beat his chest.

"If you didn't, you'd be back at the top of the list of suspects. Mine's a lager. See you in a couple of minutes."

Chris waved as he disappeared into the crowd.

"Chris, it's your round," Paul shouted at the top of his voice, then sheepishly looked round as he remembered where he was, "He always does that, every sodding time, it really gets to me."

David shrugged.

"I mustn't get pissed, last time I was at a funeral I had one hell of a hangover."

○ ○ ○

It had been twenty-three years earlier and they were burying his grandfather, the Reverend Anthony Coxon-Dyet. That funeral had been different from Larry Beckinsale's in a number of ways, but there were also similarities. The icy weather then had been as raw. David could still remember his aching hands and numbed feet. His grief had been painful too, he'd felt mangled by a depth of feeling unfamiliar to him at that stage in his young life. He had cried when he'd first heard the news of his grandfather's death and he wept again as the rites were read. He had not been the only emotional one there that day. Whereas, at Larry's burial there had been few expressions of open grief among the mourners, more a stolid forbearance. His grandfather's death had also involved the police, but they were out of the picture by the time of the funeral. One, a sergeant, had shown up though – off duty – and it turned out he had been one of grandfather's "boys" years before.

"The whole business has devastated me," he had said, "who would have believed it?"

David certainly couldn't at the time. Years later he felt he had a better understanding, yet even then his revered ancestor lacked substance, his murky past revealing only glimpses of his true self, the body of his motivation shaded by history.

In the end the "Controversy", as it was known, blew over – the Diocese finally compromised and agreed to hold a funeral service in St Botolph's before his grandfather's cremation at the local municipal crematorium – but still the journalists were there in droves. Parishioners packed the church and some of the congregation even spilled out into the cold.

The Bishop stood on the very spot where they had found the body and praised the "Good Christian."

"He was," he said, "a priest who had selflessly helped others. A man of firm beliefs and staunch principles. But," he went on, "it would be dishonest, on such an occasion, not to say that his strong views had often led him into conflict with me, his Bishop, and the wider church. However, he was always gracious when brought to book, and he accepted I had to do my duty."

The Bishop concluded his eulogy with banal platitudes, or so it had seemed to David, "This overflowing church is a testimony to the goodness of the man and to the purity of his mission. His death marks a great loss."

David couldn't cope with such idiocies and if he hadn't been enlisted as a pallbearer he'd have slipped away. Nobody brought up how his grandfather had died and there was no attempt to explain why. No talk of the unseemly clash over what should happen to his remains, only resolved by the last minute intervention of the Archbishop. Maybe, thought David, these people aren't here for the best of reasons. In the end, the organist played the hymn, "Abide with Me," David helped carry his grandfather out of the church to the waiting hearse. There was a two-minute silence and everyone went home. David had got very drunk.

○ ○ ○

The Reverend Anthony Coxon-Dyet, or plain Tony Cox as he was known then, had almost died years earlier. As his life turned out he chose his own time to bring it to an end and left others to dispose of his remains. It could so easily have happened the other way round.

He had just opened a bottle of beer. It was a glorious Indian summer day in late September. A warm breeze was disturbing the partially closed curtains in the living room, a haze of dust danced in the bright shaft of sunlight that spotted the floral wallpaper on the party wall. Outside it was quiescent and the house was empty. Eric was lying in the garden. Tony returned to work clutching his beer in a mood of intoxicated well-being that he had, in happier times, associated with languorous afternoons of endless cricket, sprawled in the green shade, surrounded by smiling, chattering girls.

He enjoyed tunnelling. The strenuous exercise kept him in shape and there was a wonderful sense of achievement, when he finished. He was also out of the way. Alone. You could have too much of people. Hours scraping away with a trowel, followed by a beer and a tepid bath lifted him for the rest of the day.

His basket full of damp earth, he rose without thinking.

"Bloody hell."

Tony's head hit a wooden beam. It moved. He dropped to his knees knocking against one of the new upright supports that he'd been meaning to nail in place. It shifted. He barely had time to touch his bleeding scalp, before his body was slammed forward. The collapsing roof winded him. He was trapped buried face down on the floor of the tunnel. He desperately sucked in air through clenched teeth as blood and soil trickled into the corners of his mouth. A naked bulb swayed in the subsiding draught, casting harsh light over the ripped sand and clay. Tony swore the earth was bleeding but it was beer seeping out of the overturned bottle. He waited – how long he didn't know – for hands to grasp his ankles and pull him free. They never came.

"Where is that bastard Eric?" he thought.

He would have liked to believe that as he passed out he was thinking of his wife, his young children, his friends. Maybe even the ironic newspaper headlines reporting his death, "Englishman dies tunnelling out of English prison camp"; "An Englishman's home is his tomb"; "The hidden secrets of number 13 Ballarat Road – an Englishman dies in a desperate bid to escape." But he was thinking of none of these things. All he could see was a woman's thighs, pale and creamy, as white as the milk spilling from an overturned churn in rhythmic waves across the red-tiled floor of a dairy.

Chapter 2

BLACK HOUSE

6th June 1934

Tony Cox sat in the public bar of the Duke of York and stared out through steamy, mirrored windows across the busy Kings Road to the building opposite. A grimy facade, colonnaded entrance, u-shaped gravel drive-way and tall sentinel plane trees surrounded by high black iron railings – it was much as he had been expecting. More run-down perhaps: the paintwork was peeling in places and the gates were hanging slightly askew, wedged open by heaped gravel and tufts of grass. Several windows were boarded up on the side close to the pavement on Cheltenham Terrace and the shutters were closed on the august double windows that overlooked the buses and cabs on the main road. He knew the building had been a teachers training college, but it no longer had the feel or look of an academic institution, maybe it never had, but to Tony it seemed like the hub of something important.

As he watched, a motorbike, belching exhaust, swerved into the drive, skidding slightly on the gravel. The rider dismounted and stood by his bike. Lifting his goggles he stared expectantly out into the crowds thronging the highway. Moments later the imposing black front doors swung open behind him and two men in dark uniforms strode out. They stood to attention at the top of the flight of steps that led up to the grand entrance. In the hallway shadowy figures flitted back and forth. Tony glanced away, took a sip of his beer, and looked back. Nothing. The rider had taken a couple of steps across the courtyard and was shaking his head and shouting up at a suited man who had appeared between the two guards.

"This is a delicious pint." Tony thought. "I'll have another if Eric doesn't get here soon. Who'd have thought it, the bloody Smoke, aren't I the lucky one?"

There was a burst of laughter and somebody was clapping. A young man was on his knees at the far end of the bar clutching a table.

"Five pints and nothing to eat; your wife will have your guts for garters," the barman was shaking his head, "who's going to clean up that mess?"

"And he's thrown-up on his trousers. I always told him he doesn't know when to stop", said another man with a wide-eyed grin. He was the one slowly applauding.

Across the road a large black car – a Humber – had drawn up. One of the guards hurried down to open the rear door. A man in an immaculate black military-style uniform got out and sprinted up the steps, brushing past the group waiting to greet him. His aide carrying a large attaché case under one arm and a bundle of legal papers bound with red ribbon under the other, lagged behind. As the car door slammed shut he placed the case and documents on the bonnet and stretched stiffly before running a hand through his hair. On the portico above the entrance a dark flag stirred in the gusts of warm air that wafted across from the nearby parade ground of the Duke of York's barracks, lifting whirlpools of dust and ruffling the leaves of the plane trees.

Tony was convinced he knew the man with the case; he had met him in Manchester. Eric had introduced them he was sure. While the tall distinguished man in the uniform could have been the leader of their party. It certainly looked like him from behind but then he'd only caught a fleeting glimpse. The one other time he had seen Oswald Mosley was on stage in the spotlight, making a speech. He was sure he'd be luckier in the next few days, being this close to the very top. He had made the right decision to come South.

A double-decker bus pulled up outside blocking the view and casting a shadow throughout the bar. Passengers hurried down the stairs. It looked like they were getting off to come into the pub and a couple of them did, letting in through the open door a babble of voices and the noisy bustle of the street. The conductor shouted "there's plenty of room on top," as he swung himself back onto the platform at the back of the bus and rang the bell.

Politics and pints or pints and politics, Tony was unsure in what order they came in his life, but they had given him purpose and he was glad. For once he believed he was happy. Tony smiled smugly to himself. He rolled a cigarette and spat the loose strands of tobacco into the ashtray next to him on the table. It took him a couple of attempts to clear the fragments from his lips and his mood jarred.

"Bugger."

Discomposure made him nervous and there was a moment of doubt. He could have come down for the march like the rest of them and have caught the night train back to Blackpool after the rally. But Eric, he felt, was a good friend. He would look after him, see him right, introduce him to people who could make a difference. Tony didn't see himself as overly ambitious, but knew this was an opportunity, maybe his only chance, to do something with his life. It had fallen into his lap. He hadn't gone out looking for it. Wouldn't have known how. It didn't run in the family to push yourself forward. Now he believed he was at the centre of a vital political movement. Or close at least. The beating heart, he knew, was in that building across the road.

The Black House had taken over his life in recent months. Orders and directives arrived almost every week at his home in Blackpool. Party business made increasing demands on him. He was busy most evenings and his parents were pleased at the direction he was taking. He was emerging from his shell, making friends, and receiving important-looking letters and packages from London. It was such a difference from before, when he'd spent his time moping round the house, sleeping late, drinking too much and making no effort. His whole family was glad things were looking up for him. His parents and brother had even come along to a couple of local Party rallies. His mother had been impressed, he could see that, even though she didn't say much. His father though, hadn't been convinced and Tony sensed he'd stay away in future – he'd not ask too many questions, would keep his head down, anything for a quiet life. But Brian was different, he appeared convinced by the arguments and was his first recruit to the Party. Tony was proud of that achievement, even though Brian was his younger brother and other members had laughed at him when this simple truth had come out during a meeting. One new recruit was more than most of them had managed and he now had many more to his credit. Such things mattered, they were noticed he was sure.

Now he was across from the Black House, making his first visit to the capital. He was in his early twenties and was going somewhere. His father had only ever been to London twice. The first time on the way to France and he had spent the day seeing the sights – Trafalgar Square, Buckingham Palace, the Houses of Parliament. The second time he couldn't have seen anything even if he'd wanted too, a gas attack in the trenches had blinded him. He had spent ten days in Charing Cross hospital on his way back from Ypres, before being sent to sit out the war in a minor stately home on a cliff top in South Wales. His sight was eventually restored, but it was not good enough for him to return to his accountancy job at "Cox and Sons", a local food wholesalers run by his uncle. The firm had looked after him – everybody agreed about that – and given him work behind the counter at one of their general stores on Greenborough Road, just round the corner from where he lived in Blackpool. His father always said, "Many others who served alongside me didn't do as well. I've been lucky."

Tony hated to hear him speak in that way. What he said was true, he supposed, but it was so complacent, so accepting of the state of things. His dad was easily the equal of his uncle, who had stayed at home – "to keep the grocery business going" – while his father had volunteered and been shipped off to France. It rankled that his father never saw it as unfair the way his life had worked out and it angered Tony that whenever he tried to tell him so, the conversation would inevitably turn into a tirade by his father against his own failings. Tony had enjoyed school and done well in his exams, but since leaving several years ago he hadn't achieved a great deal. Any number of odd jobs for "Cox and Sons", but he had no desire to work there all his life, and they'd never offered him anything permanent. Tony often thought, "one Cox hanger-on was probably enough for them."

There had been offers of apprenticeships – people felt sorry for his father and what the family had been through. One in particular making bleach had led to Tony's first serious row with his parents. It was a small firm and the job had prospects. Showing willing he had looked round the premises, but the air was foul and the smell of the chemicals overpowering and he'd turned it down, saying he wasn't any good with his hands.

"You're a waster, a total waster", his father had shouted at him getting slowly to his feet, clutching the arm of his chair, positioned as always perilously close to the fire. He never quite looked at his son, or so it seemed, but slightly to the left and above his head. It helped somehow, Tony thought, as it appeared he wasn't really talking to you.

"Do you think we can go on paying for ever, feeding and clothing you, putting a roof over your head. Isn't that the case mother? You need to think again my lad. I'd been out and got some qualifications and was earning a living by your age."

He slumped into his chair and stared into the flames. It was early evening and there was a blazing, sickly sunset. The lights were not yet on and the room was bathed in a lurid pink aura. His mother was correct when she said "You're not listening are you Tony? You're miles away as usual, but your father's dead right, you've got to do something. We won't throw you out on your ear. Dad wants to, you know, but over my dead body, I tell him. You've got to do something."

Tony had no idea what that might be. He had retreated to "The White", taken the edge off his frustration with a few pints and set himself up for a long hike along the seafront to Fleetwood and back as he'd done on many occasions before. It had been about this time, maybe even that same evening, as he walked looking at the sea, watching the distant breakers across the vast moon-steeped expanse of sand, that he had first felt the need to talk to someone. On a quiet night you could hear the faint whisper of the waves, but at this season of the year natural sounds were crowded out by the hordes of holidaymakers swarming along the promenade, shouting and laughing over the ringing clatter of trams. Their raucousness was hard to ignore, yet in his solitude all Tony could hear was the rushing tide.

He went to church almost every week. It kept his mother happy and he found it a structured distraction from the randomness of his days. The Reverend James Evans was a Blackpool FC supporter, like Tony, had even had a trial period as an apprentice with the club when he was young. Had broken his toe in one of the practice matches and never regained his form, or so he said. This was all they talked about during their first "little chat." His mother had suggested it.

"If you can't talk to your father, how about the vicar? He's not that much older than you. Go and see him, love. It can't do any harm."

He hadn't of course. The vicar came to him. It was the day of the local derby with Preston North End. Blackpool had won two-one. Tony was distracted and happy – he'd enjoyed the match – and was leaving the stands at Bloomfield Road, already in "The Rose", in mind if not body, when he felt a tap on the shoulder.

"What a match. Jimmy Hampson is truly one of the greats."

The Reverend Evans was elated, his cheeks glowing red. He looked to Tony as if he had been out on the pitch himself for the ninety minutes. He couldn't help smiling.

"The closest thing Blackpool has ever come to having its own saint," Tony said. Quickly adding, "so they say."

James Evans laughed.

"I'll have to see what I can do. It would certainly boost the attendances down at St Michael's."

Then almost to himself he chuckled.

"The two Jimmy's playing a blinder for Jesus."

Then to Tony.

"Don't tell your mother I said that, or anyone else I know for that matter. Your mother said you wouldn't mind a chat. I'm off to Marco's for a coffee, do you want to come? I treat myself on a Saturday you know."

They'd met a few times after that, once in "The White", saloon bar of course, but Tony had been impressed by the sincerity of the man. They had talked about football, fishing, his parents and, of course, what he was going to do in the future had come up. But the Reverend Evans was good at his job and Tony hadn't minded in the least, hadn't felt the ache in the temples, the tension in the stomach that he usually did when his family mentioned the subject. He hadn't even laughed when the vicar had casually introduced the idea of joining the church.

"How about it? It's not as ridiculous as it sounds."

Tony had listened.

"Why not?" was his initial reaction. They'd talked a little about the practicalities. James had contacted a friend at his old college and sounded him out. Things would probably have gone further if Tony hadn't stumbled across a different path.

Eric Baines was an inspiration and, Tony believed, his friend. He'd met him recently in Manchester. In two hours in the "Castle Arms" Eric changed his life. Tony, for the first time, saw a future for himself and began to believe he could achieve something worthwhile. He described it as his "blinding light on the road to Damascus." His mother said he was a "daft bugger" every time he mentioned it; his father, who had given up going to church years before, said he should stop talking nonsense and that he would get the vicar to make him see sense. Meeting Eric had been the most exciting night of his life.

Blackpool Central to Manchester Piccadilly by train took a little over an hour. Tony occasionally made the journey at weekends. It got him away from his parents. He stayed overnight with Uncle Alf and Aunt Enid in a small flat above their fish and chip shop in Droylsden. He used to come home smelling of beer, cigarettes and lard and was always packed off to the baths on Monday morning. His mother pushing him out of the house with the words, "I don't know how Enid stands it, she always used to be so tidy when she was young."

Alf was still a Blackpool fan, even after living away for thirty years, and Tony always visited him when the "Seasiders" played either Manchester City or United. In the evening after the match they sometimes went to a lecture or concert at the Free Trade Hall, but more often he accompanied his uncle to Stonybrook Workingman's club. Alf said it was an excuse to get out, Enid said he was a "lazy old sod," disappearing on the busiest evening of the week. Tony was not sure if she liked him visiting, but she never said anything.

Uncle and nephew got on well, could talk about anything, and enjoyed their time together. Tony was treated like the son Alf never had and always felt a twinge of guilt when he told his father what they'd been up to. The two men couldn't have been more different: his father tall, gaunt-featured, solitary much of the time, uncommunicative and depressed; his uncle short, stocky, a round cheerful, smiling face and never one to hold back with his opinions. So Tony was not surprised when one weekend in March Alf said, "How about coming to a political meeting with me? You might enjoy it and you'll certainly learn something. It'll last a couple of hours that's all."

Tony had rarely heard Alf talk in detail about politics and he'd never suggested going to a meeting before. It was true he'd recently started occasionally mentioning the New Party over a pint. "Their policies made a lot of sense," he reckoned, "Understood the small businessman while Labour had missed that golden opportunity. Mosley was a clever man and one hell of a speaker he'd heard." But Tony had thought nothing of it, having no particular interest himself. He supposed he was a Labour supporter like his whole family.

"Action! Action here and now! That's their slogan. And about bloody time, something needs doing," Alf, to Tony's surprise, gripped his arm as he spoke.

"They didn't do too badly for a new party in Ashton last election. Held on to their deposit and shook things up a bit," he went on. His uncle rarely got this animated about anything other than football and the price of fish and potatoes.

"Mosley really caused a stir here in Manchester the last time he came. I wish I'd gone along. Come on, Tony, a bright boy like you should get something out of it. I'd like to know what you think." He smiled, "There's always a lively crowd when he speaks and there's been quite a lot about him in the paper. We could have a couple of pints before we go in, then pie and chips on the way home. It would be a good night out. Go on."

It was a cold evening. Tony had thought so when they were waiting for the bus, watching cigarette smoke mingle with the misting breath of the crowd huddling in the shelter. He knew so as they walked up Windmill Street to the Free Trade Hall. He should have worn his thick overcoat and brought his gloves, but it was too late now. Smiling he remembered his mother's last words to him as he had left that morning. "You daft lump take your coat. You'll catch your death. It's mid-March. It's still winter. You've no sense, never have had." Waving he'd ignored her and she had stood wiping her hands on her apron, watching him walk down the street until he disappeared round the corner.

There were at least a hundred people jostling to get in when they arrived at the main entrance to the Hall. They weren't late and it looked as if it was going to be a full house. There were policemen standing in groups of two and three outside the building and on the pavement on the opposite side of the road. Several others were trying to stop the crowd from pushing against a barrier that had been erected at the bottom of the flight of steps leading up to the foyer. Individuals were being allowed to pass along in single file. Tony caught a glimpse of two tall men in distinctive black uniforms ushering people through the swing doors. They joined what they thought was the end of the queue and moved slowly forward.

Uncle Alf said there had been talk of an earlier march across the centre of town in military formation. He would have liked to have taken part, but they couldn't have left the shop any earlier than they did and so would have to make do with the speeches. Tony was disappointed as he enjoyed army parades. He had once thought of joining up, but his father had, not surprisingly, been against it. Or rather, his opposition had been a surprise, given how much he claimed he wanted Tony out the house doing something worthwhile. Enlisting would have been a perfect way to annoy his father even more, but Tony had never got round to it.

They had made it through the doors and out of the cold, when the garrulous man in front of them was stopped and one of the officials in black started going through his pockets. He did not object but continued singing softly under his breath and swaying gently from side to side. Tony was not surprised when two bottles of stout were discovered deep in the lining of his heavy overcoat.

"You can't take these in there sunshine. There's no drinking inside and more's the point there's no weapons allowed."

Both the security men laughed as a couple more in identical black uniforms joined them from the stairs off to the right. The drunk lurched to one side and tried to push his way past, calling out, "Let me go. I'll lose track of my mates. Hold up there Stan."

He waved to a couple up ahead who were waiting on the stairway and turned round. It was over in a second. His outstretched arm was twisted behind his back, the other was grasped by the wrist and elbow and he was bodily lifted off the ground and carried out through a side door, the toes of his black hobnail boots bouncing rhythmically across the dark red carpet. The door swung backwards and forwards, then shimmered to a halt. The silence held for a second. Tony and Alf were impressed by the slick efficiency of the bouncers.

"I'm sorry lads, we can't be too careful. Let his sort in and who knows what will happen. If you don't mind."

Tony raised his arms, thinking there was no need for an apology. The search over, he stepped forward into the ornate foyer and waited for Alf. A young man handed him a flyer.

"Read this mate, it'll interest you. Tells you why this Government's selling us out here in Lancashire. And what can be done to get our people back to work. Most important is what you can do about it."

Tony murmured, "Thanks."

As they passed through the narrow passageway into the stalls he crumpled the leaflet and pushed it into his pocket. A babble of voices enveloped them. The auditorium was over half full and there were a good number of people behind them waiting to get in. They moved down towards the stage. Tony glanced up into the circle and saw black-shirted stewards standing at regular intervals along the front of the balcony. Behind them he could see people slipping into their seats and thought, "A popular man, this Mosley". With some surprise he also noticed that many of the rows were occupied by men and women in formal evening wear. One of them, a blond-haired man, his long white scarf trailing, was leaning out precariously over the edge of the balcony, trying to read the large sign that hung below him. As Tony drew level he could read the words "Lancashire Awake" and almost called out, but he held back. On the opposite side of the hall a similar banner exhorted the audience to "Mind Britain's business."

Tony and Alf found two empty seats close to the central aisle in the middle of the concert hall. The house lights were up. It was chilly and most people had their overcoats on. The air was heavy with the smell of damp wool and mothballs. In the orchestra pit, hidden from view, a small string ensemble began playing Elgar's Pomp and Circumstance March number 3 in C minor. The music's pinched air of repressed solemnity imbued Tony's heightened sense of expectation with a feeling of invulnerability that made a profound and indelible impression on him. He would remember the moment as the true beginning of his quest.

The stage was bare except for a speaker's rostrum covered in a dark standard. A spotlight picked out a gold emblem comprised of an axe and a bound bundle of wooden sticks circled in black. The huge organ at the back of the stage was draped in a vast Union Jack, obscuring all but a couple of gleaming brass pipes that framed the flag.

The hall was filling up rapidly. As they stood to allow three young men in brown leather jackets to squeeze past them into empty seats further down their row, Alf nudged Tony.

"A couple of minutes to go. They'll start on time I know it."

It was almost seven-thirty according to the large clock on the rear wall of the hall.

"Something's happening already. Look, who are these people?"

Two columns of men in black collarless shirts and dark trousers, a few with medals on their chests, were marching slowly down the central aisle. Heads turned and the babble of voices dimmed. Tony noticed the orchestra had stopped playing and the space seemed darker. His excitement swelled, as it always did in anticipation of a performance – lights fading and the first images flickering on the screen – and he strained to see what was going on. The men in black had halted and were standing to attention almost shoulder to shoulder on both sides of the aisle. They had their backs to the audience blocking Tony's view. The Free Trade Hall had fallen silent. Now was the time, he felt it intensely, now was the moment for action. Tony held his breath.

Seconds passed, but nothing happened. He exhaled, the woman next to him coughed, across the hall, feet began shuffling. A few rows behind an old man stood up and took off his coat. "Sit down," someone snarled, but the man was looking through his pockets. He was irritated, "I need my glasses, give me a chance." One of the men in Tony's row, one of those in a leather jacket stood up and shouted, "Don't you…"

A fanfare drowned him out. Two spotlights flared from high above the stage. The audience turned in the direction of the main door. The men in uniform stiffened, coming to attention. Then with a slow deliberate action they as one raised their right arms thrusting their palms forward into the air in defiant salute. Down the aisle strode Oswald Mosley, leader of the British Union of Fascists. He was alone. Dressed like his followers in a black shirt, black trousers with a razor-sharp crease, highly polished black belt and boots, he wore no medals or badges. His dark heavily greased hair was combed straight back with no parting and he had a small neatly trimmed moustache.

Rigidly erect he strode unyielding down the aisle, resolutely ignoring his seated supporters – all they could clearly see was his distinctive profile as he passed in and out of sight between the serried heads of his honour-guard, eyes fixed firmly on the stage – his apparent disdain an appropriate adjunct to his undoubted sense of authority. Tony noticed he was receding slightly at the temples – an incongruous observation of imperfection in an otherwise flawless being that snared him as an interested observer and then reeled him in as a convert. A man of integrity, a brilliant leader of men and still only in his thirties, so Alf had told him, he certainly acted and looked the part. Tony was impressed with the powerful spectacle and the inveigling charisma of the leading man.

Across the hall, people were rising to their feet, some even saluting. There were scattered cheers. Mosley began to climb the steps at the side of the stage and the reserve of many in the audience gave way. There was shouting, wild applause and a scattering of banners and flags were unfurled. Swept up in the mounting euphoria Tony and Alf stood and clapped enthusiastically. It was only as Mosley approached the podium and the full glare of the spotlights that he acknowledged the crowd. He lifted his arm in a part salute-part wave and looked out across the hall. When he reached the elevated platform in the centre of the stage he stood to attention for several minutes as the cheering reverberated around him. Then raising both hands he brought the gathering to silence.

"Will you please sit down. My Lords, ladies and gentlemen. People of Lancashire…"

A photographer's flashbulb popped.

"I have come to warn you of a grave danger, to alert you to the risks faced by this great country of ours. We all must be on our guard. Wake up, you men of England! We must keep Britain for the British!"

There were a few scattered cheers. Mosley leant forward thrusting his face towards the audience, both hands resting on the sides of the lecturn.

"The key", he shouted, "is freedom of speech. There are thousands of you here tonight who have come to listen to the creed of Fascism. You have come to listen with an open mind and an open heart. But", he paused, "you are not alone. There are those who do not want to hear what I have to say, they are afraid of the message I have for the British People. Their sterile ideas are no match for the integrity and intellectual honesty of Fascism. I speak of the Reds, of the communists in retreat across Europe, in the face of the fascist onslaught. Their tactics of disruption and violence will not work here. Their terror squads will not deprive the British people of the freedom to hear and discuss ideas critical to their survival. Britain is at a crossroads, we must not take the wrong turning at the prompting of a movement built on tired and failed ideas. It has succeeded but once, and only once and that in the most backward corner of Europe."

Mosley stepped away from the dais, as his eyes swept the hall. He raised his arm and pointed to the central aisle. His tone of voice was conversational, almost intimate.

"You have all seen with your own eyes, the discipline and order of the Men of Fascism. I need, we all need, men of character, men of integrity who will stand up to protect the things that we value, the things that we hold dear, the things that generations of Britons have fought to achieve and defend. Top of that list is the freedom to speak one's mind without fear of interruption or retribution. I demand that right and I expect it to be honoured in a civilised society. To that end we have a Fascist Defence Force to protect the British way of doing things. Let no one, neighbour or friend, tell you otherwise. Let no one in the Old Gang government tell you it is a private army out to serve my personal ends, they are only interested in saving their own political fortunes, do not believe either the orgy of lies told by the Yellow Press. For the politicians and the newspapers are in league with each other. They are united by only one thing, the real fight of the old world for its existence against the forward march of Fascism. They are not interested in the truth."

As he spoke a number of spotlights played across the stage casting vast gesticulating shadows against the Union Jack backdrop. Crouching, springing forward, arms flung apart, finger jabbing impulsively into the air, a pace to the left then to the right. A careful orchestration of movement, composed to punctuate his speech, underline key words, and emphasize his main points. The timbre of his voice, the pitch of the words, the pace of delivery came together to create a symphony of seductive, honeyed meaning. His message was almost secondary, but was in accord with what many in the hall wanted to hear. Tony, when asked afterwards, couldn't recall much of what had been said. "He'll create employment by banning foreign goods," was the best he could do, "Safeguard Lancashire's cotton industry, keep out the alien menace who control financing of jobs, protect the small businessman, and crush the large chain stores." He supposed this had stuck in his mind, because when Mosley had just concluded his speech fulminating against the threat from foreign elements, and asked for any questions from the audience, the trouble had started.

Entranced by the persuasive rhetoric of the orator on stage Tony was oblivious to all else happening around him. People were laughing as Mosley tore into what he called, "the pink pansies of Bloomsbury who were sobbing away the Empire." The crowd was febrile, conflicting voices could be heard hijacking the narrative momentum of the speech and challenging its logical trajectory. Angry words were shouted out close by, there was a commotion to Tony's right, one of his neighbours hissed, "Be quiet, sit down, wait your turn." Tony paid no attention, straining to hear what was being said above the discordant growling background noises.

Again a man shouted, this time Mosley stopped speaking and scanned the crowd, looking in Tony's direction before carrying on seamlessly with his exhortations to action. The heckler was one of the men in the brown leather jackets seated in the same row as Tony. He was on his feet, gesticulating wildly. Tony was irritated, "Sit down, give him a chance to finish," he called. The man and his two companions turned and looked at him grim-faced. One raised a finger and pointed at Tony. A black-shirted steward at the end of the row had stood up and was waving to others at the back of the hall.

"Why do you blame the Jews for everything that is wrong with this country?" the leather-coated man shouted. "It's the aristocracy, the ruling classes and the capitalists that are to blame." There were cheers from people sitting nearby. "Blaming the Jews for everything is just an excuse. You're just a Jew-hater."

"Sit down now or we'll make you," the steward called out as he began edging his way along the row of seats. People stood to let him pass. He had been joined in the aisle by several other black-shirted men, who crowded behind him.

"See the true face of Fascist free speech," called out the heckler, "Long live the unity of the workers against Fascist terror. One question that's all I ask, just one question?"

His two companions were now standing and yelling in support.

"Fascist terror, Fascist terror, Fascist thugs!"

On stage Mosley was carrying on, raising his voice, splenetic, his words forceful, ignoring the interruptions. The steward was a couple of seats away from the hecklers.

"Sit down every bloody one of you or we'll put you out."

Two of his colleagues were edging their way down from the other end of the row. They had almost reached where Tony and Alf were sitting. People were muttering, coats slid to the floor and were trampled underfoot. Somebody muttered, "Oi watch my hat." The disruption spread. Heads were turning to see what was going on. A few members of the audience at the front of the hall were standing and looking back, trying to see if there was serious trouble. At the rear of the hall a policeman was peering round the heavy curtain draped across the main exit and watching intently. He had a whistle in his hand.

"I'd like to see you try, you lousy bastard."

The heckler screamed as he jumped onto his seat.

"Don't you call me a bastard, you red swine."

The steward drew a truncheon from his inside pocket and lunged forward. A woman screamed and clutched her head as she ducked down into the arms of her husband sitting beside her. The man in the leather jacket lashed out with his fist, missed, lost his balance and toppled backwards over the arm of his seat. His companion who was facing the opposite way, watching the approach of the flanking stewards, lost his footing and fell to his knees. His forehead caught the back of a chair and blood began to flow into his eyes. All around people were standing up, shouting. Some tried to scramble over the seats to escape. A steward managed to grab the foot of a heckler as he sprawled across the row. But a boot in the face sent him reeling backwards, clutching his nose.

Stewards converged from all sides. Tony and Alf were caught up in the melee. There was no escape.

"Out the way, mate", said a short stocky man as he tried to elbow his way past Alf, "Let me at 'em."

Tony could hear Mosley calling for order from the stage.

"Let's have no trouble, please behave yourselves."

Suddenly one of the hecklers leapt from his seat towards the encroaching stewards, screaming at the top of his voice. He landed on top of Tony, his elbow catching Alf on the side of his head. "Bugger me," was all Alf said, before slumping back. Tony felt a rib cracking as the arm of the seat dug painfully into his side. His hands clawed at the man's hair as he struggled to get to his feet. Pushing himself free, Tony leant back and punched the kneeling figure in the stomach, who groaning rolled over and slid into the gap between the rows of seats. Dazed the man tried to crawl forward to escape but was blocked by Alf's buckled legs. Tony, who was now on his feet, grabbed him again by the hair and hauled him into a squatting position. A truncheon blow across the face raised a squeal of pain and blood spurted from the man's broken nose. Alarmed, Tony let go as the steward rained blows onto the heckler's head. Glancing round, Tony saw a mass of flailing limbs as Blackshirts battled with protestors, dragging them struggling one by one into the central aisle. But the demonstrators were not alone, at the back of the hall more of their number had ripped up seats and were using them as clubs to repel a group of stewards, who were trying to force them out of one of the side exit doors. Three other men had made a dash for the stage, two of them had been caught on the steps and were being beaten in the full glare of one of the spotlights. The other made it on to the platform, where he stopped and faced Mosley who was standing with his arms folded in the centre of the stage. He hesitated, then dashed to the base of the organ and pulled down the large Union Jack, trampling it with his boots.

Tony heard a shrill whistling. The red curtain had been thrown back at the end of the hall and policemen were surging into the auditorium. As the house lights flickered on, Tony sensed the excitement ebbing away. Everything was calming down. The stewards next to him released his semi-conscious attacker, who they'd been trying to drag away and were retreating to the aisle. The injured man lay where he had fallen for a few seconds, wedged face down between two seats, groaning. He then began crawling slowly along the row, the few audience members remaining standing to let him pass. In the central aisle one of his companions was still struggling with three blackshirts. They were trying to force his arms behind his back and frog-march him from the building. A young policeman shouted at them to release him, his truncheon at the ready. They reluctantly obeyed.

The police were everywhere. The violence subsided. Tony saw one blackshirted steward being arrested. On the stage Oswald Mosley stood impassively, saying nothing, his arms crossed. A plainclothes policeman in a long brown overcoat, belted tightly at his waist and wearing a Homburg hat joined him. He paused, looked contemptuously at Mosley, before reaching round him and dragging the microphone across the dais in a loud burst of static that had everyone turning towards the stage. He said nothing as he caught his breath, relishing the moment. The officer was relieved it had come to this. He had no time for the Fascists, especially those led by an arrogant member of the aristocracy and defector from the Labour party like this character, he had no time for Tories either, and liberals, or men in uniform. Violence should be reserved for the ring, drinking was a tool of the devil and he should never have to work on the Sabbath. Only a few arrests tonight, he thought, and I should get away before midnight. I'll show them about freedom of speech, he smiled to himself and tapped the microphone.

"Your attention please, I'm Chief Inspector Jenkins of the City of Manchester police. There will be no more trouble here or I'll be obliged to close the meeting."

He cleared his throat and went on.

"Return to your seats, if anybody has been injured my officers will deal with them. Now, all members of the Fascists Union who are in uniform will line up and leave the hall, they will not gather outside, they will not march away together but disperse immediately."

He then grabbed Mosley by the arm and pulled him away from the table towards the back of the stage. After a brief animated discussion, he returned to the microphone and announced that, "Mr Mosley has told me he wants no more trouble, so I repeat will all Blackshirts leave the building!"

Pause.

"Now, if you do not leave the meeting will end. I'm sure most of you would not want that to happen."

The vast hall fell silent. Mosley had turned away from the audience and was looking into the wings. Nobody stirred. Tony was exhilarated at the thought of the Blackshirts taking on the police. He felt they had the strength to do it. But would they? He knew he would side with them if they did. Alf, he was certain, would be feeling the same way and turned seeking confirmation. His uncle was crumpled in his seat. "Alf, what's up?" he whispered and shook him gently. He was dribbling. For the first time Tony noticed the wound on the side of his head, where his hair was matted with blood that was oozing from a cut behind the ear. Tony felt sick.

"Oh my God, Alf," he shouted. "Somebody help me, my uncle's hurt."

One of the stewards heard him and started to edge along the row towards them. Across the floor of the stalls, members of the Fascist Defence Force got to their feet and began lining up in the aisles. Then, as if in response to some unspoken order, they began marching out of the hall. There were a few cheers and sporadic clapping. Then the chanting started. A group of men and women seated in the circle, and who had not been involved in the violence, began shouting "Down with Mosley, Down with the Fascists."

"Don't you worry about them," hissed the steward as he bent down to inspect the unconscious Alf. "We'll sort them out later. You get to know their faces after a while."

"This a friend of yours?"

"Uncle."

"Better get him some help. It's a nasty cut, the bastards. They're always at it, razors, coshes, I've seen the lot."

He placed his arms under Alf's, cradling his head against his chest.

"You take his legs."

"Leave him alone! You, I said leave him alone. We'll deal with it. Get out with the rest of your lot."

A policeman waved his truncheon in their direction. The steward hesitated and Tony could sense his fury.

"Do it now or you're in trouble."

"Here, my name's Eric, Eric Baines. Thanks for your help. I saw what you did. We could do with more of your sort in the movement."

He thrust a piece of paper into Tony's hands.

"I'll be there tomorrow at that address, come if you can, I'll buy you a drink."

With that he eased himself back along the row, apologizing as he went. When he reached the aisle he turned and called out.

"Hope your uncle isn't too badly hurt."

As Eric sauntered defiantly out of the hall, Tony could hear the fragmented taunting words of the "Red Flag" drifting down from the balcony.

Two policemen helped carry Alf into the foyer, where a doctor was bandaging one of the protestor's heads. As they left Mosley was speaking again, trying to lift the audience, haranguing them with a tirade against the "Red Threat… loyalty to no flag but the hammer and sickle…Red rowdies… threatening the freedom of the men of Britain with bludgeons and razors … see what we have to put up with."

It was a difficult task even for a politician as experienced as Oswald Mosley. His rhetorical spell had been broken, the impression of invincibility tarnished.

The jeering continued.

"Down with Mosley. He's a foreign stooge, smash the Fascist terror."

A smattering of people from all corners of the hall were joining in the singing of the Red Flag. The audience began to drift away, the police were everywhere, but they did nothing to halt the barracking and there was the threat of renewed violence.

Alf regained consciousness lying on the floor of the crowded foyer, Tony shielding his body from the hurrying crowd. They cleaned up his cut and when he was steady enough to walk took him to the manager's office and gave him a cup of tea. He said he couldn't remember a thing when the Chief Inspector asked him if he knew who was responsible. Tony said, "It all happened so fast and I was looking at the stage when it happened."

It was after midnight when they were driven back to Droylsden in the Inspector's car.

"If you remember anything, you know how to get hold of me."

The policeman hesitated for a second observing the two men, leaning one against the other and shuffling towards the front entrance of the chip shop, before slamming the car door and heading home.

"It had been worth putting a bit of pressure on those two. They didn't look like hardcore activists and they might have told him something. Ah well! It would have to be another day that he got one of those bloody Blackshirts up in court."

Enid was not surprised that Alf didn't get up early that morning, she assumed that he had been drinking and left him alone in the spare room to sleep it off. She tolerated that on a Saturday night, but gave her husband hell if it happened at any other time. She was taken aback, however, to find Tony up, the fire set in the kitchen and a pot of tea already on the go.

"It's not like you to be down this early, mind you", glancing at the stove, "I'm not complaining. You can come again." Laughing she said "I won't tell your mother as she'd never believe me anyhow."

Tony smiled, his pale face bloated and eyes leaden. He was euphoric despite the damp, lowering dullness of the day, which normally would have darkened his mood. He'd lain awake for most of the night mulling over the evening's savage events. It had been a wild adventure, one he'd found inspiring. A single event in his life came close to replicating the feelings he'd experienced at the Free Trade Hall and that was the recent fifth round FA cup-tie between Sunderland and Blackpool. And even that hadn't matched the elation he now felt because Blackpool had lost in the final minutes of the game. Alf's injuries only quickened his sense of gratification. His uncle wasn't badly hurt and it had been his idea to go to the rally in the first place.

"Uncle Alf was in a fight. Got knocked out."

"You what? Why didn't someone tell me?"

"He's alright, he got hit over the head, but nothing too serious."

Enid was about to get up and go back upstairs.

"Don't worry. A doctor saw to him and said all he needed was to rest. We got a lift home."

"What happened? It's not like Alf to go getting into trouble. He's a soft old sod at heart. Only time he got in a fight, over football or something, he lost his front teeth. What did he do, swear at a City fan?"

"No, no. We were at the Trade Hall for a political rally. There were speeches and some trouble started. Yobs started shouting. Communists I think. Wouldn't let Oswald Mosley finish speaking. They started laying into people who were asking them to leave. We got swept up in it. Uncle Alf caught a punch. I didn't notice till afterwards. We were just trying to keep out of the way."

Enid snorted and almost choked on her tea.

"Huh, typical."

She leant forward and studied Tony for the first time.

"You don't look too good yourself. Did you get hit?"

"No, I'm fine. Didn't sleep too well that's all."

"Is that right?"

Shaking her head she reached up to a peg on the back of the scullery door and took down a pale-blue check work coat, which she buttoned up absent-mindedly as she moved slowly around the kitchen table to the sink.

"Serves him right really, he's mad keen on those Blackshirts. Thinks Mosley is some kind of Saviour. But he knows they're a violent lot. Only last week he was reading out loud to me, from that paper of their's, about the trouble that follows him everywhere he goes. He thought it showed the Party was on the right track. Getting up people's noses as he called it."

Tony was surprised.

"He's a sly one Uncle Alf. I had no idea. Bet you he's joined them hasn't he?"

"Been a member for a while now. Sells the paper every free moment he has. Tried to sell it in the shop till we had a bit of bother with some Labour lads who live in Sedgemoor Road. Keeps them hidden away now, until he can go out in force, case he runs into them again."

"Has he got the full uniform? A Blackshirt?"

"No. He keeps going on about it though. I'm not keen. My old dad was solid Labour. He wouldn't have been happy. I don't know what to think. Keep your head down I reckon. You've got to stay well in with your neighbours in our line of business, don't you? I mean there's a good many other places to get your chips and fish round here. Enzoni's are only too keen to take any new customers they can, what with them selling ice cream as well. But, Alf swears Mosley's the man for the small businessman, like us. Has our interests at heart, he reckons."

"Spoke a lot of sense yesterday. You know about the need to look after your own and that. I can see why people follow him. What's Labour ever done for the man in the street? Look at me, never had a proper job. All I've ever done is serving the trippers for the odd week here and there."

"I know love, I know. Was Alf trying to talk you into joining? He says loads have followed his example round here. He thinks as he was one of the first in, he will get a promotion soon. He's got high hopes at the moment, as we just heard that the Party's head man here in Manchester was locked up down in London for thieving only the other week."

"What's that?"

"Didn't Alf say? Not like him. What I heard was he was in one of those fancy shops near the party headquarters and was caught shoplifting. A watch I think. Caused a bit of a stir. It was said he gave Mosley's name to the police. Didn't make him popular. Be surprised if he turns up round here again in a hurry. Know his mother, she works in the Co-op on Heckie Street. He was always a tearaway, always in bother when he was young. Alf's latched on to that right enough, keeps going on "there's always the odd bad apple, doesn't mean the whole crops rotten." I dunno, really makes me wonder when someone like that gets to be so high up and important. Can't have been more than twenty two, twenty three."

Shaking her head slowly she began filling a small pan with water.

"Boiled egg?"

"Er, yes please," Tony called out, "Uncle Alf's probably right, you can't check everyone, and anyway he may not have done it. The police really have it in for the Blackshirts you know – saw that yesterday – they may have fitted him up. Wouldn't put it past them."

Tony watched Enid slice the bread. It was getting light outside. He could clearly see a black cat crossing the roof of the shed at the end of the small cobbled yard where Alf stored his potatoes. A boy was yelling in the alley and Tony heard the sound of a bottle smashing, followed by a laugh. Sparrows were squabbling over a piece of bacon rind on the peeling black guttering outside.

"No, he hasn't," he said almost to himself.

"Sorry love, missed that. What did you say?"

"Oh, nothing. I was just thinking that Uncle Alf didn't say anything to me about joining up. Didn't say anything at all about that."

He looked round for his jacket. It was hanging over the

back of one of the chairs. His right sleeve above the elbow was spattered with dark matted patches of dried blood.

"Damn it, it must be Alf's."

The flyer from the night before was still crumpled in his pocket.

"What was that bloke's name?" he thought to himself as he smoothed it flat and read aloud.

"Britain First. The leader of the British Union of Fascists, Sir Oswald Mosley, speaks at the Manchester Free Trade Hall on "Fascism and the future of Great Britain". March 12th 1933. Doors open 7 pm. Speeches at 8pm. All seats in the stalls are free to members of the public. Special reserved seats in the balcony for subscribers. Join the British Union of Fascists today. Apply for membership, in person or by post, at the BUF headquarters – Deansgate House, 274 Deansgate, Manchester. Read "The Blackshirt", one penny, weekly."

Without hesitation he turned to Enid.

"I might just do that Auntie, before I go back home. I might just sign up."

And he had. Deansgate House was easy to find. There had been three policemen in the street outside and two uniformed members of the BUF Defence Force checking people at the door. Tony had not been alone. He'd had to remain in the entrance hall for nearly half an hour before being allowed into the waiting room, which held about twenty people. He had to stand. He didn't recognize anybody, not that he had expected to. There was only one woman and she seemed to be with her husband, who appeared to be in his forties. He was the only one wearing medals. Everybody else was much younger, early twenties, most of them. All were smartly dressed in suits and ties, a number had flowers in their buttonholes. The walls were covered in posters – larger versions of the flyer he had been given advertising the previous day's rally at the Free Trade Hall, others giving details of Oswald Mosley's meetings around the country. A banner – "Fascism, King, Empire" – was pinned above the doorway into the adjoining room. A series of pictures of a gesticulating Mosley making a speech in front of a large crowd were hanging along one of the walls under the slogan: "There is but one aim, one method and one leader." A small table in the centre of the room was piled high with the latest edition of "The Blackshirt." Almost all those waiting were reading a copy. Tony picked one up and leafed slowly through the pages.

They were moving people through quickly and Tony soon had a seat. It was next to a large scuffed brown radiator. Initially he relished the warmth but rapidly began to overheat. Perspiring he was too embarrassed to take off his jacket or loosen his tie. Beads of sweat trickled the length of his back and made him shift uneasily. He fanned himself with his copy of the Blackshirt, but stopped when his neighbour looked at him strangely.

"I'm not feeling too well. I'll come back another day," he muttered, smiling weakly. He wiped his brow with the back of his hand and stood to leave.

Revived by the chill air in the entrance hall, he raised the collar of his jacket and promised himself he would come back the next time he was in town.

Outside, Eric Baines was getting out of a specially adapted black Austin Light Twelve-six, used by senior Party members to travel round the country to meetings, when he spotted Tony coming down the steps of Deansgate House.

"You took my advice then, good. If you can hang on for a few minutes we can pop across the road for a drink if you've got the time."

He held out his hand.

"How's your Uncle? Got a sore head I bet. We've a good idea who attacked him. We'll meet him again sometime soon, don't you worry."

Tony shook his hand and tried to remember his name.

"He's not too bad, he's sitting up in bed making the most of all the attention."

"Good, glad to hear it. He looked like a game old bird."

Eric nodded at the building behind them.

"I hope you signed up for Division Two in there? As I told you yesterday we need all the good people we can get up here. They're planning a big recruitment drive in the next few months, should keep you busy. Anyway can you hang on?"

Tony flushed slightly.

"I don't think…I haven't actually um … I'm in a hurry and there were lots of people ahead of me. So I'll come back some other time. I'm over in Manchester about once a month or so."

Eric laughed.

"It's always like this after a rally. Everybody keen to join up. Look, come with me, I'll fix it."

With that he strode up the steps, hurried past the guards and disappeared through a side door. Tony reluctantly followed and stood in the hallway feeling awkward. The door opened and Eric beckoned him over.

"My old mate Les will see you now. What are friends for, eh?"

The room was much smaller than Tony had been expecting. Les was sitting at a narrow table set against the far wall beneath a map of Britain showing party membership by county in scrawled red ink. At a glance London and Lancashire looked to be doing well. Two other men were in the room, one in uniform, the other in a black suit.

"They're the witnesses," Les said, "This is Archie Payne, he's the local treasurer, he'll be chasing you for your subs."

"Pleased you decided to sign up," said Archie, "any friend of Eric's is welcome. He says you were at the meeting yesterday and had a spot of bother. Start as you mean to go on eh?"

Everybody laughed, even Tony.

"I got off lightly. It was my uncle Alf who felt the worst of it. Maybe you know him Alf Sawyer?"

"Alf? Know him well. Runs a good little chippie. Not known him go looking for trouble in the past though. Thought he was a bit long in the tooth for the rough stuff? Well, the old dark horse. This'll do his standing no end of good. Wait till the lads hear about it."

Archie looked pleased. Tony thought there must be a bit of a history between the two of them. He would ask Alf.

"So, you'll know all about it then. No need to spell out the rules and regulations, yet again, thank Gawd."

Les passed over three forms.

"Just sign on the dotted, swear allegiance and you'll be across the road in no time. I wish I could join you but there's still a few suckers to go, joking of course."

Tony felt happier with the way things were going.

"Well this sucker's not from round here, I live in Blackpool. Is that a problem?"

"No way. In fact all the better," said Eric "Not much of a party organization out there, only a couple of members so far, if I remember correctly. It was going to be one of our recruitment target areas. We were only discussing it at the last strategy meeting at the Blackies. You could play a key role if you're really committed. It'll be hard work mind you. Can take over your life, eats up time. What do you do by the way?"

Tony was angry with himself afterwards, but at the time it seemed the only thing to say.

"I run my own small business, household chemicals, this and that – keeps me busy."

"Whiter than white eh!"

Les laughed loudly. Everyone else smiled, Tony as much out of relief as anything else. Being caught out in a lie early on would not have been a good start.

"He's a right card our Les. Keeps everyone going. Come on get a grip. We're all getting thirsty."

Eric sounded irritated, but when Tony looked up after signing the forms he saw he was grinning.

"Have you quite finished? Put your mark at the bottom of all three ... the date March 13th. You know the year. Thanks. You probably know this already, but I'm supposed to spell it out for everyone. You've signed on as a Second Division member. What this means is you have to work for us at least one night a month, that's all. But by what I've heard I'd say that wouldn't be enough, keen lad like you. With an uncle already in and friends like Eric here, you'll soon be bumped up into the First Division. That's when the fun really starts, eh lads?"

Les smiled, looked round at the others then stamped the three forms, clipped them together and tossed them into an overflowing tray on the corner of the desk. He stood up and faced Tony.

"Now this is the serious bit. Straight faces everyone. Raise your right hand. Do you Tony Cox pledge, in front of these witnesses, to give your undying support to our King, George the Fifth, to the British Empire, and to the leader of the British Union of Fascists, Sir Oswald Mosley?"

"I do."

"Do you pledge to accept the rules and standing orders associated with membership of the Fascist movement?"

"I do."

"Do you promise not to associate with any other political organizations on pain of expulsion from the movement?"

"I do."

"That's it, you're in. Relax. There's only the hardest bit to come. It's a bob a month in your division, I'm afraid, paid in advance. Archie here will be only too glad to relieve you of this month's subs, won't you Archie?"

"It'll be a pleasure."

Tony handed over a shilling. It was everything he had. All he was thinking about was how he could get out of going to the pub.

"Here's your membership card and badge. Alf should be able to fill you in on the uniform. You're entitled to the basic kit you know, only get everything else when you're promoted. Welcome to the BUF."

They shook hands. Archie slapped him on the shoulder and said "Good to have you with us. Give my regards to Alf. Tell him I'll be along to one of his meetings before long to see how he's getting on."

Eric grabbed him by the arm and led him out through the waiting room. As he was leaving he turned and said, "Nice touch, Les, the flowers on the table. Gives it a homely feel," he winked at Tony.

"Wasn't my idea, believe me. Don't have flowers in a vase where I live, I can tell you. Supposed to make us more appealing to the ladies, as if we needed that," he chuckled. "Would be nice to have a young lady come through, brighten things up a bit, but haven't seen hide nor hair of one all day."

"What's new eh! Anyway, it's an absolute picture Les, an absolute picture."

"Get away with you, you young bastard. Tony take him out of my sight."

Tony hadn't been sure about Eric Baines at first, thinking him overbearing, loud and just too friendly. However, after four pints in the "Castle Arms" he had changed his mind. He liked him and Eric seemed to have taken to him. All they had in common was a love of football and the Party. Eric had played in the youth team of a London club, when he was in his early teens. He hadn't got anywhere but had kept himself in shape ever since. He was keen to get a BUF League going, but was being kept too busy, so he said, by Union business. He'd been in more or less from the beginning and was already a unit leader in "I" division of the Defence Force or "Mosley's Biff Boys" as he called them.

"Got this scar on my face fighting the Reds in Stepney. Tried to stop us selling the Party rag. We showed 'em, but one bastard caught me with a razor. Still hasn't healed properly and that was a couple of months ago. Any way my mate, Stevie Briggs, did for that particular swine. Doubt if he's out of hospital yet."

His booming laugh echoed round the small snug and brought the landlord in from the public bar.

"Go on, tell us the joke – it's been a dull day in here so far."

He stayed leaning across the bar listening to their conversation until a bell rang in the saloon.

"No rest for the wicked."

"The Biff Boys is the only place to be for me. It's where you get noticed. Old Mosley's not averse to a spot of fisticuffs himself if no one is looking. He's quite handy. I've seen him sort out a number of hecklers who got up his nose. Can't do it so much now. Too risky. Police and press everywhere."

He downed his pint in one, wiped his mouth, belched, and stood up to look for the landlord.

"Never here when you want them, all over you when you don't," he steadied himself against the bar, "Same again?"

"I'm fine thanks, still got most of this one."

"Too polite, laddy, too refined. We'll soon sort that out. Let me tell you from my vast experience of life that there are three things you need to get on with us lot: one a loud mouth, two the fists to back it up and three the ability to drink any man under the table. And I mean any man including the old man himself, Sir Oswald. He likes army lags like me who've seen something of the world. Done their bit for King and Empire. Thinks we'll inherit the earth and won't have a thing said against us. Suits me fine."

He sat down with two more pints of beer.

"I have another thing they like. I'm a convert to the cause. I know the enemy."

Tony was puzzled.

"I used to be a Communist myself. Yeh, you're right to look surprised. I was a signed up follower of old Comrade Joe. Hard to believe, innit? Find it hard myself at times. But they were bloody useless, so disorganized, no discipline. Not something they'd have you believe, but it's true. Seen it with my own eyes. Lived the life and couldn't stand it. Hang on, I'm going for a piss."

Tony was overawed. He had never met anyone as animated, as alive, who had done so much with his life and was prepared to talk to him about it. His father had fought in the war but never mentioned it, kept everything buttoned up. The closest match to Eric of the people he knew was Alf, but Archie was right, Alf wasn't a man of action, a leader of men, he was very much a follower. Tony wasn't really sure about himself. He knew he was unhappy with the way things were going, but it was a timid, uncertain, unfocused feeling. Maybe things were about to change. He felt ready and was flattered.

"Woah I needed that. You know what I really hated about those red bastards, don't you?"

Tony shook his head.

"The leaders were Jews, or nearly all of them anyway. They kept joining, recruiting more of their own. It sickened me in the end. I had to get out."

Tony said very little. He sat, sipped his beer and listened to Eric talk. He'd been right about his scar, it hadn't healed. It was still a flaming red gash across his left cheek. Not unattractive, thought Tony, like the man himself. Eric was medium height, stocky, well-built and looked as if he could take care of himself. He had a square weather-beaten face, from his time as a cabin boy in the Merchant Navy spent staring at the horizon, so he said. His eyelashes were long, and many women had been distracted by them, not noticing his dull brown eyes. He wore his greased black hair swept back from a heavily furrowed forehead. And he had a thin dark moustache. This was, as Tony had noticed, as much a part of the uniform of a British fascist as the blackshirt itself.

Tony remembered it as one of those rare timeless afternoons. He felt as if he could have sat there forever, but his reverie had ended abruptly. Three men in blackshirts came in looking for Eric.

"It's time to be heading back to London. Train leaves in half an hour."

Eric had introduced Tony to them as, "our latest recruit. One who is bound to go far."

One of the men had been a Major General and was an important figure on the top body of the BUF, the Policy Directorate. He seemed to know Eric. Tony was impressed.

That was the man Tony had just seen entering the Black House with Oswald Mosley. It was time for another pint. Tony was at the bar placing his order, when Eric burst in through the double doors, smiled and clapped him on the shoulder.

Chapter 3

DEAD AND BURIED
4th March 1995

"Can I book you in for tonight?"

David was sprawled across a compact highly patterned red and yellow sofa staring through half-closed eyes at the television. He was watching the news, but his head was leaning so far back that it was very hard to tell if he was awake.

"Maybe, it depends what time you come to bed."

"Oh, come on, it's Saturday night. Say yes."

"Depends how I feel."

David shook his head and looked away. Feigning an expression of baleful dejection he spoke to his wife in a whining falsetto.

"Susan, I've been here before. This booking system is not worth the paper it's written on."

He burst out laughing and took a sip of red wine.

"I'm feeling quite pissed."

A brief smile passed across Susan's tired face. She was holding back her long blonde hair with one hand as David spoke and let it fall as she looked up from the book she had been reading to reply.

"Alright, just for you."

"For you as well I hope?"

"You never know my luck, it may be in tonight, maybe not."

"Recreational sex, don't you just love it?"

"With you darling?"

The dark wooden rafters of the small bedroom always unnerved David, causing him to duck involuntarily as he came through the door. It was unsettling, because it was unnecessary. He'd been coming here all his life and many years ago had tested the height of every beam with his brother and it was only in the corner next to the window that he had to bow his head. David stood there now, slightly hunched, staring out on to the deserted moonlit street that ran down the hill towards the village church. His grandfather's church, as he always thought of it, even though the man himself had been dead for twenty years. He'd go there tomorrow, on his "regular pilgrimage" as Susan called it. She sometimes came with him out of a sense of duty, but then she had never known the old man, never fallen under his spell.

Pleasantly drunk, David swayed slightly and tried to remember when he had last seen his grandfather. It should have been easy, he had died so unexpectedly and in such peculiar circumstances that the date of his death was etched on his memory – December 3rd 1975. He had been sixteen years old, in emotional turmoil, unhappy and uncertain. At odds with his parents, forever fighting with them, he frequently disappeared from home for days, often ending up here at his grandfather's flat in the village of Dumpton Gap. These escapes had helped calm him down, his life starting to make some sort of sense, in large part due to his elderly relative's ability to listen and advise. David had eventually taken his words to heart and stopped running away, buckling down at school and starting to work for his looming O-levels. This change in attitude happened only a few months before his grandfather's death and ever since he had deeply regretted the time he had missed spending with him, thanks to his good behaviour. His final recollection of the man was bittersweet and imprecise.

Why he had died was one of the imponderable questions that plagued him when drunk or depressed. It was a source of intense frustration. For David was a strong believer in personal progress. He was reconciled to getting older, but only if the reward was a greater self-awareness, coupled with insights into his past. Age and increasing maturity, however, were not providing any answers to the questions about his grandfather, who as the love of his life was never far from his thoughts even now and still hurt him, twisting his powers of recall. He knew it was why he kept coming back to stay in his flat. It was a holiday rental now. He had so many disparate memories that he could never let go.

David sat on his grandfather's battered brown leather sofa in front of a raging fire in the high-ceilinged sitting room of the old Vicarage. He was dressed in green-striped pyjamas and a blue and red dressing gown pulled tight round his shoulders. A steaming mug of cocoa rested perilously on the stained arm of the settee, while his grandfather sat smoking and reading the Daily Telegraph in his favourite armchair illuminated by a tall standard lamp with a threadbare tan shade. Beside David, balanced on the brown cushions, was a pile of his grandfather's Mickey Mouse comics. He knew them all by heart and savoured each and every one of them. He was happy, thumbing through the pages, not reading the words just looking at the cartoon figures. Impressions of that time were indelibly fixed in his mind: the popping of the logs on the fire, the smell of wood smoke as it blew back into the room every time the wind gusted outside, the ticking of the carriage clock on the mantelpiece, the sweet chocolate residue at the bottom of the mug, that he used to scrape up with his finger and then lick clean. It had been a magical time that he would willingly have revisited. Or so he had thought. Now he was not so sure. A grown man in his fifties, intelligent and knowledgeable, owning and treasuring so many childish comics had recently started to seem strange to David. It wasn't as if they had been old comics from when he was a boy in the Thirties. After their grandfather's death, David and his brother Freddy had squabbled over the magazines and his father had said no one was going to have them, as they were worth "a bob or two." David could still remember his own sense of triumph, tinged with disappointment, at the look of annoyance on his father's face when he returned from a special trip to London where he had attempted to sell them, with the news that they were valueless as they weren't that old. He'd dumped them in a bin in disgust rather than carry the heavy bundle all the way back home.

David had asked his grandfather once why he had so many children's comics. He had replied that they were for his boys to read, whenever they stayed with him.

The light suddenly came on and David started.
"Oh God, the windows are wide open."
The room plunged back into darkness and he fumbled to find the cord that closed the curtains.
"There's no one out there, you know."
David turned, massaging his aching neck. Susan stood there with two cups of tea in her hands, her black cotton dressing gown hanging open.
"Oh you never know in places like this."
She smiled.
"By the way there's not much hot water left if you want a bath."
"Thanks."

"Don't look so sad, I don't mind. Where do you want your tea?"

"Over there. I'll have one in the morning."

As David sat on the end of the bed and undressed, Susan stood in front of the full-length mirror on the door of the wardrobe and gently prodded her stomach with her fingers.

"What do you think – not too bad for someone of my age?"

"Let's see."

Susan slipped off her dressing gown and turned to face him, her right hand hovering tentatively by her side.

"Not bad. A nice pair."

Susan laughed.

"You never give up do you? You're so predictable."

"It helps if you breathe in though."

"You bastard!"

Self-consciously she hugged her balled-up dressing gown, before throwing it at David and rushing over to the bed.

"I don't know what you expect after two children?"

Susan slithered beneath the bedclothes.

"Move over. You're bloody lucky I don't have any stretch marks."

David stood up.

"You don't know how lucky you are."

He slipped off his underpants and threw them into the corner of the room. He then lay across the bed. Susan pulled her legs out of the way and he crawled forward until his forearms rested on the floor and the top of his head touched his hands. He then raised his feet.

"I don't know why you bother. It doesn't do any good."

"How do you know?" David muttered as the blood rushed to his head and he began to feel the pressure build up behind his eyes. The veins in his temples throbbed.

"At my age you can't afford not to try anything that might do some good. I think it's stabilized."

"Yeah, yeah."

"It has. I should know. Nowhere near as much hair comes out when I wash it as it used to."

"That's because there's less to come out."

"Shut up, will you. I'm busy."

Susan leaned back against the wooden headboard and sipped her tea. She stared at her husband's naked body; it had been his strongest suit when they had first met and it had very nearly not been enough for her. If she was honest his whole demeanour had put her off. It had taken time and effort on his part before she'd begun to see him in a better light, and his muscular physique had been the deciding factor. Susan smiled to herself. Thinking back she did wonder how they'd got together. He wasn't really good-looking then – his face thin and angular, with a large nose, framed by long, dark wavy hair. His eyes though had attracted her, soft sugar-brown, staring, ever attentive, framed by long thick curling eyelashes. Many times she'd had to look away, embarrassed by their intensity. He was much more handsome now with his receding hair cut short, a few wrinkles around the eyes and a crease or two across the forehead. Ageing had made him less austere-looking, fuller in the face, friendlier. When they had first met he'd seemed blinkered, forever brushing hair back from his face, introverted and reticent. Whereas in truth, he'd been something different, behaving towards her with a confidence and intense physicality that were overwhelming. The first time they slept together, three or four weeks after they had met – it annoyed both of them that they couldn't remember the exact date, couldn't celebrate the anniversary properly – he had picked her up and carried her up the stairs before flinging her onto the bed, an old door, resting on piles of bricks and covered in a thick sheet of foam rubber, that had knocked noisily against the wall as they wriggled and giggled with delight. Six feet tall with strong forearms, in the end he'd been impossible to resist.

He was still in reasonable shape. This recent fixation with his thinning hair was faintly ridiculous, as she didn't care. She'd told him, but he hadn't believed her, and it had spurred him on to experiment with even more outlandish remedies.

She put down the mug on the bedside table and smiled, then lunged forward and slapped his naked buttocks. David cried out in surprise, his body stiffening momentarily before writhing away and almost rolling off the bed. Susan retreated beneath the blankets and stared wide-eyed as he slowly crept towards her. She screamed when he grabbed her.

"Leave me alone, it was just too tempting."

She struggled as he pinned her to the bed with his arms, then lay still.

"Do you surrender?"

"No, never."

Kicking out she managed to topple him over on to his side of the mattress. Grinning he tried to grab her wrists again, but she shoved her hands into his armpits and began tickling him. Convulsed by laughter, he thrashed around, his body quivering. Susan climbed on top of him and smiled.

"Do you surrender?"

"Maybe."

"Grasping her buttocks with both hands, he began gently kneading them. Susan relaxed, closed her eyes and arched her back. Her body moved in rhythm with the circular motion of his hands. Unnoticed he edged one of his fingers between her cheeks and with a sudden cry of triumph thrust it deep inside her.

"There, see how you like that."

With a yelp of pain Susan rolled off him and covered herself with the bedclothes.

"That hurt David."

"Oh come on."

"It bloody did. You know I'm sensitive down there. You never know when to stop do you?"

David sat up and held out his arms.

"I'm sorry. I just got carried away."

"Leave me alone and drink your tea."

"Please don't let it spoil things. Susan?"

"I could've woken the kids. You're an idiot."

"That would have been a pain."

"Oh give over will you. You can always bloody win me round. Drink your tea and we'll see."

The two of them sat side by side in silence, the only sounds the dripping of a tap in the bathroom next door and the intermittent snoring of their eldest son, punctuated by the occasional heavy thump as his feet hit the thin party wall as he turned over in his sleep.

"I knew there was something I had to tell you."

"What?"

Susan sounded irritated. She was already starting to feel drowsy and David's voice wrenched her harshly back to full awareness.

"At work there are rumours we're getting a new managing director. Derek told me. It never bloody stops, does it?"

"Who is it, do you know?"

"No idea, although Derek thinks it will be someone from outside. A new broom, as he puts it."

"How does he know?"

"He heard it from one of his sources. The new bloke, he reckons, is being brought in to carry out all the recommendations in that departmental review those management consultants did for a vast sum at the end of last year. So God knows what will happen. They've kept the results of that one close to their chests."

"You should be all right though, shouldn't you? You've only just signed a new three-year contract."

"Yeah, should be. It'll mean more bloody work though. These things always do."

Susan put down her empty mug and slid over to David, placing her head on his chest and looking up at him wide-eyed.

"David is not afraid of a little bit of hard work is he?"

"No, David is most definitely not. In fact he wouldn't mind some hard work at the moment. Are you still on?"

Susan blinked at him.

"On for what?"

"You know … for it."

"I may be, if you treat me right."

David snuggled down beneath the blankets, hugged his wife and kissed her fleetingly on the lips.

"How's that?"

"Is that it? Is that what you call foreplay?"

"Yep."

He nuzzled her neck with his lips and caressed her breasts and nipples.

"A lady likes to be wooed. That's better."

"Can we go all the way?"

"What do you mean? I'm a virgin."

David placed his hand between her legs and began to slowly probe the moist matted hair with his finger.

"Don't worry, you're safe with me. I'll treat you gently."

"You won't go too far will you?"

"No, not at all. What position do you want to adopt?"

Susan sighed and began nibbling David's ear.

"How many do we have to chose from?"

"Lots and lots. Let me see there's missionary… jockey… spoons… rear… and many more. That's enough to be going on with."

"You choose. I'm too tired."
"No, it's your choice."
"I don't know. I can't make up my mind."
"Go on."
"Will you go on top?"
"Alright."
"Missionary then."
"Roll over…"

"They've taken down the Limes. It really opens things up."

Susan looked quizzically in the direction David was pointing. It was raining and they were sheltering beneath the covered porch at the entrance to St Botolph's church. Their two boys, Richard and Mark, sat gloomily on the gnarled wooden seat leafing their way through a bedraggled copy of the Beano and glancing up occasionally to glare malevolently at their father.

"David, this looks pretty set in. I'll stay here with the boys if you want to visit the grave. We don't mind do we? As long as Daddy doesn't take too long."

Richard nodded his head without looking up, while Mark steadfastly ignored his mother. David was about to say something, when out of the corner of his eye, he caught sight of Susan shaking her head.

"OK, I won't be long."

Raising the collar on his jacket David ran up the gravel path towards the northern end of the graveyard, but quickly slowed to a walk. The rain soaked his hair and began running in cold rivulets down his neck. With the trees gone – only gashed stumps were left – he had a clear view across the park to the wooded slopes beyond. He'd often walked over there with his grandfather, looking for bird's nests and wild flowers, and at the top of the ridge they would stand and look back, trying to pick out the church steeple among the trees. The burgeoning graveyard Limes had made it almost impossible, but there was one spot where you could just make out the golden weathervane glinting above the waving green canopy. He'd always spotted it first and been so pleased. To think of those times now, brought tears to his eyes.

The grave was overgrown and the grimy headstone heavily weathered. If you didn't know who was buried there, it would have taken an effort to find out and David was certain nobody ever bothered these days. It was the final grave in the last row of graves in the churchyard, close to a small wooden gate that he'd often used to get into the parkland. He remembered it had a powerful spring attached to it and always slammed shut with a sharp retort. His grandfather said he could hear him coming, well before he ever arrived. That was when he lived in the rundown Old Vicarage next to the church, in the days before he moved, somewhat shame-faced, David recalled, into his small flat in the village. The benefice was demolished and not rebuilt and now there was a car park on half the site, the rest overgrown and wild. David couldn't believe enough worshippers came to church to justify a car park that size, but then he'd never been a great believer. He'd stopped going to listen to his grandfather give his sermon on Sundays when he was thirteen or fourteen and had hardly ever been to a church service since. His grandfather had teased him mercilessly.

"Here I am, a man of God, raising a heathen. You'll never get to heaven you know."

He had gone on and on until finally David snapped.

"What makes you think you'll get to heaven yourself, there's no monopoly on goodness."

His grandmother, Emily, had been buried here, around the time he was born and he wasn't sure she had ever met him. He guessed probably not as his father and grandfather were barely civil to each other and his family had not visited Dumpton often.

That had been part of the attraction for David when he started having problems of his own with his father, a common bond of estrangement, which had rapidly grown into something much stronger, one of mutual respect and then love. It had irritated his father.

"I don't know what you see in him, he's an old charlatan. I'd steer well clear of him if I was you."

It was the only parental advice David had ever been given and he didn't understand it and as a result paid it no heed. Every time he came to Dumpton he thought he must ask his father what he had meant, and every year he never did.

His grandmother's name was barely legible in the centre of the headstone: "Emily Coxon-Dyet, loving wife of the Reverend Anthony Coxon-Dyet." At the bottom engraved in a clearer slightly different script was his grandfather's inscription: "In memory of Anthony Coxon-Dyet, 1910 – 1975." They were the only words that the church authorities would allow and none of his family had been prepared to argue with them. The problem had been that his grandfather's body hadn't been buried here, they'd held a funeral service in the church, then had him cremated. His youngest son, Freddy, David's uncle, had finally agreed to dispose of the ashes and had come here with his nephew on a damp winter day and scattered them over the grave. For David this was his grandfather's last resting place. But even that was not as he remembered it. Everything was changing. He took one last look at the grave, then headed across the soaking grass towards the gap in the hedge that led to the site of the old Vicarage.

He had loved this place. Some of his happiest memories were of roaming around the ramshackle Victorian house and its overgrown, lush-green gardens with one or more of the boys who were always staying with his grandfather. "Rooming with him" was the phrase and they always seemed to David to have been a "cutthroat" bunch, all outlaws on the run from the authorities. He remembered unlimited supplies of cigarettes, bottles of Strongbow cider, marijuana and pills. Naturally conservative, David initially hesitated, scared of losing control, before finally taking the hedonistic plunge with a boy called Jamie. They spent a gloriously sunny afternoon speeding, while his grandfather was out on his pastoral rounds, smashing every pane of glass in the old conservatory on the side of the house. It had been hilarious and a giggling Jamie owned up and was sent away, David didn't and had relished this guilty secret ever since. The glass had never been replaced and the cold biting autumnal rain quickly killed the palms and cacti that had flourished there for years, while rats gnawed their decaying trunks, scattering fibrous honey-coloured husks across the tiled floor.

The boys, his itinerant friends, had come and gone, yet he could still see their wild faces milling around in the drenched vegetation that had reclaimed the derelict site. They had been runaways, thieves, arsonists, petty criminals. St Botolph's vicarage was the sink into which all the local magistrates poured their problem cases, the boys they had seen just once too often, the boys who they considered beyond redemption. But all had been welcome.

David had watched as they gradually wrecked the place, taking advantage of his grandfather, abusing his hospitality and generosity of spirit. David joined in, exploiting a freedom he had never known before and would never experience again. He had his first sexual fling with a fat blond-haired boy hidden in the middle of a huge rhododendron bush at the end of the garden. The shrub was still there, twice as large as he remembered it and as lush and forbidding, but now parishioners parked their cars in its shadow before evensong and Holy Communion. David smiled as he gazed at the dark glistening mass and remembered his horror as he undressed later that night and discovered his penis had turned green. The algae were still there, he noticed, as vivid as ever, clinging to the trunks and branches, staining everything that brushed against it a bright powdery emerald. The smell of coal tar soap was for him the aroma of release, as the viridescent lather trickled away down the rusty plughole of the stained white enamel sink in one of the vicarage's outhouses.

The vicarage was known locally as "Fagin's Den". The police were regular visitors, bad publicity led church congregations to tail off, letters were written, and finally the Bishop intervened. But it had been a fun-filled rite of passage for David and his grandfather appeared unperturbed by the criticism. His sermons berated the "uncaring" for their lack of charity and his weekly newsletter in the parish magazine hit out at a country whose moral backbone had been weakened by years of Socialism, which had destroyed any concept of self-help and left the care of the sick, the poor and the outcast to an inefficient, unfeeling state. His strident views on politics and every other topic imaginable, together with his willingness to court controversy by putting them down on paper, meant that the magazine was popular. It always sold out and over the years they printed more and more copies to meet the demand. As his grandfather used to say, "people prefer to take their medicine in private, rather than be spoon-fed in public." David remembered him chuckling to himself in his study on Saturday evening as he tapped out the following day's sermon or the next week's editorial on his old Olivetti typewriter. Clouds of cigarette smoke hung in the air and the light from his desk lamp outlined his hunched body in a yellow smudged haze. David would sneak into the room, sit quietly in the narrow gap between the wall and the bookcase and imagine he was watching the word of God being made real. He was sure when he thought back, that he would wake up, tucked safely in bed, the light streaming through the partially closed curtains of his bedroom. The one he always slept in during his stays at the Vicarage, high in the roof, with a glorious outlook over the chimney pots of Dumpton Gap. He knew the view so well, that it floated before him: it was always sunny, a brisk breeze blowing, the silvery undersides of the leaves twisting and glinting, the clouds scudding across an azure-blue sky. There were days he had scoured the countryside with his grandfather's old telescope probing the woodland edges, the stacked hay bales, the long grass in the meadow by the river, the windows of the houses in the village, but only once found what he was looking for. It was as vivid to him now as the day it had happened. A young woman stood framed in an upper casement window, slowly unbuttoning her white blouse. She had a distant look in her eyes. The white cotton slid from her shoulders revealing a white brassiere, David could clearly see a red weal on her shoulder where the strap had cut into her skin. He held his breath. She stepped back, shut the curtains and disappeared from view.

David shivered, he felt chilled to the core, the damp air intruding, his body sodden. The Vicarage was gone and so was his grandfather. There was so much he didn't understand. He didn't know why he had died. He still couldn't remember when he had last talked to him, could not resurrect that final image. After his death he had discovered there were very few photographs of his grandfather. The local paper had a number of him opening fetes, holding babies awkwardly in his arms or judging a vegetable or cake competition, but they were all in black and white and he didn't want to remember his dearest relative that way. David's memories were vivid and alive – silver-grey receding hair, cut short; brown limpid eyes that unnervingly held your gaze; yellow nicotine-stained fingers, nails manicured – a plethora of detail even if the whole man escaped him. The odd thing had been the indifferent reaction of his father, who had shown little interest in

David's pleas for help in fixing this shifting figure, referring him brusquely to an old cardboard box stored in the attic. It had been damp and cold up there and many of the jumbled photographs were curling and fading, the chemicals eating away the images they had originally preserved. The photographs were all of his grandfather when he was young, recognizable, but not the man he had known. He looked more serious in his youth with an angular, less attractive face and more hair. His grandfather had been one of those people whose appearance had improved with age, his face filling out and softening his harsh features. A distinctive youth had matured into a handsome old man.

In only one of the photographs was his grandfather looking at the camera, and he seemed slightly bemused. David didn't recognize him. There was something about the eyes that made him appear distant, evasive and unfriendly, a stranger.

David had been depressed after his grandfather's death – the news had deeply shocked him, it had been sudden and unexpected – and then to find out there was little of the man that was tangible seemed particularly unfair. Even more galling was that nobody seemed to care. It was as if there was a conspiracy to erase his grandfather from history. His name had never been added to the ancient wooden panel with its ornate frame hanging in the nave of St Botolph's that listed the vicars of the church and their dates in the parish in a more or less unbroken line from the eleventh century to the present day.

He took one last look at the site of the old vicarage and walked slowly back towards the church. The rain was easing off and the sky was brightening, he thought he could hear voices calling out to him. He shouted, "I'm just coming, give me a couple of minutes."

David had complained at first, saying that the list of clergymen was an historical record and shouldn't be tampered with, for the sake of future generations. He had thought at the time that he had made his case and the parish clerk had not argued with him.

"The matter will be taken up by the Parochial Church Council and the due procedures will be followed," was all he said. That was years ago and as of last July nothing had happened, he knew that for sure.

The church frightened him and he rarely went inside. He approached the large black wooden door now with trepidation. The covered entrance was cool and totally silent. He stamped his feet several times, hesitated, then grasped the iron door handle – it was cold to the touch – and turned. The heavy latch lifted noisily on the other side of the door and David pushed. Nothing. The door was locked.

"Bastards."

Chapter 4
OLYMPIAN HEIGHTS
7th June 1934

Eric's room in the Black House was narrow, barely wide enough for a single bed and a small cabinet. It was one of ten similar "dens", which opened off a corridor that was wider than the rooms themselves. It had once been a dormitory and had been subdivided when the British Union of Fascists took over the lease of the building.

"At least I've some privacy, even though anybody walking through can just peer straight in. The other poor sods have to sleep fifteen to a room. Had to pull rank to get in here. It pays to pull it when you can and believe me I pull it."

Eric laughed and threw himself on the bed.

"Look, I've got half a window. Some of my elders and betters live in semi-darkness. But not me, I'm woken by the warm caresses of the rising sun. Not so sure about what'll happen to you though, sleeping on the floor."

There was barely a flicker of a smile on his face as he nodded at the worn mat at his feet.

"Make yourself at home. 'Fraid there's nowhere else. The place is packed out with people ready for tomorrow. You'll have to make do with my threadbare Persian unless you fancy the bed, but it would be a tight squeeze."

He chuckled to himself. Tony, too drunk to care, was silent.

"There might be some room in the cupboard if you've got anything valuable. Don't leave it lying around, they're a bunch of thieving bastards in here. Oh, and there's a hanger for you in my dressing room."

He pointed to a hook and a small brass rail attached to the wall at the side of the bed. He then doubled over in a fit of giggling. Tony, standing beside him, rocked forward and back, clutching his stomach.

"Shut up for Christ's sake. I'm going to throw up."

"Not all over me you're not, you little swine. Can't you hold your drink up North?"

Tony lunged at Eric and they fell back on to the mattress. Tony was tall and sinewy and had long since given up any serious exercise, unlike Eric who was stockier with a strong muscular frame, but he had the advantage of surprise. He forced Eric's arms back above his head and pinned him down with the full weight of his body. His knees dug into Eric's chest.

"Take it back, you bastard or you'll never get up. Go on, take it back."

Eric's eyes gleamed as he stared up at Tony's flushed face. He didn't move for several seconds and then whispered, "Are you threatening me, you drunken Blackpudlian git? It'll take a battalion of your lot to make me take it back."

He quivered and Tony tightened his grip.

"Getting worried? You never looked like a fighter to me, more the bookish type. Won't help you much now, will it? Be a difficult one to talk your way out of."

Tony smiled.

"You think I'm jesting? Obviously you haven't read the BUF regulation handbook. It's a serious offence attacking a senior Party official. Fine, instant expulsion, the shame, you name it."

Tony felt unsure, he didn't really know this man. Was he joking?

"And that's not even taking into account what my mates will do to you when they get to hear about it – which will be in about five minutes – unless you're a tougher man than I imagine."

It was over in a second. Tony loosened his grip and Eric grabbed him, flung him hard against the wooden partition, leapt up and pinned his shoulders to the bed. It moved slightly away from the wall.

"What's it like this way round, eh? Not so brave now? Not feeling so clever?"

Tony's eyes were watering. He could feel very little. Eric's behaviour was a surprise, he was uncertain, but he was not scared. He was thinking would they accept being drunk as a defence?

Eric suddenly kissed him on the forehead, then flung himself down beside him on the bed. The two of them, their heads together on the pillow, stared at the ceiling.

"I had you going there, didn't I? You looked as if you were going to piss yourself."

He nudged Tony, and laughed.

"I told you it was always a good tactic to pull rank, works every time. If you fancy your chances against me you'll need to get in shape."

Relieved, Tony was breathing heavily. The room kept spinning, the garish blues and greens of the River Rhine, flashing before him. He shut his eyes, but it didn't help.

"Have you ever been to Germany?" he asked trying to focus by nodding towards the tourist poster pinned on the wall above their heads.

"Changing the subject, are we? Yes, I was there a couple of months ago on a cycling tour. Got as far as Berlin. Had a great time. Lots going on there, in all sorts of ways. Really enjoyed myself. We're planning to go again soon. You could come."

Tony slurred his words of assent.

"God, I'm hungry, haven't eaten all day. Bet you could do with some food, sober you up a bit. There's a mess room here, grub's so so."

Eric got to his feet and held out a hand to Tony.

"Come on, let's hope we're not too late."

The sound of a bugle cut the still air. It was dark. Tony was confused. He was freezing cold. There was a bitter taste in his mouth, a dull throbbing pain in his temples. His body ached and he couldn't move his head. A momentary panic – there was movement above him – he was paralysed. He desperately needed to relieve himself.

Someone grunted.

"Eric?"

"Yes."

"What time is it? Feels like the middle of the night."

"Just gone six. Usual time for reveille. Better get going or we'll be late for the run – the streets are pretty clear this time of the morning. Then we'll just have time for a cold bath before breakfast."

Tony groaned.

"You're welcome to it. Is this how you Biff Boys spend your time? Bloody masochists."

As he was speaking the lights in the corridor came on.

"Hands off cocks everyone, hands on socks. Time to rise and shine. Busy day today."

"Sod off Beazley. I told you if you said that one more time I'd cut yours off."

"I'd like to see you try you arrogant little bastard, at least I've got one to cut off."

There was a yell from along the corridor and seconds later

a naked figure rushed past the open end of Eric's den. A door slammed and a man screamed.

"You've broken my fucking toe, you…help me someone. The swine's broken my toe."

Eric smiled down at Tony.

"Just another day at the Black House. Don't worry about them they are always having a go at each other. Goes back a long way. They were either in the same regiment or the same prep school, I can't remember."

Tony's head was wedged between the wall and the small cabinet. He was completely naked. His clothes were scattered under the bed and out into the corridor.

"What a sight first thing in the morning, what a body."

"Give over, I feel terrible."

"You look a bit peaky. You could run along to the sick bay. But," he leaned over the edge of the bed, bringing his face close to Tony's, "take a tip from one who knows, don't tell nurse you had too much to drink, she can't keep a secret, It'd be all round this place in hours and wouldn't do your reputation any good at all." He winked, "Don't say I'm not your friend."

"Thanks for nothing. How about you, how are you feeling?"

"Never better."

Eric rose unsteadily to his feet and began bouncing up and down on the bed. He was also naked and Tony watched transfixed for a moment before glancing away. Seconds later he sat bolt upright and covered his groin with his hands. Eric grimaced and began leaping higher into the air. The bed creaked ominously. Tony edged nearer to the wall.

"There's no need to be shy", Eric shouted, "I've seen it all before."

"Baines, why don't you shut up? Some of us like a bit of quiet when we get up in the morning."

"Good morning to you too, Jimmy. Oh my, what's that you're doing? You'll be wearing specs next if you're not careful."

A tousled haired man stuck his head out into the corridor and looked aghast as he saw Eric waving at him.

"You sod", he grinned and disappeared back into his "den", returning a second later with a shoe. He lobbed it at Eric. It missed its target, hit the wall and dropped into the "den" next door to Eric's. There was a muffled yell.

"Sorry Bert, my old mate, apologies. Just mucking around."

Eric breathing heavily bounced slowly to a stop.

"Jimmy the silly sod he believed me. Christ, I'd have to have been hanging from the bloody ceiling to have seen him handling his piece. Guilty conscience if you ask me."

He collapsed on to the bed and pulled a sheet over his head.

"God, I feel faint."

Tony meanwhile had slipped on his underpants, got unsteadily to his feet and was leaning against the entrance to the "den." Materially present, but emotionally absent, he registered the frenetic activity around him but didn't care enough to participate. Gripped by unsettling cramps in his stomach and intense pain deep behind his eyes, he was incapacitated physically. It was an effort to stand and with his mental capabilities befuddled by erotic thoughts he was barely able to function. The progress of his hangover had a reassuring inevitability about it – he was going to throw up. He had some control over the timing and the place, but could do nothing to alter this simple truth. Years of suffering from the condition and over-familiarity with the consequences had yielded no remedy. He had tried pints of tap water before bed, black tea, warm water with lemon and spoonfuls of sugar, dry toast, aspirin, stomach powders, cold baths, hot water bottles on his stomach, dark rooms, fresh air, long sea-walks, a shot of brandy and finally in extremis, yet more beer. Some of the cures delayed the crisis long enough that he thought he had got away with it, some hastened it, but none could halt it. He was resigned to his fate.

Obfuscation was now his sole aim – how to get away with being sick, without embarrassment. It was obvious that his new friends would be an unforgiving bunch. Not being able to hold your drink was, he was sure, a major failing. At home it was easy. Creep along to the bathroom, get down on your hands and knees in front of the toilet bowl and imagine: a knife slitting open the yolk of a soft fried egg, an overflowing gut bucket in the covered fish market on the front at Fleetwood, the smell of the ship canal on a hot summer's day or the sensation of walking across the slippery, bloody sawdust strewn, black and white tiled floor of the back room in the local butchers, Slopes of Mafeking Street – "suppliers of fine cooked meats and sausages to the working man."

Sitting down on the bed Tony was happy to wait for a while.

"How long are you going to be lounging there? We've got to get going, you know, if we want anything to eat before the parade briefing."

Eric was standing and reaching for a neatly pressed uniform that was hanging on the clothes-rail. Tony noticed that his back was criss-crossed with faint ragged scars.

"Don't mention food," Tony whispered half-heartedly, "give me a few minutes."

He shivered as he watched Eric put on the full BUF dress uniform. Tony had never seen one up close before. Although he had recently been promoted to the "First Division" he hadn't been able to afford all the extras. Eric certainly had the physique and colouring to carry it off well. Black suited him.

"Can you see my shoes down there? They were under the bed, before you started messing around."

He tucked the tails of his collarless black shirt into his pressed black trousers and looked down at Tony. With his right hand he did up the three buttons on his left shoulder.

"Any luck?"

"They're right at the back, a towel or something has fallen on top of them."

"Thanks. What do you think of these then?" he said showing Tony a pair of gold cufflinks, shaped like a lightning flash striking across a circle, that he had taken from his locked cupboard.

"Nice aren't they? Our new party emblem. I prefer it to the old one."

He pointed to the buckle of his thick black leather belt.

"Bloody Italians use this one. Just a bundle of sticks and an axe, which they stole from the Romans. Whereas, this is home-grown, truly British. How do they put it, "a flash of action in the circle of unity," that's more like it. Looks good on flags and stands out at rallies."

"I like it too but isn't that what the Communists call the "flash in the pan"?"

Eric laughed.

"True, true. That's bloody funny. What's it they say about the devil having all the best lines. Well, it's true in this case, the bastards."

Grinning he thumbed the cufflinks through his heavily starched shirt cuffs.

"Still it won't put me off. It's just one more thing for me to hate them for. Now where did you say my shoes were?"

"They're at the …Oh no. I'll be back in a minute."

Eric waved his finger and smiled as Tony staggered down the corridor.

Twenty minutes later Tony found Eric in the mess room eating a large plate of bacon, eggs and fried bread.

"I've just been thinking of breakfast," Tony said as he sat down.

"You'll have to be quick if you want anything, most people have already eaten."

"Just tea. That'll do me fine, thanks. Can't face anything else."

"Tony and I had a basinful last night," Eric said to the woman sitting opposite him.

"But he's not had quite as much practice as I have."

He elbowed Tony.

"Won't take you long to catch up though will it?"

The woman was smiling at Tony.

"Eric has no manners. I'm Emily Carstairs. Pleased to meet you."

"Sorry, Emily, you know me, dragged up. This is Tony Cox, a good friend of mine from up north – Blackpool. He's a district leader or at least soon will be. He's down for the rally. Thought I'd have him tag along with me, see how the real bastards live. Tony Cox this is Emily Carstairs. She's a women's district leader from … must be somewhere near you, Cheshire isn't it?"

Emily nodded.

"But she's been down here for six months or so acting as assistant to old Brock-Griggs, the Chief Women's Officer. An influential lady our Miss Carstairs, well worth getting to know."

Tony and Emily shook hands across the table. Her palm was hot, the fingers cool to the touch. Clear blue eyes stared intently, holding Tony's gaze. He felt he should look away, but was transfixed, hazily absorbing all before him. Black hair pulled back in a tight bun framed a round pale face, a loose wisp softening the severity of the white slash of her central parting, red lips half-smiling, the only colour. Lightly powdered skin, unblemished except for a small mole on her left cheek, highlighted her charm. A blink of the eyes, a flutter of curling lashes, set him free.

"It would be my pleasure," said Emily, "maybe after the march?"

She stood up, brushed the front of her grey skirt with both hands, picked up her empty plate and mug and carried them over to the scullery.

"Look after yourselves," she called across the room, "they're expecting trouble."

"What's new?" Eric cheerily called back, then lowering his voice said almost to himself, "She's a good-looking woman, don't you think Tony? Tall and slim, your type, eh Tony?"

He laughed.

"You're probably not in a fit state to notice anything are you? Even beauty before your eyes."

"No. She was very nice. How do you know her?"

"I've got to know her quite well since she's been here. She's unattached. And I've always said there's something about a women in uniform."

Tony smiled. Eric's a coarse bugger, he thought. Trouble was he never knew if he was poking fun or not.

"Are you seeing her?"

"Noooo."

Eric grinned inanely.

"She's all yours. If you've got the balls."

He drained his mug of tea, belched silently onto the back of his hand and stood up, his chair noisily scraping the floor.

"If you're not having anything we best get going. Don't want to be late on duty do we, not on your first day."

"I was hoping for a tea."

His voice trailed off and he got unsteadily to his feet and followed Eric.

"Look, I should fill you in on a few things before we get going on the march."

Eric and Tony were standing at the top of the wide staircase that swept down to the cramped entrance hall of the Black House, which was already a seething mass of jet figures. Except for, and Tony was watching him intently, a white-haired man who moved slowly across the room, like a rolling cue ball on a billiard table of dark baize. He disappeared through a side-door. With a start he realized Eric was speaking.

"...stick with me. I've cleared it with old Piercy. We'll be the advance squad, four others will follow from here later. Our job's to organize security when we get to Olympia. You can make yourself useful sticking up posters and the like. During the rally you'll be with me. We're one of the "Biff-Boy" flying squads. Any trouble we're straight in. Sort it out or sort them out more likely. There's no messing around. Any hecklers get shown the exit. Others will be waiting there to help them on their way. All clear?"

Tony nodded. He had been concerned, when it dawned on him, that he was likely to be in the thick of anything that happened. Now as his headache lifted and life began to take on a renewed clarity, unfiltered by pain, he acknowledged his own sense of anticipation and felt the excitement building around him.

"All very clear. Look, thanks Eric, I appreciate what you are doing for me."

"It's nothing. But just you remember who your friends are. Which reminds me," and he thrust his hand into a trouser side pocket and pulled out two brass knuckledusters, "these are a couple of my best friends, never go anywhere without them. Feel naked if I do. Here have one of them. Wouldn't want you naked and vulnerable twice in one day would we?"

Tony cradled the warm smooth metal object in the palm of his hand. It was heavier than he expected. His fingers fitted comfortably through the worn rings.

"I do," he mumbled.

"Till death us do part, eh? Come on don't flash it around. Everyone will want one. We leave here at four, on parade at three thirty. I've got to go to a briefing so amuse yourself for a few hours will you. Take a look around, get a feel for the place. Meet up here at three fifteen."

With that he ran down the stairs, taking the steps three at a time. Tony watched him disappear into the crush of people in the hall and then turned and made his way slowly along the landing to Eric's den. He gathered up his scattered belongings and stuffed them into his small canvas suitcase. He lay down on the bed and immediately fell asleep. He was awakened by laughter in the corridor. He sat bolt upright.

"Were they laughing at him?"

He'd been dribbling and hastily wiped his mouth. But there were no sneering faces, no pointing fingers, just a dim light bulb swaying gently in a draft. Tony shivered. Then looked anxiously at the small alarm clock on the cupboard beside the bed. Ten to two. He bent over and tried the cupboard door, but it was locked. He pulled the drawer, it opened easily and he just caught the tray before its contents spilled onto the floor.

"Bugger."

He lifted it back and slid it into place.

"Ahh, thank God."

He took out an open packet of Ardath straight cut, placed a cigarette in this mouth and rummaged through the drawer looking for a match.

"I don't believe it, there's a bloody medicine chest in here."

He reached across and patted the pocket of his jacket, he then peered back into the drawer. There were numerous medicine bottles and pill boxes: Dr White's Kompo for colds, Cephos tablets, Philip's Dental Magnesia for smokers fur, Doans backache kidney pills and a half empty bottle of Milk of Magnesia; a bar of Bodyguard soap, a crumpled bag of mint humbugs, a crimson velvet cloth folded around three medals, a couple of black and white photographs – one showing a smartly-dressed man and a women in a fur coat standing by a lake, the other two men on a beach in swimming trunks smiling at the camera – a dirty handkerchief, an advert torn out of a newspaper "Kill Rats with Rodine", but no matches. Tony slipped the cigarette back into the packet, "The Navy's favourite cigarette."

"It's certainly not mine", he muttered.

He had slept deeply, but was uneasy, concerned that he had missed something, let someone down. He still felt slightly nauseous. The air was stuffy and heavy with dust. He watched the motes dance in the sunlight streaming through Eric's half window. It was a beautiful day outside.

"Fresh air is what I need. A curse on the noble weed."

Before leaving he checked his appearance in the mirror. He looked pale and tired. Tony slapped himself hard on both sides of his face and a red hue suffused his cheeks. His clothes were creased but, he thought, as he combed his greasy hair, "no one will notice", that was one of the advantages of wearing black.

Tony was slightly over six feet tall, lean, muscular, yet with a bulky softness that diminished the impact of his physical presence, making him appear ponderous. He had thick dark brown hair, tinged with auburn, that he liked to let grow so that it curled over his collar. He also wore it long at the front and swept it back from his forehead in a grand gesture that he slicked down with Brylcreem, an act of sleek defiance that set him apart from everyone but his fellow fascists. He had pronounced features, a hard jaw-line and a large thin nose, "a Roman nose, if ever I've seen one," he'd been told innumerable times, and piercing brown eyes. He was vain enough never to have grown a moustache, even though it was fashionable in the Party, but not conceited enough to think he was good-looking. He saw himself as open and approachable, but had a face that in repose, appeared stern and aloof. He would never reconcile himself to this conundrum, and throughout life would be disappointed at the barrenness of all but a few of his friendships.

Outside, the sun was achingly bright and there wasn't a cloud in the sky. It was a hot afternoon. Tony stepped back into the shadow of the grand doorway of the Black House and looked out across the "parade ground" to the King's Road. A small crowd was milling around at the entrance and several passersby were reading a notice pinned to one of the gateposts. A blackshirt guard was giving directions to an elderly gentleman dressed in a dark overcoat and hat. Two policemen strolled by and Tony noticed there were others standing together on the opposite side of the road. He desperately needed a cigarette. It was a wonderful day and he was finally starting to feel human again.

When he had peered out of the window of Eric's den earlier that afternoon, down on to Cheltenham Terrace and the exit ramp for the underground garage, Tony had seen a couple of men in overalls working on the roof of a "battle" van. One had been smoking. Descending the steps he turned right and headed for the narrow passageway that ran between the railings and the side wall of the Black House. The plane trees moving in the breeze cast sun-stippled shade shimmering across the red bricks. In the Duke of York's barracks a platoon of soldiers in full service uniform was marching back and forth, the barked orders of the Sergeant Major harshly audible. There was a police van parked in the street, five constables leaned on the railings, talking, their helmets in their hands. They looked across when Tony appeared at the corner. He nodded.

"I wouldn't do that if I was you," said one of the mechanics when Tony reached the garage, "some of them can turn quite nasty. Them lot's regulars, will have marked you down for sure."

"I was only passing the time of day, any way I'm not from round here."

"Take my advice and keep your eyes open if you're on the march today."

"Thanks, will do. What I was hoping was you might be able to spare me a smoke, I'm gasping?"

For the next hour Tony stood and talked to the two men. They were wiring up speakers on top of the van and checking microphones.

"Some of them never miss the chance to tell people what's what. I've seen old Mosley up on top here, speaks for hours sometimes. Bloody marvellous, moves 'em to tears he does. Never known him at a loss for words. Not like some of 'em, gor blimey they're all over the place. But it's not for me to say, my job's to keep this running smoothly, drive 'em here and there and get 'em out of wherever, sometimes bloody quickly I can tell you. They may not look it, but these vans are specials – bloody powerful engines under that bonnet."

"Look I've got to go. Thanks I feel a whole lot better now, I was hung over when I first spoke to you."

Eric was waiting for him at the top of the stairs.

"Word is we can expect trouble today," he said. "The Communists are planning something special. Seems they're angry that the Albert Hall meeting was such a success. They've been bleating about it in their rag. At the briefing they showed us some clippings from the Daily Worker. Usual load of cobblers, but they're calling for a "counter-demonstration" at Olympia to meet, how do they put it, "Mosley's challenge to the working class". For God's sake I'm working class, most of us are, they don't know what they're talking about. It really makes me angry …"

He dramatically pummeled the wall with his fists.

"I must have been an idiot. Oh, that reminds me, there was one good bit, you'll like this, I saved it for you."

He took out a folded piece of newspaper from his pocket and read with a slow slurred accent.

"Mosley's tune is the old capitalist one dished up through new instruments – the knuckleduster."

Eric smiled.

"And we were just discussing that very political point weren't we, comrade. Not more than two hours ago."

He looked at Tony.

"What do you think comrade?"

"If that was meant to be a Lancashire accent, it was rubbish. Would get your head kicked in by any self-respecting Lancastrian, let alone Communist, in any pub in the north. Don't think of going on the stage."

Eric clapped him on the back.

"Enough, we'd better get ready. Here put on this arm band, makes you an honorary Biff Boy for the day."

"How many are they expecting?"

"The "Worker's" talking about tens of thousands, but then they would. The best guess seems to be there will be a few thousand. The problem comes if any of them get into the hall. That's where we come in. Get them out fast with the minimum of fuss. Mosley doesn't mind the odd interruption, gives him a chance to go on about the threat to the freedom of speech, the depths to which our opponents will sink and so on. But not too many, breaks the flow, you know. The key this time round is firm but fair, at least while people are watching."

Outside on the parade ground the Blackshirts were drawn up in marching order when Eric and Tony arrived. There were three columns of at least two hundred men and about fifty women, all dressed in black. Many wore medal ribbons, the only flash of colour. Eric saluted the senior team leader, who had been drilling the squads, and Tony was directed to a place in one of the outside ranks close to the front of the first column. Eric then addressed the assembled company in a sonorous, commanding voice unlike anything Tony had heard from him before.

"This is one of the most important occasions in the short life of our movement in this country. This meeting at Olympia will be the largest in our history, in the audience will be peers of the realm, politicians, business men, and the working man, they will be coming to hear what we have to offer this great country of ours. We must not disappoint them. We must be disciplined, well ordered and we must, under no circumstances, under whatever provocation, whatever insult, break ranks and react either verbally or physically. We can expect trouble, and believe me it is out there looking for us, but, and I must make this absolutely clear, we will not go looking for it. We are in the vanguard of a new beginning for Great Britain. Let's march. God save the King."

All in the columns raised their right arms in salute. There were cheers from the windows of the Black House and a few boos from people in the street. Foolish, thought Tony as he saw a couple of Blackshirts chasing three boys round the corner into a side street. Eric took his place at the head of the parade.

"Attention. Quick march. Left, right, left, right, left."

They moved smartly out into the King's Road, halting traffic on the busy thoroughfare, horns blared as the marchers headed towards Sloane Square. Policemen immediately joined them, taking up positions on either side of the snaking column. Tony was amused to see that they were soon walking in step. A few children stopped to watch, but Blackshirts were a common sight in this part of London and most people paid little attention. A taxi driver gave the thumbs up sign, waved and continuously blew his horn as he overtook the procession. His passenger gaped, open-mouthed through a side window. The cab was followed by a crowded double-decker bus, belching exhaust fumes as it rattled past, ranks of pale faces staring through grimy glass. Tony felt invigorated. He had only been on one other BUF march and that had been in Manchester on a wet Saturday earlier that year, hardly anybody had turned up and they had broken up and gone for a drink as soon as the pubs had opened.

A disturbance in the air marked their progress up Sloane Street away from the Square – shouts and catcalls intermingling with the resolute tramp of parading feet amplifying the chaotic noises of urban life into a confused din – a noise that inexorably rolled forward announcing their presence and threatening their imminent arrival.

Two schoolgirls began running alongside trailing scarves, cheering and clapping. People appeared at windows, some waved, others just watched. Near the junction with Pont Street an elderly women appeared on her balcony and threw down a bunch of red roses. Tony had to stop himself from catching one, to save it from being trampled under the marching boots.

At the top of Sloane Street the column turned left into Knightsbridge, distracted shoppers stared, pedestrians slowed. A cameraman snapped pictures, before running ahead and speaking to Eric, who nodded. The column slowed almost to a halt, the photographer quickly set up his tripod, adjusted the camera, peered through the lens and waved.

"Quick march!"

They were almost upon him.

"Eyes right, salute."

The Blackshirts stiffened and raised their arms. The shutter clicked noisily, the flash bulb exploded, a white cloud enveloping the stooping figure. Tony felt immensely proud. He was part of something important, his individuality subsumed into a greater identity, beyond his puny imagining. It was a unique feeling to be invincible, able to sweep all before him. Tears filled his eyes. He looked away, hoping no one would notice this failing. Across Hyde Park the sun was shining through the tall trees, riders on the bridleway reined in their horses as they approached the road, seeing the Blackshirts for the first time, giving way, as Tony thought, to the tide of history.

The marchers, buoyed by their brush with the press, began to sing as they drew level with the Albert Memorial.

"Comrades: the voices of the dead battalions
of those who fell that Britain might be great.
Join in our song, for they still march in spirit with us.
And urge us on to gain the fascist state."

Tony had learnt the lines of the Party marching song from the pages of "Action", but had never heard them sung before. He was a diffident singer and in church had mumbled his way through the hymns, his head bowed. Even here among this group of fellow-travellers, on a busy noisy street, he lacked confidence and silently mouthed the words.

"Gainst vested powers, the Red front and massed ranks of reaction we lead the fight for freedom and for bread.
The streets are still; the final struggles' ended;
flushed with the fight we proudly hail the dawn!"

As their voices swelled in volume, drowning out the city hubbub, a marcher in the centre of the row ahead of Tony raised the banner of the British Union of Fascists, it hung limply in the still warm air. Further down the column two Union Jacks were unfurled.

"See, over all the streets the fascist banners waving – triumphant standard of a race reborn."

Ragged cheers rang out. They were passing the grounds of Kensington Palace.

"Eyes right, salute."

The column picked up pace. The rhythmic beat of the marching boots carrying Tony along, swept forward by the surging presence and physical power of the massed ranks, an encompassing entity outside of his experience and within whose ambit he felt secure. Absorbed, he could watch the relentless passing – precipitous buildings, ornate facades, peeling trunks of leaning London Plane trees, their leafy branches silhouetted overhead, hazily obscuring the vivid blue slash of sky, the faint silhouette of a wheeling flock of pigeons catching his eye.

Shouting close by. His mood punctured. The column tensed, men immediately alert. A pack at bay.

"Fascist swine, get off our streets. Blackshirt vermin get back to your sewers. Off, off, off our streets."

The man striding next to Tony nudged him, "Here we go, keep your eyes open… There they are, over there."

He pointed. A group of men were standing at the junction of Campden Hill Road, waving their fists and chanting.

"Off, off, off our streets, fascist swine, get off."

One of the protestors, a tall thin man, dressed in a long overcoat with weighted pockets, dashed into the road ahead of the column and gesticulated wildly. He backed slowly down the centre of the street shouting abuse. Nobody in the front row took any notice of his protest.

"You jumped up little Hitlers, you junior Mussolinis, you Jew-haters, you sewer-rats, crawl back to where you came from. Bastards. Damn you all. We'll break your heads don't you worry, bastards. You at the front I'll remember you, the biggest bastard of them all."

He veered off, retreating across the road, shouting as he went. Eric called out, "We know you, we know who you are."

The jeering and booing continued as they strode down Kensington High Street. A glass bottle shattered on the road, a woman ran up and spat on one of the marchers. He swore at her. Suddenly, a large flat-bed dray drawn by two black and white shire horses pulled slowly out of a narrow side street ahead of them. Angling the cart across the road, the drayman reined in, dismounted and went to the rear of the wagon, where his assistant was lowering the tail-board. It was too late for the Blackshirts to manoeuvre around the obstacle.

"Halt."

They came to a ragged stop, those at the back bunching up on those in front. The order of the march was broken and the three columns fragmented, men spilling onto the pavements, cursing. They all sensed momentum had been lost. There was mocking laughter from those observing nearby.

"Spoiled your fun have they?"

"Should know better, all of you, grown men and all."

"Lost your way? Should ask a copper, there's plenty round here. They'll be only to pleased to help."

Eric went up to the delivery men.

"What the hell do you think you're doing? Move this thing at once."

"Hang on a minute mate. Just dropping off a couple of barrels of beer to this pub. Won't be two tics."

"You can march round, there's plenty of room", said the man standing on the cart as he balanced a barrel precariously on the rim of the wagon. Two constables walked up to see what was going on, but didn't interfere. The barrel thudded to the ground, landing on a small stained mat, before being rolled to the gaping cellar entrance in the pavement and stood on its end.

The offhand civility of the draymen drained the colour from Eric's face, his jaw muscles twitched and he clenched his fists. He thought better arguing back. There was a crowd gathering, now was not the place for an altercation.

Reverse if you can," he called out, "make some room."

He whispered to a young Blackshirt standing beside him.

"Make a note of the brewery – it's on the barrels – then have a word with the publican, there's a good lad. Watch yourself, we'll meet up later."

The Blackshirts slowly edged backwards, milling, colliding, turning, ranks dissolving, reforming, amid a cacophony of confused voices. It was several minutes before the cohesion of the columns was restored and under the watchful eyes of the two policemen they wheeled past the stationary cart.

The onlookers on the pavements grew more numerous as they approached Olympia, their demeanour subdued, apprehensive and often disapproving. In among them were supporters of the march whose mood was also mooted and low key, the visible signs of their approbation limited to desultory clapping. In marked contrast the railway bridge at the end of Kensington High Street was lined with raucous demonstrators waving Communist Party and trades union banners. The police had corralled them behind crude wooden barriers at the side of the road away from the main entrance to Olympia. As the marchers approached the bridge a policeman with a loud hailer slung over one shoulder stepped off the kerb and signalled for them to stop.

"Seems the opposition got here early then," called out a Blackshirt standing behind Tony.

"How much are they paying you?"

Others joined in the jeering.

"Keep it down back there."

"Bastards," called out a demonstrator. Then the harracking began.

"Workers against fascism – Mosley out! Workers against fascism – Mosley out!"

The noise was deafening in the narrow street. The policeman took Eric by the arm and led him out of earshot of the marchers. They talked briefly. When they returned Eric was holding the loud hailer and clearly unhappy.

"The police have requested that we do not proceed to Olympia as a group." His voice was distorted and high pitched. "They are concerned that there may be trouble. Given that we are the advance party and given that we want to co-operate with the forces of law and order."

There was consternation among the Blackshirts and a number shouted out in frustration at this unwarranted interference in their plan.

"Quieten down…co-operate whenever possible, I have agreed that the first ten files will follow me to the front entrance of Olympia, the rest of you under the command of Arthur Hammond will turn left up ahead there, down Olympia Way, and enter through the Grand Hall entrance. We will then meet up again inside for a briefing. Is that clear?"

The incessant chanting mangled his words and many marchers couldn't hear what was being said. They crowded forward. Disquiet spread through the ranks, undermining the equanimity of the military body, weakening its defensive unity, fraying tempers, crazing its resolve. Eric was forced, for the continuing benefit of the enterprise, to emphatically repeat his order.

"We're a disciplined force, let's not forget that. Our opponents obviously don't believe in the freedom to say what you want and to go where you want. Let's not let them stop us from doing exactly what we want. We're going to Olympia. Later tonight our great leader will tell the British people what we stand for, what we represent. There is nothing they can do to stop that. Minor battles, mere skirmishes do not make a war. Our time will come sooner than they would like. Much sooner."

As he finished speaking, he swung round to face the demonstrators, snapped to attention and saluted. His right arm a pointed symbol of defiance aimed directly at their heads. There was noisy outrage among the spectators on the bridge. The Blackshirts cheered and began to rally, hastily regrouping into two units.

"You fascist bastards. You make me sick," screamed a young bespectacled woman who was shaking with rage and trying to force her way under the wooden barrier. She was restrained by two friends as the Blackshirts marched past.

The approach to Olympia was more or less clear of people. Traffic had been diverted and was moving slowly along the Hammersmith Road, and the police were keeping away all pedestrians who did not have business in the hall.

"What a magnificent place," said the man marching beside Tony as they neared the main entrance of the building. It was only the second time they had spoken.

"That's the sort of thing I'd like to build given the chance – the architecture for a fascist future, for the state. Powerful and awe-inspiring, built on the grand scale. Just look at those columns in the centre there."

"Is that what you do then?" asked Tony.

"Student in my second year at Cambridge. Studying architecture. Name's Albert, Albert Cummings."

"Mine's Tony Cox. I come from Blackpool."

Tony looked afresh at the building towering over them. It reminded him of the ocean liner he had seen the day he had visited the docks at Liverpool. The fresh white paint, the rows of small windows running along the side, the railings, the Union Jack fluttering on its flag-pole and the name Olympia in large block capitals. H.M.S Olympia sailing the seas for fascism, flying the flag for Britain, the "Honourable Mosley's Ship Olympia" launched in 1934 to bring fascism to a welcoming world and a grateful Empire.

Eric was in a bitter mood when they finally got inside the hall. The police had held the marchers on the pavement outside while they checked with the building management. Everything was behind schedule.

"It's bloody humiliating. That prig of a police inspector had the cheek to tell me that he needed more than my personal guarantee before he could allow us to proceed. I ask you what sort of bloody word is proceed? Then tells us we have to split up or walk away and wait for Mosley, or someone else in authority. You can see that can't you, he'd have my bloody guts for gaiters, he would. I fought for my country, I know how to organize a bloody campaign, more than he probably does, jumped up little nobody. Then did you see those people outside? The sooner we get to grips with things the better it strikes me, sort this lot out I can tell you."

He stopped, clutched his forehead and looked around for somewhere to sit down.

"I get migraines sometimes," he said quietly, "See that everyone gets positioned round the building, will you. Cover all entrances, then send all the stewards from the main hall to me in about half an hour. Need to run through it all one more time. I may have a bit more intelligence on who we can expect in here by then. I hope to God it's some of those from the bridge, or even that bloody brewery man. Tony you stick with me, it should be lively. I feel like banging some heads together tonight."

"Mosley out, Mosley out. Death to Fascism, death to Fascism. Socialism lives, free the workers."

The chanting was clearly audible in the hall. Tony looked out at the seething, encroaching mass from the first-floor window of the manager's office, there was an emptiness in the pit of his stomach and his heart was racing. A catch in his breathing accentuated his natural anxiety, a headiness that clouded his thinking and made him nervous. Under siege he discovered he was frightened, but could barely admit it to himself. He knew he wasn't preternaturally brave and was aware he shouldn't be there, he wanted to leave yet understood he had no choice but to remain. His father had been a weak man but had gone off to war. He would do the same, his resolve was clear. There was only one way forward, feed on the excitement, thrive on the fear.

Hundreds of people were now outside, chanting, taunting, jostling with the police. They were being held back from the entrance as BUF party members and supporters streamed in – dinner-suited men, women in evening gowns, army officers, high-ranking dignitaries, so Tony had been told, Lords and Ladies. Bentleys, Humbers, Daimlers, the occasional Rolls Royce drew up, disgorged their passengers and pulled away to cries of "Bloody murderers", "Fascist bastards", and "Mosley's monkeys". Occasionally some of the demonstrators would break through the police cordon and surge forward, forcing the guests to hurry towards the entrance.

"Looks like a full house tonight, not bad. Shame they're not all paying," the hall manager snorted. He was a short plump man wearing a tight khaki-coloured linen suit and was standing beside Tony, smoking a pipe and looking down on the mêlée.

"Can't say I have much sympathy with your lot, with any of the political parties for that matter if I'm honest, but old Mosley can certainly pull them in. Must say something. Though that bunch out there look like trouble to me. If any of them get into the hall, it could get interesting. Mind you, I see you've come pretty mob-handed. Have to keep an eye on 'em though."

Tony nodded.

"We know who the troublemakers are, so don't expect a lot of bother tonight."

"Not my problem mate, unless you start smashing up the place. Can't see that myself. You'll be lucky to get this crowd in their seats by eight o'clock, particularly as you're using your own stewards, not my usual lads. The hall can accommodate twelve thousand you know, that's a lot of bums to get on seats."

"Mosley's always late anyway. A tactic he uses for raising expectations supposedly. They've got a band playing all the old favourites, which'll keep people happy."

"Should do the trick for a while, yes."

The air was heavy with tobacco smoke, a pungent variety Tony didn't recognize. He needed air. He left the office and walked through to the main hall. It was almost full. The bustle of multiple small movements and the garbled words of myriad conversations filled the vast space with sound, the inconsequential scraping of the pit orchestra sited below the stage barely an undertone. Tony strained to pick up the melody. Rows of chairs had been laid out in the central arena and this was seething with people. Four large searchlights, positioned in the open areas that bordered these seats, pointed at the stage at the far end of the auditorium. The permanent seating was banked up around the perimeter. Tony could see very few empty places. He was uncertain what he was supposed to be doing. Eric had assigned him to one of the roving "Biff squads" and told him to keep his eyes open for trouble, helpfully adding that if there was any he was to pile in and sort it out. This was madness, he knew it, he had never been a fighter. He turned and Eric was beside him.

"Mosley's here, he's in the office being briefed. A couple of the other columns ran into trouble getting here so he wants to know our side of it. Usually works it into his speech – threats to freedom, blah di blah. Seems to be limping, sad to say it's nothing to do with fighting the good fight, more to do with fighting the gentlemen's fight. Fencing apparently, strained a muscle. Wouldn't put it past him to say he was injured on the way here tonight. We'll see. He'll be out in five minutes or so and that's when the trouble will really get going. Need to keep your eyes open. I'll join you as soon as I can."

There was a ragged fanfare. Tony glanced at his watch. It was eight-forty. The audience turned, heads craning. A ten-man Blackshirt honour-guard was slowly goose-stepping down the central aisle, bearing Union Jacks and fascist banners. Sympathizers around the hall were standing and saluting, arms outstretched, as most present looked on intrigued. Sir Oswald Mosley came into view, there was a cheer, and scattered applause, which built in intensity as he moved closer towards the stage. He acknowledged those around him with a slight sideways movement of his head and an effete salute – his right arm raised, slightly crooked at the elbow and the palm of his hand bent backwards – which set him apart. Such a manifest display of confidence in his ability to lead, larded with upper class arrogance and wrapped around with the latent trappings of power elicited a visceral response that was difficult to ignore. Beguiled, Tony raised his arm and saluted out of respect for the man, his position and his supreme dominance. Momentum was building, a virtuous circle of pageantry, symbolism and ideology that inflamed the enthusiasm of the masses present, choreographing their actions and forecasting their responses.

The house lights dimmed. The searchlights burst into life, punching cones of yellow light through the darkness, the dazzling beams sweeping erratically around the hall, before one by one they pin-pointed the marching figures and steadied, incandescent polished leather and burnished metal, flaring. The spectacle possessed a visceral dynamism matched by the excited appreciation of the crowd which, feeding on its own lustful desire for change, built towards an overheated crescendo of adulation.

Attuned to the temper of the moment Mosley reached the front of house and halted, his back to the assembly, while his flag bearing escort divided right and left and marched up the steps onto the stage, the exuberant rhythmic accompaniment to their progress undiminished. They formed up along the apron coming to attention with their banners tilted towards the audience. The vacant rostrum, stage centre, gleamed in the beam of a solitary spotlight. Mosley turned and at that point, the constrained clapping exploded into a babel of wild applause, cheers and wolf whistles. Staring straight ahead he accepted the rapturous acclamation unabashed. Overhead foils of light slashed the gloom as the spotlights broke away from the central drama, weaving crazy reflected patterns across the glass roof and iron rafters of the hall. Refracted rainbow colours burst forth from eruptions of light scarring the eyes of the awed onlookers with ragged glowing stars.

Mosley, the accomplished performer, held the hall in fervent suspension, existence subverted for minutes, until the right time for action arrived. Then brusquely the connection with his audience was severed and Mosley turned and limped after his honour guard, his infirmity now more pronounced. Stepping out of the light into the shadows at the edge of the stage, his absence inverted the jamboree atmosphere allowing the seriousness of the enterprise to impinge on the gathering. This subtle collective shift occurred in the briefest of moments and sober applause greeted his reappearance on the stairs. Discipline restored, the spotlights ended their anarchic dance and focused their intensity on the immaculately composed luminary as he crossed to the rostrum.

There was a staccato burst of cheering as he scanned the audience. He raised his arm in wan salute and it died quickly away. He nodded in the direction of the orchestra. The thin opening notes of the National Anthem were heard before they were drowned out by the rush of the vast audience getting to its feet. Their combined voices, spurred on by an enhanced patriotic fervour and a sense of righteousness, ensured a rousing three-verse rendition of "God Save The King". Tony mouthed the words. As the music died away, Mosley motioned for quiet.

"Ladies and gentlemen, this meeting, the largest indoor gathering ever held under one roof in Britain, is the culmination of a great national campaign in which audiences in every city of this land have gathered to hear the fascist case…"

"Fascism means murder: Down with Mosley, Fascism means murder: Down with Mosley."

The hecklers were in the banked tiers of seats to Tony's right a hundred feet or so from where he was standing. He could see several groups of men and women on their feet, yelling and waving their arms. They were surprisingly loud, the acoustics of the hall working to their advantage, and he could no longer hear what Mosley was saying.

"Get ready. Wait for a signal from the stage. We've to deal with the first few by the book."

Eric was standing behind Tony with four other men he had never met before. They were lean, refined enforcers physically attuned to violence unlike the muscle-bound, overweight chucker-outs Tony saw patrolling many Blackpool pubs during the summer season.

"This is my crack squad, only just got here. Had a spot of trouble outside to deal with."

They nodded at Tony.

"Move around the side and get above them. Don't worry if the bastards see you. Then wait. I'll give you the signal."

On stage Mosley was exclaiming about the freedom of speech and warning the protesters that they would be ejected if they didn't stop interrupting him.

"Fascism means murder: Down with Mosley, Fascism means murder: Down with Mosley."

One of the spotlights played across the demonstrators and they were visible to the entire hall. Many of those close by were watching them, ignoring the speech. Tony stood feet above them in one of the narrow gangways between the seats. They didn't appear to have noticed his approach. He was sweating profusely and the tightening in his stomach made him nauseous. He didn't think he could act, his motivation seemed purely self-serving, designed to save face rather than coming from some deep-seated commitment to the cause. Did he care enough to turn violent at the drop of a hat, as seemed to be required? He wasn't sure. The only person he had ever hit was his brother and that had been a justified retaliation. He chewed his lower lip, tasting blood.

"...everyone here has seen that I have been unduly tolerant of your behaviour. Have given you due warning of the consequences of your actions. My patience is exhausted. Stewards will you please remove those people."

"Go, go", shouted Eric, waving the squad forward. The protesters, angry committed men and women, turned to face them. People seated nearby struggled to get out of the way, pushing and shoving, faces contorted with effort, largely silent except for their agitated breathing. Tony froze, momentarily incapacitated by the glare from the spotlight and his own fear, before being physically swept into the fray. The imperative of the contact was relentless and unforgiving and his attention focused on a young man with a red scarf around his neck that he had noticed standing at the end of the row of seats.

"You're coming with me."

He grabbed his arms. There was no resistance, which was a surprise, just physical compliance and a disconcerting air of composure that undercut Tony's own feigned aggression.

"No need to raise your voice, I'm not deaf. Not like you must be. How can you listen to this rubbish, you must be my age. Hey, watch what you are doing will you."

The reasonable words modestly delivered were disquieting and Tony was aware that his response was banal and ineffective.

"Shut up, just shut up."

It was a game, a farcical pretence, with both sides playing their part. There was no fire to their captives' protestations, no vigour to their struggling, as they were manhandled down the steps into the maze of corridors below the auditorium. Around them the chanting grew louder, the abuse more explicit.

"Going to be a busy night for you, I think", the young man said grimly, "We're not going to let Mosley have his say, however many of us you throw out."

The underground passageway was dimly lit, the damp painted brickwork glistening in a pallid green light, the air stale and fetid. It was crowded. Writhing figures indistinct in the gloom threatened and imparted violence, their slow motion grappling a ballet of flailing limbs, slamming bodies and butting heads. Swirling around Tony the madness of the action, each pairing a tableau of impetuous force and rash judgement. Eric was in among them, his tensed form hunched over a cowering body, bunched fists lashing, the dull thumps of angry contact resonating in the narrow space and underscoring the shrill cries of fury and pain.

"Look I've had enough of you, keep quiet or else."

Eric had grasped his victim by both arms, a brown tweed jacket pulled back over his head.

"Take them down there. We'll chuck them out by the back exit on Beaconsfield Terrace. Quieter that way."

Up ahead a Blackshirt was struggling with a prone demonstrator who was refusing to get up off the ground.

"Leave me alone, you have no right", he screamed as he was dragged slowly towards the exit doors. Tony could see an upended leather holdall and black beret lying on the dusty concrete floor. All around struggling figures hove in and out of view, a cast of characters peripheral to, but critical for, the central drama.

"Time to teach you a lesson in politics, you little bastard."

Eric had thrust the young Communist up against the brick wall of the tunnel. Holding him by the lapels of his jacket he hit him hard once, twice in the stomach. The man collapsed onto his knees with a feeble gurgling cry. Eric struck him again with his fist on the side of his head. Incensed, Tony's prisoner broke free and ran towards Eric.

"You animals, you fucking animals", he cried.

Without thinking Tony followed, lunging forward to grab an arm, the momentum swinging the man forcefully into the wall. There was a sickening thud and his body lost resilience, sliding slowly to the floor. Blood frothed from his broken nose and open mouth, gobbets of pink-tinged mucus spraying outwards in stuttering bursts.

"Look out, Tony!"

He whirled round. A demonstrator was struggling to reach him, but couldn't free himself from his assailant. He was held by one arm, the other flailing wildly.

"Watch out."

Tony tried to push him away but he kept coming forward.

"I can't hold him much longer, do something for Christ's sake."

Tony lashed out hitting him in the mouth. The pain in his hand was excruciating as splintering teeth lacerated his knuckles. Angry he punched repeatedly until the man collapsed at his feet. The exhilaration was intense. Looking down at the prostrate body, he noticed a beard, shot through with grey. He had beaten an old man.

"He'll be fine, you can hear him groaning, he'll just have a sore head for a few days that's all. Come on, let's throw this lot out and get back in there for some more."

One of the stewards had drawn a switchblade.

"I want to deal with these two first, make sure they don't think of returning any time soon."

The struggle ceased, a stillness prevailed as all in the vicinity focused on the weapon being waved threateningly in the air. A protestor, muttered, "Please, no."

The Blackshirt smiled, his arm flicking deftly forward, the knife cutting cleanly through the man's braces. His loose baggy corduroy trousers slumped to his knees.

"That should slow you down," he sneered as he leaned over and cut through the thick black leather belt of the man standing next to him.

"Nobody likes showing their bare arse."

He turned and faced a man who was crouching against the wall.

"Stand up you Jew lover."

The man, in his late forties with receding hair, rose slowly to his feet. His face was deathly pale as he stared defiantly at the steward. He spat into his grinning mouth. The Blackshirt recoiled in horror, gagging as he frantically wiped his lips with his hand.

"Hold the bastard."

Coughing he slowly drew his blade across the man's cheek, tracing a fine vermilion line strung with glistening ruby-red beads.

When Tony returned enlivened to the auditorium the ambience was electric, the tumult overpowering. The clamour of protest reverberated throughout the hall and the volume of the public address system had been turned up in an attempt to drown out the chanting. The din threatened to overwhelm Mosley's speech, diminishing the effect of his words, distorting their meaning and diverting attention from his performance on stage.

"…we have in England low wages, long hours, rotten houses, unemployment, and poverty, all absolutely unnecessary!"

Mosley thumped the rostrum with his right hand and paused, aware he was losing his audience.

"With the vast Imperial resources which are the heritage of this country, in this age when scientific progress and technical advance has vastly increased production, the problems of poverty and want can easily be solved by a government empowered by the people to carry out their will. While democratic governments are giving away the empire which our fathers won…"

The chanting continued.

"Down with Fascism, Down with Mosley, Down with Fascism, Down with Mosley."

In frustration, Mosley halted his speech and berated the hecklers, inciting further jeering and shouting. The outnumbered stewards targeted those who were out of their seats and forcefully escorted them from the building. But the protests continued in a co-ordinated manner – flaring up in disparate banks of seating as other areas were cleared of protestors – and members of the audience began to leave fearing further violence. Tony heard whispers that Blackshirts were being roughed up and suffering serious injuries. His own squad had been obstructed and abused by audience members sitting near a protester they had been trying to remove. The stewards were on edge and tempers were fraying.

"…it is the force which is served by the Conservative Party, the Liberal Party, and the Socialist party alike, the force that has dominated Britain ever since the War, and which ruins the economy of many parts of this country – the force of International Jewish finance."

There was uproar across the hall, the chanting and taunting redoubled. A tin can lobbed from the stalls bounced across the stage.

"Ah, I thought they wouldn't like to hear their master's name. The Labour party squeals about capital doing it. It is those who have accumulated great holdings in financial houses who sit in London, not developing British industry but exploiting foreign industry, not lending money to assist British industry and re-equip our mills but going where they can get quicker returns and profits, going into the Orient, where there is a great virgin field of labour un-employment, where women work in the foul slums of Bombay and Madras, for one purpose and one purpose alone – that Lancashire may be destroyed in order that the City of London may wax fatter and fatter."

Mosley was shouting.

"This is bad," thought Tony as he leaned against a gold, green and red painted iron pillar, catching his breath, "there are too many of them." His arms ached, his hands were sore and his shins badly bruised. He was thirsty.

Suddenly there was shouting from high above him and yellow leaflets began fluttering down out of the gloom like confetti. People looked up as the papers began drifting in to land amongst them. A few stood up, concerned, and called to the stewards. The roof void was in darkness, but the shadowy iron ribs of the arched glass ceiling could be traced against the red-tinged, star-flecked sky. There was no sign of demonstrators.

"…the Empire belongs to you, the People of Britain! Thousands of Englishmen won this great Empire, which has been the glory of the world; their sacrifice and heroism…"

"Liar, liar, Mosley a liar, liar, liar, Mosley is a liar."

Mosley faltered and glanced up, then turned and looked questioningly at the stewards standing on the side of the stage.

"Ladies and gentlemen, I apologize for this latest interruption. It appears some of our critics have climbed up into the roof in an attempt to prevent me from speaking. Now this is taking things to an extreme. I appeal to them to come down peacefully, there will be no trouble."

"Death to Mosley, death to Fascism. Make us Mosley, come and get us, send up your bully-boys, if you dare. Death to Mosley, death to Fascism."

There was scattered applause and shouting and screaming broke out again across the hall. Mosley flung his arms wide in an appeal to the audience.

"Ladies and Gentlemen, this is what we have to deal with. I assure you we will sort this out immediately, there is no cause for concern. Stewards please apprehend those people. There must be no violence."

He paused and consulted his notes on the rostrum.

"Yes, the Empire, the British Empire it belongs to you, the people…"

A searchlight that had been fixing Mosley on the stage was directed up into the roof girders, its beam obscuring all not caught in its searching yellow eye. It was a dazzling display as the spot traversed the curved glass roof, shards of light reflecting back on to the floor of the hall. Many in the audience stared upwards, watching the luminous show, ignoring the speaker on the stage. Captured fleetingly in the skittering glare they would look away, hands raised, shielding their eyes. All the while the flyers drifted down out of the darkness, efflorescing briefly in a sweep of the beam, diminishing into the gloom as it passed. People grabbed for the them as they emerged floating within reach, standing on the seats, leaping into the air. The searchlight was unwieldy and the operator struggled to control it. Gradually the beam's erratic course slowed and it began to systematically quarter the roof: illuminating grey painted iron girders, each bolt clearly defined; the diffuse glare from the glass panels; the narrow iron cross-ribs; girder, glass, rib, girder, glass, one followed another. The audience mesmerized by the spectacle, waited. Mosley had stopped speaking and was looking up into the roof space. The hubbub died away. The protesters had stopped chanting and nobody stirred, there was barely a rustle of people getting to their feet, making their excuses, heading for the exits, people with coats over their arms stood in the gangways and at the doors, peering into the air. The spotlight began its second sweep, aided by the blanched illumination from the partial moon that had just risen over the lower rim of the glass arch and was casting a silvery patina over the girders.

"Where are they?" muttered Eric as he came up behind Tony, "I want people up there as soon as we spot them, this is beyond a joke. The whole bloody meeting's at a standstill."

He tapped Tony on the shoulder and nodded towards the centre of the hall.

"They must be somewhere near here if you look where most of those handbills are coming down. God, I don't know what that idiot on the spotlight is playing at. It shouldn't be too hard, should it? After all they're not going anywhere. You stay here and keep an eye out. I don't want the climbers getting away. Be careful though, they'll certainly have friends on the ground."

He moved off towards the searchlight. There was a gasp. People cried out, pointing.

"There they are; on that girder; back a bit; you've gone past; I only saw one man; how many are there? They've missed them."

The beam shimmered to a halt – catching a red and gold shield, the coat of arms of the Iron-masters in its ghostly tremulous light – dimmed slightly and then began to retrace its passage. A dazzling burst and there they were, two men, spotted in the blaze, seated on either side of the central support of the arched roof on one of the main iron girders that made up the ribs of the building. They were shielding their eyes with one hand, holding on with the other and energetically swinging their dangling legs. As the light settled on them they waved then shoved their remaining piles of leaflets into space, sending them showering down on the upturned faces. Around the hall pockets of supporters clapped, cheered and waved coats over their heads. Whoops of triumph came from the front of the auditorium, where two men and a woman were attempting to climb up onto the stage. They were dragged back by stewards.

"Gentlemen, this is a reckless escapade. I demand that you come down. You are endangering yourselves and members of the audience. Enough is enough."

As Tony's eyes grew accustomed to the glare, he realized that the men were sitting on a girder supported by the pillar he was leaning against. Without thinking, he leapt up and grasped an overhanging ledge of metal that protruded just above his head, kicked his legs and hauled himself up. The iron collar, which was wide enough for him to sit on, formed part of the building's anchoring foundations, acting as a brace, securing the two large beams which formed the outer edges of the roof truss and which had bolted onto them a framework of lesser struts. This open mesh-like structure allowed for a two-foot wide access space through its centre.

"This should be easy to climb. That lot up there aren't as daredevil as they look," he thought.

The metal bridge arched up above him into the gloom. Getting tentatively to his feet, he reached up and sought out a handhold. He sneezed. There was dust everywhere, coating surfaces in a furry accretion that felt unpleasantly greasy. He wiped his fingers then his palm on his trousers.

"I must be careful."

On stage Mosley was trying to re-engage the crowd and divert attention from the drama unfolding above their heads.

"…you the pioneers of the British Revolution shall be remembered and honoured wherever English men and women are gathered together. In days to come your children shall call down the blessings of Heaven upon your heads because you had the courage in these days of our struggle to stand up with us."

Tony began his ascent unseen, his climb shrouded in shadow. He gained height rapidly, keeping his eyes firmly fixed on his hands as they moved purposefully upwards from bolt to bolt. Stopping to catch his breath and clear his throat, he found he could see more clearly in the reflected light. The iron beam was leveling out, which meant he must be getting close to the protestors. He glanced over the edge of the girder.

"Oh no…no."

Shutting his eyes, he clutched the metal and rested his head on his forearm, gasping in lungfuls of dusty air.

"It's too high, what am I doing, it's too high."

Cramp seared the muscles in his calves and he was conscious of a sharp pain in his knuckles. He feared he was unable to move.

"…that is what the Labour Party was saying this morning. Everything was perfect till a man like Mosley came down and stirred up trouble. Everything was peaceful and happy until the wicked Blackshirts came. You were all living in paradise until then. Why, today they are more conservative than the conservatives…"

Tony could only ascend, one deliberate handhold after another, his feet carefully placed. The dread of failure was a spur. He crawled slowly into the full glare of the spotlight and was a yard from his quarry, before he was noticed. The two men had been concentrating on events below and were taken by surprise.

"Stone me Jack, there's one of them up here."

Jack peered round the central pier.

"So there is. Mind you he looks like a scared rabbit, he's got his eyes closed."

"Anybody coming up your side?"

"No, can't see anyone. Hang on I think there's something. Yes, we're cornered mate."

"What happens now?"

"Dunno, let's wait and see what they have in mind."

Tony opened his eyes. There was an iron-shod boot sole, he could clearly make out the pattern of the leather stitching, and noticed the frayed end of one of the laces. The man was wearing brown corduroy trousers with muddy turn-ups and was staring at him.

"Not got a head for heights then? Me, I was in the navy, tall ships."

Tony closed his eyes.

"They sent you to bring us down, did they? How you gonna do that? Fly?"

The two men smiled.

Down below people at the back of the hall had caught sight of Tony – he was hidden from those directly underneath him – and were calling out.

"… the forces of political corruption and all the hatred of the old world…"

Mosley hesitated and looked up.

"Ah, I see my stewards have reached those perched in their aerie high above us. I think this has now gone far enough. Come down and there will be no trouble. I do not want any fighting. This is a dangerous situation, people could get hurt. My stewards will not harm you, but will assist in helping you down."

"More the other way round I should think. Come on sonny, you heard your master, give us a hand."

He reached towards Tony, holding out a grimy khaki military-issue canvas knapsack.

"Here, you can carry my bag for me."

Tony shook his head. His hands tightly gripping one of the cross ribs. The man looked away.

"Time to call it a day Jack?"

"Yeh mate, we've shown these Blackshirt bastards. See you on the ground."

Shouldering his bag the man started to slither feet first towards Tony.

"You'd better move," he said, grinding the fingers of Tony's left hand beneath his heel.

"I'm not waiting for anyone."

"You'll bloody wait for me."

Tony screamed, as he grabbed the boot and, driven by the intense pain, twisted. The man, caught off balance, toppled from the girder, hanging on by his hands and one foot. The colour drained from his face and he stared wildly through stricken eyes. There were gasps and cries as people clambered from their seats directly below them. The canvas bag slipped from the man's shoulder and plunged to the ground, where it lay crumpled and untouched between the empty seats.

"Please gentlemen, be careful. I want no more violence. Come down now."

Straining the protestor hauled himself back onto the girder and clung face down to the solid span, shaking. Tony, tears streaming, began to slowly retreat, he could barely grip with his bruised hand and his legs were numb. Alert to danger he stared fixedly at the man's boots, as his antagonist gingerly began to follow him. There were cheers and applause as they descended, the spotlight tracing their progress. As Tony lowered himself to the ground, he was grasped round the legs and helped onto his feet. It was Eric.

"Well done lad, well done."

Hazy figures rushed to shake his hand, he was slapped on the back, offered cigarettes, he stood there in a daze.

"Here he comes, get him."

A pair of muddy boots dangled before his face. Hands grabbed them and pulled violently. The man resisted, then fell, collapsing in a heap at Tony's feet. He was mobbed by Blackshirts, beating and kicking him.

"Stop, he's mine," cried Tony as he pulled bodies away, "leave him to me, I've got him."

The attackers backed off. Their mark was lying curled up on the floor, his hands shielding his head. As the circle around him widened, he looked up and saw Tony.

"You and me is it?"

He got up on one knee, rapidly glanced at the malign faces in the crowd around him, wiped his hands on his shirt and then staggered to his feet.

"I'm all yours."

Tony lunged at him, swinging a wide wild punch with his uninjured right hand. The man parried the blow easily with his left arm and then jabbed Tony hard in the face, once then twice. Tony reeled backwards, his legs giving way, blood pouring from his damaged nose and mouth. He stumbled into a steward standing behind him, then fell into the arms of another, who slumped to the ground under the sudden dead weight, cushioning Tony's fall. His assailant was bodily lifted up and carried struggling from the hall into one of the side corridors. He was set upon by Blackshirts who broke both arms, his nose, three ribs and partially tore off his left ear, before themselves being attacked by a group of communists, who had seen their comrade dragged off, but had been unable to reach him in time to prevent the beating.

Tony was unconscious for minutes. He came round seated on the floor, leaning against a pillar his head protected by a folded overcoat. Bodies seethed around him, a mess of legs blurring his vision. The noise was deafening; people were talking across each other, shouting, calling for help. It took a while for anyone to notice he had come round.

"He's back with us. Any sign of the doctor?"

Tony felt cold and sick. His world was black and white, colours disconcertingly absent. The sensation of slipping from the girder and falling was real. Reflexively he turned his head to one side and vomited – dry retching convulsions that burned his throat and strained the muscles in the wall of his stomach. There was parting suddenly, a movement away, a perception of clarity. Tony shivered and wrapped his arms tightly around his body. He closed his eyes. The yawning drop was there. A warm hand touched his forehead, another loosened the shirt buttons on his shoulder.

"Tony? Tony? Can you hear me?"

Spinning below, rolling into that space, head first.

"Tony? It's Emily, Tony? Tony?"

Emily Carstairs had been on first aid duty all evening and had tended to a procession of the walking wounded – cuts, broken noses, fractured ribs – but Tony was her first unconscious patient. She had watched his climb into the roof and was amused that the "hero of the hour" should be that quiet, good-looking, hung-over boy from the mess room in the Black House. She was mildly taken aback at the pleasure she felt that he now needed her help.

"Can you hear me, Tony?"

Emily reached into a black medical bag and took out a bottle of smelling salts. Tony groaned and opened his eyes.

"How are you? It's Emily, remember me?"

She motioned for the stewards guarding them to move back.

"Can someone see if there is any water? Clean if possible."

She held Tony's hands as he came round.

"How are you feeling?"

"Terrible," he mumbled, "I can't see."

He tried to stand, but she held him down firmly by the shoulders.

"Stay there, there's no need to move. Doctor Abbott is around here somewhere, he should look you over first. You've taken quite a hammering."

"I'll be fine if I can just get going. Eric'll be needing help."

"No, no," she stated firmly, "No you don't. Eric can take care of himself. Anyway, the meeting is nearly over. It's all running way past time but Mosley is building to the grand finale. The worst is behind us, most of the "red agent provocateurs", to quote dear old Eric, are outside. But not down and out unfortunately. There could be problems on the way back to the Black House. But that needn't bother you. Foot soldiers wounded in action get special treatment."

"What?"

"...me to look after you, bathe your wounds, strap up your broken limbs, massage bruised egos," a fleeting smile crossed her impassive face, "mop your fevered brow, that sort of thing."

"I want to get back on my feet. March out of here with everyone else."

"Come on, you've done your bit, no one expects you to."

Tony tried again to get up, his eyes searching for a gap in the crowd. He grasped her arm.

"Steady on, we'll see."

He slumped back against the pillar, strangely relieved, and closed his eyes. There was a commotion in the crush behind them and Eric pushed his way through, breathless.

"How is he, our hero? Taking it easy, I see. The doctor'll be here any minute."

He then leant in close to Emily.

"This is a shambles, the police are everywhere. Can I leave him with you? I've got things to sort out. If they ask what happened to him, say he fell or something. Haven't seen them taking anybody in, but you never know."

Emily stared at Eric incredulous at being told what to do.

"Yeah, yeah, fine. I wasn't born yesterday. I've been doing this longer than you have, you know."

She knelt down and spoke softly to Tony.

"He gets excited sometimes. And truth is, he doesn't think that much of women, for all his charm. Not long to wait now, then we can leave."

"...take its wealth, organize this mighty heritage. The message of the Blackshirt Movement to the people of Britain is, arise and enter your own realm of opportunity, and be great, happy and wealthy once again!"

There was scattered cheering and clapping.

"Thank you for coming to Olympia this evening. I hope our message has struck a chord with some of you. I apologize for the interruptions tonight, which have delayed the proceedings, but I hope you will appreciate the depths to which our opponents will now sink to prevent the great British people from hearing about and reaching their true destiny. Let it be a lesson to us all. Thank you and good night."

Mosley mopped his brow with a white handkerchief he took from his pocket, then waved both arms, acknowledging the audience, many of whom were now standing. The ovation had grown, there was shouting, whistling and sustained applause. Others were already streaming towards the exits. The National Anthem brought the stragglers to their feet, but didn't entirely halt the exodus, people were afraid there might be more trouble. Mosley appeared irritated and as the last notes of the anthem died away strode across the stage, surrounded by his bodyguards. He exchanged a few heated words with Eric before disappearing behind a curtain in the wings.

Tony heaved and sighed before again throwing up. He felt hot and hemmed in. There were people everywhere. A flustered elderly man tripped over his feet and swore at him. He was alone. The stewards had been called away and Emily was searching for the doctor. Tony didn't know it, but he was obstructing one of the main entranceways into the Grand Hall.

In the street, demonstrators were barracking the crowd as they left, thrusting leaflets into their hands. The Hammersmith Road was jammed with cars and taxis, crowds milled across the thoroughfare causing greater congestion. The traffic moved fitfully in both directions, the police were concentrating on keeping the communists and fascists apart, but people were streaming out of the many exits of Olympia and they were over-stretched. The demonstrators ejected from the hall by the Blackshirts had congregated in the "Hand and Flower," opposite Olympia on the corner of the Hammersmith Road and Addison Bridge Place. The police had already moved on a large gang who had been standing on the pavement outside, bottles in hand. They had gathered on the other side of the railway bridge and were waiting to ambush the departing Blackshirts.

"God, it's a crush. Can't find the doctor. Are you alright? Here have some of this, it's been keeping me going."

Emily raised a battered silver hip-flask to Tony's lips and poured.

"Cognac, can't beat it."

Tony coughed convulsively, Emily drew back, fearing the worst. He grinned weakly, wanting more. The pain in his limbs was easing and he felt deliciously light-headed.

"A miracle," he mumbled, "a French bloody miracle."

"I believe in them too," she said, offering him the flask, before taking a swig herself.

"Daddy would have slapped my legs for that, you know, he's strong on taking the Lord's name and all his good works in vain."

She giggled to herself as she took another sip.

"He's a vicar, the right reverend A.W.B. Carstairs, heard of him? You should have. You read the "Blackshirt", well he writes their weekly morality column. You know the sort of thing: "Why Fascists are Christian?" "Fascist faith or communist atheism?" It's all good stuff. Try to keep it quiet though, thugs like Eric never let up once they find out about the connection. Don't know why I'm telling you really. But I don't expect you'll remember much of this evening by the look of you. Bloody hell."

She clutched her ankle.

"Watch where you're going."

A disheveled man in a dinner jacket apologized curtly, then muttered, "Drunks, disgusting, blocking the exit."

Emily stuck her tongue out at him and then nudged Tony.

"Do you think you can move? We're in the way here."

He nodded.

"After one more sip I'll be fighting fit."

The hall was almost empty, the air thin and bruised. House lights feebly illuminated the cleaners who were sweeping up between the long rows of seats. A scattering of Blackshirts manned the exits, the rest gathered in the basement corridors ahead of the march back to the Black House. Oswald Mosley and key party dignitaries had already left in his black Humber escorted by one of the armoured vans, packed with bodyguards. The official plan was for the main force of Fascists to depart through a number of adjacent exits, hopefully dividing and confusing their opponents. The "I" squad was to leave by a side exit off the Hammersmith Road and retrace the route along Kensington High Street they had taken to Olympia earlier in the day. Tony was determined to accompany them. Emily had helped him to his feet and he had stood rather uncertainly, holding her round the shoulders for several minutes before limping off down the ramp.

"If you go with them I'm coming with you, after all I'm your nurse and I outrank you, so I can do what I like."

Tony wasn't the only one injured, a man had broken his arm and was carrying it in a crude sling lashed across his chest, others were cut and bruised, but he was the celebrity.

"Well done, mate."

"Bloody brave going up there, I couldn't have done that, no head for heights."

"We took care of that bastard that was up there with you, he'll be limping home."

A bantering jollity temporarily bolstered the column's friable morale. Tony smiled.

"Here let me shake your hand, well done."

Everyone was tired, their faces sweat-streaked and grimy, hair ruffled, shirts and trousers ripped, torn and misshapen, shoes scuffed.

"What a good scrap that was, a few pints inside me and I'll sleep well tonight."

"Could do without the bloody walk back, how did those lucky sods get onto the vans?"

"Seems there's quite a few of the bastards hanging around outside. You were on the door earlier, see anything?"

"Not a lot, but I was at the rear entrance, where there wasn't much trouble. There's plenty of police out front though. Dick, over here had a good look and said they were pretty mob-handed there. That's the way we're going out."

"Where were you hiding then? Lazy …"

"Give over, you'll give a soldier a bad name. I was in there with the best of you. Look, listen to this: we was near the front of the hall, we had this right little madam. You know you have to be bit careful with the ladies, but this one had a bloody hat pin this long, no kidding. Old Reggie took it straight in the backside. You can laugh, its true. Never heard anybody squeal so loud in my life. Sticking pigs out in India had nothing on this. Took four of us to get her out and that was after she gave me this," he pointed proudly to a ruddy-black bruise around a half-closed eye, "smashed me right across the side of me face she did. I tell you keep away from her if she's waiting outside. Got on a red top, brown skirt. Oh yeah and curly red hair. Can't miss her."

Tony was suddenly grasped round the chest from behind and squeezed firmly.

"Watch my …"

It was Eric.

"We love him, don't we lads? He's a real hero. Good stuff Tony. You've done yourself no end of good with your monkey exploits. I'll set you up with a few drinks when we get back. And what a man we have here lads. Miss Carstairs tells me you're marching with us."

Tony nodded, embarrassed to be the centre of attention. Eric pulled him aside and said quietly, "Mosley was very impressed with what you did. Asked me who you were. I, of course, told him you were a good friend of mine. Excellent recruit, been doing sterling work up in Lancashire, potential to go far, you know all the usual baloney. He seemed to buy it. Wants to meet you before you go back up North."

Eric could barely contain his excitement and rocked animatedly back and forth.

"It couldn't be better," he mumbled to himself. Then taking Tony forcefully by the shoulder he walked him into the shadow of one of the barred doorways. They were out of earshot of the squad.

"Look," he glanced round, "there's bound to be a comeback after this shambles. Your little escapade gives me a chance to get out from under it all."

He nudged Tony.

"You understand me, don't you?"

Tony wasn't sure he did and looked on blankly. Eric turned aside in exasperation.

"You've been knocked around a bit, I suppose, but come on Tony, all you have to do when you meet the great man is mention me. Puff up our actions today, with just a touch of humility of course, but make damn sure he thinks we were the ones who saved him from an even greater disaster, understand?"

"Disaster?"

"Oh Tony, pay attention, will you. Lots of people saw the hammering we gave the commies and many won't like it. And you've got to give it to the bastards, they were pretty well organized. Never seen them like this before and it's not finished yet. Listen, it'll be all over the papers, mark my words – the stinking gutter press will not miss a chance like this. Probably find we laid into one of their reporters or photographers or someone. It'll be the usual story, together with photos, all across the front page. Plus there were at least a couple of MPs poking their noses in. God knows what they'll be saying and where. Questions raised in the House, that sort of thing. All calculated to get right up Sir Oswald's nose. I tell you, there'll be hell to pay. This was supposed to have been the crowning moment of the campaign, finally taking our message to the masses to show how politically respectable we are. I think it will be seen very differently. I've invested a lot in this and I don't want to go down just yet, so make sure you do your bit to help your old mate Eric. Right?"

Tony nodded. He was feeling exhausted, his head hurt and his body ached. He didn't want to hear what Eric had to say, or what anyone else had to say for that matter. He needed to sleep.

"Don't worry," he said and smiled reassuringly, "I won't let you down Eric. Anyway, I'm sure it won't be as bad as you think."

Eric patted him on the back.

"Don't bank on it, you've not been around the court of King Oswald like I have, anyway thanks. I'm sure you'll do your best. Don't mention this little chat to anyone else, will you? That's a good lad."

Emily smiled at them as they returned arm in arm.

"What are you two so pleased about?"

"Guess who's been summoned to meet our leader then, and it's not me?"

"Tony, that's wonderful."

She flung her arms around his neck and kissed him on both cheeks.

"I told you, didn't I? Derring-do will always see you through, especially in the dear old BUF. Congratulations. Now, let me guess?"

She leaned her head on one side put a finger to her lips and looked directly at Eric.

"Your old friend here took you aside and told you to put in a good word about him in case the Biff Squad gets itself biffed for messing up today. Am I right, Eric?"

"When are you ever wrong, dearest. A boy's got to look after himself, you know that only too well."

"Oh, I do. Wouldn't want to come a cropper, when one is this close to the top, would one?"

Shrugging his shoulders Eric leaned closer to Tony and said in a stage whisper, "Take no notice of her, she's just bitter and twisted and jealous of my success. It's not really very becoming in a lady."

Emily frowned.

"Give over, will you."

Turning to Tony she said coquettishly, "Eric is right, you will put in a good word for me too, won't you Tony? Tell Sir Oswald how I nursed you through thick and thin, restored you to full health so that you could return to fight the good fight whenever the call is made, whenever the trumpets blare. I know I am but a mere woman, but I did my duty. Stood resolutely with the best of them...1 ..."

"He'll have you first Lady of his Bedchamber if you go on. The state Tony's in, he'll probably repeat every word and then God knows, look."

Laughing he pointed at Tony.

"...we've lost him way back. Take no notice of her."

"Take no notice of him, rather. "Lady of the Bedchamber", indeed? There are worse things to be."

"Oh I see, like that is it."

Tony was confused, he'd stopped paying attention and was hazily watching the Blackshirts gather in the corridor in front of him, ready to take the salute before marching out of the building.

"Enough of this it's time to go. Tony, come on. Are you sure you are up to this?"

Tony started on hearing his name and nodded.

"Never felt better."

"Liar."

Jeers and catcalls met the Blackshirts as they emerged from the Grand Hall onto Olympia Way. They began to form up in military order in the narrow street sandwiched between the towering outer wall of Olympia and a high mesh fence that ran along the railway line. The underground station opposite was shuttered and in darkness. There was little light. The moon, that earlier in the evening had irradiated the hall, was now hidden by clouds and the only functioning street lighting was the gas lamps on the Hammersmith Road. A volley of stones ricocheted off the brickwork and bounced across the cobbles – it was too dark to clearly make out where the missiles were coming from. A young Blackshirt stumbled, clutching his head, blood flowing through his fingers. The column started to break up, nerves frayed by the uncertainty, people fretful and afraid.

"This is the last sodding thing we need."

"Christ, that was close, did you see where that came from?"

"Think they're on the other side of the railway, the bastards."

"Oh no, look at that lot. There must be hundreds of them. Sir, have you seen what's coming up behind us?"

"What are we waiting for?"

"Let's leg it."

The Fascists were lined up, facing the Hammersmith Road, where they knew they would meet opposition, they had not expected to be outflanked. But a large number of Communist demonstrators had been deployed in the streets at the back of Olympia – Blythe Road, Beachford Terrace Road and Macliser Road – to cut off any Blackshirts who tried to leave that way. They had already surprised Oswald Mosley and his entourage, screaming abuse as his convoy sped away, but after that it had gone quiet. Tipped off that the Blackshirts were massing in Olympia Way, they had gathered out of sight in Sinclair Road. On a signal they marched in silence round the corner of the exhibition hall and came up behind their adversaries.

Inconspicuous in the gloomy street between the soaring brick buildings they were about a hundred yards from the rear of the fascist column before they were spotted. There was a yell, high-pitched, almost a squeal, and a tremor ran through the Blackshirt lines. Discipline collapsed – men vainly pointed as others faced their attackers, anxiously determined, their faces grim masks, ranks splintered, individuals scattering to the sides of the road, backing away, colliding with those behind them – seeding confusion. There was much pushing and shoving. Hearing the warring cries, Eric ordered the four "I" squads, who were in the vanguard, to deploy to the tail end of the column.

"We'll hold the bastards while the rest of you get up to the Hammersmith Road, it's too bloody dark and narrow here for a serious set-too. Mason take charge. Wait for us on the bridge."

"Yes, sir."

Eric then pulled a rubber cosh from his belt and raced along beside the railings, following his squad. Tony was about to join them, when Emily grabbed his arm.

"Tony for God's sake, you're in no fit state. You've done enough today. Come on."

The column edged forward, making scrappy progress, the random nature of the bombardment and the imminent threat of attack agitating their cohesiveness and weakening solidarity between the ranks. Men inured to violence and indifferent to the consequences of their actions sensed the danger and the lengthening odds. Their hardened sensibilities were incapable of completely controlling their anxiety. Stones and bricks rained down, bloodying heads and bruising limbs.

Blocking the street in a line of men, two deep, Eric and his squad squared off against the communists. He was agitated and angry, snarling his words.

"Come on, you bastards, what are you waiting for?"

The jeering and chanting continued, but no one moved.

"Come on, what are you afraid of? Don't you like the odds, eh?"

"Fascist thugs, Fascist thugs."

"Shut up, for fuck's sake shut up. Yes I'm looking at you. What are you smiling at? You think it's funny do you?"

Eric sprinted forward and coshed a middle-aged man, wearing an open necked shirt and a beret, who appeared to be one of their leaders. He then retreated gesticulating violently.

"Bastard, that'll teach you to grin at me."

The man fell to his knees clutching his head. There was a groan from the crowd.

"Anybody else want a taste?"

He raised his cosh and pointed it at the kneeling man, whose white shirt was darkening at the shoulders.

"Or are you all just a bunch of sniveling invalids. You make me ..."

The words were drowned out by a deafening roar from the crowd, which surged forward, overwhelming Eric, who disappeared under a mass of lunging bodies. Without hesitation his fellow Blackshirts piled into the fight, screaming and lashing out indiscriminately.

The head of the retreating column had reached the Hammersmith Road, and was being funneled through a narrow gap between the police lines. The confused disturbance behind them in Olympia Way was a frenetic audible presence and three mounted policemen, with batons raised, pushed their way through the marchers and clattered across the cobbles towards the commotion, their horses' iron-shod hooves sparking. Constables followed on foot, their shrill whistles piercing the air. Facing the marchers on the opposite side of the main road was a noisy crowd of demonstrators who had gathered again outside the "Hand and Flower" public house. Up ahead, others blocked the road across the railway bridge.

"It's an ambush, we're bloody trapped," Tony muttered to Emily, "And the police are running away from it, down to where we've come from."

Emily moved close to him and tightly squeezed his hand. He looked down at her and smiled.

"Stick with me, you'll be alright. There are lots of us."

The ragged column had come to a halt, the apprehensive Blackshirts uncertain of the threat they faced. Their nervousness was infectious, indecision spread insidiously through the lines. The Hammersmith Road was momentarily quiet before a barrage of abuse shattered the calm. The decision to move was taken and the command to "quick march" given, but heard by very few. Order disintegrated. Individuals moved forward, others remained standing, looking around, alert to danger. Challenged on all sides the cohesiveness of the marchers gave way as waves of attackers broke against them. The tumult was deafening. Tony was pushed violently in the back and stumbled, painfully twisting a muscle in his knee. Turning he saw Emily tripping a lunging man, who fell heavily to the ground. She kicked him between the legs and he rolled, howling in agony, beneath the feet of a wrestling couple, bringing them crashing to the pavement. Tony pushed away their writhing bodies and staggered upright, only to be grabbed round the neck. Short of breath from his fall, he couldn't breathe. He clawed helplessly at the hard sinews of the man's arm, sweat flooded his stinging eyes, blinding him. His feet left the ground and he was enveloped in a harsh suffocating cloud of bitter Virginia tobacco. The bulging veins in his temples quivered. Stretching artfully, searching for the ground, he passed out. There was a scream nearby, an animal bellow, a nightmare's prelude. Falling, he could breathe again.

Tony was sitting on the road, his right leg twisted beneath him. It was raining. Heavy droplets smacked onto the ground beside him and spotted his face and arms. A fine spray, reminiscent of the sea mists swirling across the promenade at home, intermingled with the downpour. The rain would clear the air, there would be brilliant views of the ocean. He would walk out to where the breakers crashed onto the sand, far away from the day-trippers, and watch the terns. They would be fishing at this time of year, to feed their young. Soaring and arcing through the air, then plunging downwards like a spear, shearing the surface, before rising again, shedding water, a rebirth fuelled by the dying. And so it would go on. Tony lay down, he wanted to curl up and sleep, but something was sticking into his back.

"Tony, Tony, for Christ's sake, Tony."

It was Emily's voice, he felt her hands in his, tugging.

"Come on Tony, come on, get up, you must get up."

He heard the yelling and moaning. Could see the milling legs, behind the crouching figure of Emily, who glanced anxiously above his head, then pleadingly at him.

"Now Tony, now. I mean it now."

Pushing himself up from the tacky tarmac with one hand – as she pulled him with the other – he stumbled to his feet and looked round. Her fear was sobering. They were caught in the middle of the mêlée, the violent grappling spurred by undimmed anger and hatred. Tony saw he had been leaning against the legs of a stockily built man – the one who had grabbed him round the throat – who was standing immobile, clutching the right side of his face and whimpering. Blood ran freely from his damaged eyes, through fingers, over lacerated cheeks and into his overflowing mouth, from where it dripped onto the ground in heavy shining globules. His fractured, laboured, breathing sprayed a fine mist of blood and saliva into the air, which shimmered in the orange glow from a nearby gas lamp, crowning his bowed head with a sulphureous halo.

"Come on Tony, let's get away."

Tony held back, grasping her hand.

"What happened? Why is he just standing there?"

"Tony, please."

She tugged on his arm.

"He was choking you, trying to kill you so I scratched his face. Come on, before he comes round, he didn't get a good look at me, come on."

Tony pulled himself free, thrust his hand into his pocket and pulled out Eric's knuckleduster. He punched the blinded man in the stomach and watched as he subsided, without a sound, onto his knees. Then turned and hit another man, who was struggling with a Blackshirt against the wall of the "Hand and Flower", hard in the midriff. He felt immensely powerful.

"You shouldn't have done that Tony, come on, please, there are too many of them, we don't want to get arrested."

Head down she pushed him through the swarming mob of swinging, lunging figures, and down a dark side street that ran alongside the railway. It was calm and much quieter.

"There was no need to hit him Tony, I think I took his eye out," she stifled a sob, "I didn't mean too, but it felt like it. Let's go. I've had enough."

"Don't worry about him, he deserved it. Come on, you saved my life, I owe you."

He embraced her and she put her arms around his waist and looked up at him.

"You're right I suppose, but it was horrible, it just sort of gave way. There was nothing there."

"Forget it. I'm sure it wasn't as bad as you think. Anyway we won't be around to find out."

Tony hugged her again. Elated and still feeling strangely invincible, he knew he could do anything. He stared down at Emily, her face barely visible, and it came to him that he had no idea what she looked like. In the dim light he could make out a centre parting in her, he supposed, dark hair. She must have brown eyes, he thought, although there was no way he could tell for certain. He bent forward to kiss her. Their lips had barely touched when there was a loud yell from the direction of the Hammersmith Road. They were instantly alert.

"Over here. They're somewhere down there, they went this way."

Caught in the hazy glow of a streetlamp, Tony and Emily could see a man pointing in their direction. He was standing close to a group who were squatting on the ground beside a hunched body. Behind them the fighting appeared sporadic, the violence diminished, scuffling cartoon figures casting giant shadows on the wall of the public house. A mounted policeman galloped past, clattering onto the bridge, scattering Blackshirts and communists.

"Quick," Tony whispered, "I don't think they've seen us."

Holding hands they ran further along the street away from the lights on the main road. On one side there were high iron railings and a row of sycamore trees facing the railway cutting and on the other a terrace of early Victorian town houses, three stories high, all in darkness, the gates to their basements securely padlocked. They had covered only a few yards before they realized to their horror that the road was a dead-end. A block of flats marked the end of the terrace. There was a small courtyard in front, with a car parked in it, surrounded by a low fence. Tony tried the car door but it was locked.

"Bugger."

"I think there was an alley back there on the right, let's go there."

As they retraced their steps they could see their pursuers walking cautiously in their direction. It was obvious they were uncertain about what to expect. Tony and Emily found the passage and hurried down it, hoping it would lead into a neighbouring street and allow them to escape. It was unlit and they could only see a few feet in front of them.

"Damn."

"What's the matter? Keep your voice down, they can't be far behind."

"Thanks a lot. I've grazed my ankle on a cart or something lying in the middle of the bloody road."

"Here hold my hand. I'm following the wall. It seems to curve round behind the terrace. Let's hope it goes somewhere."

"These doors, they must be workshops or something. Ugh what's that? It feels disgusting."

They crept slowly forward. The road was unpaved and deeply rutted and their feet scuffled noisely in the dried mud and gravel heaped along the verge. Whispered voices could be heard at the top of the alley-way. Emily and Tony froze. Agitated they held their breath, but were soon forced to exhale.

"Shhhhh, they'll hear us."

"I know, come on."

They stumbled further along the track. On the opposite side they could make out the block shapes of a number of small cottages. In one of the upstairs windows a faint light was visible through a chink in a curtain. Above them towered the black silhouette of large factory or warehouse clearly picked out against the blue-black of the night sky. The still air was humid and smelt of mould and decay. The wall they were following was covered in a dense cascade of ivy, which scratched their faces and bare arms, and forced them out into the middle of the lane. They started as a small animal scurried away.

"Perhaps they've missed us and given up."

"Maybe. Wait here, I can't see a thing up ahead. I'll go and check."

Tony disappeared into the gloom, Emily heard him scrabbling his way forward. He returned a few minutes later.

"It seems to be a dead-end too, can you believe it, a dead-end," he sighed heavily, "the wall runs right up to the houses, there's not even a gate."

"Couldn't we try the house with the light, they might let us in."

"Keep your voice down. We'd be lucky, they won't open up at this time of night, not if they heard all the trouble. No, we'll just have to hide in that doorway we passed and hope they go away."

The entry was set slightly back from the alley and one corner was overhung with ivy. Emily slid behind it, shuddering as she brushed cobwebs from her face and hair. Tony stood in front of her, slipping Eric's knuckleduster agitatedly from one set of fingers to the other. Emily grasped him round the waist and pulled him tightly into the recess.

"I feel safer now," she murmured.

Minutes passed in silence. Their breathing eased and they began to calm down. Emily gently pinched Tony, once, then twice. He reached back and did the same to her. She squirmed.

"What a hero," she whispered, "all the girls will be after you now."

Her breath felt warm on his cheek, his skin tingled, sensitive to every touch, his body tensed then relaxed.

"Just remember all I've done for you today. We're comrades in arms, don't you forget, I'm first in the queue."

Tony smiled, the idea of a woman, let alone women, lining up for him seemed faintly ridiculous. He half turned towards her and was about to promise, "he wouldn't forget," when they heard voices and movement.

"Cor, its bloody dark down here. Can't see me own feet."

"They must have come this way, unless they got into one of the houses, but I'm sure I didn't see any doors opening, no lights or hear any voices, they must be around here."

"Keep it down. See if we can hear anything."

Silence. Scared, Tony and Emily held their breath. There were at least three trailing them, maybe more. As far as they knew none of their fellow Blackshirts had seen what had happened and followed them. They were on their own.

"Can you get out this way?"

"Dunno."

"If you can, we'll have lost them, the bastards."

The men came closer, moving slowly, cautiously finding their way.

"Oh, what's all this stuff?"

There was a rustling close to where Emily and Tony were hiding.

"That's ivy. Come on, you idiot they could be anywhere."

Tony couldn't see their stalkers but could smell perspiration and strong tobacco. Were they as obvious? He was sweating profusely and his heart was beating noisily. He was sure they would hear and be on to them. Emily had let go of his waist and was resting her clenched fists on his back, alert.

"Aagh, what's that?"

One man had passed them, Tony could now make out his faint silhouette. His nose itched, it was unbearable, but he daren't move. The two other men drew level with the first.

"Are you alright?"

"I think so, caught my foot in a damned pot-hole."

"Need a hand?"

"Yeah, just my luck, not a scratch brawling with those bastards. Do my leg in walking down a road," he laughed, "Oh sod it, I've had enough of this. You want to carry on? We've lost them I reckon. Couldn't catch them now anyway."

"No you're right," the younger sounding man appeared relieved, "I'm knackered, Bert what about you?"

"Yeah, I suppose so. Would have liked to have got my hands on them, though. Come on, give me your arm."

Their disengagement from the chase was a relief. Aware that luck had been on his side all evening Tony entertained the notion of stepping out of the shadows and proving himself yet again to Emily, but after brief consideration chose caution. He had no real choice as their pursuers' retreat from the alleyway was slow, measured and vocal.

"Do you think he'll ever be able to see again?"

"Honestly, I dunno. It looked very nasty, blood all over the place. I couldn't see the state of his eye."

"Bastards, how could anybody do that? He reckons it was that woman."

"Only seen something like that once before, years ago. It was in the ring, knuckle fight back of the George in Deptford, you know the place?"

"Yeh."

"Old Stan Barrymore, it was, taking on all challengers. Some poor bastard gets up and fancies his chances. Total mismatch. Should have been stopped, but you know what it's like. Everybody's tanked up. Anyway, he got beat so badly his eye came out. Hanging by a thread it was. Honest, blood everywhere. Dunno turns my stomach even now to think about it. Old Stan didn't get back in the ring for a bit after that, an' he'd seen a few things in his time I can tell you."

"What happened to the bloke's eye? Was he blind after that?"

"I can't remember the …"

Their voices faded away as they stumbled back along the alley. It was only when all was quiet that Tony and Emily relaxed. Sighing they sank to the ground with their backs to the wooden door.

"I need a drink. I hope I haven't lost that flask."

She rummaged around in her bag.

"Where is it?"

"God, that was close. Boxers!" Tony shook his head," Getting ideas above my station."

"What?"

"Nothing, just mumbling."

Emily shivered.

"Here it is, always right at the bottom."

Unscrewing the top she raised the flask to the gibbous moon that was emerging from behind a cloud, its glowing outer rim kissing the roof of the factory block.

"We were very fortunate Mr Moon, that you stayed hidden away until now. Cheers."

She passed it over to Tony, who drank deeply.

"Comrades in arms," he said quietly and Emily rested her head on his arm. They sat and drank without speaking, watching as the alley materialized before their eyes. The chilling, silvery light illuminating the commonplace details of what had been not long ago a place of danger.

"E.J. Hancock – metalworking", "Addison Saddlery", the two-storied cottages opposite, numbers one, three and seven, the flower box with the wilting flowers outside the downstairs window of number three, the bedroom light flickering in number seven – they must have fallen asleep with it on, or was it a child's room? – the weeds growing along the central ridge of the rutted track.

"What's the time, do you think?"

"Must be way past midnight, but I haven't got my watch with me."

Emily involuntarily shuddered.

"I can't believe I did that. It sounds like I really hurt him."

Tony gently brushed her cheek.

"It was me or him," he paused, "no two-ways about it."

"I know, you're right," Emily's response was tentative, "but it was a horrid thing to do."

She swallowed hard, took a deep breath and resolved to drive it from her mind

"How long do you think we should wait before moving?"

"I could sit here for ever."

Emily nudged him.

"Come on, we can try and find a cab. It doesn't feel safe to me round here. What would my father say? His darling out all hours, brawling in the streets and with a man she barely knows to boot."

"He need never know. I won't tell, I promise."

"Dead right you won't, there's lots he doesn't know already, don't want you spoiling things."

She stood up and held her hand out to Tony.

"One last swig."

"Finish it, there's more at the Black House."

He got unsteadily to his feet.

"Lead on."

"Keep your eyes open, there may still be Reds on the loose."

"Yes sir!"

They walked slowly hand in hand along the length of the alley, each stepping awkwardly between the ruts. At the top of the lane where it met Addison Bridge Place they stopped and peered cautiously towards the brightly lit Hammersmith Road. All appeared muted and subdued. There was little traffic, just the occasional pedestrian. A lone policeman leaned against the parapet of the railway bridge on the opposite side of the road. Tony glanced the other way. Darkness. The bright gleaming eyes of an animal stared back at him, otherwise nothing. As they approached the lights they let go of each other's hand and the policeman watched them as they hesitated before turning right and crossed the bridge, heading towards Kensington.

Several taxis passed them by before they managed to flag one down. They sat close together during the journey to the Black House, arms entwined. Tony stared out at the near deserted streets. This was his first ever taxi ride, and he hoped Emily had some money. He seemed to have lost the little he had sometime today, or maybe he spent it all last night, he couldn't remember and he didn't care. A rare feeling of heedless freedom.

The Black House was a blaze of lights when they drew up.

"I don't feel like going in just yet, do you? I fancy some fresh air."

Emily looked at him as she paid the taxi-driver.

"Well, it's a stroll with me or more male high-jinx, the choice is yours?"

"A stroll."

Emily smiled.

"Good, come with me."

Hand in hand they walked down Cheltenham Terrace, a gentle cooling breeze moving the branches of the plane trees, moonlight glinting on the sandy parade ground of the Duke of York's barracks. A cat slunk across their path and disappeared into the basement well of one of the imposing Georgian houses on the other side of the street. All were shrouded and closed, basking in the weak glow of the street lamps that was dimly reflected on the black-painted iron balconies set at intervals along the terrace. Somewhere in the distance a milk train rattled into Victoria Station, the metallic screech of its wheels audible, as it slowed down, crossing points. At the end of the road Tony could make out an open space stretching into a misty distance, a line of tall trees barely etched in the haze. He nodded ahead of them.

"Is that where we're going?"

"Mind your own business," a little later she added, "isn't this park lovely. If only London could be as quiet as this all of the time I could bear it then. I'm a country girl at heart. That's why I always try to come here when I have the chance. You can look up at the sky, almost make believe you can see to the horizon, watch the weather sweep in and pass over you. All the things I've missed from home since being down South. Not that I've not enjoyed it here, but there are some things … the air even seems fresher away from the roads and the buildings."

"I know what you mean. In the middle of that fight I found myself thinking of the sea back home, of terns fishing, ocean mists. It was very strange."

She pressed herself closer to him.

"I swear you can smell the old briny here sometimes. Must be when it's high tide on the Thames. The river is only just over there behind the hospital."

"Having such feelings probably means I'm not cut out to be one of Eric's Biff Boys. Fighting was never really my thing, even at school."

"Oh, I don't know, they're not all the muscle-bound thugs they like to make out they are. Take John Blade, I don't know if you've met him, he's a published poet. Quite a good one actually. So there is always room for a more sensitive soul. But I expect they'll want you working up north. Fertile territory there, you know. That's where I'm going next. I'm in line for Women's Organizer for the North, or something like that."

"Good, I'm glad."

"Why?"

"Oh it would be good to … you know, keep in touch."

"I'm only teasing, sorry, don't get embarrassed."

She stretched up and kissed him on the cheek. They stopped and turned to face each other.

"I'm not very good at this."

"Don't worry. There are very few experts."

She placed her hands on either side of his face.

"You're very good looking, you know. Although I suspect you don't realize it. I want to tell you something, I was attracted to you the first time I saw you in the mess room."

She smiled, laughing to herself.

"Romantic eh? We won't be the first or the last I wager."

In a delightful reverie of his own, Tony said nothing.

"You can kiss me, you know."

Hesitating, he leant forward and their mouths met. He grasped her firmly round the shoulders and pulled her close. Her flicking tongue gently moistened his dry lips, slowly prizing them apart, while her hands caressed his cheeks.

"Not here," she said, "I know just the place, come with me."

Taking his hand she led him across the road and through a narrow gateway onto a path that led diagonally across the open grassy parkland.

"Burton's Court, where all good Blackshirts come to play."

She giggled.

"Football, cricket, bowls, athletics, everything you can think of."

Grabbing Tony round the waist, she started to push him firmly across the grass.

"I bet you can think of a few more, can't you?"

Tony nodded and started to run.

"Catch me and I'll tell you."

With a shriek Emily chased after him. They weaved back and forth trailing dark intertwined tracks across the damp, moon-struck grass. Gasping for air Tony stopped, turned, his hands on his knees.

"I'm going to let you catch me."

"You're too kind, noble sir. Not much further now. See that ridge and the bushes?"

She pointed up ahead of them.

"My lair. That's where you'll catch me and not a moment sooner."

With that she raced past Tony, who lunged desperately in her direction, before spinning round and sprinting after her. Seconds later she disappeared among the bushes. Tony followed into the undergrowth and was lost. Everything appeared the same in the gloom. He frantically circled looming clumps and peered into one of them, parting the leafy branches with his hands, but she was nowhere to be seen.

"Damn it, Emily, where are you?"

Holding his breath, nothing stirred and he could hear the vast sounds of a senescent city, sense the echoing volume of concrete, bricks and glass, the flux of a great conurbation pressing in, filling him with disorientating joy. A new territory opened up before him – he noticed his shoes and trouser bottoms were soaking wet, mundane details trespassing – and his focus was precise, marred only by the stipple of laughter. She was close by lying against the sloping earthen boundary of the bowling-green, waiting for him.

"Isn't this a more secluded spot? No one can see us. Come here Tony, are we still friends?"

Emily held out her arms. Tony walked slowly across, grabbed her round the waist, hauled her to her feet and they roughly embraced, their bodies colliding, mouths discordant as they kissed – her teeth gouging Tony's lower lip – tasting blood. She pulled his shirt loose and ran cool hands over his back. He closed his eyes, his body charged.

"Touch me," Emily whispered as she fumbled to undo Tony's belt and unbutton his flies. Tenderly he caressed her breasts and through the fabric of her blouse teased her nipples. Absorbed he licked the corner of his mouth, savouring the warm metallic taste. Chilled air wafted around exposed legs as his trousers slid to the ground and bunched at his ankles. Emily lay back on the grassy mound and smiled up at Tony, who stood awkwardly exposed. Holding him at arm's length with one hand, she blew him a kiss as she began pulling up her grey skirt with the other. Tony was transfixed as the hem rose higher. Her blanched calves, knees, thighs shimmered in the pale liquid light. Kneeling down he placed his hand on her inner thigh and slowly tracked the skirt as it crept upwards, the barely perceptible roughness of the silk charging his gliding fingertips. He was breathing heavily. Emily flinched – her bristling skin rough to the touch as his hand slid over the rim of her stockings – a faint spasm embracing a whisper. Hesitation – he wanted this to be the end – but apprehension was a spur. He sensed her presence for the first time and had to act. Then a rapid intake of breath as his fingers again brushed silk. He rested his head uncomfortably on Emily's hip. He was beyond caring.

Grasping him gently by the upper arm she drew him on top of her. Spattering his face with kisses, she took his hand and guided it under the waistband of her girdle and down between her legs. She sighed deeply and laid her head back on the grassy bank, baring her pale fragile neck. Tony was unable to act, enervated by inexperience and the beauty before his eyes. Lying close to a woman, his first, was better than any imagining. Gazing at the dew-drenched bowling-green in a London park luminous in the moonset he saw a lake, a silvery grey mirror, reflections of his dreams. It was an earthly paradise. He had always believed he would find it.

Emily moaned as she moved her hips against his rigid, immobile hand. Staring through hooded eyes she whispered, "I need you," and threw her arms around him. Tony kissed her bare neck, throat and mouth, he nibbled her ear before burying his face in hair, perfumed with sweat, tobacco smoke and a sweet essence unfamiliar to Tony. It was, it seemed to him, the fragrance of Elysium.

"Tony, my darling move over a second, will you."

He rolled off her pliant body onto the bank, feeling the chill of heavy dew soaking through his shirt. He shivered.

"I'm very damp," laughed Emily as she lifted her hips, unclipped her stockings and pushed her knickers down to her knees. Leaning forward she rolled them to her ankles and eased one foot free. She let go and was about to lie back when she thought better of it, and reached out again to free the other foot. Lying back she waved her underwear in the air before tossing them aside.

"I'm yours."

They embraced passionately, Tony eager, all inhibitions abandoned, Emily calming, controlling, guiding. It was a brief coupling. For Tony was diving into a vast tropical lagoon, he had no idea in which direction he should be swimming, no inkling of where the shore lay. For Emily it was not so profound, yet she enjoyed the excitement, relished the danger and was smitten by Tony, which by her own taxing standards was a surprise. Afterwards, they lay close to each other on the bank, the raw damp forgotten.

"Do you have a cigarette?"

"Yes, but they got crushed in the fighting. Only fit to roll your own now."

"Ah well, you can't have everything I suppose, although you can always hope."

She leaned over and kissed Tony on the cheek. He stared at the sky. It was getting marginally brighter, a faint reddish tinge along the horizon bleeding into the blackness.

"What a perfect day," muttered Tony, "what a perfect day."

Chapter 5

GOD WILLING
13th June 1995

The office had recently been refurbished. Out had gone the old formal hardwood desk, the austere solid upright chairs, painted metal bookshelves and the functional brown carpet tiles. In had come a narrow pale pine desk complete with computer workstation, a high-backed black leather swivel chair, a wall of almost invisible shelving that could accommodate any combination of books, files, television screens and audio-video equipment. Banks of low comfortable seating were arranged around a glass coffee table with a permanent display of white lilies in an elegant twisted stainless-steel vase and the daily newspapers neatly arranged one on top of the other, their mastheads clearly visible. The walls had been painted a pale bluish-white and the framed certificates and pictures of past executives receiving awards, meeting local dignitaries, presenting employees with merit cups had all been replaced by two large original abstract paintings in narrow brushed metal frames. A blue deep-pile carpet and a new clear-fronted Tonelli drinks cabinet with its own fridge completed the makeover.

The room smelled of freshly ground coffee and seemed lighter than David remembered it. He had only been here once before as part of his induction programme when he joined the company just over a year earlier. The view was unchanged – the traffic surging down High Holborn ten floors below – otherwise he wouldn't have known it was the same place.

He had arrived early, just by a couple of minutes, but he was the first one there and the secretary had shown him into the office in silence. His department had been given no advance notice of the meeting, just a terse top-line message when they had arrived that morning – "Briefing in Larry's office on the future at 1300 today, all should attend. Sandwiches will be provided" – and he wasn't sure all his colleagues would be able to make it. David had a feeling this was going to be the "crunch" meeting when their fate would be revealed, others had not been so sure – "He'll just be laying out his plans for the future of the company", "How we fit into the corporate strategy, that sort of thing."

There had been rumours of changes ever since Larry Beckinsale had been appointed Chief Executive a few months before. David had decided he'd better take a note of what was said, but realized that he'd brought a pad but no pen. The office was bare, as he looked furtively round, all surfaces clear. It was annoying. David trusted his instincts even though they were wrong as often as they were right, largely because he was a pessimist and enjoyed looking on the dark side of things. He now felt uneasy and as the minutes ticked by he became more and more depressed. His discomfort put David in mind of another meeting many years before – it had been the week of his seventeenth birthday and he was still unhappily at school re-sitting his O-levels – that had started with the same nervous wait, the same sick feeling in the stomach and, as he remembered it, had ended in profound disappointment.

The offices of Messrs. Evans, Barmthwaite and Craddock, Solicitors, were located above Millers, the local grocer on Bridge

Road, the main street of Dumpton Gap. A narrow black door with a shiny brass knocker opened off the pavement directly onto a steep stairway that led up, via a sharp right-hand bend, to the cramped reception area, where a Miss Collins had her desk, typewriter and a large brown Bakelite telephone. She had seemed flustered when David, his brother Daniel, their mother and father and Uncle Freddy had arrived out of breath, fearing they were late.

"There was no need to rush," she snapped, "Mr Evans sends his apologies but ummm…" She coughed loudly and dabbed at her mouth with a handkerchief, cheeks flushing she continued, "… he's tied up with another…er…client. He shouldn't be long, please take a seat. I would offer you a cup of tea but we've run out of milk."

She sat down and began typing a letter. The percussive tapping of the keys reverberated around the wood and glass partitioned ante-room as the Coxon-Dyet family sat in embarrassed silence. David fidgeted with his collar – it was too tight and he was not used to wearing a tie – and watched a fly buzzing in tight circles around an electric fan set in the clouded glass panel above Miss Collins' desk. He was happy to be missing a day of school, but nervous of anything to do with his grandfather. He didn't want to be here.

"It's important you come David, it really is," his mother had said when he'd pulled a face at the news of the family trip to the solicitors, "he would have expected it. He really would. Come on, you liked him. He certainly had a soft spot for you."

David did agree with that.

His uncle Freddy suddenly broke in.

"It's bloody typical Stephen, everything to do with this business of Dad's is a problem. I'm fed up with the whole thing."

"Please Freddy, not now, the children are here."

"It's all very well."

"I'm not a child," said Daniel. He was three years younger than David and sensitive about his age. Perplexed Freddy glanced at him and then continued.

"It's alright for you Helen, but you didn't have to put up with him all your life. You think you've come to terms with everything. Never see the old bugger and then he springs all this on us … it's bloody…, bloody too much I can tell you."

"You didn't have to come, you know, if it's too painful. Stephen and I could have sorted it out."

Freddy looked at her aghast but said nothing. He then stood up.

"I'm going out for a fag, give me a shout when he turns up will you."

They listened to his heavy footsteps descending the stairs and heard the front door slam shut. Then his mother turned to David and spoke in a whisper.

"He's only jealous you know. He's come all this way out of curiosity to see how much his father was worth, but he knows he'll get nothing. Mind you neither will your dad. Both of them never had much time for the old man, but you love, you were his favourite, you should do alright. You mark my words."

"Oh Mum, I'm not bothered."

"Don't be daft, this could set you up nicely. A tidy little nest egg to get you started when you leave school. You can't go on sponging off your old mum and dad forever you know. Mind you, you'd better bear us in mind if you get it all. Remember everything we've done for you."

She leaned over and pinched David's cheek shaking it roughly.

"Mum, that hurt."

"What about me, won't I get anything?"

"Oh Danny darling, I'm sure there'll be something for you. You got on with old grandad didn't you?"

"But I hardly ever saw him. You wouldn't take me. It was David who got to see him. It's not fair. I always miss out, 'cause I'm the youngest."

"Come on Danny it's not like that. I've told you before. Anyway, whatever happens David will share whatever he gets with you, won't you son?"

David had been feigning lack of interest, but was intrigued at the prospect of getting his hands on some money. He had been sitting there pondering what he would spend it on – a motorbike and record player were top of the list. As his mother spoke a wondrous thought struck him, he would buy Penny the necklace she wanted and then he could ask her to spend the night with him over at John's one weekend. It was a delight dwelling on the prospect of seeing her body, long legs and pale skin, all his to do what he wanted with.

The thought of sharing his new found wealth with his brother was not a happy one and he almost cried out at the prospect. He got on with Daniel, but the idea of his brother coming between him and a naked Penny didn't bear thinking about.

"We'll see, maybe," was all he said as he crossed his legs. There was the sound of steps on the stairs. Freddy appeared cigarette still in hand, "He's here." Close behind him was the solicitor, Mr Evans, sweating, an anxious look on his ruddy face. He was breathing heavily and leant against his Secretary's desk to regain his composure. After adjusting his tie and glancing at a mirror hanging on the wall, he took out a comb and ran it swiftly through the thin strands of hair plastered across the top of his bald head and patted them gently into place. Satisfied he turned to face his clients. Freddy bent over and stubbed his cigarette out in the green metal wastepaper bin under the desk. He took great care to extinguish it, all the time staring at Miss Collins' legs, which were stretched out either side of the bin. She was too absorbed in her work to notice, but Mr Evans caught

Freddy's eye as he stood up. David had never seen his uncle so florid before and thought he should cut down on smoking.

"Mr and Mrs Coxon-Dyet, Mr Coxon-Dyet, David and Daniel, that's right isn't it? I'm very sorry to have kept you waiting. I had to check something with an associate and it took much longer than I anticipated. Do forgive me. Please come into my office."

He opened a door in one of the partition walls and held it open as they passed through.

"Has Daphne been looking after you? I do hope so. Tea everyone? I know I could do with a cup. Daphne."

"Mr Evans, we haven't any milk."

"Get some will you. Use your initiative."

"But Mr Evans."

"Look, these good people would like some tea, so can you please see to it."

He shut the door, shook his head in a co-conspiratorial way, straightened his tie, pulled down the front of his suit jacket, then walked across to his desk, positioned in a large bay window that overlooked the main street of the village. The Coxon-Dyet's sat down on chairs arranged in a row facing him.

"It's just like school", muttered Freddy and Daniel, who was sitting next to him, giggled.

Leather bound legal books lined the walls and piles of papers and rolls of documents, all tied with ribbons, were heaped on and beside the desk and along the partition wall behind them. The air was heavy with dust and David sneezed.

"It is a problem all these papers, but I'm afraid it's an occupational hazard." Mr Evans laughed self-consciously. "Here let me open the window, it's such a lovely day."

David managed to blurt out his thanks, before he was again convulsed by sneezing.

"I must be allergic to something."

"Would you like to get some fresh air? We could reconvene again in a few minutes when you're feeling better?"

"No, no I'll be fine."

"Very well then, if you are sure."

David nodded. Mr Evans reached into the top drawer of his desk and took out a folder, glanced inside, then placed it on his desk. Then he very deliberately opened a battered black spectacle case, took out a gold-rimmed pair of half-moon reading glasses and placed them carefully on his nose. He looked up and waited until he had everyone's attention.

"Let me begin by saying how sorry I am at your loss of a dear relative. It is particularly painful for me as I knew the Reverend Anthony Coxon-Dyet very well. Indeed I had known him for many years, ever since he came to the village as a young vicar, and I don't think it is too presumptuous of me to say that we had become friends. It was therefore a great shock to learn of his death, particularly as I am almost certain that I was the last person to see him alive. He came to me you know just before he died. The very day, just before Christmas last year. Funny it seems just like yesterday. It was most irregular."

He took off his glasses and polished them on a starched white handkerchief he plucked from his breast pocket.

"I never see clients at home and certainly never in the evening, but you know he was a friend and as it happened I wasn't doing anything in particular, so I thought I'd make an exception in his case. Anyway Anthony, I hope you don't mind me calling him Anthony?"

"He preferred Tony," David said his eyes watering.

"I never knew that. In all those years he never said anything. Well, I am surprised."

His voice trailed off and he stared out of the window. David's father glanced at his wife then said, "He answered to both and no, we don't mind you using either. Now can we get on."

It was the first thing he had said since they had arrived in the village.

"Yes sorry. Where was I? Yes he was good company, Tony, so I agreed to see him. But it was a surprise when he told me what he wanted. That he needed to change his will."

Freddy leaned forward and looked at his brother.

"You mean he changed his will just before he died?"

"Yes, obviously at the time there was no way I could know that was the case. He did seem a bit on edge and I tried to talk him out of it. I told him it was late and couldn't we do it in the office in the morning. But he was most insistent and appealed to our friendship, so in the end I agreed. My wife and I witnessed the whole affair and he was with us less than an hour and then he was gone, pleading work to be done and that was the last time I ever saw him."

Freddy was shocked at what he had heard.

"Did he say why he had to change it then? Why it couldn't be done in the morning?"

"Well, he just kept saying he'd had a change of heart and he wanted to sort things out. Simplify things as he put it. If he didn't do it now, he might forget. He said he needed to rewrite his will and please, as a friend, would I do it and not ask any more questions."

"But he couldn't do that could he? It's not legal is it?"

"It is. Anybody's entitled to change their will as they see fit, provided they are, of course, of sound mind and not under any duress. And there was no reason at the time to think that was not the case with Anthony. Obviously, in the light of events I was obliged to report what had happened to the police. They are satisfied that the change to the will had no direct bearing on Tony's death and I am, therefore, able to read the will to you."

"I'm not happy about this."

"Freddy shut up will you. I doubt either of us were going to get anything under either will, so let's hear what's in it and then we can be gone."

"Look I understand your concerns, but let me assure you that as things stand this is a legal and binding document. Relatives obviously can challenge a will, but they do need very firm grounds for doing so. It is not something that should be entered into lightly as it can be an expensive business."

"We understand, now let's get this done with."

Mr Evans peered over his glasses and looked at each person in the room in turn.

"If we are all agreed?"

He took a single sheet of paper out of the folder on his desk, coughed once and began to read in a deliberate, sonorous voice, clearly enunciating each word. David couldn't help smiling, the tension was excruciating and it was hard for him to contain his excitement. He would soon be rich.

"This is the last will and testament of the Reverend Anthony, William, Sidney Coxon-Dyet, currently residing at Flat 2, Penrose Mansions, the High Street, Dumpton Gap, Somerset and dated the 3rd of December 1975. I revoke all previous wills and codicils and I appoint as my sole executor Peter Erskine of 39 Macclesfield Terrace, Birmingham and I leave everything I own to him. Signed Anthony Coxon…"

"Hold on," Freddy's voice was questioning, surprised. He was looking at his brother as he spoke. Stephen gazed back with a puzzled expression on his face.

"…Dyet, witnessed by Peter Gareth Evans and …"

"Look, who the hell…"

"… please let me finish."

David was confused. He couldn't believe what he had heard. He knew his grandfather loved him. But he'd been left nothing. His left eye began to flicker.

"… and Dorothy Patricia Rosemary Evans. I understand this must be a surprise."

"You're telling me, who is he?"

"He's one of his boys, isn't he?"

David's mother covered her mouth with her hand as the shocked realization of what she had said sank in.

"Oh my God."

The room fell silent. Mr Evans shifted uncomfortably in his chair.

"I'm afraid I know very little about him. I have no recollection of him ever having stayed at the vicarage. I assume that's what you are referring to?"

Blushing, Helen nodded her head.

"As the local solicitor I dealt with most of them – the boys as you call them – at one time or another. When they came before the courts that sort of thing and I have no records of him. He's certainly not a local lad. I'll be writing to him at the address that's given and doubtless I'll learn more. The police have been in touch with him, but they've not told me anything. You obviously don't know him?"

David's father shook his head.

"Never known an Erskine, the name means nothing."

"Me neither."

Freddy was leaning back in his chair, a faintly disgusted expression on his round full face.

"He had all sorts of boys there, didn't he? Is it one of those that took him to court?"

David's mother was deeply ashamed of what she was saying, but couldn't help herself. Her hands twisted convulsively in her lap as she spoke and a hint of perspiration glistened on her top lip. David had never seen her so agitated.

"Oh my God."

"Mrs Coxon-Dyet, I acted for your father-in-law in both the cases to which you refer. In the first – the allegations of gross indecency were shown conclusively to have been a tissue of lies concocted by two young lads who Anthony had taken in and encouraged to join the choir. They abused the confidence he had placed in them and he suffered for it. It was deeply embarrassing for a man in his position, but the verdict of the court totally exonerated him. There was never any question in anybody's mind in the village that he could have done such a thing. The boys in question have long since left the area and I can assure you neither of them was called Peter Erskine. A handkerchief Mrs Coxon-Dyet?"

Helen was crying quietly to herself.

"Mum?"

David touched her gently on the back.

"Give over Helen, we can do without the waterworks. It's not as if we were expecting anything from the old git anyway."

"Stephen, please."

"Leave her alone will you Stephen, that's not the point. It's family money, we don't want it going to any old Tom, Dick or Harry."

"That's right Stephen, what about David? He liked David, why's he got nothing?"

"I dunno. I'm just sick of all this. He got up my nose when he was alive and he's getting up it again now he's dead."

"You didn't fall out with him, did you David, and not tell us?"

Barely able to hold back his tears, David shook his head and mumbled something about not being bothered.

"Grandad probably had a good reason to leave it to this boy."

"That's bollocks. He didn't give a damn about anyone else but himself, he just wanted to have a final pop at his family after he'd gone. He'll be up there laughing at us now."

Freddy snorted.

"You mean down there, don't you bro?"

The two brothers nodded grimly, in agreement for the first time in many years. Helen blew her nose and glanced at the solicitor, who at that moment was staring back at her thinking that she was a very attractive woman for her age, with her short curly ash-blond hair and ruddy cheeks. Wasted, married to this oaf. Anthony had always sung her praises, never said much about his sons and he now understood why.

"Mr Evans, I'm sorry."

"Don't worry my dear, these occasions are often very emotional."

Helen responded to the warmth in his voice, sniffed a couple of times and then smiled weakly.

"The second case you mentioned, Mr Evans, you're sure that's nothing to do with all this?"

It was his turn to smile.

"Mrs Coxon-Dyet that was a silly prank that went wrong. Anthony admitted he had made a mistake and paid a small fine. There was nothing more to it."

"Oh come on, who are you kidding."

Freddy was becoming increasingly irritated by the solicitor's glib tone, and frustrated by the fact that once again he couldn't understand his parent's actions, that for a final time his father had put one over on him, had missed the opportunity to make amends, to recognize him, to acknowledge his sons.

"He was a laughing stock. What was that notorious headline? God I'm embarrassed thinking about it – "Vicar: I didn't drive with boy on my lap" – can you believe it?"

"What's going on? Did you know about this?" Daniel whispered to David.

"Shhhh, keep quiet. He's going to tell us."

"Mr Coxon-Dyet, the loc…"

"Call me Freddy, for God's sake."

"If you insist. Freddy, the local paper made a big deal of it as they do with such things. Always looking for the sensational in everything. They had it in for him, if the truth be told. The case itself was, in my opinion, one that should never have been brought to court, but we had a stand-in constable that summer and he was keen to make an impression and not so concerned with local sensibilities as old P.C. Sanders would have been. The evidence was not strong, the police claimed Anthony was driving his car with a boy sitting in his lap and not exercising proper control over the vehicle. Your father denied this of course, but because he couldn't remember the particular incident in question he pleaded guilty, on my advice, because technically if anyone else is touching the steering wheel while you're driving then you are not in proper control of the car. And your father did admit to having boys in his car on a number of occasions, as part of his care responsibilities of course. So nothing particularly untoward there and just to reassure you further, the boy in question was not Peter Erskine."

"I've had enough of this, Helen. I think we can take it as read that Mr Evans knows nothing about this Erskine character."

"That's correct and if I did I'm afraid I wouldn't be able to tell you anything without his permission."

"So how much does he get? Can you tell us that much?"

"Yes, I can tell you that. Hold on a second, I have the estate valuation here."

The solicitor took a second sheet of paper out of the manila folder and again cleared his throat before speaking.

"Your father, as you know, rented his flat in the High Street so that has now passed back to the leaseholder. All in all, Anthony left a total of, let me see, just over sixteen thousand pounds. Sixteen thousand, one hundred and fifty-seven pounds to be precise. That's gross of course."

"What?"

All the Coxon-Dyet's were stunned, unable to believe their ears.

"Say that again."

Freddy was on the edge of his seat.

"How did he get that much, he was just a local vicar?"

"Sixteen thousand, one hundred and fifty-seven pounds."

"That's unbelievable. I had no idea he had that much. He didn't appear to live that well."

"You didn't know him like I did. None of you ever bothered to come and see him. He was very generous and kind."

There was undisguised bitterness in David's voice.

"Oh yeah, he's been dead generous to us all, hasn't he? He must've really liked you."

"Daniel stop it, your brother's upset. David do not react. Daddy and I need to think about this."

"There's nothing to think about, as far as I'm concerned. He thought little about us when he was alive and he obviously couldn't give a toss what we think about him now he's dead. It's all over as far as I'm concerned. Let's go."

David's father stood up and made for the door.

"Hold up, Stephen."

"Thank you for your trouble Mr Evans, goodbye."

"Stephen, please. I just want to find out how he got so much money, Mr Evans?"

"Well, I'd have thought you would have known. He was one of the highest paid vicars in the country. I don't know exactly what he earned, but it was over five thousand a year."

"I had no bloody, sorry, I had no idea vicars were paid so much."

"Well they're not normally, but your father was, I suppose you'd call it, lucky. The problems he had with the vicarage eventually turned to his advantage. You look blank?"

"I'm afraid we've no idea what you're talking about. The vicarage was pulled down, wasn't it, because it was almost in ruins? That's what we were told, as you know we didn't visit much."

"That's right. The vicarage was demolished after it was purchased by the local council. It was in very bad condition. Your father's generosity, others said naivety, had been abused by many of the boys he had staying with him over the years. They had basically wrecked the place. The final straw was the theft of all the lead from the roof one weekend. Once water started getting in, then it didn't take long to become virtually uninhabitable. Anthony moved out and the boys ran riot. The council stepped in, paying over £100,000 for it. All bad news so far, you would think."

Mr Evans smiled and took off his glasses, realized he no longer had his handkerchief, and put them back on again.

"But the good news for your... for Anthony, was that during a vicar's tenancy any benefits, such as the sale of church property automatically accrue to him. In this case the capital from the sale of the vicarage reverted to the Church Commissioners, who invest it as they see fit. The interest on the investment comes to the vicar, that's to say, your father. With interest rates as they've been he must have been making over £2,000 extra on top of his vicar's salary."

"Well, I never would have thought."

David wanted desperately to leave.

"Hello."

Unsettled, David looked up. For a moment he struggled to make sense of his surroundings. He smiled wanly. Towering above him was a tall blond-haired man wearing an expensive dark suit and small circular gold-rimmed glasses. His light blue eyes flitted across David's face, his clothes and shoes, before darting around the room, returning seconds later to stare directly at him. He was grinning.

"Hi, I'm Larry Beckinsale. We haven't met."

He held out a tanned manicured hand. David levered himself

up awkwardly from the deep cushions of his low seat, almost falling back, before staggering to his feet. He shook hands, the man's grip was cool but firm, his smile unwavering.

"David Coxon-Dyet, pleased to meet you."

"The others are right behind me, so we'll soon have the meeting underway. I'm running late already so I won't be able to stay long."

The smile dissipated, his bevelled features settling into a mask of disinterested geniality. He unbuttoned his jacket, walked behind his neatly ordered, uncluttered desk, grasped both arms of his swivel chair and trundled it round to the front of the desk. Then as members of David's department and others he didn't recognize filed into the room, Larry Beckinsale took off his jacket and slung it over the back of his chair and then proceeded very deliberately to roll up the sleeves of his immaculately pressed white shirt. He motioned to the seats around the coffee table in front of him and, when everyone was in place, he himself sat down.

"Welcome, are we all here?"

A man standing at the back of the room, a clipboard clasped across his chest, nodded.

"Thanks Dick. Could someone close the door. Right, this shouldn't take too long. For those of you who don't know me I'm …"

There was a knock on the door and instantly the soft contours around Larry Beckinsale's eyes hardened into an expression of intense exasperation.

"Come."

A young woman entered carrying a small tray of sandwiches, covered in cling film and a pile of paper plates.

"On the table, everyone help yourselves."

The door closed. Nobody moved.

"Right, I'm Larry Beckinsale. At the back there is Dick Sanders, Head of Human Resources, Steve Percival, my deputy and, of course, most of you know Jane, she'll be taking the minutes of the meeting."

Jane shifted in her seat, uncrossing and crossing her legs, smiled briefly at no one in particular and turned a page in her A4 ring file. Larry leaned forward, rested his elbows on his thighs, resolutely clasped his hands together and then paused. Elaine Parker, one of David's junior colleagues, her stomach audibly rumbling, had been about to get up and take a sandwich, but thought better of it and sank back into the soft over-comfortable seating, mumbling her apologies.

"No, please do."

Elaine smiled sweetly, but didn't move.

"I've been with this company nearly two months now and I've spent my time very productively. I've been looking at how we do business here and I've been very impressed by what I've seen."

Across the room people visibly relaxed, looks were exchanged and there were faint smiles of relief.

"But, and I suppose there is always a but, this doesn't mean that things can't be improved. In the current business climate the company that stands still is the company that goes to the wall. A truism you all may think, but one that is easily forgotten and, I have to say, I believe it had been forgotten, to some extent, in areas of our operation."

He glanced at his watch. The tension in the room was again palpable. The ill-judged confidence of moments before banished. David grimly anticipated the impending drama.

"In short, I believe changes are necessary. But, and I must stress here, these will be exciting changes. If we can make what I propose work then we'll be entering a vital period of expansion and growth for the company that can only benefit all those involved. Let me underline this is a positive process, a forward-looking process. I am not interested in looking back, that's over with. I'm not interested in how things were done in the past, that's history. My concern now is for the future – the future for you, for me and for this company. The way ahead for us will involve, I believe, something, radical – a complete break with everything that has gone before."

Larry Beckinsale looked directly at David.

"I can see that some of you are perturbed by what I'm saying, that is only natural," – a nebulous air of contention troubled the room and Larry Beckinsale raised his hand in tacit acknowledgement of the disturbance – "let me finish, there will be plenty of time for questions afterwards. But I must stress that for all of us, if we are to survive into the next century and beyond as the lean, hungry organization that I know we can be, if we are to be a serious player, then we must reinvent the way we carry out our work. I believe, and I have the complete backing of the board of management on this one, that what is needed is a complete re-engineering of our business operations. It sounds dramatic doesn't it? And it is. I'll need the co-operation of all of you for it to work. Together we can make this happen, people."

Smiling he leaned back, the leather of his chair squealing as his body shifted.

"A good time for coffee I think, let what I've said sink in. Jane, will you be mother? Excuse me for a minute I have a call to make."

He stood up and left the room. The coffee was served in delicate china cups emblazoned with the new company logo and drunk in silence. Ten minutes later Larry Beckinsale returned.

"Sorry guys, a problem I had to deal with, you know how it is."

He sat down, took a couple of sips of coffee, placed his cup back on his desk, eased back into his chair, crossed his legs and faced them again.

"You've probably been asking how I came to the conclusion that a radical redesign of our company was necessary. It's a good question and I intend to give you an answer. You deserve an insight into my thinking on this one. As I told you, I've spent my time since I arrived here looking at every aspect of our business model. I was brought in to make changes, refocus the company and, it goes without saying, boost our profits – you all know they've been down over the last quarter – and that's what I intend to do. That's what business is all about after all."

A few people round the room laughed along with Larry.

"This company is not going to follow the path taken by so many other businesses I've known. You know the story; profits start to drop, so called radical changes are made – de-layering, decentralization, downsizing, corporate flattening – call it what you will, they're all fads. Just tinkering with the problem in my opinion. They rarely have any significant impact on the key problems, so what started as a blip turns into a trend and the company is on the slide. That won't happen here people, not on my watch, believe me. We're talking radical here, and by radical, I mean radical."

He motioned towards Jane and pointed at his coffee cup. She stood up immediately, placed her notepad face down on the table, and took the cup, it rattled in its saucer as she filled it with coffee. He smiled intently at his personal assistant as she handed it back to him and in that instant, David imagined, or thought he did, that he winked at her.

"As you know I have been helped in my task by an excellent report from Braziers, the management consultants. I thank all those who co-operated so fully with those guys when they were here. Their thinking is very much in tune with mine. They identified many areas of, how shall I put it, friction in the otherwise smooth running of our company. These chimed very sweetly with my own analysis of the problem. In short we were pulling together on this one. It was a long report, far too long to detail here, but I think I can summarize briefly their conclusions and, of course, mine."

He again looked at this watch and then at Jane.

"What time is my lunch with Sir Richard?"

"Two o'clock, the car will be ready for you when you finish here."

"I'll be brief."

He again smiled at her.

"Basically, and I think what I have to say is fair and I believe many of you will agree when you give it some thought. Many of the tasks you do, and I don't just mean in this department, there are others with similar problems, are simply being carried out to satisfy the internal demands of the company's own organization. They are being done this way or that way simply because that's how they've always been done. In short, they're an historical hangover and, as I said earlier history is exactly what it says it is, history. There is a particular problem with our regional organization. It makes no sense to me now we are dealing with a global market. Information is universal, we can't impose time-bound, space-bound categories on something that is fluid and ever-changing, just because it suits our internal auditing system. It's madness and more importantly it's an ineffective way for us to do business. It has to change if we're to achieve significant improvements in performance. Let me ask you, what is the most important thing for our business?"

His eyes strafed his audience, blazing defiance. Nobody moved.

"Let me tell you. It is concern for our customer. The customer is God. That's G.O.D. If we don't believe in him we wither and die, remember that. I do, every hour of every day. It's not important to look up to me your boss, nor sideways at other departments, where you look is outwards to the customer. You give him what he wants," Larry nodded his head, "and I'll tell you what that is, shall I?" Others in the room sheepishly followed his example and nodded. "He wants a flexible company that can respond instantly on a global scale to his demands. He doesn't want one that is slow, unresponsive and more concerned with its own bureaucratic structures and power arrangements, than it is in dealing effectively with him."

Larry raised a flaccid fist to his mouth and coughed silently.

"As a manager I've had to fundamentally rethink how I do my job, for you too there'll have to be a root and branch reassessment of what you do. There must be, if you're to have a part to play in this firm's exciting future. As I see it there will be no more task-orientated jobs in this company, no more specialists. Our twenty-first century employees will be generalists dealing with the entire process of our business – from the commissioning of the contract to its completion. We will be streamlined, efficient and profitable. We will be a player."

Triumphantly he sat back, hands firmly clasping the arms of his chair, which he then began to swivel from side to side in apparent excitement.

"As you can see, I'm enthusiastic about the future and you should be too. Although I'm sure you'll have realized that what's planned does have an impact for you …"

He surveyed the room, his audience was frozen, anticipation fuelling a creeping anxiety.

"… well you've had enough of me. I think the person to tell you what this'll mean for you personally is Steve Percival. He's been right with me throughout all of this, Steve."

David stared hard at the man, who raised himself slightly in his seat as way of an introduction, then slumped back emphatically crossing his legs. He was slightly younger than

David, and less than six weeks ago had worked alongside him in his department. He was tall, good-looking and had long silky brown hair that he would push back from his forehead with a languorous gesture of his hand, that David knew drove at least one woman in the office wild. He watched him now and couldn't see it. The flush of success was annoying, particularly in a bearer of bad news, which he almost certainly was. David was resigned to hearing the worst, he had listened to such a speech before, but he was already inwardly fuming, a slow-burning anger kept in check only by the abject hopefulness of the condemned man desperate for a last-minute reprieve.

"Larry thank-you. People. As has already been clearly spelled out, our aim here is total quality management. You should have no doubt about that. This will be achieved in two ways: firstly by restructuring the company and second by increased efficiencies. To that end we propose to do away with all departments and reconstitute them as divisions. In the process certain departments will be redefined and their separate identities lost. As you will have gathered, yours, being a regional entity, is one of those…"

There was a perceptible movement in the room, bodies subtly adjusting to an uncomfortable new reality, a collective exhalation of breath. Roger McCarthy, the head of department, looking visibly ill at ease, asked the question on everybody's mind.

"What will this mean for us, my colleagues? I wasn't told anything of this. I had no idea."

"Roger."

All attention turned to Larry.

"I want only team players on this one, you understand? This is not a consultative process. The decisions have been made and approved at the highest level. No muddying of the waters now, Roger. Sorry Steve."

Roger appeared about to respond, his mouth wordlessly

open, his body positioning combative, but he thought better of it and sank back into silent passivity. Steve stared at him then continued.

"As I was saying, your department is to be subsumed into the new "Global Division," and I don't think I'm speaking out of turn," he glanced at Larry, who smiled and nodded, "to be headed by myself. This is a sign of the high priority placed on our overseas business by the directors, in that they've appointed one of their number to head this division."

"Smug bastard," thought David, "this is going from bad to fucking worse. Now I've no chance. I'm finished."

"As to what will happen to individual members of staff, well as you know the company operates a redeployment policy, it doesn't simply make everyone redundant. Let me assure you that is not our intention. This scheme will come into immediate effect and everybody will be given careful consideration for every company-wide vacancy that comes up over the next six months."

"How many of us will be made redundant?"

"Roger, it may not come to that. Six months is a long time in business as you well appreciate. But you've been around long enough to know the score, so let me put the cards openly on the table. Greater efficiencies can't be achieved without some pain, we aim to minimize it, but there will be pain for some of you I'm afraid. Bottom line …"

Steve Percival paused for a second, his blank eyes and tanned face radiating contempt.

" … we estimate there will be a small head count reduction."

"When will this happen?"

"We aim to have the new structures in place by October, so in just under four months."

"What have the unions had to say about this?"

"Roger, come, come, today marks the beginning of the formal consultative process. But as Larry made very clear the company can't afford not to implement these changes at once. The competition doesn't stand still. The days of continuous incremental improvement, I'm afraid are over, and no bad thing in my opinion."

"Well said, Steve."

Larry was again looking at his watch.

"Has anybody anything else they want to ask?"

David couldn't contain himself.

"Larry mentioned that the company no longer needed specialists. But I was recruited just over a year ago on a three-year contract to be exactly that, a specialist. I was told at my interview that the regional departments were being expanded," his voice faltered, clipping his words and he swallowed hard before picking up his thread, "they were being seen as the focus for the company's stepped up drive to win new markets in these areas. Now that appears to have changed, where does that leave me?"

"Well, I think Larry made the case well for the company's change of policy. There is no question in anybody's mind about the need for such a development. As to your contractual position I think that's one for Dick."

The small balding man looked up suddenly and turned to face David.

"I don't know your name?"

"David, David Coxon-Dyet."

"Well, David, the position is this. Contractually I think you'll find the company is obliged to give you one month's notice of termination of employment. After that your length of service will determine the level of redundancy payments you are entitled to. Basically for someone at your level, on your type of contract, it amounts to one month's salary for each complete year of service. Tax free, of course, up to a maximum of 30K. And believe me that is generous. The legal minimum is much less than that – a week for each year, I think. But, in your case, and I would need to check your files, it sounds as if you'd be entitled to nothing, I'm afraid, as you haven't been with us two years – that's the minimum service before you're eligible for redundancy."

"But I signed a three year contract. It sounds as if you're saying you're not going to honour it, that it's not worth the paper it's printed on?"

"No, I wouldn't say that David. If you bother to read it carefully you will find that it is all there in black and white. We're not pulling the wool over anybody's eyes, I can assure you."

Larry lifted his jacket from the back of his chair and began putting it on as he spoke.

"Look folks, I have to leave. Thanks for coming. I know it must have come as a shock to some of you but if you have any further questions, Dick's door is always open. It's a brave new world we're entering and I'm excited about it and you should be too. In your heart of hearts, if you ask yourself honestly, you will see the inevitability of all this and give thanks that decisions are being taken now that will safeguard the future of this company of ours for many years to come."

He stood up.

"And don't think I don't know what you're going through. When I was younger I was let go by the company I was working for. It was devastating. I had two young children, a mortgage, believe me, I understand."

Chapter 6

TRAITOR

4th June 1940

The hammering on the door, sonorous and prescriptive, was an anomaly in the pitch dark void of the blackout. Silence followed, an interlude, empty and intimidating. Tony sat bolt upright in bed. Emily stirred beside him. He'd been expecting this but for the life of him he couldn't remember why. Bad news? Invasion? It couldn't be good at this hour. What time was it? Tony turned in the direction of the bedside table and the alarm clock, but he couldn't see anything. Those bloody curtains, he thought as he fumbled beneath the blankets for his pyjamas. The pounding resumed and there was the sound of glass shattering. Tony tumbled from the bed, entangled in the sheets.

"What's happening?"

Emily blearily murmured as the bedclothes slithered to the floor and the chill morning air swept over her curled body.

"Hey, what you doing?"

"Get the children. It's happening."

"What?"

A rapid series of dull thuds shook the house. A child cried out, closely followed by the uncomprehending screams of another.

"The bastards."

The front door loudly cracked as it gave way. Tony hopped across the bedroom floor frantically pulling on his pyjama trousers. There was a brief pause. Tony stood on one leg listening.

"The boys," he hissed to his wife.

Light flooded under the bedroom door then everywhere shouting, the rush of bodies, pounding boots in the hallway, on the stairs, doors crashing open, wood splintering.

"Their bedroom's the one at the front. Constable, get in there, try and stop the children crying."

Tony turned to face the door as it was flung open. A tall thin man in shirtsleeves strode in, closely followed by two police constables, truncheons in hand. He switched on the bedroom light. The room tepidly lit filled with the noisome smell of gamy perspiration.

"You were expecting us then?"

He gesticulated at Tony, looking round at his men, who nodded back at him affirmatively. They were watching Emily who was sitting on the edge of the bed pulling her nightdress over her knees. She glared up at them.

"I thought you lot were well-organized. They told us you'd have been tipped off. That you'd have scarpered or been ready to put up a fight. But…"

He looked again at his captive audience.

"…we seem to have caught you with your pants down."

All three policemen smiled as Tony hastily tied the cord of his pyjamas and buttoned up the jacket.

"Can I go to my children?" Emily asked coldly, getting unsteadily to her feet.

"What are you looking at?" she sneered at the youngest policeman, who had been following her every move, "never been so close to…"

"Hold on, hold on, a few formalities first," said the plain-clothes officer. He coughed self-importantly and went on, "You must be Emily Cox?"

Emily stared silently back at him.

"Playing silly buggers will do you no good at all, co-operating with us is to your advantage, believe me."

He smirked. Emily said nothing for a moment and then asked quietly.

"My children?"

The smile faded from the policeman's face, his cheeks flushed as he stroked his chin and glowered first at Tony then Emily. Any trace of good humour dissipated.

"I'd expect nothing less from a pair of traitors and fifth columnists like you. Should've rounded you lot up a darn sight earlier than this in my book. But better late than never, I suppose. Now, let's start again, shall we?"

He stepped over to the heavy mahogany chest of drawers that stood along one wall of the room and looked into the walnut jewelry box that was open on top of it. He rummaged through the individual compartments before lifting out a pair of ear-rings, small silver replicas of the flash and circle symbol of the British Union of Fascists.

"Very nice, very nice. Lads, it doesn't look like we've come to the wrong house, does it?"

He held the ear-rings up to the light.

"Put those down, they're mine, you've no right."

"Shut it, I've every right, madam."

He tossed her jewelry onto the top of the cabinet.

"You're the one without rights. There was a day when we used to execute traitors, but the world's gone crazy, upside-down. I'm supposed to treat you with the due respect of the law. Fine, but no more. And, lady, we'll be back here tomorrow to question the neighbours, and remind those heavy sleepers, who haven't been woken up by our little visitation this morning, just exactly who you lot are."

A child screamed then began crying inconsolably. Emily winced and tried to leave the room, but was pushed roughly back onto the bed.

"Sit there and keep quiet."

"You heartless bastards, there're just children. They've done no harm to anyone."

"Right, I've had enough of this."

He pointed at Emily.

"You must think we're stupid, but let me assure you we're not. We've got you lot taped. Our intelligence is very good."

Frowning he drew away from her, his disdain explicit.

"You are Emily Cox, formerly Carstairs. You've been Women's Administrative Officer for the North," as he said this he raised his eyebrows and shrugged, "for the British Union of Fascists for the last three and a bit years. You joined the party, if memory serves, way back in the early thirties. Seems to run in the family doesn't it? Your dad's also a keen member and a man of the cloth, no less. Well you won't be seeing him for a while, so I've been told. What gets me though, is that you can't get much lower than this. What is it with you people? Bit of a family tradition is it, being a traitor? Comes up regularly over Sunday lunch, does it? Or maybe you just say a prayer before you tuck into your roast beef asking God to overthrow King, Country and Empire?"

"You're wrong."

"Shut it, now. I don't want to know."

He walked over to the bed and scowled at Emily, who ignored him and continued to stare at the wall.

"The time for talking to you lot, listening to you lot, is long gone. Lock you all up, I would, throw away the key. But, and this is why today is your lucky day, you may not think it now madam, but believe me it is, the powers that be have told me not to pick you up, just your old man."

Emily looked up aghast.

"Yes, no need to seem so surprised, it's true. Left to me though you'd be inside, children or no children. In my book you're as bad as he is, if not worse. Women shouldn't be getting involved with politics, their place is in the home, raising kids. You, lady, crossed that line, but lucky for you, it's not up to me."

"Bloody disgrace", muttered one of the constables as he thrust his truncheon back into his belt.

"Not a popular decision I suspect round here. People don't like those with ideas above their station and you fit that bill in my book. You're free to go. Go on, get out of my sight."

Emily glanced across at Tony, who was standing at the end of the bed clutching his pyjamas at the waist, his eyes dark studs in a face bleached and grimly set; his mouth, twisted with fury was barely visible. He nodded at her and she got up, grabbed a dressing gown from the back of the bedroom door, and left the room. The crying stopped almost immediately. The tension eased – it was as if everyone paused for breath – and for an instant the only sound was the discordant din of the dawn chorus.

"Now, back to the real business of the morning."

The policeman nodded his head in Tony's direction.

"You, you fascist bastard."

He stepped menacingly forward, tripping on the tasseled edge of the bedside rug – which shifted on the black polished floorboards – and lost his balance. Warding off the lunging body, Tony staggered backwards and caught his hip on the sharp corner of a Singer sewing machine table and cried out. The policeman shoved him away angrily. In retaliation, Tony raised his fists, anger subverting his natural reticence, but the eager glint in the officer's eyes warned him off and he lowered his guard.

"What a pity. So you're a coward as well as a traitor. Wish we'd known that earlier, eh lads. The heavy mob could've stayed in bed and we could have sent a lady constable round instead to pick you up in the morning."

He turned, nodding knowingly to his constables.

"Ain't that right Bob?"

PC Robert Inglewood, who personally had ambivalent feelings about the round-up operation and was exhausted by the run of early morning call-outs, humoured his senior officer, nodding in agreement.

"Yes sir. Elsie'd have loved getting her hands on this one. She's a real pussy cat."

Laughing the policeman turned back to Tony.

"You were reported to have been some sort of hard man in your youth. What happened? Married life softened you up? By the look of her, old Emily's a tougher nut than you are. Is she the one who wears the trousers in this house? Was she wearing the trousers when we came in, eh?"

Tony stared at the pile of crumpled blankets lying beside the bed, the shirt, trousers, underwear he'd worn the day before discarded in a heap nearby. He looked anywhere but at his tormentors. He noticed a coin – a sixpence – in the shadow of the bed, he saw another, then another – pennies, farthings – they must have spilled from his pockets as he undressed hurriedly last night. He rubbed his eyes wearily with his left hand. How long before he did that again? Weeks, months, years? He sighed deeply then opened his eyes and glanced up. They were still there. He had to assert himself.

"What is it you want?" he bellowed at the top of his voice. The policemen gazed at him in surprise. One of his sons began crying in the next bedroom, Emily could be heard soothing, comforting him. A helmeted policeman stuck his head round the door.

"Everything alright, Sir? We was wondering if you needed any help?"

"No Sergeant, everything is under control. Our man here's just trying it on, but he'll learn. Once he's got dressed, we'll be out."

The policeman disappeared.

"Oh Sergeant…"

Seconds later he reappeared.

"Sir?"

"Get someone to search the back bedroom and the children's room will you, we'll check in here. You know the sort of thing, papers, letters, anything official, collect it up and take it down the station."

"Sir."

"Don't I get told what I'm being arrested for, or has the war put paid to all such niceties?"

"You're a fine one to talk about niceties, do you think we'd be standing here talking if old Adolf was in charge? No way, up against a wall my old son, no messing. A lot going for it in my book, but this is Great Britain and we still have our procedures. So here goes."

Noisily clearing his throat he took a notebook out of the back pocket of his trousers. He deliberately flicked through a number of pages before looking up at Tony.

"Now pay special attention, won't you. This is for your benefit."

"For our benefit?"

Emily had stepped back into the room and was holding in her arms their youngest child Freddy, four years old and fast asleep. Standing behind her, tightly hugging her waist, was their eldest son Stephen, who was six. His tear-streaked face peered anxiously round his mother every few seconds, smiling briefly when he caught sight of his father.

"Tony Cox, you're District Leader of the Blackpool District of the British Union. You're also prospective parliamentary candidate for that party for the Walton constituency in Liverpool. I am detaining you under, under…" he looked down at his notes, "…it's here somewhere…ah yes…You are being detained under defence regulation 18B (1A). You will get dressed immediately and come with us."

"Hang on. Why am I being detained? I've done nothing wrong."

"Well, that's where you're mistaken, my old china. In most decent people's eyes you've done a hell of a lot that's wrong. So you're going to have to lump it until you see the error of your ways. I've told you all I have to. According to the regulations I don't have to tell you anything, just take you in."

His voice dropped to a stage whisper as he leaned towards Tony.

"But between you, me and that bed post over there. They're detaining you because you're a fascist, and, in case you hadn't noticed, we're fighting them in Germany and Italy. And we don't want any home-grown traitors going around blowing up bridges, poisoning the water, setting up alternative governments, like old Quisling, while our British lads are laying down their lives for all we hold precious and dear. You get my drift?"

Tony was shaking his head, he realized, but too late.

"Save your special pleading for the Tribunal. There'll be no tears shed round here about your fate, I can tell you that for free. Handcuff him once he's dressed, we want to put on a bit of a show for the neighbours."

He walked out of the room. As he left he said without turning round, "Oh yes, and you've ten days to appeal. I almost forgot."

"Appeal, appeal?"

Tony looked across at Emily. She shook her head and shrugged.

"I don't know, I just don't know, but I'll try and find out. They can't have got everybody."

"You out. Come on now, get dressed."

Tony opened the wardrobe and took out a clean white shirt, a starched collar, studs and tie from the accessory drawer and his navy-blue work suit. Before he could close the door one of the constables barged him aside and began rummaging through the clothes hanging on the rail. Tony half-heartedly tried to stop him, but he knew what was coming.

"Sir, look what's in here."

The Inspector reappeared at the entrance to the room. The policeman was holding a black uniform triumphantly in his arms, the brass buttons gleaming, braid lustrous on the shoulders, a highly polished belt hanging down the front of the jacket like a black tongue, which seemed to Tony to be mocking him as he dejectedly dressed under the vigilant eyes of the policemen.

"This hasn't seen much use lately, what were you keeping it for?"

Tony shrugged.

"I know it must be for the day when old Adolf sets himself up at Westminster and you can be there on parade to welcome him. Saluting and cheering as he marches past with his new Prime Minister, Sir, God don't it stick in you throat lads, Oswald Mosley."

The Inspector looked expectantly at Tony.

"Well, I'm waiting. What's the answer? What use is a uniform when…"

"Sir."

"Well, well, his and hers, you would have made a fine couple."

There was a strong smell of mothballs. Tony could anticipate the onset of a migraine, the incipient nausea, the vice tightening at his temples, the interior of his skull throbbing to the pulse of a disturbed existence.

"Pack it in will you," he said wearily, "We were...we are both senior members of the Party, we don't deny that. That's the official Party uniform. It's only in public that we aren't allowed to wear it anymore. We were set on legitimately winning power in this country. We're not traitors, we're British patriots."

"Save it for later. You'll have plenty of time to spit out your pathetic excuses to someone else. Just listening to you trying to justify yourself makes me sick. Constable, keep hold of those uniforms, we'll take them with us."

Static noise – the police ransacking the house, carelessly rifling through his possessions – befuddled Tony's thinking as he moved around getting ready. Downstairs, furniture scraped across the floor, doors slammed, crockery smashed on the stone hearth, there was the sound of water flowing and then raised voices. The logic to this legalized vandalism, the formality of the wanton intrusion, he understood as part of the game they were playing – there was nothing the forces of law and order would find that would make any material difference, as a family they had been careful – yet he still felt violated. The insistent banality of a chirping sparrow, perched on the ledge outside the bedroom window, irked him. He pulled aside the heavy black drapes, and the bird dropped from view in a flurry. It was growing light, the houses across the street were starkly etched against a yellowing sky. Down below his next-door neighbours, Stanley and Grace Grimshaw, were standing on the pavement wrapped in dressing gowns, the cool morning air misting their conversation with the policeman guarding the garden gate. Grace pointed excitedly when Tony appeared at the window and he pulled back, letting the curtain swing heavily into place. Anger was, he knew, a fool's emotion, the heat of his disdain must be contained to get him through the onerous days and weeks ahead.

The Inspector grabbed Tony by the arm, forcing it behind his back.

"Violation of the blackout. Is there no end to the trouble you're in? You'd better come quietly, wouldn't want to add resisting arrest as well, would we? Constable, the cuffs."

"Do you have to do that? I'm not going anywhere."

"And why should we believe you, eh? The word of a fascist traitor isn't worth buggery in my book. Give them to me, it will be my pleasure."

He painfully yanked Tony's arms high up behind him before slipping on the handcuffs. Tony winced as the metal cut into his wrists.

"Oh, too tight are they? Don't have much call to use them these days. Out of practice. Constable, see what you can do for this soft bastard will you. I need some fresh air. Bring him out as soon as you can."

"Can I say goodbye to my wife and children?"

"Sorry?"

"Can I say goodbye to my wife and children?"

"I heard you the first time."

"Please."

"No."

"Hold on, where am I being taken then?"

"That's restricted information. Can't have everybody knowing where we're holding major security risks like yourself, can we? What do you think we are?"

"Bastards."

For the first time that morning the inspector came close to losing his temper, his contempt for Tony evident in his eyes as he sneered.

"Wait till they get you behind bars. I don't think you've got it in you. You'll soon be singing to a different tune. Constable make sure that door is shut, I don't want them talking to each other again."

Two policemen grabbed Tony, nodded at each other, doubled

him over and frog marched him head first into the doorpost. His nose, broken, instantly sputtered blood over his face and shirt as he reeled from the impact, legs faltering.

"Watch where you're going," mumbled one of the constables as they hauled him onto the landing, "nasty bruise you've got there."

Jarred, head splitting, Tony couldn't think, his faculties were diminished, overwhelmed by jangling pain. Breathing was difficult through his fractured nose, warm rivulets of blood seeped into his mouth, choking, he retched as he was dragged down the stairs. He was unable to see clearly.

Emily, anxious to know what was going on, called out as she struggled vainly to evade her captor, beating his chest with her hands as her children cried at her feet.

The neighbours standing outside in the close were silent as Tony stumbled down the garden path; others watched from their bedroom windows. A dog was whining in a kennel on the opposite side of the road, its owner standing in striped pyjamas and a sleeveless sweater, arms crossed, watching the arrest over his garden hedge. Two policemen supported Tony's limp, flexing body as they unlocked the rear doors of the Black Maria. A woman, her voice familiar, called out, "Traitor," turned her back and shaking her head, walked into her house.

Tony was bundled into the police van, where he slumped across a hard wooden bench and stared myopically out at the street though a small barred window. The familiar was unrecognizable in the hazy dawn light; an optical illusion that his befuddled brain could not make sense of. Three policemen followed him into the cramped interior, forcing him to sit up. The proximity of their bodies made him uncomfortable. Agonising minutes passed as the driver struggled to get the engine running, one of his colleagues cursing loudly as he trapped his fingers trying to crank start the motor.

"What an idiot, eh, he's always doing that."

"This bloody van should be sold for scrap."

The delay heightened the restiveness of the constables confined in the cage with Tony who, alive to his discomfort, were increasingly wary.

"Come on, I'm dying for a cuppa. I want to put my feet up for a few hours before I'm out again. Supposed to be following up on those taxi-driver robberies, you know the ones that keep losing their takings. Inside job it strikes me, but whoever takes any notice of what I say."

In the sickly mist-shrouded dawn, the short drive to Richardson Street police station along near-deserted roads passed in a confused disquieting reverie. Tony, still concussed, reflected incoherently on the intangible quality of the commonplace as it glided past – the ethereal figures of the Home Guard unit, walking home after a night manning an anti-aircraft gun on the Promenade, two of them pushing bicycles, the angry Sergeant in the middle of a tirade against who knew what; the Church Street cafe already open serving hot tea and toast to fire wardens and early rising shop-keepers, its windows partially steamed up; further along the street the Winter Gardens showing "My Little Chickadee" with W.C. Fields and Mae West, a garish billboard towering over the shuttered ticket office. The Tivoli wasn't far away. He had two tickets from there for "Bandwagon" next week, starring Arthur Askey. "Big-hearted" Arthur was his favourite comic. He'd seen him before and he'd been hilarious. The planned evening out was a surprise treat for Emily, but who would go with her now? Maybe if his arrest was a mistake it would be him. His eyes filled with tears. Mortified he understood that with his hands in cuffs he couldn't wipe them away. He looked down and shook his head in despair. They had taken his shoes. A sharp pain jolted his body – the Black Maria jounced over the kerb turning into the cobbled yard of the police station – and he cried out. Bemused the policemen looked on.

"I'm all out of clean handkerchiefs," sniggered one of them, as his companions steadied themselves as the vehicle trundled across the uneven surface.

"Come on Cox, face up to it there's nothing for you to whinge about, you'll be out when the war's over and it'll save you from doing any fighting. Look on the bright side."

The van came to a halt. The rear door swung open.

"Stick him downstairs, nobody's in a hurry to speak to him. Waiting to hear from higher up about what's to be done with them."

Tony stumbled forward, tripping over the lip of the van and collapsing onto his knees in front of the custody sergeant. He was groaning.

"God, what happened to him?"

"Slipped on the stairs, Sarge."

"He'll have to be more careful here then, lots of steps in this place. The berth at the end has just come free, put him in there and I'll see if anyone can look at his head."

Barely aware of his surroundings, Tony was hustled into one of the larger cells, his mishandled body comprehensively bruised he ached for sleep. He crawled towards the narrow bed-board suspended from the wall by two rusting black chains. The mid-section of the thin brown straw-filled palliasse was soaking wet and one end was drenched in vomit. Thin gelatinous strings hung from the edge of the bed dripping occasional liquid beads into a spreading pool on the dusty floor. Sickened he scrambled to a bucket by the door. His stomach heaved as he recoiled in disgust, covering his mouth with a hand. The room stank, but he'd lost all sense of smell. Staggering to the furthest corner he sat down, the dark green brick wall damp on his back, the worn flagstones corpse cold. He drew his legs up to his chest and massaged his numbed feet. His head sank slowly onto his knees, then retracted, the pain of contact splitting. Blood was drying on his face, stiffening the skin on his lips and cheeks, pulling at the raw edges of his wounds. His swollen throbbing nose was sensitive to the touch.

"God, what a mess I'm in."

The sun was streaming through a small window high up in the wall above him, casting a checkered shadow over the black steel door. The only sound was the incessant dripping of water, at first barely audible, then in ever-diminishing snatches of time, deafening. To escape the noise Tony clutched his ears, his head bobbing randomly.

"Oh Chriiiiiiiiiiiiiiiiiiiist."

The police searched the house for more than five hours. They took away very little, but left everything in disarray. Clothes were spread over the floors, drawers emptied, books pulled from shelves and papers strewn throughout every room. Cushions and pillows had been torn open, covering the bedrooms in feathers. In the kitchen the cupboards had been ransacked, precious bags of rationed flour and sugar cut open and the contents poured onto the work tops, cans had been emptied clogging the sink, pot plants uprooted and the earth scattered. A vase that had been in Emily's family for generations lay smashed in the hearth, carpets had been lifted and floorboards prized up. The children, who hadn't slept while the police were in the house, finally collapsed exhausted. Emily had time to think. She knew they had arrested senior Party members – Mosley and the rest – several days ago. These latest detentions must be aimed at rounding up all the key officials in the regions. There would be very few people she could contact. It occurred to her that the obnoxious Inspector had been right about one thing, she was lucky not to have been detained. But what should she do now? Go to her parents? But her father, would they have detained him too? He was harmless but had a very high profile in the Party. If they had, her mother would have to stay here rather than the other way round. All that would have to come later. Her priority was to find out about Tony and where they had taken him.

Time past was a yellow quadrilateral of dappled sunlight sliding slowly down the riveted length of the black steel door and out across the stone flags, constantly shimmering as it shifted shape and lustre. This mesmerizing pattern had faded almost to nothing as it approached his outstretched feet, it's radiance gradually dissolving into the dull paving. He had believed losing his shoes was a catastrophe, but leaving his watch behind was, he realized, insanity. Time present was a string of sentences spoken out loud, marking the seconds, minutes and, he hoped, the hours, but losing faith, he soon abandoned himself to silence. Time future was unimaginable.

As it grew dark, the hatch in the door opened and a man peered through.

"Food?"

Before Tony could respond the face disappeared. The retort of the door bolt as it was drawn back, though not unexpected, startled him and he tried to get to his feet.

"No need, me old cock-robin, no standing on ceremony here," slurred the gaoler as he sent a metal tray skimming across the floor. A chipped heavily stained white enamel mug full of steaming tea, was placed just out of Tony's reach, stewed liquid slopping messily.

"There again, it might do you some good."

He coughed, his gruff voice, gritty and strained.

"Bread and dripping, hope you like it."

He looked at Tony, clearing his throat with a series of exaggerated gulps.

"You're the first Blackshirt we've had in here. Look ordinary enough to me, but that's what they say, innit? Let's hope you're the last. Got enough on our plate, without our own kind doing the dirty on us. Could understand it if you were a foreigner or something, but you're English and they say you were born round here. One of your uncles was even mayor. I can't understand it."

As he spoke he slowly backed away from Tony, his brow furrowed in consternation. Reaching the sanctuary of the doorway, his mood lightened and his eyes glistened. He waved his hand in front of his face.

"There's one hell of a stink in here. You should open some windows, let in some fresh air."

His thin laugh echoed in the narrow corridor. The clanging reverberations of the cell door, slammed shut, died away and Tony imagined he was screaming, panic shredding his senses. Time assumed another dimension and passed unmarked. He drifted. Finally, hunger imposed an order, natural appetite overcoming despair and he began to eat – the stale greasy bread mush in his dry mouth before forming into an unshapely mass when swallowing, the lumps catching in his throat, gulps of strong lukewarm tea finally washing it down, inducing an uneasy settling in his hollow stomach. Tony had barely forced his way through one unappetizing slice before the door opened and a familiar face appeared, Dr. Douglas Macfarlane.

"Oh my God Tony, look at you. What happened?"

Tony struggled to collect the words, but his friend was not interested in an explanation.

"You need to understand I'm not here as your GP, but as the police surgeon. Emily called me saying she thought you'd been assaulted when they brought you in." He looked over his shoulder and pushed the door to with his foot before whispering, "I told her I left the Party years ago, as you know. I couldn't stomach what was being done, what was being said. With things as they are now, I don't know how you could have stayed in Tony. They're right to bring you in here in my opinion. I told them outside I didn't want to get involved, but the Sergeant ordered me, saying if I wanted to keep my job I had to do it, so here I am. You didn't keep membership lists did you? They won't be able to trace anything back to me will they?"

Tony glanced up at him and said nothing.

"I'm a professional man, Tony. Youthful indiscretion, actions of a hot-blooded young man, that sort of thing. Tony, as a friend I'm begging you not to say anything that would drag me into this. Please?"

"You've nothing to worry about," Tony said almost absent-mindedly, "You flatter yourself Dougie, they are only going after the big fish. Minnows like you always seem to get away."

The doctor sighed with relief and sat down heavily on the stained mattress. He looked around, his face contorted with distaste.

"It's fairly rank in here, what the hell have you been up to?"

"Fucking treat me and get out."

Tony's anger startled his erstwhile friend, who stood up and clutched his black bag to his chest. Tentatively reaching out he turned his patient's head from side to side, cursorily examining the clotted abrasions and swollen florid bruises.

"You'll live Tony. A broken nose, black eyes and bruising to your head and upper arms are all it is. The nose will set itself. As for the rest, well time is what is needed. Something you'll have plenty of, no doubt."

"Bloody hilarious. There may be nothing written down, that I know of, but I'll remember, don't you fear. You'd better hope I am in here for a good long time."

The police surgeon wiped his hands on a handkerchief he took from the breast pocket of his jacket and stepped back, a fear-tinged sense of superiority coupled with a desperate need to leave evoking in him an unconvincing bravado.

"You're a spent force Tony. Even if the Nazis win this war

they won't be interested in your lot, they'll bring their own people over. So stuff you. They'll be sending you away for the duration I expect, so I won't be seeing you again."

"Unless it's all been some horrible mistake."

"No chance, dream on Tony, dream on."

He tapped on the door, which opened immediately, and walked out.

"How is he doctor? Is he fit? Can they talk to him?"

"Yes, yes," he said impatiently.

Daylight had faded away, only a faint outline remained at the window, otherwise the cell was in darkness. Tony pulled his jacket tightly across his chest, hugging himself against the creeping cold. There was a naked light bulb hanging high above him and he hoped it wasn't broken, unable to bear the thought of sitting alone in the dark. What had he done to deserve this? The question was corrosive.

The loud ringing jolt of a steel bolt sliding open woke him into blackness. The harsh electric light brought him to his senses. Blinking he saw two policemen standing in the open door.

"Cox, it's time to get up. You never know you may have visitors today."

"Visitors? Emily? What time is it?"

"Nearly six, what too early for you?"

Tony had slept hunched in a corner of the cell, his body numb with cold, joints painfully stiff, he felt dirty, his skin clammy.

"Give me a hand will you," he pleaded, "I don't think I can move."

"Piss off. Get up yourself."

Tony leaned forward, his clothing peeling away from the damp wall, then rolled over onto his side, before managing to scrabble on to his hands and knees. Movement brought life back to cramped limbs, his frozen feet agony, he stifled a cry.

"Come on, time to go for a walk."

It was mortifying, but this was how it was going to be from now on, he thought, day in day out, stupid fucking bastards making stupid fucking jokes and all he could do was accept it.

"Woof woof."

"Good dog, do as you're told."

Deliberately, one considered action after another, Tony got to his feet, hand on one knee then the other, balancing delicately, stretching sore muscles, a dull ache in the small of the back, needles behind his eyes, streaking his vision with phosphorescence, his cracked lips, ragged, grazing the sensitive tip of his parched tongue. Savage gripes in the pit of his stomach made him uneasy and he needed to relieve himself. He limped over to the bucket, giving its contents barely a glance, and concentrating on the wall in front of him, urinated in its general direction. The policeman following his every move, backed away.

"Christ, Cox."

Tony turned at ease with himself, buttoning up his fly. He was resigned to whatever was to come.

"You're a cocky bastard. You can mop that up later. Now get over here, we've been told to clean you up."

They escorted Tony along a dingy corridor to a small washroom. The floor was wet and slippery, unpleasant in stocking-feet and he self-consciously tiptoed across it. There was one grimy, cracked enamel sink and a cold tap.

"Go on, wash, you've five minutes."

Tony hesitated, he sensed a smell and tasted it, the cutting chemical tang of must and putrefaction. How do these people bear working down here, he wondered, before turning on the tap and plunging his hands into the brown spluttering torrent. Splashing icy water onto his face, he bore the chill burning into his damaged skin, relishing the delicious enveloping numbness. He stripped off his jacket, shirt and trousers and standing only in his tattered black socks, doused himself, yelping and shivering in turns. He was alive. The policemen looked on, dragging on their cigarettes.

"First time I've seen anyone do that, ain't that right Reg?"

"Too true, Arthur, stupid sod, look at him."

With his head under the tap, Tony's body appeared twisted, water cascading over his neck and shoulders and streaming in rivulets across the sloping tiled floor and out into the corridor.

"That's enough, this isn't the public baths. Get dressed."

The hours passed. He flung the stinking palliasse onto the floor and lay down on the bare rough-hewn wooden slats and stared at the ceiling. He must have slept, because the next thing he knew he was being roughly shaken by another policeman.

"Why'd you do that, I was well away?"

"Grub?"

"Thanks."

Tony sat up, swung his legs off the bench and took the tray.

"Is this all there is, bloody dripping?"

"Think yourself lucky, some of the lads are all for giving you nothing, there's a war on, as they say."

"Are you one of them?"

"What?"

"That wants to starve me to death?"

"That would be telling, and we're under strict orders not to tell you anything."

The constable stood in the doorway and watched as Tony, revulsed, nibbled at the bread and sipped his tea.

"This is terrible. What are you staring at? Hard to believe anybody can eat this muck?"

"Where did you grow up? It's good enough for most people."

Tony rubbed his face and looked up.

"If you don't mind I'm tired and I'd rather not talk, not unless you can tell me what I'm being held for and whether I'm going to be charged? Otherwise, I didn't sleep very well last night and I need to rest."

"No, we're all talking about it. What makes someone like you, a local lad, turn against your own country when we're up against it like we are today. For God's sake, the Germans started this, they're evil bastards. You can't want us to be like them?"

"Look, do you know why I'm being held?"

"It's regulations, nobody knows the details. Order came from the Chief Constable. Your name was on the list."

"You mean there were others?"

"Oh yeh, they've rounded up most of your lot in Lancashire. Don't know about anywhere else, expect so though. Lots of Italians as well, a few Germans, but that's been going on for a while. We're at war with them, so it's no surprise."

"Why don't you give over. You all keep on about it, it's getting me down."

"I won't be the last. Can't you see people don't understand. I bet your wife'll get it in the neck from your neighbours, patriotic lot…"

"My wife? What have you heard? Tell me."

"Oh nothing, but when I told my Ethel we'd brought you in, she said she wouldn't want any of you living near us. She said the whole lot of you should be locked up, children and all – evil was what she called you."

"Come on, we've lived here for years. I was born in Blackpool."

"Makes it worse mate, believe me. We've not seen much of the war up here, but everybody knows someone who's away in the forces. My brother's in the merchant navy on the North Atlantic run. Makes my blood boil to think of the likes of you rooting for the other side."

"I'm not rooting for the other side. I'm a patriot, not a traitor.

For God's sake our government was dealing with the National Socialists for years, they were dead keen to get a share of the German market, they weren't interested in a war."

"But we've got a war, Poland, France taken over. Hitler's treaty with Stalin. It's all bloody bad news. Your lot went on calling for a deal with Hitler, what do you expect people to think? Them and the Nazis are one and the same thing. It's a disgrace whatever way you cut it."

"No, no they're very different, people don't understand."

"Dead right."

"Look the National Socialists, Mussolini's lot from Italy and us, the British Union, are only looking after their country's interests. We believe in protecting our Empire – it's vital for employment, markets, the lot – without it Britain is nothing. So we must, it's so important, we must be friends with our potential rivals – Germany in particular. Germany's interests in Europe are nothing to do with us, they're not in anyway vital to our economy. Britain doesn't need Europe, we have the Empire. On the contrary we should be encouraging Germany and Italy to expand in Europe, that's what they want, and it suits us, as it will lead to the collapse of the Soviet Union and that's in everyone's interest believe me. The Communists are a much bigger threat."

"That's rubbish, Germany doesn't see it that way. They cosy up to Stalin and they're bombing us."

The policeman shook his head in disbelief. Tony got to his feet and began pacing up and down his cell. He was silent for a moment then went on animatedly.

"It's all a Jewish conspiracy, Britain…"

"Oh no, not all that again. It's a load of claptrap."

"No listen, that's your opinion. Listen please?"

The policeman shrugged, he had nothing else to do.

"Go on, it'll give me something to talk about in the pub."

"The pub...," for a moment Tony was distracted, " ... no listen. All through the thirties the government wanted to deal with Germany, "peace in our time," all that stuff. No different from what we were saying. But things ran out of control. The government was in the grip of the financial markets, they were subservient to THEIR vital interests. Britain was forced into the war by a quarrel between Jewish finance and Germany."

"Come on, why would we do that? This is stupid."

"This war is a Jews war. They saw a powerful Fascist Germany as the main barrier to their plans for global domination. It was in their vital interests to stop Germany. Now who could do that? Britain, of course, the most powerful Imperial power in the world."

Tony was excited, he was back on the stump, enthused, arms gesticulating, speaking to the unconverted.

"Britain's mistake was to go to war for Poland. You know what Poland is? It's a Jewish controlled state, which is all part of their plan. You mentioned the Nazi-Soviet treaty, well that's a key component of it too – a Jewish communist plot to create war between Germany and Britain. We've been goaded and manoeuvred into it. It's all so clear."

"Why doesn't anybody else see it then? You never had much support, because people know it's all rubbish."

"Not true, party membership went up last year, after the war started and Mosley was calling for a negotiated settlement with Hitler. People don't want war, they want peace, they want security and they want work. They don't want to be fighting for somebody else's interests."

"But we are fighting and it's bloody serious in most people's book."

"I know its serious, don't get me wrong. Now we're at war we support fighting to save Britain, nobody gains if Britain loses."

"I don't believe you. Mosley would be Prime Minister in a

Nazi government. You people would gain a hell of a lot. Come on, pull the other one."

"I don't think so, there is no such agreement, and even if that did happen it would still be a German-run government. The key thing from Britain's point of view is that if the Nazis were in charge that would lead to a break up of the Empire and that would be the end of the United Kingdom. Believe me, for the future of the country we need a negotiated peace settlement that protects the Empire."

"A negotiated settlement that brought you to power."

"Maybe, but that's better than defeat and the loss of India, the Gold Coast, Nigeria and all the others. It could have been so different."

"How do you mean?"

"The Chamberlain government was right to deal with Germany, accommodate their vital interests so long as they didn't interfere with ours. Divide up the globe into spheres of influence and make it crystal clear where all the main powers stood. But they should have spent more on rearmament, they really should. Only thing they got wrong as far as we were concerned was they didn't spend enough on the military. Mosley was absolutely right on this one. He was a great believer in, what was his phrase, "appeasement through strength". Deal with Italy, Germany, but build up your own armed forces to ensure that in the future if their governments ever forgot where their national interests lay, Britain wouldn't be a pushover."

The two men faced each other in silence, Tony gently tapping his cheek with a finger deep in thought, the policeman put out by what he had heard but unable to think of a suitable rebuttal. In the end he gave up and pointed at the dinner plate lying on the floor.

"Have you finished with that?"

Tony turned and nodded.

"I've lost my appetite."

"You really believe we can negotiate with Hitler, even now?"

"Yes, I do, along with many others. It's not in our interests this war."

Tony bent down and picked up the plate, an untouched slice of bread fell to the floor, leaving a greasy stain on the stone flags, he handed it to the policeman.

"Can you do me a favour? I've lost my shoes, could you try and find them for me or ask my wife to bring a pair in?"

"I'll see what I can do. I'm not sure your wife will be allowed to visit, but I'll ask."

"Thanks, do you have any idea what's going to happen to me? You're the only person who's spoken to me since I've been here."

"Look, you keep quiet about that, nobody is supposed to talk to you. I've heard you're to be moved on fairly soon, but to where I've no idea. No one here has, we just brought you in."

Four days passed, each one identical to the others, the natural rhythm of the sun establishing the pattern: woken at dawn, two meals, a trip to the washroom and then sleep at dusk. The electric light was only switched on sporadically, no one spoke more than a few words and the highlight came on the morning of the fourth day, when a pair of brown shoes, two sizes too big, appeared with his lunch. He asked every day about Emily and the children, but was told nothing. His injuries healed slowly and when they came for him on the fifth day after his arrest, he still wasn't able to wipe his nose, without flinching.

"You're leaving today. Can't say anybody here is sorry."

"Where am I going?"

"No idea, mate. Here, we got you this bag, razor, soap, comb, stuff like that."

"That's my bag."

"I know, we got it from your wife."

"Emily? How is she? Have you seen her? And the children?"

"She's fine. A little trouble with the neighbours, but that's no surprise."

"What do you mean? Is she alright? Tell me."

"She's a tough woman. She'll have to be, the mess you've left her in."

"What trouble?"

"Oh, nothing much, windows smashed, weed killer on the lawn, dog shit through the letter box, that sort of thing."

Tony lunged at the policeman, but was grabbed and forced down onto his knees.

"Temper, temper. We should do you for assault, but what's the point? From what I've heard you won't be back round here for a while. And if the problems continue for your wife, she'll be keen to move away as soon as you get out."

Handcuffs were slipped onto his wrists as he struggled on the floor.

"If I were you, I'd watch that nose of yours. Any little knock could set it back."

The policeman grabbed Tony by the hair, signalled to his colleague to shut the cell door, and then slammed his head forward hitting his nose on the stone floor. Tony screamed. A dirty towel muffled his cries and soaked up the blood. Tony writhed, gasping for breath, but was helpless, pinned to the ground by three burly men.

"Go quietly, say nothing and there'll be no trouble," hissed one of the policemen as they hauled him through the door and along the corridor to the stairs.

"Nobody gives a damn about you and they won't believe a word you say. So don't waste your breath."

Waiting on the ground floor was a group of prison officers drinking mugs of tea, they looked round wearily as Tony appeared.

"This is the fifth one today, when will it end, eh?" said one of the men.

"I dunno, I think they've arrested most of them, so I heard from a mate in the Met," replied the desk sergeant, "What happened to him?"

"Slipped on the stairs."

"Never learn, do they?"

Tony stood impassively before them, the pain dominant.

"Where are you taking me?"

The senior prison officer looked at the sergeant, who shrugged.

"It'll be home from home for you, Walton Prison. Seems you know it well. If I've heard right you could have been our MP. Come and visited us, seen what conditions were like, asked questions in the House."

"If pigs could fly."

"Now you're going to get that experience firsthand."

"What about a lawyer? My appeal?"

"Appeal all you like, we're listening, aren't we boys? I'm only too happy to hear what you have to say. Let me make one thing crystal clear, you won't be getting a lawyer. The likes of you aren't entitled to one. We're at war remember. Take it up with the powers that be when it's all over, you bastard."

Tony was thrust against the wall, and held roughly as one set of handcuffs was exchanged for another. He began struggling when they shackled his feet.

"Forget that, we're taking no chances with you."

"I've done nothing, I tell you I've done nothing wrong, let me go."

"Shut up."

The officer smirked at his colleagues.

"Ask us nicely and we might let you off."

Tony was silent, head shaking from side to side, his eyes closed.

"Please."

"Please what?"

There was a deep sigh of resignation. But the officers didn't care, they were focused on humiliation.

"Please, don't shackle my legs. I'll not try to escape, I give you my word."

The men looked at each other.

"No."

"You bastards."

"Did you hear that?"

"Ay."

"Sticks and stones Cox, remember that, sticks and stones. We've all the sticks and stones…try this one for size."

Withdrawing a truncheon from his belt he held it in front of Tony's face.

"I call this my little bastard."

He stepped back and swung the club hard against Tony's right knee. There was a sound like a whip cracking and Tony's leg bowed outwards as his body buckled under the blow. The men let him fall and a thin high-pitched squeal issued from between his clenched teeth, like steam escaping a kettle. Hands restrained, he lay at the feet of the officers, and sobbed quietly. They were in no hurry to leave and watched him impassively.

Tony Cox had been the British Union's prospective parliamentary candidate for Walton, in Liverpool, for just over three years before the war. He had worked diligently, canvassing, addressing meetings, selling the Party's newspapers, "Action" and "Blackshirt", on street corners. He would often spend days away from Blackpool, sleeping at the homes of supporters, rarely changing his clothes. He had been both surprised and honoured when he was selected for the seat, the constituency committee citing his work in setting up and running the Blackpool branch, the record level of recruitment he had achieved, and their approval of the efforts made by his wife, Emily. Together, they were a perfect couple.

Walton had not been his first choice as he'd expected to stand in his home town of Blackpool, but the Party only planned to contest around a hundred seats across the country in the upcoming election and had to be selective. Walton – poor, working class with large numbers of military veterans and high unemployment – was seen as a winnable seat and he was determined the leadership wouldn't be proved wrong. It was a hard violent place and he faced opposition. Many of his meetings ended in clashes with political opponents and people getting hurt. He had been arrested twice for brawling, ending up with a caution on both occasions. But his campaigning efforts didn't go unnoticed. Senior figures in the Party visited the constituency and made speeches – Mick Clarke, William Joyce, even Sir Oswald had been due to come, during his next tour of the north. The war had put paid to that, the elections had been postponed and for the time being at least it looked like the British Union was in retreat.

Tony knew Walton Prison, an oppressive Victorian building that cast a pall over the surrounding terraced streets. He had once held a rally on a corner beneath its walls, it had begun to rain and the sparse audience had deserted him, people scattering, running home, leaving him standing alone on an orange box in the dank, glistening road. He had sheltered beneath the prison's imposing twin-towered entrance, shivering as the biting rain lashed his face. A passing prison officer had joked that it was "no warmer or drier on the inside, so he wouldn't be inviting him in." He'd given Tony a cigarette before disappearing through a small door that opened slightly off-centre in one of the large wooden gates that dominated the prison approach.

The streets were depressingly familiar to Tony as the Black Maria drove through the neighbourhood. It was raining again, but this time the sun kept breaking through gaps in the thinning murk. The cobbles glistened in the opaque sunlight, puddles reflecting the washed-out grey and off-white pallor of the cloud-dappled sky. He yearned to smell the rain-drenched streets, the muggy smoke of damp coal fires, the wet fragrance of sodden earth, but he was a prisoner, trapped.

They passed the street corner he had campaigned on and turned into the rutted access road to the prison. His heart was beating fast and he was short of breath. The van slowed, its horn blared, a face appeared, the large black gates swung slowly open and they drove in, passing out of sodden daylight into a dry shadow-less gloom.

Ahead in the small inner courtyard was another prison van, engine idling, its rear doors open. The air was thick with petrol fumes. Three men dressed in working clothes, one of them wearing a cloth cap, were awkwardly climbing out of the back. The guards were watching, offering no assistance. The prisoners' hands were in cuffs and their feet shackled with rusty chains. Tony recognized two of the men – Ray Ainsley, BUF District Leader in Halifax, he'd shared a train carriage with him once coming back from a rally in London, and Basil Greatrix from Leeds, who was one of the best speakers in the Party. Tony had always enjoyed listening to him working a crowd, a true rabble-rouser, he'd caused a near riot the night he spoke at the Central Library in Blackpool. Two members of the local Communist party had heckled him for attacking the Jews and he had finally lost patience and jumped down into the audience and threatened to throw them out himself. The Communists left before the national anthem and Basil made great play of that. His exploits got a mention in "Action", one of the few occasions Blackpool had made it into the headlines.

"What a place to meet again," Tony thought, "the police seem to have done a bloody good job rounding everybody up."

The three fascist prisoners, heads bowed, shuffled from the van to the bottom of a small flight of stairs that led up to a stone landing. As they passed, Tony noticed they were unshaven, their hair dishevelled and clothes heavily soiled. The man he didn't recognize had two black eyes and a heavily swollen jaw, his white shirt front was spattered with dried blood. A guard standing above them on the walkway, a pistol in a holster on his belt and a Lee Enfield rifle slung over his shoulder, barked out a curt order.

"Right, come on you bastards, let's have you up here and no trouble."

Ray Ainsley moved forward, shackled he was unable to raise his foot high enough to reach the first step, he strained, slipped and overbalanced, falling back onto Basil Greatrix, who was following close behind. The two of them concertinaed into the third man, who bore their full weight as they collapsed in a tangled heap on to the stone flags. There was no sound. Tony smiled grimly, he couldn't contain himself, it was like watching a silent film featuring the Keystone Cops.

"Cox, get out. You lot need to stick together. Help 'em up, but not a word mind, no talking."

"My hands. I can't help with my hands tied, can I?"

"Shut up and get out."

Moving in chains, unaided, was tortuous and by the time Tony alighted from the van, the men were sitting on the ground, groaning. Blood trickled from the mouth of the unknown man as, winded, he gasped for breath. The other two, shocked and demoralized, nodded in recognition when they caught sight of Tony approaching, then looked away. Basil was in pain, his right leg lying awkwardly beneath his body. Tony stood helplessly in front of them, before looking questioningly at the guards on the walkway above.

"Take his cuffs off."

The relief was intense as his wrists were freed. He wanted to wave his aching arms in the air, let the blood flow again, drive away the numbness in his fingers. But instead, as ordered, he reached down with unfeeling hands to drag his fellow detainees to their feet. The rankness of their unwashed bodies was distasteful, their breath stale, dull glazed expressions barely registered his presence. The companionable feelings that had swept over Tony at the sight of familiar faces ebbed away with the realization that these men were severely damaged and defeated. With great effort Tony pushed each in turn up the steps and then followed them onto the walkway. His hands were sticky with blood. At the end of the landing a pale yellow light glimmered through an opaque window in a green door. It opened, an order was given and another armed guard, who had been standing in the shadows, beckoned to them.

Basil found it difficult to walk, so Tony grabbed one of his arms and supported him as they staggered forward. The glare was blinding after the gloom of the transport bay – it was impossible to see the dimensions of the room or how many people were present, but Tony sensed there were a good number – and there was the faint smell of disinfectant. For the first time since his arrest he felt completely helpless, temporarily unsighted it became obvious he was losing control, his weakness evident in the stabbing pain in his abdomen and a loosening of the bowels. It was as if his companions were dragging him down to their level of incapacity, crippling him. The door slammed and was locked.

Faculties awry the four men stood swaying, raggedly bracing each other, in front of a trestle table that had been set up at one end of the long narrow room beneath a barred window high in the wall. Sitting behind it were two men, one dressed in a black suit with a blue tie, the other in a white laboratory coat. Prison guards, some armed, were posted at intervals along the walls.

In the centre of the room stood an empty battered tin bath. The prisoners were led up to the table and their restraints unlocked. The shackles fell noisily to the floor and were dragged into a corner. The release was invigorating and there was a reorientation – sight clarified and base instincts asserted themselves.

"Leave your arms alone, stand up straight. Come on, you're not on some fascist parade ground now. Right, get undressed, fold up your clothes and pile them in front of you."

The four men glanced at each other and hesitated before Basil slumped across the table. A guard instantly approached, placing an outstretched hand on his shoulder.

"Step back in line."

"You've no right to make us strip. I've been hurt." He slurred. "This is blatant discrimination. I demand to see a person in authority."

The man in the suit raised his hand as Basil was pulled back into line.

"I am Deputy Governor Briggs. Let me assure you we have every right. Prison Regulations clearly state that every inmate on arrival at the prison must be given a medical inspection by a qualified doctor, and then must be offered the opportunity to take a bath or shower. As should be only too obvious you need to undress for both, so please proceed."

His quiet acerbic tone expressed an authority that tolerated no objections and he was surprised when Basil spoke again.

"But in front of all these guards, that cannot be in the regulations."

The Deputy Governor's reply when it came was barely audible, but it was clear he was losing patience.

"Look, you are considered to be some of the most dangerous prisoners we have in Walton. I deem it necessary that each of you should be accompanied by at least four guards, whenever you are out of your cells. So you can see all these people are, as you put it, perfectly within regulations. Enough, now carry on."

Basil was about to respond when Tony nudged him. "It's not worth it," he mouthed and began to unbutton his shirt. The others grudgingly followed suit. When they were naked a guard picked up their clothes and shoved them into a dirty hessian sack. He tossed the bundle into a corner and then circled the men eyeing them critically. It was cold and the four of them began to shiver. Basil covered his genitals with his hands. When he had finished his inspection the guard nodded at the Deputy Governor, who ordered the prisoners to stand to attention.

"Seeing as you are great ones for regulations, you will be pleased to hear that I am obliged to give you some indication of why you are being held here."

Clearing his throat he picked up a sheet of paper from the table. A second after glancing at it, he put it down, reached into his jacket pocket and took out a pair of wire-rimmed spectacles. Carefully placing them on the bridge of his nose, he deliberately coaxed the flexible textile temple tips of the glasses behind each ear in turn and then looked up at the prisoners over the top of the circular lenses.

"You have been detained under section 18B, subsection 1a. of the wartime defence regulations."

He stared at Tony and the others.

"This was promulgated under the Emergency Powers Act of 24th August 1939, and amended on the 23rd of November in the same year. It states that the Home Secretary has reasonable, please note the word, reasonable cause to believe that the organization, of which you are members, that is the British Union of Fascists, has hostile origins or has recently been involved in actions seen as compromising national security."

He paused for breath and looked down at the document lying on the table.

"Or you yourselves are seen as capable of carrying out acts prejudicial to the public safety or the defence of the realm or to put it into language we can all understand, you are seen as traitors."

He removed his glasses and peered myopically round the room, seeking approbation from his men. A number nodded in his direction. He replaced his glasses and continued reading.

"All detainees have the right of appeal to an Advisory Committee. All appellants will have to appear in person and will be allowed no legal representation from counsel or solicitor. All very clear, I think, self-explanatory. Now this is Doctor…"

Tony interrupted him.

"Can you tell us more about this right of appeal, how do we…"

"Quiet," roared the Deputy Governor, "I said nothing about questions. I have told you everything you are entitled to know. Count yourselves lucky you have that much information."

He stood up, his chair scraping across the stone floor, and glared at Tony.

"Your name?"

"Tony Cox."

He shuffled the papers on the table, identifying a paragraph with his finger.

"Ah yes. Wife a fascist too I see, what a pair. Sired a couple of young fascists as well, they must have been proud of you. Right, you can be processed first."

Sitting down he almost missed his chair, pulling it under him awkwardly. His pale watery blue eyes fixed Tony over the rim of his glasses.

"As I was saying," he tried unsuccessfully to clear his throat, then raised his fist to his mouth and coughed loudly, "before I was interrupted. This is Doctor Ryan, he will carry out the medical examinations."

Standing the doctor was thinner and taller than he had looked sitting at the table, his white coat was several sizes too large for him and he had rolled up the sleeves to make them fit more comfortably. There was dried blood smeared down the right side of the garment above the pocket. He smiled weakly at Tony and came round the table to face him. He was holding pale translucent surgical gloves, which he pulled on as he spoke.

"Any history of serious illness?"

Tony shook his head.

"Answer the doctor," interjected the Deputy Governor, "clearly. We all want to hear what you have to say."

"No."

"No what?"

"No, I've no history of serious ill…"

"Stop this. You really are trying my patience."

The Deputy Governor was on his feet and scowling at Tony. His hands, pressing hard on the table, whitened at the knuckles.

"No SIR," he blared.

Tony felt warm spittle spatter against his face and closed his eyes.

"Look at me when I'm talking to you. Christ, I'm so tired of you people."

He raised his eyes to the ceiling and sighed deeply. Retrieving his chair he sat down and anger contained, stared at Tony. He was again barely audible when he spoke, "It's always sir to you, whoever you are speaking to in this prison, is that clear?"

"Yes Sir."

"Louder, I want everyone to hear."

"Yes Sir."

"Good. Doctor, please continue with your medical examination."

"Open your mouth …wider."

The Doctor's breath smelled faintly of whisky as he

scrutinised Tony, a bemused expression on his face. His fingers tasted of rubber as they probed and searched. Tony stared back into the dark unblinking eyes and fought the temptation to bite the man's hand.

"Tongue out. Good. Head forward."

Fingers raked back and forth through Tony's hair, before roughly squeezing his neck. Muttering to himself the Doctor ran his hands over shoulders, armpits, chest, and stomach, before leaning forward and slipping a grasping hand beneath Tony's scrotum. As he straightened up Tony moved forward to relieve the uncomfortable pressure but was stopped by a firm hand on his chest. The Doctor appeared vacant.

"Cough."

Unembarrassed at his nakedness until that moment, Tony suddenly felt acutely vulnerable. His fate had never seemed so arbitrary and so dangerously out of control. Anxious, he broke out in a fine sweat, shivering uncontrollably. The pressure in his groin increased.

"Cold? Well the sooner we get this over with the sooner you can get something on, so cough."

Tony obeyed.

"Once more."

He coughed again, his mouth filling with phlegm. Spitting it out, debased as he was, seemed a foolish act of defiance and swallowing he winced with disgust. The Doctor released his testicles and stepped back, his lips mouthing words, forming silent sentences. He passed the back of a gloved hand over his forehead and spoke out loud, a slight rasp in his voice.

"Turn round and bend over."

As Tony reluctantly changed position the Deputy Governor shifted slightly in his seat, leaning forward to rest his elbows on the table. The guards seemed to have moved closer and all to be staring at Tony, while his three fellow prisoners, pale and diminished in their own nakedness, averted their gaze.

"I said, bend over."

Intensely self-conscious Tony closed his eyes, his body vibrantly alert to any approach, skin susceptible, a heightened appreciation of his defenselessness raising the hairs on his bare limbs. His exposed back tensed. He felt the Doctor's hand rest on his left buttock, then apply outward pressure. A tingling anticipation, then the violation: the thrust of two fingers, the flinching of muscles, the probing search, the tearing, the withdrawal, then the stinging aftermath.

"Straighten up and face the front."

As he spoke the doctor wiped his fingers on a discoloured towel hanging on the back of his chair. He nodded at the Deputy Governor. Tony brushed tears from his eyes and gently touched his buttocks.

"Buck up man. Right, time for your bath."

A guard grasped Tony by the arm and led him to the tin bath in the middle of the room. It was empty.

"Get in."

He stepped into the bath, the metal felt warmer on the soles of his feet than the stone flagstones. The Deputy Governor, meanwhile ticked the medical and bath boxes on his record sheet and handed it to the Doctor for initialing.

"Get out."

Tony was then ordered to walk to a door at the far end of the room and to stand to attention. Sensing everyone was watching him, he seethed with hatred at his tormentors, but prayed that outwardly he showed nothing.

"Basil Greatrix step forward. What sort of name is that?"

Averting his eyes, Tony stared at the tired yellow wall opposite – slowly traced the jagged crack in the bricks that snaked from the ceiling to slither from view behind the shoulder of a guard – closed his ears to the barked orders, and silently humming, attempted to disappear. He quickly discovered there was nowhere to hide. A gasp, an intake of breath, a whimper forced his return, weaving him ever more tightly into the fabric of humiliation that blanketed the prison. He would discover over the coming months of his detention that this stuff was the only covering in the institution able to keep him warm. But for now the ritual of abasement seemed unremitting to Tony.

"The bastards."

A novice in the art of self-negation he had no idea how much of this treatment he could withstand – it was an agonizing assault. A siren, loud and close, wailed in sympathy. There was frenetic movement around him, close to panic. The prisoners buckled as the pandemonium engulfed them, fear being mutual, the tumult only calmed when the lights suddenly failed, plunging the room into darkness.

"Switch them on for Christ's sake, we can't see a bloody thing."

The bulbs flickered back to life.

"Get the detainees to the cells," yelled the Deputy Governor, as he dashed out of the room, followed by the doctor. The door slammed as another swung open behind Tony. Bent double and breathing heavily a red-faced guard struggled to speak. All activity ceased as attention focused on his efforts. He straightened up and babbled, "It's an air raid, they're overhead. Get to the shelters."

Handcuffed, the prisoners were frog-marched down a long barely illuminated corridor, which grew appreciably brighter and less stuffy after they turned a corner and approached an open door that led into a walled yard. The party halted and the guards peered out, looking upwards. The sky was a paler grey than the black undifferentiated shadow of the prison building, a pink essence frosted the top of the boundary wall. It was an unheralded visual confection, stunning to the eye. The fresh air too was an elixir, warm and faintly cinder-scented and Tony greedily inhaled as they were hustled across the exercise yard. The pathway worn in the sparse patch of turf by generations of inmates was sodden and gritty, the protruding stones painful for their bare feet. The keening of the siren ceased and as the echoes died away there was calm. Then everyone tensed as they heard the monotonous drone of aircraft. Standing in the open, vulnerable and exposed, the bombers sounded to be upon them.

"Bugger this," hissed one of the guards, "Run."

The group broke up in disarray – the prisoners standing rigidly still, uncertain what to do – as their escorts sprinted towards a dark shadow in the wall over on the right. A bright orange light flashed in the slate-streaked space above the wall, followed by another and another. They heard the dull crump of a single explosion and felt the tremor beneath their feet, it was instantly superseded by another distinct crack then the percussive sounds merged into an ugly rolling dissonance as the bombardment tore up the neighbouring streets, the ground quaking. In panic they followed the guards, who could be dimly seen disappearing through a door ahead of them.

"Hey, wait for us," screamed Ray.

The prison shook and the ground bucked as bombs exploded close to the walls. Fiery columns erupted high into the air as houses burst apart and gas mains ruptured. Acrid dust billowed everywhere materializing from the shaking walls and cracked earth in roiling clouds, searing lungs and lacerating eyes. Blind and choking, Tony's alarm at being a target of the German aircraft was accentuated by a powerful sense of his imminent death, inducing a state of pure terror. Acutely aware of a growing inability to act, a sinking down, he was saved by the crashing animal momentum of his companions, which overrode individual paralysis and swept them all forward. Maddened they coalesced – it was difficult to stay upright as they scrambled with hands cuffed behind their backs – their bodies colliding and stumbling. Tony grazed his knee on the gravel as he struggled to keep his balance, the sharp pain penetrating the fug of fear, clearing his mind. He heard Basil repeatedly muttering, "Oh God," as he overtook him and cried out, "This way, over here." He stopped, stepped back and touched Basil on the shoulders, offering fake reassurance as he hauled himself to his feet. Together they shuffled forward.

At the doorway the guards were agitated. The heavy tang of seared metal hung in the air.

"What the fuck are you lot playing at? You may want to get you heads blown off, but we don't, get over here."

Weak torchlight illuminated a dusty corridor, strewn with debris. Shards of glass glinted as the beam swept from side to side in the smothering gloom.

"Stick them in the first one you come to and then we can get to the basement," shouted a guard from the doorway as desperate hands grabbed the prisoners, pushed them roughly into a cell and slammed the door. The precise turning of the lock was heard above the compressive thud of the bombs. It was pitch dark and the terrified men blundered around blindly, recoiling whenever they came into contact with a grimy body, before they each found the wall and settled on to the ground. The floor was granular to the touch and uncomfortable to sit on. They shifted as the room shook and the sound of explosions grew louder. Tony searched the darkness above his head for any sign of a window, a slight change in the quality of the blackness, an escape, but could see nothing.

Dust drifted down, stinging eyes, irritating noses and filling mouths. Coughs and sneezes punctuated the incessant thumping of the bombs. Tony shook his head, the uneven tempo of the blasts, the threat they posed was beginning to possess him. He counted the detonations. They occurred in clusters of eight, then they would stop, raising hopes that the raid was over. But they would start again. On and on. The building never stopped shaking.

"One, two, three, four…"

A massive explosion plucked the words from Tony's mouth and sucked the air from his body. The cell physically moved, plaster and bricks showered down, pressing the prisoners to the floor. A flash seared the torn blackout curtain covering the window high up in the wall, illuminating for a moment their wrecked surroundings. There was a sound of falling masonry and the faint echo of a scream. The roar faded into the distance. In the lull, Tony heard a sobbing, disconnected voice, one he didn't recognize.

"Oh Lord Jesus, oh good Lord."

That was not the last raid on Liverpool that night, for several more hours the Luftwaffe bombed the city, but Walton prison escaped further damage. Guards and volunteer firemen fought the blaze that raged through part of D-Wing. They had only a couple of hoses and one functioning water-hydrant and made little progress. Five prisoners had been killed when a bomb hit their cell block, two others escaped with minor scratches and burns. The four detainees cowered in their cell listening to the hubbub outside. The darkness heightened their senses – the acrid smell of burning filled the room, every cry and shriek cut through them. Fear obliterated hunger, the savage cramps in their bound wrists and arms, and all shame. No one slept.

A naked bulb brought them round, the light piercing dust-encrusted eyes like needles. Blinking they heard the guards cursing as they struggled to open the encrusted lock and shift the rubble-jammed door. It gave way after much hammering.

"Look at these bastards. They've got nothing on. Sam, you'd better go and find their clothes."

"Right ho."

"Come on, you lot get up. Count your blessings it wasn't you that burned up eh? Some poor sods weren't so lucky."

The prison officers tentatively kicked the hunched naked figures, their hair and bodies coated in a thin dusting of white powder, faces marked by a darkening around watery eyes and moist traces of saliva dribbling from the corners of open mouths.

"Come on, rouse yourselves. We're moving you, it's not safe in here. The ceiling could come down at any time."

One of the guards blurted out, "Oh Christ, who left them in cuffs?"

"We was in one hell of a hurry last night. There was no time to look after this bunch and make it to the shelters. Sod it, who's going to find out. Corkhill's not going to give a damn about this lot, is he?"

"Steady on lad, we won't breath a word. Have you got the key?"

"No, they aren't mine. It'll take a bit to sort this out. We was all over the shop when the bombing started. I really don't need this."

He stormed out of the cell in search of the keys.

"You're already making a lot of friends, aren't you?"

Another guard stood above Tony and stared pitilessly at him, before nudging him in the side.

"Up all of you, I've been here all night and I wanna' go home, come on stand."

He bent over and hauled on Basil Greatrix's arm and he rose groggily to his feet.

"Ughhh you're in a state."

Basil struggled to reply, but could only manage an abusive croak. The others staggered up unaided. As their eyes grew accustomed to the bright light, they saw that the room was a shell, empty except for a pile of dirty rags heaped in a corner. The floor was strewn with plaster and brick fragments, the walls stained and scuffed. Mould flourished verdantly on decaying plaster peeling from a segment of brickwork near the door, sustained by a ruptured pipe seeping rusty water that constantly flooded a quadrant of the cell.

The prisoners' stupefaction elicited sympathy.

"Not up to your standards? Well things are better on the upper floors, which is where you're going. You've got beds, running water and, oh yes, your very own chamber pots. You boys are lucky you're the first to be put up in there. The old women's quarters are being opened up."

"Re-opened you mean."

"Of course I do, re-opened specially for you. Keep all your lot in one place, where we can keep an eye on you. You'll have cells of your own for a while. But I hear they're bringing a good number of your friends up here, from down south."

In the corridor there was a strong smell of charred wood and as they were led up a dusty flight of stone stairs the prisoners could hear the distant disparate sounds of picks and shovels removing rubble. The lower steps were splattered with bird droppings and they stepped forward gingerly. The corpses of emaciated pigeons littered the floor of the stairwell – broken feathers scattered everywhere – the birds trapped by the metal grill that lined the stairs from the ground to the third floor of the building. A window on the first landing hung open on broken hinges, letting in a warm breeze. The courtyard was carpeted with broken bricks, roof tiles and splintered timbers and there were piles of sodden clothes and footwear heaped everywhere. The pages of a discarded newspaper fluttered across the debris, slowly opening and closing, catching on broken pipes, guttering and a washbasin untouched by its fall from an upper floor.

A thin plume of blue smoke rose from the shattered remains of D-wing. The end of the building had been completely destroyed, the interior of the cells, some with pictures pinned to the walls, stood out starkly against the scorched brickwork. On the third floor a swaying bunk hung by a single chain. A gang of prisoners was clearing a blocked doorway, their exhausted escorts sitting on large slabs of masonry nearby, smoking. The sun was bright and a number of the prisoners had taken off their shirts, their grimy sweating bodies glistening in the clear morning light. Tony caught sight of the Deputy Governor standing in the shade on the opposite side of the courtyard talking to another man in a dark suit – was that the Governor he wondered? Last night's bombing wouldn't help their chances of an early release.

"Damn it."

"Poor sods, most wouldn't have known what hit them. Come on, move away from the window, we haven't got all day."

They climbed the remaining half-flight of stairs to a dingy landing.

"Here we are," called out one of the guards, "Take your pick."

The four prisoners stood indecisively, looking up and down the corridor.

"Only joking," the guard grabbed Tony and pushed him into the first open cell, "in you go."

He was greeted by the crack of wings and a flurry of feathers, as a panicked pigeon crashed through the bars and out of the broken window. No one followed Tony.

"Thank God," he thought, "I'm on my own."

There was a cry from the bottom of the stairs.

"Hold on, don't lock them in. I've got the keys and Pete has found some uniforms."

Seconds later a breathless young man appeared at the

door of Tony's cell. Behind him another guard, who tossed a grey washed-out tunic onto the floor and disappeared, only to reappear seconds later with a pair of lace-less black shoes, which he threw against the wall. Tony flinched as the shoes bounced across the room. The boyish guard frowned.

"I hope this is the right key."

It was dark when Tony woke up. He was lying on soft musty bedding and he was clothed. It was deathly quiet and the air was frigid. He thought of his wife and children, would they sleep through the night? Would they be undisturbed? Get a lie-in in the morning? A cup of tea in bed? It felt like the weekend. He fell asleep.

He sat bolt upright. It was light. There was a commotion in the corridor outside the cell.

"Slopping out lads, buckets at the ready. You've got five minutes for that early morning shit, make the most of it."

The voice faded away and the rattling and hammering diminished. Dazed, Tony stared at the rusting metal door, its scuffed mute solidity demoralizing. Outraged as he felt at the injustice of his incarceration and at the indignities he was suffering, he was too drained to move. He dutifully sat and waited until he heard the guard returning, then grabbed his bucket and stood by the door. The twisted metal handle cut into his fingers and he lauded the return of feeling to his hands. The day before when his handcuffs had been taken off, his upper body had been numb. Relief forced a smile to his face.

"Someone's happy this morning. Privvies are at the end of the corridor, wash up, straight back here and no talking. Grub in half an hour."

Basil and Ray were already in the washroom with two other prisoners Tony hadn't seen before.

"Wash up, there's no fucking water," one of them snarled as he came in, "and there's even more of us. I really am fucking fed up with this. How many of us are there on this fucking wing? How many more are they going to cram in here?"

"Shut up will you, you stupid," Basil hissed, "We're all in the same boat. The last thing we want is some thick …"

"Basil keep it down for Christ's sake, we'll get it in the neck if they hear us."

Tony grabbed Basil's arm and pulled him back towards the door.

"Leave it, he's not worth it. How's the leg?"

Basil was uncertain he wanted to act reasonably, but Tony refused to release him.

"Is it true there's no water?"

Basil stared directly into his face.

"Yes it's true, no bloody water. I'm going to forget how to piss if this goes on much longer."

He threw an arm around Tony, simpered, his narrow pinched face contorting, yellowing teeth exposed and said, "I'm glad to see you, it's good to see a friendly face. When did they nab you?"

Excited, he didn't wait for an answer.

"They bloody grabbed me in the pub in front of my mates, the bastards. Can you believe that?"

"It was three in the morning …"

"Quiet in there. No talking. Quiet, any more and you'll be locked in for the day, so shut it."

The guard appeared at the door, his black uniform immaculately pressed, a wooden baton in his hand.

"There's no water," one of the prisoners said sheepishly. The guard laughed, a scar on his left cheek blood red, almost raw.

"The state this place's in, you're lucky to have taps. Anyway I wouldn't worry, you won't be here long."

The prisoners looked up expectantly. The guard sneered, revelling in the power he held over them. He called to his colleague.

"What do you think Fred, should we tell the bastards what's going to happen to 'em?"

Fred was armed not only with a wooden stave, but also with a pistol in a holster. Initially surprised he nodded in agreement, scowling with an obdurate intensity that should have signalled a warning, but the prisoners' desperate need for information made them gullible, and it was ignored.

"This is not official, of course," the first guard said conspiratorially, "just something I overheard, passing the Governor's office."

He lowered his voice to a whisper and the prisoners drew closer.

"Keep it to yourselves, won't you?"

They all nodded and stepped nearer.

"Steady on, not too close. Get back."

Submissively the men retreated, opening the circle, but still leaning anxiously inwards. The only sound, an ominous clunking in the pipes.

"It's not good news, I'm afraid."

Pausing, he savoured the shocked, disappointed, expressions of the prisoners.

"Not good news for some of you."

His outstretched arm swept the room in a large arc, his pointing forefinger briefly admonishing each dismayed face in turn.

"Maybe even all of you in here."

Tony felt the jolt of anxiety behind his eyes, the prickle of concern, first in the small of his back, then across his shoulder blades.

"What? For pity's sake, tell us."

"Well, I shouldn't be talking to you like this. What do you think Fred? Have I said too much?"

Fred looked thoughtful and then shook his head.

"Go on, they'll find out soon enough, may as well tell 'em."

The other guard looked doubtful, then sighed and went on, "Fine, but don't breath a word," and he looked at each prisoner, waiting for their nod of assent.

"Good. I mean I'll deny I ever told you anything and Fred'll back me up."

Fred mouthed his agreement as he absentmindedly tapped the wooden stave against his leg.

"I understand that given the seriousness of the charges against you, the authorities …"

"What charges? Nobody's said anything to us about charges," blurted out Basil Greatrix, "I mean it's all very well."

"Do you want to hear what I've got to say? I'm not doing this for my health you know."

"Yes, shut up Basil. Let's hear him out," cut in Ray firmly.

Basil, angry, threw up his hands in resignation.

"Go on, go on, I won't breathe another word."

"As I was saying, given the seriousness of the charges and the current state of hostilities with the Germans, the Government is not prepared to look kindly on traitors."

Basil made to move forward, but was restrained by a prisoner. The guards stiffened.

"Watch it. I'm getting mighty pissed off with you lot. I'm only trying to help."

"Go on, there will be no more trouble," stated Tony, "Put us out of our misery."

"That's exactly what might happen," said the guard at the door.

"Bluntly, the powers that be feel a few examples need to be set, discourage the others, know what I mean?"

The prisoners looked at each other, the implications of what was being said, dawning on them. Ray started to shake.

"You mean they're going to execute …?" his question trailed off as he swallowed hard and turned away. The guard, grim-faced, nodded and pointed vaguely in the direction of the window.

"You remember the high wall in the courtyard you passed on the way in here?"

There was silence. Then Tony quietly said, "It was dark, we couldn't see a thing and there was the air-raid. It was impossible to make out anything."

"It's hidden from the rest of the prison. It's ideal the governor said."

The prisoners looked on blankly, breathing heavily, mouths open, their faces ashen-white.

"Firing squads, like in the army?"

Ray slumped onto his knees with a sigh, his shoulders heaving. Tony watched for a moment, his own thoughts incoherent, then crouched down and cradled him in his arms. Basil, staring grimly at the guards, placed a reassuring hand on the back of his neck.

"They can't do that," he said, "things haven't got that bad. You're fucking lying, just saying it, you bastards."

"Watch it, Sunny Jim."

The guard then drew out a whistle and blew it. Tony shut his eyes as the piercing notes reverberated around the room.

"This is a nightmare," he thought, "I'm going to die for nothing, God help me."

Fear shorted out linkages in his mind, stripping him of the ability to think, leaving him distraught, clutching pathetically at Ray's shaking body for support. They could be bluffing but he was uncertain, too frightened to trust to luck.

A door banged shut down below, the hurried clatter of hobnail boots could be heard climbing the stairs, drawing near along the corridor. A voice called out, "What's up Fred, where's the trouble?"

Fred nodded malevolently into the room.

"This lot have had some bad news and aren't too happy about it. Thought we'd need help getting them back into the cells. One of them is a right mean bastard."

He waved his truncheon at Basil. Three guards burst into the washroom, agitated, aggressive. They were disappointed all was calm. Hesitating for a moment, reassessing, then two of them grabbed Basil and dragged him out into the hallway, his cries of pain dying rapidly away as they hustled him back to his cell.

"Anybody else looking for trouble, because if they are, they've found it?"

Nobody moved. Ray sobbed quietly, his tears soaking the leg of Tony's trousers.

"You get up, you sniveling little sod, on your feet."

The guard lunged forward and kicked him in the small of his back.

"You're supposed to be hard men, not girls. Christ, you make me sick. The Governor's right, why are we wasting time with you lot? There's a war on and we have to deal with wretches like you, prepared to sell us out. You deserve all you get."

"Firing squad is what's coming, I told 'em."

"Ay, a firing squad that's what they need," and the guard sniggered, "A firing squad, that's a good one."

He poked the other guard in the stomach gently with his stave.

"Right you lot, back to your billets. Any trouble and you'll be mine to deal with."

In Tony's cell a battered metal tray lay on the floor – a chipped enamel mug half-full of earth-brown liquid rested beside a hunk of bread it soaking in a pool of slopped tea.

"I'm alright," Basil called out from the adjoining cell.

The sound of his voice was obliterated by the crashing of solid iron doors and the ratcheting slide of metal bolts. Tony grimaced as he sat down on the floor beside the tray, the sharp darting pain in his back a locus for the tremors racking his aching body. He poked at the bread, which disintegrated, he then picked up the dripping mug and sipped cautiously. The tea was lukewarm and tasted bitter. He was ravenously hungry and gnawed at the soggy crusts, washing them down with the tea. Then he picked up the tray, raised it to his lips and poured the glutinous slurry into his mouth. He retched, his stomach heaving. Tepid liquid ran over his chin, percolating into the stubble and splattering onto his grey prison uniform. He belched and wiped a cupped hand over his face, then licked his palm clean. For a moment he was overtaken by a feeling of peculiar indifference, his hunger quelled, and all his other needs suppressed.

Tony shuffled backwards across the floor and leant against a dry patch of wall stretching out his legs. He dozed. His thoughts were fleeting and ephemeral, apprehended only between blank swirling spans of indeterminate time but their clarity of purpose, when he could be bothered to pay attention, was uplifting in a way that was satisfyingly self-deluding for the false optimist he had become.

"I can do this. I don't believe those bastards, they're having us on. Playing with us. I won't be here long. I don't believe they'd put us up against a wall and shoot us, no way. I've just got to get used to doing nothing. They won't leave us here to rot, I know it. Emily'll be trying to sort something out. She's a fighter, tenacious, she won't take this lying down."

Chapter 7

TWO SIDES OF THE SAME COIN

1st July 1995

Great Uncle Brian looked like a taller, thinner version of his brother, Tony, but only at times. It was disconcerting for David, an expression, a flick of the hand, a distant look in the eyes conjured up his grandfather, then he was gone. David's memories of the most important influence in his young life were hazy and he found, to his surprise, that with this new connection to the past he was hungry to conjure the man up again, to bring him back from the obscurity he had inevitably sunk into since his death, keen to rekindle that old friendship. It would ultimately prove to be a frustrating and personally damaging re-acquaintance.

The two brothers had not met for nearly thirty years before Tony died and had barely communicated with each other in that time. Only the death of their parents had brought them together, and that only in acrimony. Brian had not come to Tony's funeral, had not sent any message of condolence, a wreath, or even a card.

"The west coast of Canada put just enough miles between me and my brother to suit me," was how Brian described their relationship to David, "there was never any time during those years when I felt the need to change that."

It was Brian's first visit to England since he had turned his back on the country in the late forties and emigrated to British Colombia in search of a better future. He was now retired, a life running his own janitor's business had left him lean, tanned and fit, and his wife had been on at him for years to take a vacation in the old country. There was now no reason for him to refuse. David had barely heard of Brian or his family over the years, just passing references to the mundane antics of these exotic-seeming overseas relatives at Christmas, and had been surprised when his mother had called to say he was in the UK and keen to meet him.

"Take him to one of those country pubs near you, dear, he'll like that. It would help us out. And when are you coming to visit? I see so little of the boys. They'll be grown up before we know it."

David put down the phone.

"Oh fuck."

"David, not in front of the children, please. How many more times?"

"Leave me alone will you. It's just what I need, some distant relation offloaded on to me. I've enough on my plate, what with everything at work."

"I know, David, but you must watch it, they'll copy you. Richard has already used the word B.U.G.G…"

"Oh, for God's sake, is that all you're worried about?"

"It's important David, it's important to me. I really can't take this negativity all the time."

"Don't be so pathetic."

"Oh, you're always nasty to me, I can't bear it. You're a real swine sometimes."

Susan threw a tea-cloth violently across the table at David. It swept a half-full mug of coffee on to the floor where it smashed, spreading a dark stain across the red tiles. She glared at her husband, tears welling in her eyes, before dashing out through the back door, slamming it behind her. Richard, who had been playing by himself on the floor let out a scream, hauled himself to his feet, kicked a pile of bricks out of the way and hurried after his mother. Guilt briefly staunched David's anger – he hated punishing his innocent children – but his fury flared again as his obsession with events unfolding at the office took hold. He resented it but was consumed by it nonetheless. He felt powerless.

Larry Beckinsale's announcement of his plans for the restructuring of the company had rapidly been followed by a letter to David and his colleagues.

> Dear David,
>
> I am writing to confirm to you the outcome of the discussions, which were held today, with Larry Beckinsale concerning the future of your department. It is proposed that with effect from 2 October this year the work of your department will be carried out by the newly created "Global Division". Therefore, your unit will close on 29 September, as a result of which, a number of jobs would be made redundant. You will know by now that unfortunately your job is likely to be one of these.
>
> The relevant Unions have been notified of the proposals and we shall now begin a process of consultation involving the Unions and, of course, all of the staff of the units may be affected by the changes.
>
> If you have any queries about this proposal please do not hesitate to contact Steve Percival. If you wish to discuss how this proposal would affect you personally, if implemented, you should contact Dick Sanders in Personnel.
>
> Yours faithfully,
> Larry Beckinsale.

David had read the letter over and over again, unable to believe it.

"Yours faithfully, Larry. The man can't even write fucking English."

To be told that it was all over in this illiterate manner was galling for David, who prided himself on the quality of his work. Here he was for the second time, in his working life, being told he was not wanted. But at least the first time they had not promised so much when he joined. At least the first time his expectations had not been so high. It was always the same, the bastards. Just when you felt you were getting somewhere, making a favourable impression, getting your nose out ahead of the pack, starting to enjoy yourself and what do they do – kick you in the teeth. A bloody great size ten comes and takes out not just your incisors, but the whole fucking set. Leaving you toothless and raw. Warm phlegm and spittle staining your shirt-front pink as you gasp out your gratitude for any little human kindness they may show you. Feel free to use the phones, the printers, the fax, anything that'll help sell yourself to the next bunch of fuckers. That's if you're not too old, too experienced, too expensive. God what a prospect. The swine. It made you so fucking mad, it really did. All this tight-lipped, controlled, acceptance of their fates. It was sickening. How many times had he heard from colleagues, "you don't want to burn any boats do you", David could have sworn it was bridges, but fuck it who was he to say, he understood well enough, "you never know when you might want to come back or need a reference." So it went on. God.

The longer David thought about Great Uncle Brian, mulling over who he was, the more the prospect of meeting this unknown relative began to appeal to him. It became something of a balm. Opening up the possibility of revisiting, at least briefly, a happier less complicated time, throwing up the chance of meeting his grandfather one last time, and if not him at least some echo of the man he had admired most in the world. The only human being who had ever really cared for him.

Brian looked the part. A vigorous eighty-year old. Tall, wiry, a full head of greying, black hair and greeny-brown eyes, like his grandfather in so many ways, yet warmer or duller, David couldn't make up his mind. His memory was far from perfect. The only identical feature, of this he was certain, was their noses. "Roman" was how his grandfather used to describe his, Brian would not have disagreed. He spoke softly in a mid-Atlantic drawl tinged with a faint trace of his Lancastrian roots that on occasions would bring David up with a start. It was, he discovered, comforting to have that link established so emphatically and he was reassured by Uncle Brian's assumption that all they both really wanted to talk about was their relative.

They chatted about his life in Canada as they strolled along the narrow country lane that wound its way between high fragrant hedgerows towards the "Elephant and Castle." The pub was located in a small hamlet well away from any main roads, surrounded by woods and fields, where affluent city dwellers stabled their horses and hunted at the weekends. David often parked on a stretch of common land nearby and walked the short, undulating three-quarters of a mile to the pub, breathing deeply and feeling virtuous. Uncle Brian leapt at the chance of some exercise.

"I've been cooped up for days, with all our relatives. Don't get me wrong, but it's good to get out. I'm very glad you asked me."

"My pleasure. I've had a fair basinful lately at work, it's good for me to get away too."

Their stroll was a gentle prelude to the serious discussions both seemed to know would follow. As soon as Brian had sat down with his pint of beer, half drained it, and wiped his mouth, he began.

"God, it's been a long time. I expect it isn't all as good as this, but this particular pint makes me wish I hadn't gone away."

He laughed quietly to himself, almost, David thought, at some half-forgotten sadness rather than at anything remotely funny.

"Cheers."

"Cheers."

"He used to drink a lot you know, your Grandfather, Tony. I don't know where all this pretentious Anthony stuff came from, beats me. He was always so straightforward as a lad. I tell you it took me a few seconds to figure out who'd died when they called to say Anthony Coxon-Dyet was no more. Honestly, it took everything I had not to burst out laughing on the phone. Just made me realize I never really knew the bastard. Here's to him anyway, my brother."

He raised his glass high into the air.

"…wherever you are."

"Your brother, my Grandad."

Their glasses touched briefly.

"You know, David, I've disliked him for so long, hated him even, that it's good to sit with someone who saw him differently. Your mother told me you were very close, at least when you were younger. At my age I feel it pays to settle old scores rather than let them fester all the way to the grave. Missed my chance with him, but you're a good substitute. Bet that makes you feel good eh? This sort of thing makes one a happier boy, believe me. If you don't know that already it won't be long before you do."

He laughed again.

"Here, drink up, let me get you another. What's it you ask for, bitter is it? I'm a bit rusty."

A faint breeze was rustling the pale silvery-green leaves of the tall willow that cast a wide carpet of speckled shade over half the pub garden. Disconcertingly a cockerel, caged and frustrated, crowed manically every few minutes disturbing David's sense of equanimity.

"He's taking his time," he thought, "Oh God, hope I haven't got to go and bail him out of some embarrassing fracas with one of the locals."

He was half standing, ducking his head below the leaning umbrella and edging his way between the wooden bench and table when his great uncle appeared, the pub door slamming suddenly shut behind him, beer slopping over his hands and clothes. As he frantically shifted his feet to avoid drenching his shoes he yelled out in a voice tinged with amusement.

"Bugger, what a waste and what are you grinning at my boy? Think your old uncle isn't fit to fart his way out of a paper bag? You'd probably be right, but you'd better not say anything in my hearing."

"Fighting talk, eh?"

Brian carefully placed two pints on the uneven weather-worn trestle table, then shook his wet hands violently before sitting down.

"Dead right, our family knows no other. Not really true, although life wasn't easy for Mum and Dad, particularly for Dad with his war wounds. He needed careful treatment, you had to make allowances, but Tony knew exactly how to rub him up the wrong way. He was a hard man you know, Tony. You wouldn't think it to look at him, at least not when he was at school, nobody really realized for a long time, but I suppose as a brother you get an insight into these sort of things earlier than most. Maybe it's not so much seeing it as feeling it. God, I took some beatings from him."

Brian drank deeply, the glass trembling imperceptibly. David sat transfixed his own pint untouched.

"He got emotionally harder as well as time went by. I suppose on reflection it was largely him growing up, maturing, but joining the Party certainly didn't help mellow him. He took to it like a duck to water. Mum and Dad were glad at first, it got him out of the house, stopped him moping around all day and you couldn't really blame him. He'd never had a proper job, just grudging handouts from the family, all temporary, short-term, nothing with any prospects. Not good for the morale of a proud young man like Tony, and they were such a pompous self-satisfied lot, the "Grocery Cox's" as they were known. Thought they were superior to us lot."

"What Party was that?"

Brian looked bemused for a second, his chain of thought broken. He had to search back, retrace his mental steps. His brow momentarily furrowed.

"I lost it for a second. Couldn't remember the name, even though I was in it myself for a while. Old age is bloody awful in many ways. It was "The British Union.""

David looked at him blankly.

"What's that then, a trade union?"

Brian shook his head and smiled.

"Oh no, my boy, far from it. Oswald Mosley's lot. That name ring any bells?"

David couldn't believe what he had just heard, it was his turn to frown.

"THE Oswald Mosley?"

Brian nodded.

"I'm ashamed now to say yes."

"Grandad was a fascist?"

"Yes, and so was I for a while."

"I don't believe it."

"You never knew?"

"No, nobody said a word. Christ."

"I'm sorry David, I just assumed you all knew. God. Tony was in so deep I doubt if he ever gave it up, at least in his heart of hearts. He was a true believer. He never said a word to you?"

David shook his head.

"That was the difference between us. He was dedicated, committed to the cause. I was in it initially because he was, there were lots of trips, socials, drinking that sort of thing. It was all mates together, plus a few women if you were lucky. They went for the uniform you know, it's all true. It was a good time. I was less enthused with all the meetings, the selling of the newspapers that sort of thing. I was more happy go lucky, but their ideas were attractive at the time, they seemed to have answers for many of the ills of the day. And Tony, well, when he got going he was a bloody good public speaker. He believed and it came across in everything he said and did and he won people over. It definitely helped him get on in the Party, as performance counted for a lot in those days. Out on the stump all weathers, you had to do it. It was the days before television – all this sound bite politics has changed everything – then you had to argue your case from A to Z, face down the hecklers, win them over with your arguments. Why are you looking at me like that?"

The two men sat in silence for a moment, holding their pints and gazing at each other.

"Yes, well you had to have the muscle to back your words up if things got out of hand. And, as I said, Tony was a hard man to the core, he wasn't shy at coming forward. It wasn't really true at the beginning, when I was in, there wasn't much need for strong-arm tactics in Blackpool. Worst that happened was a few over enthusiastic drunks would go too far, that sort of thing. Nothing really nasty."

Brian sipped at his drink and looked intently at his great nephew over the top of his glass. A car braked heavily in the car park, skidding noisily on the gravel. The cock crowed.

"You look shocked David, what can I say? I thought you would have known. You have a right to know, after all."

For brief seconds he seemed uncertain, to have again lost his way, and he gazed into the distance. David studied him closely. The clear tanned skin, barely a blemish after more than sixty years, the wrinkles around his eyes, the single deep furrow that bisected his brow, his swept back hair, curling around his ears and along his collar. He seemed relaxed and at ease with himself, but his next words betrayed his disquiet.

"If you want me to shut up just say so and we can talk about Canada. I can bore for hours on the subject of Canada."

David shook his head.

"You let the bloody genie out. Another? To show what a fair man I am, I'll even drink with a fascist."

"Come on, it was a long time ago. I was young."

"And only obeying orders."

"Sorry?"

"Never mind, same again?"

"Aren't you driving?"

"Oh, sod that, I need one. It's not everyday you discover a black sheep or two in the family."

Brian laughed quietly to himself and then smiled at David.

"Go on then."

He stood in the empty bar. The landlord was in the cellar changing a barrel, he could hear the clattering of a metal cask as it rolled across the stone floor. Smoke billowed into the room from a fire newly laid in the ancient walk-in fireplace, the gaping chimney repelling the choking clouds rather than swallowing them up. David was irritated by the fumes, his lungs always painfully sensitive to the quality of the air he was breathing, but was glad to be alone for a moment to reflect on what he had just learned. Absentmindedly, he jangled the loose change in his trouser pockets. As he stared at the blustering grey-green bands of smoke that were drifting across the bar, he felt a veil lifting. He remembered the last time he had seen his Grandfather. It had been on television, in an item on the local news bulletin, a few weeks before he died. It was the time of all that fuss about his article in the parish magazine. There was nothing much else going on news wise, it was the summer "silly season" in the media, if there had been the story would never have received any coverage. Nobody normally gave a damn about what was written in a parish magazine, even if it was very popular with parishioners – snapped up like hot cakes, his Grandfather always used to joke – but this particular vicar had made a bit of a habit of attracting press attention over the years. This, however, was his relative's first appearance on television that David could remember.

The report was about a leading article his Grandfather had written on Europe where he had laid out his dislike, verging on hatred, of the Common Market. Venting his spleen once more against the then Prime Minister, Ted Heath, his one-time hero, in the manner of a lover spurned. The man who at the time was planning to take Britain into Europe was beyond the pale, as far as the Reverend Anthony Coxon-Dyet was concerned, and his parishioners were in no doubt about his views. For a while he had written incessantly on the subject featuring it almost every week in his editorials until people had complained saying enough was enough, but he remained unbowed and on this particular occasion, David inadvertently shuddered at the recollection, he had brought Oswald Mosley into the argument. Saying in no uncertain terms that the disgraced fascist leader had been right in his views on Europe and that Britain would not be in the mess it was in now if the people had listened to him. It had caused a storm.

St Botolph Thunderer – August 1972

"Parishioners, I've told you many times in these pages that I am a conservative with a small "c" and that I am always open to any well-reasoned argument. The privacy of the ballot box is the cornerstone of our democracy and I have never breached that confidentiality in this or any other illustrious organ. But the observant reader will not have failed to notice that my sympathies lie more with the "true blue" of the Conservatives than with the "red flag" of Labour. So you will all appreciate my torment when I tell you that over the issue of the Common Market my loyalties are reversed. Labour has got it right are not words I utter lightly, but in this case it is true. Our Prime Minister, an honourable man in so many things, has got it so unbelievably wrong on this issue that I am almost at a loss for words. But fear not dear friends, not completely. Mr Heath maintains with a great deal of eloquence, and in French too – Sacre Blue – how Britain's future lies in Europe. If we are not part of Europe, he tells us, this once great nation will fade into insignificance and became a tiny island state feeding off the scraps falling from the table of our giant neighbour – the United States of Europe. That is the price, apparently, we will pay if we stay outside the Common Market, but what of the price we pay if we go in? Answer that Mr Heath. I almost said Ted, but I'm afraid that will no longer pass muster with me.

If the Prime Minister balks at a reply, rest assured I do not feel so shy. The price is we can wave goodbye to the Great in Great Britain almost immediately and then over a period of years we will wave goodbye to Britain itself. We will disappear into this huge super state, never to be seen or heard of again. The "mother of parliaments" will haemorrhage powers to some faceless bureaucracy in Brussels, your vote will be worthless, you will have very little say over the people who rule you, make the laws you live by and spend your taxes. Is that what you want? Having known many of you for years I know I speak for all of you when I say I think you do not. Any Briton with a sense of history must see the folly of the course now being followed by our government, and a Conservative government to boot.

I hang my head in shame when I think of the hundreds of pages I have written, the thousands of words I have spoken over the years, in support of these very fellows who are now stabbing us in the back. I feel personally betrayed.

(In case you all think I am nothing but a windbag of a wordsmith. Let me assure you in black and white, on the record, that my annual turn at the Dumpton Gap Conservative Association Autumn Fete will be cancelled this year and henceforth until the party sees sense on Europe.)

Briton's awake, or at least the people of Dumpton Gap should prick up their ears, and listen to me, and many others I should add. (I'll say it quietly, in a whisper, but many of the most effective voices of dissent are in the Labour Party – there I've got it out. Never let it be said that the "St Botolph Thunderer" doesn't admit its mistakes and tell it as it is.)

I can assure you and I don't understand why this isn't obvious to everyone, but Britain outside Europe can be and will be great. It is not inevitable that we will be reduced to some small insignificant water-bound basket case. What of our Empire? what of the Commonwealth? what of our special relationship with the United States? All this is ignored by the Europhiles, as if looking back at our long history as a major power is somehow wrong, irrelevant, and the most patronizing thing of all, a sign of old-fashioned thinking. People who think as I do, as you do, are not modern, that most serious of crimes, but out of date, mere dinosaurs. More power to large extinct reptiles I say.

Let me ask you a question – where have the greatest dangers this nation has faced this century come from, and not just the last hundred years either? It doesn't take much to come up with the answer, does it? Europe. Now, any supporters of the Common Market out there, and I believe there are some, even in this quiet tranquil village of ours, will be saying, "Ah, we have him. That is exactly one of our arguments. To be safe we must join up with Europe, embrace our former enemies, ensure we never go to war with them again." Sadly, you have not. I can wriggle free with ease. A Common Market may, and I only say may, stop all conflict in the future, but I say the price is too high. The end of Great Britain as we know and love it, almost certain domination by that economic colossus, Germany, that is too much. What I propose and in this I follow in the footsteps of one of the most misunderstood men this country has ever produced, Sir Oswald Mosley, will not compromise our security, far from it. Sir Oswald said many years ago that, "Britain should be less prone to anxious interference in everybody else's affairs and should concentrate more on the resources of our own country and Empire. Britain", and this is the critical bit, "should keep out of the tangled skein of European rivalries and animosities." Hear, hear, I say.

Not joining the Common Market doesn't mean we can't trade with our neighbours, they need us as much as we need them, but we won't jeopardize our unique and preferential relations with our former colonies. Security should be left to our well-resourced armed forces, we are a nuclear power after all, and our special links with the United States and our membership of NATO. We have nothing to fear staying out of the Common Market, everything to lose going in. Outside Britain will prosper and grow, inside we will die."

David and his family had been surprised at the media frenzy that blew up over this article. It in fact brought them briefly closer together. They all relished their relative's discomfiture, but for different reasons. David's father enjoyed seeing his father in trouble. "Finally getting his just desserts," as he put it. David was amused at his grandfather's embarrassment, looking forward to meeting him again and teasing him over it. He foresaw hours of heated conversation as the old man stoutly defended himself against the charges. They were all bemused by the opinion of an elderly woman interviewed by one of the newspapers. She was a parishioner of the Reverend Coxon-Dyet and claimed to know him well.

"This is so unlike our vicar, he's such a pleasant man. When you meet him, normally, he wouldn't say boo to a goose."

This was not how his family saw him, but they laughed nonetheless. Throughout the weeks the story was in the news, they didn't bother to get in touch with him to offer their support or to commiserate, it never occurred to them.

David ordered the drinks, haunted now by his memory of the look on his Grandfather's face as he ran the gauntlet of the cameras that final time on television. The man had looked scared, something his grandson had never seen before. At the time, David had put it down to the actions of the reporters, who hounded his Grandfather for days disrupting church services, staking out his flat, and generally making life a misery. He knew the local Bishop would have told him to say nothing, as had happened before, and he would have found this request difficult to go along with. His Grandfather was nothing if not argumentative when his views were challenged. David had attributed his atypical behaviour to his shock at the predatory snooping of the national press and to a lack of understanding of the ways of the modern world. He believed his Grandfather was out of his depth and he'd sympathised with him, even though his views had often made his own blood boil. But now David knew the truth, and he felt ashamed of his own naivety, at the betrayal of his love. His Grandfather was frightened alright, but not at the crude determination of the journalists dogging his every move, but at the threat of his unmasking – the public laying bare of his duplicity and deceit. His exposure as a lying hypocrite.

"Cheers, David."

Brian raised his glass, took a sip and then carried on their conversation as if there had been no interruption.

"I wasn't at it long you know. I was a member of the Party for a couple of years at the most. I remind myself, which isn't often these days, to tell the truth, that I packed it in when they started blaming the Jews for everything."

David puffed out his cheeks and exhaled slowly.

"You're right to be sceptical. I know I would be. But David, to be frank, and I only came to this decision while you were in getting the drinks, I don't care what you think."

David was taken aback and he sat up and paid attention. When he realized what he had done he was amused, his discomfort tempered by a desire to get as much information as he could out of a man he was rapidly coming to see as an "old fart." Brian went on.

"This is for my benefit as much as anything, you're just along for the ride if you're interested. I'm sorry, but I'm not going to sit here and not be believed by someone who seems to know nothing. So either you buy it, take it home and digest it or sick it up at your leisure, but hear me out without any more of the pouting and silly asides. To be honest, justifying it all to myself is enough without having to do it all a second time for your benefit."

David thought "You old fuck-head," but said nothing "bugger me up, shaft everything I hold sacred, won't you. But you'll get no fucking absolution from me."

He was happy for a moment.

"So, anti-semitism was my reason for leaving the party. That's official. Dad argued with both of us, it made him ill. Dad was

Labour through and through, he couldn't believe you needed anything else but Socialism to explain what was going on in the world. We betrayed him, simple as that. That mattered to me. I could see what it was doing to him. The Great War damaged our father physically, we were wounding him emotionally and it took its toll. Tony wouldn't compromise, I would. He called me weak, I said much worse. I left home and we hardly spoke again. The family ganged up against Tony, but Dad never recovered. He was heartbroken, ashamed. He stopped going to Labour party meetings, couldn't face his old comrades. His eldest son a "Blackshirt", it was too much. He died in March 1938. Tony did visit him just before the end, but Dad refused to see him and passed away in bitterness, railing to the last. I could never forgive Tony for that."

Tears welled in his eyes and he wiped them quickly away.

"Mother survived him by eight years and three months, but she had more or less given up. She watched your Grandmother struggle with her children and couldn't reconcile it in her own mind. Tony, her eldest son and probably her favourite, if the truth be told, behaving like that. It was all too much. Parricide and matricide are heavy burdens for anyone to bear don't you think? Especially for a man of God. That's when I went to Canada."

His laugh crackled like newspaper trampled underfoot.

"The truth? You want the truth I suppose? I did have my doubts about blaming all society's problems on the Jews. Nothing too intellectual of course just a gut feeling. It didn't seem right somehow, but the main reason at the time was I was getting bored. I'd done the trips to London, the rallies, the marching up and down, it was all getting to be old hat. I was also becoming heavily involved with girls, which was far more interesting. Blackpool was a great place in those days for a fling, heaving with mill girls out for a good time and only there for the week to boot. Also, if I'm honest I was getting a little scared. Things were turning serious. Tony was rising up the Party ladder. He wanted me along but I was useless, introverted and tongue-tied. I hated getting up in front of people. Then there was the violence. It got worse as the Communists became better organized. More and more meetings and marches ended in trouble. Tony was in the thick of it and he loved it. A bloody nose was as good as a tonic for him and he had a good few of them in his time. I told you he was a hard man, I wasn't. I didn't really believe, I suppose, was the truth of the matter. But he did, he really did."

Chapter 8

FASCIST MAN

12th May 1941

The deck moved unsteadily beneath Tony's feet; he clutched the wooden guard-rail and breathed deeply. The fresh sea air was tainted with smoke billowing from the ship's funnel and he could barely move as men crowded around him. The view was sublime, but he felt nauseous, for nearly a year he had seen nothing so beautiful, but he knew he was going to be ill. The sky was a blaze of incandescent reds, pinks, yellows and purples, the looming coastline blackly silhouetted along the horizon. Tony, his head spinning, fever ridden, his body weakened by hunger was sure he had seen such vibrant colours before. They shimmered in the blood spilling from Basil's bruised body, rippling in waves across stained floorboards and soaking into straw-hued sacks. He remembered it now, his knuckles whitening on the rail, he vividly recalled the sick black joke his death had been. A razor, everybody wanted to own one. Official regulations stated that there should be one blade available for every twelve men, Tony smiled, Basil had got hold of his own cutthroat.

The ferry lurched in the erratic swell. A space opened up beneath him and he felt a spasm of pain, a concavity in the stomach, his sweat chilling in the squally gusts, head aching, then the sea rising rapidly upwards, submerging the starboard side of the vessel before breaking over the rail, flushing the deck, his feet awash, foaming before his eyes, then the shiver of saltspray lashing his face shocking him into welcome remission.

A simple razor – purloined then secreted away – had meant the world to Basil and his pleasure at having one in his personal possession far outweighed all the other tribulations of his corralled existence. The dignity of a regular shave was important to him. It had been his way of coping with the grinding humiliation, the daily fear and ever-present uncertainty. He attached great importance to being smartly turned out and had been clean-shaven and wearing a jacket and tie when Tony found him propped up against a pile of powdered cement bags. He was in an empty room on the top floor of an unfinished house on the building estate in Huyton, outside Liverpool, that had been used as an internment camp since the early days of the war. The pair of them had only been detained there for three days before Basil took his life, the banality of the damp ramshackle buildings, mere shells lacking basic facilities, exerting their malign influence with horrific certainty. Blood formed a vast pool, tranquil in its turbid viscosity, lapping his statuesquely rigid corpse, bloodshot eyes wide open, startlingly blue orbs staring out from the ashen exsanguinated face, wrists protruding from pink stained cuffs scarred with jagged clotted crusts. He was a man emptied out, a corpse, and the first Tony had ever seen close up, the raw pungency of the killing floor enshrouding the grim scene.

Tony was ailing with a persistent chest infection. Nearly all the inmates were sick in some way, but not Basil. Once his injured leg had healed he had been physically strong, immune from illness, seemingly unaffected by the deprivations of prison life. Tony had come to depend on him as they were moved around the country, from prison to prison, camp to camp. As the likelihood of release faded, Basil had seemed resilient. He was always telling jokes, bouncing back from any setback. But this strength had been an illusion, at the end his vitality seeped away within seconds. They had been friends, together constantly since their arrests and yet Tony hadn't realized how fragile Basil's fortitude had been. Weakened by illness, overcome with grief, Tony had collapsed by his companion's body and had lain there for hours, watching the blood congeal, darken and dull, before they had been found and help called, too late.

"Was that less than a week ago?" thought Tony, "if only he'd held on a little longer this move might have saved him."

The ship lurched violently and a crush of bodies pushed him against the rail, bending him double. He could clearly see the water rushing by thirty feet below. Basil would have seen the funny side of all this, even of his own death, thought Tony, he would have told a joke about it in that upper class voice of his.

"There was this wake. All the family of the deceased were present, eating and drinking, talking about the good times. Then up pipes Aunt Mabel, "I must go and pay my last respects, you coming George?" The body was laid out in the front room, the curtains were drawn and a single candle was flickering dimly in the corner. "This won't do," said Aunt Mabel, who'd left her glasses in the back room, "I can't see a thing." So she throws back the heavy curtains and lets the sunlight come streaming in. There was great uncle Arnold in his best Sunday suit lying peacefully in the open coffin. Aunt Mabel walks over and stares hard at him. "My God, George," she says, "he's looking well, his trip to Blackpool must have done him good."

Tony could hear Basil's shrill laughter reverberating around him as he vomited into the green churning waters of the Irish Sea.

It was dusk as the "Lady of Mann" steamed into Douglas harbour. The tall white tower of the lighthouse on Douglas Head had been visible to the prisoners for hours and now the beacons on the harbour wall and inner quays burst into life, defying the blackout, to guide the vessel into dock. Close to the sea wall several fishing boats, bobbing violently in the heavy swell, waited for the ferry to pass, before following in its wake and mooring in the inner harbour to unload their catch. The sky, deep purple fading to magenta and red, framed the dark mass of the hills looming above the port. Here and there in the gloom of the town pinpricks of light glinted, mirroring in their steely brightness the stars revealing in the darkening haze overhead. The promenade was a blaze of yellowing light, blurring into a misty distance and the air was heavy with coal smoke and the fishy tang of the sea. With two deafening blasts on its horn, the steamer juddered to a halt in mid-harbour, its engines thrown into reverse, its propellers thrashing the water. On shore a crowd had gathered at the gates of the quay, held back by police. Other uniformed figures, many armed, were dotted along King Edward Quay watching.

"You wouldn't know there was a war on would you, with all the lights and that lot milling around? You'd think they'd have better things to do."

Tony whirled round at the sound of a familiar voice.

"Eric, what a surprise. God, it's good to see you."

"Tony."

Without hesitation the two friends embraced, holding each other close before letting go.

"I thought it was you as soon as I saw you clutching the side, that had to be Tony Cox."

"You don't change, do you Eric?"

"Oh, but I have. This is all starting to wear me down. I half expected to bump into you sooner than this, I thought they must have picked you up. What about Emily?"

"No, they didn't intern her. Left her to look after the boys, thank God. Only seen her once in the last year, the bastards. Have been moved about so much before this – Walton, Ascot, York and then back to bloody Liverpool."

"Boys?"

"Yes, we've got two now. Stephen is the oldest, he's a right handful by all accounts. Driving his mother spare. It's different with the youngest Freddy, he's just four, birthday last month. He's a little angel in comparison. Trouble is he won't even recognize me when I get out. It's a bugger. What about you?"

The two men leaned on the wooden rail and looked across at the rough-hewn quay as their vessel edged closer.

"Oh, nothing like that for me. No domestic ties if you know what I mean. No time. I was in the first lot to be rounded up. Went straight to Brixton with Mosley and the others. Been there ever since, apart from a stint out at Latchmere House, on Ham Common."

Eric shivered and shook his head.

"God that nearly did for me, I can tell you."

Tony placed a hand on his shoulder, Eric turned and smiled.

"It is good to see you Tony, It's been a long time."

"It must be five years or more, but what happened to you?"

"It was military intelligence, interrogations. No holds barred. Bloody torture to tell you the truth. They woke you up at any time of the night, took you to a darkened room with a bright light, questions for hours, no food, no water. They were bastards."

"I thought we'd had it bad. But there was nothing like that. Why you? What did they think you'd been up to?"

Eric shrugged, the ship whistle blew and the ferry nudged gently against the sodden, splintered pine trunks that lined the dockside. A white rope snaked through the air and landed on the cobbles, stopped and then began to slide with ever-increasing speed back towards the quay's edge. A young boy ran out and grabbed it before it dropped into the harbour. A cheer went up from the boat and the boy looked around sheepishly before pulling on the rope. Two men joined him and they hauled the dripping cable on to the quay and slipped it over a huge iron bollard.

"Tony, they thought we were a bunch of traitors. Still do. Thought we'd been dealing with the Germans and Italians. Were planning to take over and put Adolf or Benito into Number 10. They kept telling me that Mosley and the others were all naming me as the go-between. Saying I ought to be protecting myself by telling the truth. Fuck, I almost bought it, Tony. After two weeks of that treatment I was ready to tell them anything. They knew a lot about what I'd been up to. My role in party security, intelligence gathering, strategy and all that stuff. Remarkably well informed. There must have been a spy at the Black House, is all I can say. God, I almost told them what they wanted. One minute it was, they'd go easy on me, even let me go and give me "substantial remuneration," that was the phrase the upper-class bastard used, "substantial remuneration," the next it was, I was going to be shot and my body buried in quicklime. I believed them in the end Tony, I believed them."

Eric wiped his face and turned away.

"I wonder if we'll get off this bloody boat tonight," he murmured, "we should have been here a lot earlier. It was only those bastard porters in Fleetwood refusing to handle our bags that slowed us down. They had me carting stuff back and forth for hours, you know."

Tony laughed.

"It's good for you."

"What is?"

"Exercise, lifting weights, that type of thing."

"You're right you know, keeping healthy, keeps you sane, keeps you going, that and Lady Luck."

"What?"

"They let me go Tony. Just as I was about to spill everything, they let me go. Came in one morning and said, you're leaving. We all ended up back in Brixton just as before. They obviously got nothing, but it was never the same again. You know, the suspicions, who said what, who told them about me. Glad to be here I can tell you, back with the lads."

"Well, I'm glad you are as well. It's good to see you."

"You too."

"Is Mosley here?"

"Don't think so. They'll keep him safely locked up in London away from his troops, I reckon. Keep him in comfort mind you, in the manner to which he's accustomed; his wife being a relative of Churchill and all. He certainly didn't come with me."

The crowd at the entrance to the quay had grown, two men perched precariously on the top rail of the iron gates were trying to climb down to the dock. A policeman attempted to catch hold of their feet to push them back, but they kicked out causing him to duck. The catcalls and booing grew louder and people pointed at the steamer. Tony leaned out over the guard-rail and looked up. Along the rusting green side of the upper deck was chalked the words, "Mosley for Peace", in large crude letters. Smiling he nudged Eric.

"Have you seen what's up there? Who would do something like that?"

Eric grinned back at him.

"I was wondering how long it would take them to notice."

"You?"

"I can claim some credit. It wasn't me who climbed up there though."

"But you said you'd had enough?"

"Of prison, yes, not the Party. Our time will come, you mark my words. Churchill's going to lose this war and that will be our opportunity."

"You believe that?"

"I do and you've got to let them know we know it, otherwise we're finished. There's no halfway house any more. This is a fight to the death."

He stared hard at Tony, who looked into his eyes for a second, then turned away abashed.

"Tony, I'm serious. It's not going to be the death of me I can tell you. I can see you need to polish up your commitment."

Eric reached across and grabbed Tony by the upper arms, forcing him to look directly at him again. His face was pale and his gaze piercing. Tony wanted to get away, uncertain of his own feelings. It had been a long time since he had given the Party and its policies any serious thought, he no longer knew what he believed. Such intense scrutiny was unwelcome and left him uncomfortable. In an instant it was over as Eric smiled and patted him on the back.

"Only joking, my old china. My crystal ball gazing has been markedly off in the past, so who knows? But I like to think the fires' still burning. Hey, look at that."

One of the protestors, a young man with striking red hair, had scaled the gate and was running along the quay waving and shouting. Two policemen were in hot pursuit, backed by choruses of cheers and jeers from the crowds on the ship and on the other side of the fence. He easily outpaced the older men. They gave up, hands on knees breathing heavily, he doubled back and ran alongside the ship waving his fist and yelling, "Fascists go home – you're not wanted here," at the top of his voice. A crush of prisoners gathered along the rail, jostling and pushing, shouting obscenities at the man, waving and whistling. The demonstrator grinned at them and running backwards, waved both arms wildly before veering off and sprinting for the fence. The policemen stood and watched him climb back over and disappear into the cheering crowd.

"Ladies and Gentlemen," the deafening crackle of the ship's tannoy caused everyone to look round, "I'm Lieutenant William Ashford, officer in charge of this contingent of internees. I hope you can all hear me."

The jeering and shouting died away.

"Thank you. I just want to say a few words to reassure the people of Douglas. I can promise you that every effort will be taken to minimize the disruption these prisoners will make to life on this Island."

The crowd erupted and there was laughter as the Lieutenant's words were drowned out in a screech of feedback.

"What an idiot!" Eric whispered to Tony, "This is what we have to put up with. I'll fix him, you wait here."

"… are the first of a number of prisoner contingents arriving over the next few weeks that will be taken to Peveril camp at Peel. I trust there will be no trouble when we come to transfer the men, nothing will be served by making my life more difficult. I know some of you feel strongly about …"

His words were lost in a storm of abuse from the agitated crowd.

"Please, please hear me out. I understand your concerns about your own security, but everything's being done to ensure that no one will escape. You have my word on that. In wartime everybody has to make sacrifices, no one can avoid doing their patriotic duty. Looking after these internees is vital to our national security. See it as the people of the Isle of Man's – your – contribution to that endeavour. I fully understand it is not something to be taken lightly or with a happy heart, like so much we have to do these days. But believe me it is not unappreciated by the authorities. The Isle of Man is writing its chapter in the history of Britain's glorious war effort."

The crowd began rattling the chained iron gates, the metal jangling cutting through the human uproar.

"Ship's company, soldiers of the eighteenth, and prisoners let us show our appreciation of the hospitality shown by the people of Douglas. Let's show them our true mettle. Three cheers for the Isle of Man. Hip, hip, hoorah."

The lieutenant's distorted voice reverberated around the port. He was joined in a desultory chorus by members of his own company, but ignored by the steamer crew and the prisoners, who looked at each other, smirked, shrugged their shoulders and a few spat over the side. The people of Douglas, crowding at the gates, continued jeering, unmoved.

"…hip, hip, hoorah…"

A quartet of prisoners at the ship's stern, gathered around Eric, began to sing quietly. At first no one joined them.

"…hip, hip, hoorah…"

Then as more and more heard the familiar words the singing swelled.

"Thank you ladies and gentlemen. I look forward to a long and happy association with you. Good night."

Feedback howled from the speakers as the Lieutenant thrust the microphone into the hands of the steamer's radio operator, a burst of static, then silence. The mocking cries of the crowd on the quay grew to a crescendo, then slowly died away as they heard the prisoner's singing.

"…fearless, faithful unto death.

All to dare and give.

For the land that we love and the people's right, for Britain we shall live."

Every prisoner was standing to attention, facing the crowd onshore and enthusiastically singing the words to the "Song of the British Union".

"Mosley leads us in Britain's name.

Our Revolution sets man's hearts aflame."

Tony blurted out the words, recalling the warm summer

sunshine and comradeship of those marches through the Lancashire countryside. Kissing and cuddling with Emily in the woods, when they stopped for lunch. The warm beer, the sense of optimism, the feeling of progress, it seemed an age ago.

"Lift high the flag,
on with the fight.
Strength in the Union,
Let the land unite."

Clapping and cheering, Tony felt elated. He was not alone. Flushed with a renewed pride in their cause the prisoners shouted and gestured at the increasingly angry crowd. Armed soldiers began to form up on the upper deck. The Lieutenant appeared and stared down at the jostling crowd of prisoners before issuing an order to his sergeant. Eric, spotting what was going on, called out to his men.

"Give me an 'M'."

A few voices joined him.

"I said give me an 'M'."

"MMMMM."

"Give me an 'O'."

"OOO."

"Give me a 'S'."

"SSS."

The prisoners could barely hear themselves above the booing of the crowd. Stones ricocheted off the metal hull of the steamer. Soldiers moved along the guardrail pushing back the prisoners. Another squad surged towards Eric, who was standing on a bollard at the stern of the ship.

"Give me an 'L'."

"LLLL."

"Stop this now," yelled the Sergeant, "move below decks or there will be trouble."

Two soldiers grabbed Eric and hauled him down. Over his

shoulder he called out, "Give me an 'E,'" before a gloved hand was placed firmly over his mouth.

"EEEE."

Tony followed close behind the small group as they descended the iron steps to the large lounge, where the prisoner's belongings had been stacked when they came aboard. It had been the saloon for second-class passengers before the "Lady of Mann" was commandeered into military service at the time of Dunkirk and there was still a smell of spilled beer and stale cigarette smoke. The ornate wooden bar at the far end of the room was blocked off by an iron grille, the optics empty and askew, the large engraved mirror that filled the wall behind, stained and dusty. The Lieutenant, a young man in his early twenties with a scrubbed, anxious face, stepped in front of Eric and gestured for him to be released. Tony stopped at the bottom of the stairs to watch, but was hustled into the room by the press of bodies streaming down the steps behind him.

"That was uncalled for. These people on the island have done nothing to you. They are upset enough about you lot being here. You goading them doesn't help. What's your name?"

Eric eyed the lieutenant before shouting it out.

"Eric Baines."

There was a cheer from the prisoners as they gathered round and a few began to clap their hands. The Lieutenant raised his right arm, looked round anxiously, searching for his sergeant. Seeing him standing in the room with a couple of men he went on.

"That's enough. Baines, don't think you're getting away with this. I'll make my report to the camp governor at Peveril. We'll deal with you there."

Eric stared impassively at the young soldier.

"Do you understand me?"

Eric nodded his head.

"Good, I've got your number, so be careful."

Affronted, the lieutenant's pale countenance hardened, his expression scornful, brown aqueous eyes flaring with contempt – his dislike of Eric and his compatriots compounded by a disdain for their class, politics, and treachery – and his quiet, finely modulated, voice was for a moment tinged with menace.

"I want no trouble from you."

He jabbed Eric hard in the chest and then shoved his way through to the bar.

"Now listen to me. I've just about had enough."

There were scattered jeers and an indiscriminate jostling in the crowd. Uncertainty among the prisoners at the Lieutenant's resolve engendered disquiet and prevented any greater disruption, order briefly prevailing while the officer struggled to speak.

"You are all staying on board tonight. The fine people of Douglas have seen enough of you for one day."

Angered by this news, the manner and tone of voice in which it was delivered and bolstered by frustration at their continued incarceration, the throng coalesced around the figure of Eric standing resolutely facing the soldiers in the centre of the room – the fascist hard men forming a wall of defiant opposition either side of their leader. Incensed the Lieutenant pulled his service revolver from its holster and pointed it at the crush.

"Step back, now. That is an order!"

The mob surged, a residual hostility bearing it forward, before retreating, its cohesiveness rapidly dissipating. The soldiers stood their rifles at the ready. Voices fell silent and the shuffling of feet died away as the room stilled, the throbbing of the ship's engines vibrating through the hull and rattling the loose fittings of an open porthole. Outside the manic cry of a solitary gull tore at the quiescent air of the falling dusk, picking at shredded nerves.

"You will disembark tomorrow morning at six am. Till then any more trouble, any disturbance of any kind will be dealt with severely. Not just here, but also at the camp. You lot aren't going anywhere anytime soon. You're the dregs they've decided to keep locked away for the duration of the war. So get used to it, we'll break anybody who doesn't."

As the soldiers backed out of the room, padlocking the doors behind them and switching off the lights, there was a perceptible easing of tension among the detainees, their brittle morale buoyed by an indeterminate sense of authority bested, a collective relief that an engagement however slight had been won. Their triumph was short-lived as the practicalities of spending the night in cramped quarters intruded and there was a rush to find a place to sleep. Most of the seating from the saloon had been removed so the favoured spots were in the half of the room that was still carpeted. The only illumination came from the masked harbour lights shining dimly through the ship's picture windows and there was confusion as the men stumbled around in the near darkness pushing and shoving. With the help of former members of the "I" squad who Tony hadn't seen in years, Tony and Eric managed not only to grab a place with carpet but also close to the wall.

"Isn't rank wonderful," Eric was smiling as he flung himself onto the deck, "remember I told you Tony, years ago, you can't beat it. I make damn sure I make the most of mine, I can tell you."

Tony sat down beside him.

"Eric, I feel so much better after that. I haven't felt so well since they locked me up."

"I know. God I enjoyed that too. Well you've got to haven't you? Or else you'd go mad. That Lieutenant's a right … "

Eric shook his head.

"For once I'm at a loss for words. I don't know where they get them from."

Tony nodded in agreement.

"I don't suppose we get anything to eat on this cruise?"

"You'll be lucky."

Laughing they both lay down and quickly fell asleep, oblivious to the shuffling movement and whispered disputes carrying on around them.

Tony woke up hungry and with a headache. There was a rustling beside him. In the faint orange light he watched as the rhythmic movement gathered pace then subsided. He listened as Eric quietly sighed under his breath and then rolled on his side and almost immediately began gently snoring. Tony turned away, closed his eyes, and thought as he drifted back to sleep, "My friend is much braver than I'll ever be."

It was a relief to be allowed back onto the upper deck, to escape the humid fetid air of the ship's lounge. The chill dampness of dawn, tinged with the salty decay of low tide, cleared Tony's head and lifted the pall of depression – a hangover from the euphoria of the evening before – that had entangled him since waking. Hunger pangs and the parched yearning of an insistent thirst were familiar burdens to Tony, but the beauty of the sunrise diminished such trials. He stood awestruck by the immensity of the sky, the sensuous variety of the natural palette that subtly shaded the landscape, investing it with a substance independent of physical mass. He had never imagined that such joy could exist in his diminished world, where gratification was of the basest kind, and could barely comprehend that his pleasure had no down side, no price to pay. Transfixed he absorbed the glory of the morning, ignoring the hacking and belching of other prisoners as they emerged into the clear air. The harbour, draped in mist, glowed in the ochre light of the unseen sun. A gentle swell rose and fell beneath an unbroken surface of burnished metal, embellished by slashes of iridescent colour mirroring the celestial drama overhead. The changing tide agitated a line of trawlers moored along the inner harbour, the rhythmic slapping of rope against steel mast and the creaking of their tired wooden hulls played in counterpoint to the atonal human orchestra building around him. High above the outer sea wall dozens of terns spiraled crazily through the misty air, one by one they peeled away and plummeted like darts into the sea, rising again through a shower of liquid pearls, a fish struggling in their beaks. Douglas lay silent, hidden from the world, white smoke rising from one chimney in the town. There was no one outside the locked gates of the dock and the quay itself was deserted save for a single sentry, stamping his feet in the cold. A shaven-headed man standing wrapped in a blanket beside Tony coughed, cleared his throat and spat noisily over the side. The ripples spreading out from the boat died rapidly in the syrupy oil-slicked water.

"Oh God, nothing lasts forever in this bastard world of mine," muttered Tony as he stepped away from the rail rubbing sleep-encrusted eyes. His neighbour looked at him suspiciously.

"What did you say?"

"Sorry, nothing, just talking to myself. You know how it is."

Unconvinced, his incomprehension turning rapidly to resentment, the man let his blanket slip to the deck. Tony was not in the mood to get into an argument and wearily tried to mollify him.

"Look it was nothing."

"Who you calling a bastard, you fucking …," his anger was consumed by a fit of vicious coughing, that shook his wiry frame, bending him double. Tony walked away.

The gangplank was lowered and soldiers trooped off the steamer and formed up in two columns on the damp quayside. A black police car had drawn up outside the dock gates and a policeman was talking through the iron bars with an army officer, occasionally waving dismissively in the direction of the moored steamer. A man walking his dog stared at the boat as he passed by, then with a shake of his head disappeared down a side street.

The order was given for the detainees to collect their belongings and congregate on the deck. A reluctance to obey was tempered by a desire to escape the stifling confines of the ship and a crowd quickly gathered, coalescing around a brawling pair fighting over the ownership of a hat. No one stepped in to break it apart and the melee swept back and forth, catching up all who were nearby. Shots were fired in the air as the press of bodies threatened to overwhelm the guards. Jeers greeted the barked threats from the sergeant as he ordered everybody to step back. Unabashed the prisoners fell away to reveal bloodied figures cowering on the wet planks, grazed hands protecting battered heads. One of the men bruised and bleeding profusely from the nose lashed out blindly at one of the privates who had pushed their way through the crowd. Reinforcements arrived, their steel-capped boots ringing out as they clattered up the iron steps from below deck, and order was finally enforced. The prisoners were lined up, hard against the railings and held there until stretchers had been brought for the two injured men, who were then carried off the ship by four soldiers. Following two by two the men were shepherded onto the quayside, where they gathered in small groups, staring sullenly at their escorts. The sun was now visible above Douglas, lifting the morning chill and burning off the early mists drifting across the town. At the last minute Eric appeared, pushed in beside Tony and handed him a Union Jack armband.

"Here, wear this. I think we should put on a bit of a show for the good citizens of Douglas after all that palaver yesterday. Show them the British Union is far from a spent force. It will rise again, phoenix-like from the ashes of war. Should give them a few nightmares, don't you think?"

His cackling laugh was infectious.

"You never give up do you? You're a stubborn bastard."

"Hey watch it, who are you calling a bastard?"

Still laughing he grabbed Tony around the neck and wrestled him to his knees.

"Oh hang on, looks like it's time to move out."

Tony got up, straightened his shirt and jacket, smoothed down his hair, picked up his battered suitcase and began to edge towards the gates.

"Where were you this morning?" he asked as the ragged column passed out on to the North Quay.

"That prig of a Lieutenant hauled me in early. Wanted a word he said. God help us. Said, as I was the senior Party official here, he expected better of me. He wanted no trouble during today's transfer and if there was he would hold me personally responsible."

Eric raised his eyebrows and shook his head in mock disbelief.

"Charming, isn't it? Anybody would think we were here of our own free will. I don't know who he bloody well thinks he is."

The Lieutenant was taking no chances. The column was flanked by two lines of soldiers, and along the route to the railway station local policemen had cordoned off the side roads. A few passersby stopped to watch the prisoners. They were silent until some of the detainees gave the fascist salute and called out, "Mosley for peace, the Isle of Man awake. Mosley for peace, Britain awake." An old lady, dressed in a black woollen coat and long red scarf, shouted back, "You should be shot the lot of you. You filthy traitors."

"Mosley for peace, Britain awake. It's too late for you old girl."

"You're not fit to call yourselves British, cowards the lot of you."

"Shut it," barked one of the soldiers as he aimed his rifle at the saluting prisoners, "Drop it or I'll fucking blow it off."

"That's right, do as you're told, you flea-bitten animals," called out the breathless woman as her grandson helped her away.

"Come on Grandma, don't fret yourself, they're not worth it."

Wiping the spittle from her chin she muttered under her breath.

"I hate them."

A group of fishermen, heading for their boats, noticed the distraught old lady, registered the smirking faces of the marchers, stopped and turned their backs on the column until it had passed. Then one of them ran after the old woman and threw his arm around her.

"Don't worry Gracie, they're all bastards. If any of them turn up round here we'll sort them out."

"Oh Dick, when I think of our Stephen away fighting in North Africa, and I see that lot, it makes me so angry. And they have to bring them here. I don't know, I really don't know."

She shuffled off shaking her head.

A squalling flock of seagulls rose into the air as the marchers approached and swooped noisily back and forth above the column. The birds had been feeding on heads and entrails thrown overboard from a trawler, listing awkwardly on the exposed sand of the inner harbour, and barely visible from the dockside. The stench of fish scented the still air and the inane whistling of the hidden fisherman gutting his catch formed a stark discord to the shrill cries of the gulls. This cocktail of smells and sounds was intoxicating and Tony, overcome, thought of walking along the Promenade in Blackpool, hand in hand with Emily and their children. Often they walked as far as Fleetwood to buy fresh fish from the quayside market, then back home, their house only one street over from the beach. To be detained here on an island in the Irish Sea, just across the water from where he'd grown up and still had his home, seemed so ridiculous, it was the only conclusion he could come to, so bloody absurd he could scream. The rising sun was warm on the back of his head, he felt the prickle of perspiration breaking out across his back and the damp chill on his forehead. In his discomfort he irritably discounted any personal responsibility for his predicament and blamed the world around him. Looking up into the pale blue sky he took a deep breath and yelled at the top of his voice, "Fuck you all."

Immediately, there was an echo from a young man in blue stained overalls coiling rope ahead of them, "Fuck yourselves, you bastards."

Catcalls from the prisoners drowned him out. Eric clapped Tony on the shoulder and smiled, as a soldier pointed his rifle towards Tony and bawled at him.

"Shut it you, any more of that and you'll be in trouble."

Seeing Eric beside him he said grimly, "I might've known, we were warned about you."

"Nothing to do with me mate, I'm just minding my own business."

"Don't mate me, it's Sir to you."

"Nothing to do with me, Sir."

Turning again to Tony, the private prodded him in the side.

"Remember, you've been warned."

The flood tide was running in the inner harbour. A line of small rowing boats roped together in a snaking line along the water's edge started imperceptibly to rock back and forth as the current began to flow. A black-headed gull that had been perching on the lead boat fluttered several feet into the air at the sudden movement, before settling again, its ruffled feathers catching a breath of wind blowing in from the open sea as it landed. Tony cast a backwards glance at the distant skyline as the column shuffled forward into a narrow cheerless street of terraced houses – Croft's Circus he noticed – the weather appeared capricious, banks of dark clouds were building, their drifting bulk shading a dark strip of ocean below the horizon, white caps flecked the intervening green vastness. His mood demanded that the elements be kind, but he was fearful and ill-prepared for disappointment. He shuddered as the buildings closed in around him.

A whistle blew as an ancient steam engine – the name "Pender" resplendent in peeling gold letters on its green liveried boiler – shunted five carriages slowly across an intricate system of points – sparks flying from screeching wheels – into Douglas Station. Smoke and steam poured from its chimneys and billowed above the blackened roof of an imposing red and white signal box, before being wafted inland. Amber overtones tightly enveloped the ornate Victorian red brick railway buildings, as the rising sun bathed the morning in glowing light. Twin towers, four storeys high, framed the low-lying booking hall and loomed over the ramshackle column, casting the detainees in chilly shadow, as they approached the terminus up a slight incline from the quay. They halted in the cobbled station yard, hemmed in by a cordon of soldiers and a camouflaged, armoured vehicle which was parked across the bottom of a flight of steps that led up to two gilt-topped brick turrets which marked the main entrance to the concourse from Peel Road. Nobody was allowed onto the platforms and the porters and ticket collectors had been instructed not to speak to any of the prisoners. A small crowd of onlookers had gathered under the iron and glass canopy of the ticket office and they jeered as the detainees swarmed in front of them. A policeman walked smartly up to the head of the column, saluted and then spoke a few words to the Lieutenant; who returned the salute and ordered the prisoners to march through the waiting room onto the platform.

There was a hiss of steam and a squeal of brakes as the locomotive edged the carriages into position. A guard waved a red flag and the train clanked to a halt, sending thick grey clouds of choking smoke roiling beneath the shingled roof that covered a section of the platform. The soldiers followed the detainees and lined up along the back wall of the station facing the carriages, the prisoners formed straggling groups in front of them, their baggage strewn at their feet. Tony sat down on his case, reached into the inside pocket of his jacket and took out a battered tobacco tin. Inside was his dwindling supply of tobacco and a couple of cigarettes he had rolled back in Huyton. It was always a major decision when to smoke, but he had been feeling uneasy since his outburst on the quay and he knew it was what he needed to calm his nerves. Placing the cigarette between his lips he compacted the shreds of tobacco with his tongue, tasted the bittersweet flavour and smelt the pungent aroma. Aware that others were watching he took the cigarette from his mouth, held it prominently between nicotine-stained fingers, and said to no one in particular.

"I know, I know, but God I need it."

Ray Ainsley sat down beside him on the case.

"Don't we all, move up and let me sit here, so at least I can breathe in the fumes."

As Tony lit the cigarette and drew in his first delicious lungful of smoke, the public address system crackled into life then immediately died.

"I bet it's that bloody Lieutenant again," smirked Ray, breathing deeply, "no wonder he's been sent over here, he'd be useless on a battlefield." He exhaled slowly and just had time to hoarsely whisper, "Oh my God," before collapsing in a fit of coughing. Tony, laughing, thumped him hard across the back.

"Here have a drag on this, it'll make you feel better."

"Attention."

Eric, who was sitting on his trunk nearby, leapt to his feet and stood crisply to attention, before saluting smartly in the direction of the ticket office. Many of the prisoners around him could barely keep a straight face and even some of the soldiers inadvertently smiled.

"I can't help myself sometimes," said Eric in a tone of mock concern, "I think it's a medical condition I've suffered from for a long time. Is there a doctor around?"

"…leaving in approximately fifteen minutes. It should take us about an hour to reach our destination, which is the town of Peel. The front four carriages are for the detainees, the last one is for the military escort. Sergeant, will you see to it that the prisoners get aboard."

Tony managed to find a window seat in one of the compartments. The wooden benches were packed and men sat between the rows and on the floor in the corridor. Baggage was piled precariously in the racks above their heads and a soldier stood by each carriage door, which was padlocked as soon as everybody was aboard. The windows were wired shut and it quickly became stuffy inside the coach, with condensation streaming down the dirty glass. Tony spent the journey peering through the smears at the small rural stations of Union Mills, Glen Vine, Crosby, and St John's as they trundled by. He glimpsed rivers, herds of black and white cattle, a galloping roan mare, followed by its piebald foal and women bent double working in the compact fields that dotted the narrow picturesque valley. After St John the land opened up, flocks of sheep grazed the undulating grasslands, there was a man fishing by a foaming weir and then they were pulling slowly into the city of Peel, on the west coast of the Isle of Man.

"As far from the bloody war as you can get," pointed out an old man glumly. He was wearing medal ribbons from the First World War and had been silently sitting at Tony's feet throughout the journey.

"That's without leaving the country," he added as an afterthought, "back of bloody beyond."

He looked up at Tony and nodded.

"But look on the bright side, I saw little enough of my wife when I was living with her. I'll see a damn sight less now. You couldn't give me a hand up could you? My bloody leg's gone to sleep."

Peel's Art Nouveau railway station, with its steeply pitched slate roofs and windows, and stone surrounds picked out in black against white pebble-dashed walls, sat incongruously at the head of a picturesque harbour. The platform was deserted except for a police constable in his shirtsleeves sitting on a bench next to a row of steel milk churns. His bicycle was upended beside him, its back wheel slowly revolving, and a puncture repair kit lay scattered across the ground. As the train approached he leapt up and called out, grabbing his jacket from the back of the bench. The station-master and a police sergeant appeared almost immediately at the door of the ticket office and watched as the train pulled into the station.

Alighting first the soldiers formed up slowly along the platform. Compartment by compartment the dishevelled, complaining prisoners were released and ordered to line up facing the sea. One of the last to leave the train, Tony, breathing deeply, smelt the pungent aroma of smoked fish. Stretching his cramped limbs he looked around at the dark creosoted wooden smokehouses stretching in a line along a small lane at the back of the station. Beyond, the lush green patchwork hills that surrounded the town were partly obscured by dense clouds of smoke rising lazily into the still air above the pitched, tar-covered roofs.

"Get in line," barked the sergeant, "we're not moving until we have a decent show. Come on, we haven't got all day."

Tony gazed at the haze drifting imperceptibly inland as it spiralled upwards. High above the pale dispersing wisps he spotted two birds of prey circling on the warm air, almost invisible to the naked eye, he stared hard before looking away, blinded by the bright light. Blinking, he slipped in among the other prisoners as they dawdled on the platform, their belongings piled haphazardly beside them.

"This must really annoy these army types, used to everything in its place," thought Tony and he smiled as he remembered a saying of his father's, "A disorderly kit is a sign of an untidy mind." He had heard it so often in his youth that it seemed the words were ringing in his ears, "You'd better buck up your ideas young man or you'll come a cropper, mark my words."

His mother had written and told him his father had been mortified by his arrest. He'd received letters from her and Brian, and he'd seriously fallen out with his brother over the Fascists and the Jews and he'd bothered to write, but he'd heard nothing from his father, who was unable to forgive his son for proving him right. It was funny though, mused Tony, he was the person he thought of the most. The old bastard never gave an inch.

"Column, quick march. Left, right, left, right."

The harshness of the order grated, and with his father's voice admonishing him, Tony joined the ragged group that ambled along the platform and on to the quay. Passing out of the station's shadow they could see the towering red sandstone walls and the blockhouse of Peel Castle rising vertically from a rocky outcrop that dominated the narrow entrance to the harbour. A flag hung limply from a pole on the highest battlement and people – only their heads visible – could be seen peering over the ramparts and looking down on the marchers as they approached the corner where the quay met Shore Road.

The expanse of Peel Bay stretched out dazzlingly to a misty blue horizon. The men at the head of the column raised their hands to shield their eyes from the glare, while others glanced away. The tide was out and a vast expanse of yellow sand ran in a sweeping arc to the low brown cliffs in the distance. The deserted beach was sandwiched between a black meandering line of seaweed washed up on the low water line and the boulder-encrusted concrete wall of the promenade. Mirroring each other they ran together until, in a trick of the eye, they coalesced in the middle distance and vanished in a daub of light. Emerging from this haze at the far end of the promenade – a point of fascination for the prisoners – was their destination, Peveril Camp, the rows of newly uncoiled barbed wire, raw glinting gashes scarring the face of the quaint Victorian seaside town.

The seafront was quiet and the occasional sightseer curiously surveyed the detainees as they approached noisily along the promenade only to glance away as they drew level, avoiding eye contact, and continuing to look out to sea. It was as if the men were phantoms, an anxious frisson greeting their presence but once they had passed they were dismissed as beings without form or substance. Encased in this bubble of unreality the column floated along the front – overhead a flock of gulls raucously climbed and swooped – passing fisherman's cottages, guesthouses, small hotels, cafes, a boarded up amusement arcade, a sandbagged Home Guard post and a row of shuttered beach huts, before approaching the camp. Close up the high wire fence dominated the esplanade and searchlights were mounted on old telegraph poles at regular intervals along a section of the sea wall. Tangled coils of razor wire, higher than a man in many places, were piled along the base of the fence.

"They're not taking any bloody chances are they," muttered Eric tugging at the wire mesh as they passed, "even if you could get over this lot, you've still got to get off the sodding island. It's enough to bring a good man down."

He leered across at Tony, who was staring grim-faced at the enclosure.

"Come on Tony, me old mate, look at it as an extended holiday by the sea, which should suit you. A holiday camp with good sea views, its own beach and all the amenities you could ever want. Only trouble is, as you well know, it pisses down here nine days out of ten, but still, you can't have everything."

Tony glanced at Eric and smiled wanly. The column had halted on Marine Parade in front of the main gate to the camp. Beside them, only feet from the wire that ran inland along the middle of Walpole Road, stood the Creg Malin Hotel. It was a massive three-storied building in drab brick, its frontage onto the sea buttressed at each end by a round neo-gothic tower, surmounted with a steep sloping lead-faced roof, topped with a triskelion weathervane. Much of its paintwork was stained and peeling and the iron railings on either side of the steps up to the main entrance were spotted with rust. A "Vacancies" sign hung at a slight angle in front of a set of dusty net curtains in one of the downstairs windows.

"Bet the camp's been good for his business," said Tony as he dropped his suitcase onto the sandy road, "very reasonable rates for long stayers, especially for British Union members. Families and pets welcome."

Those around him laughed.

The gates swung open and a contingent of soldiers marched smartly out, linking up with the column's escorts to form a heavily armed corridor into the camp. Beneath their gaze the prisoners shuffled forward, passing in front of a beachfront terrace of nine small two-storey houses, before gathering on an expanse of flat land that had once been clay tennis courts and a public bowling green. They were ordered to face inland away from the sea. In front of them a grass-covered slope, criss-crossed by sandy paths rose steeply up to a long terrace of white-painted houses. Behind them the wire fence ran along the promenade to the low rocky cliffs on their left before turning inland and continuing up the rise to disappear from sight behind the buildings on the ridge at the top of the hill. It reappeared at the other end of the terrace and was visible to the prisoners for a short distance as it followed the incline down a paved road before passing out of sight behind the tall seafront houses immediately to their right.

"Spacious innit?" muttered a young man standing next to Tony, his brow deeply furrowed as he squinted in the bright sunshine, "Don't look like there are any bastard tents for us to sleep in, like in Liverpool. I was fucking freezing there I can tell you. Looks like I might get a decent night's kip here, that's something."

He held out a clammy hand, which Tony grasped firmly, only to let go instantly.

"Name's Sid, Sidney Stiles from West Ham," he laughed, a shrill high-pitched cackle that had people turning to stare.

"I'm a long bloody way from home, there's no way my mates are going to make it up here."

He looked questioningly at Tony.

"Beg pardon?"

"Sorry, I'm Tony Cox from just across the water there, Blackpool, but it feels like a long way home to me too. Why are you here?"

"Good fucking question. Ask meself the same thing every bloody day. I was one of Mike Moran's boots in the East End. Mixing it with the red Jewish bastards, day in, day out and twice at weekends. Brought me in when they nabbed him. Never got round to letting me go, the bastards."

"Is he here?"

"Don't think so. Last I heard he was down in Brixton with old Mosley, but you never know. What about you?"

"I was District Leader in Blackpool. Down to be the parliamentary candidate for Walton in the election that didn't happen."

"Never? I bet you felt home from home in the nick there then. Bloody hell that's the best tale I've heard in a while, fuck me."

Sid shook his head in disbelief, pulled out a dirty grey-coloured handkerchief and wiped the sweat from the back of his neck and forehead, then folded it neatly and put it back in his trouser pocket.

"Bloody sand gets everywhere. Look, I don't know how they are going to sort it here, but I don't know anybody, so how about we bunk up together? Eh?" he nudged Tony with his elbow, "Come from a good home, only a few bad habits."

Taken aback, Tony hesitated and then nodded unenthusiastically.

"Cheers, you'll find I come in useful. Handy with me hands, if you know what I mean. No bad thing I reckon once they start packing 'em in here. Stone me who's this old geezer?"

A grey-haired army officer, carrying a swagger stick, was limping towards them from the direction of the Promenade. His right leg, dragging across the sandy ground, threw up clouds of fine dust that coated his boots. Several paces behind two other officers followed, one of them was unconsciously mimicking his limp.

"He'll go far," whispered Sid when he noticed, "obviously got his head so far up the old bugger's arse, he can't see what he's doing."

The prisoners' escort snapped to attention and the Lieutenant stepped forward and smartly saluted. Barely acknowledging him the Camp Commandant shuffled past and stepped up onto a low wooden dais, placed on a grassy mound that had marked the edge of the bowling-green. Tucking his swagger stick firmly under his left arm, he drew off a pair of black leather gloves and stood motionless and absorbed with his hands behind his back. He peered imperiously at the men lined up in front of him, his flitting gaze intense, then he grabbed his swagger stick and began beating time with it in the palm of his hand.

"I'm Captain Sebastian Faulkner," he paused, "I'm the ultimate authority here, you don't need to know anything else. In over thirty years of service to God, King and Country, I have stood for no nonsense and I'll stand for none now. You…" and he pointed the ornamental metal head of his swagger stick at the prisoners, "…are considered a threat to said King and Country. So, ipso facto, you are a threat to me and I'll treat you as such. There'll be no trouble here, is that clear? No trouble at all. If there is, your lives and I mean all your lives will not be worth living. The authorities have deemed that you should have freedom of association and so you will, you can share accommodation with whosoever you want, speak to anyone you like, but only so long as I believe you are not abusing the privilege. If I think otherwise it will end immediately, make no mistake about that. Carry on Lieutenant."

Captain Faulkner stepped down from the dais, saluted the guard of honour and hobbled off towards the promenade.

"Choose people you can't stand," announced the sergeant, becoming more amused by his own wordplay, the more often he repeated the phrase, "you're going to be with them for a very long time."

The prisoners milled around aimlessly, bemused at being given an unexpected modicum of personal responsibility.

"If that bastard comes with us I'll end up kicking his head in before we get off this parade ground," whispered Eric to Tony,

"Here, I've got just the companions you need, Biff Boys all of them, good and true."

"There's Ray, of course."

"And there's me," said Sid thrusting out his hand towards Eric, "pleased to meet you, Sid Stiles, a friend of Tony's."

Eric looked at Tony, who rolled his eyes but said nothing.

"Well, that's that then," said Eric, "with two of my old squad we're done. I hope they've been airing the beds."

The detainees slowly coalesced into groups of six as instructed, harried by an increasingly irritable sergeant and when finally ready were led away to the buildings, dotted around the compound, where they were going to be locked up.

"House 13 is to be your home sweet home," said one of their escort sardonically, "better than most of you are used to I expect. Give us your names as you go in."

Tony's group had been allocated a small two-storied house, in the middle of a terrace of five identical dwellings, which faced on to the wire fence that formed the inland boundary and highest part of the camp. The row had been built originally in the mid-nineteenth century as housing for agricultural workers. It was located on the slight incline where the Ballarat Road climbed out of Peel before heading off along the cliff tops towards Kirk Michael, the nearest large town. The remote position of the terrace meant that it had only been sporadically occupied over the intervening century and the houses were all in a state of weather-beaten neglect. Their exposed situation laid them open to the vagaries of the Atlantic storms that lashed the island in the winter months. Driving wind and rain had insinuated their way through ill-fitting sashes, broken windows and gaps in the roof left by lifted tiles, ensuring a permanent chill dampness permeated the rooms throughout the year. The compensation for residents, as Tony and the others discovered, was the magnificent view from the back windows of the Irish Sea and the coastline of Peel Bay, set against the panoramic grandeur of the western sky, the amphitheatre for the daily playing out of a resplendent light show, that dazzled and moved onlookers until familiarity finally dulled its brilliance into irrelevance.

Sloping away at the rear of the terrace were long narrow gardens all overgrown, except for number 13 where the previous occupants had dug it over for vegetables, but never got round to planting anything. At the front of the houses there was a gap of several feet between the garden gates and the camp perimeter fence that ran down the centre of the road. Across the street on the other side of the wire, life carried on more or less as normal. There was a row of modern bungalows, neatly tended, their occupants coming and going, studiously ignoring their disreputable neighbours, rarely looking across at the prisoners and then only furtively. The elderly couple, who lived opposite number 13, kept their living room curtains permanently drawn. They owned a large Alsatian which they chained up in the front garden and who could be heard howling mournfully late into the night. Unknown to his owners Sid, who had bred and raced greyhounds, quickly befriended "Oswald", as he was soon called, throwing him scraps of food over the wire. Running beside the bungalow was a narrow grassy path that led past some older stone built houses into fields beyond. On the other side of the path was a fenced off compound with a guardhouse, which was home to around ten soldiers when they were on duty. It was a single story wooden building, which much to the relief of the occupants of number 13 directly opposite, was windowless and had a door that faced away from them. The only light seemed to come from two skylights in the roof. In fine weather the soldiers were rarely there. The guardhouse had worried Eric when they had moved in, but after watching it for a while he came to the conclusion that it was a positive advantage to have it there. As he put it rather cryptically to Tony one evening, "They think they've got our every move covered, when in fact they haven't, which suits me."

Eric had been elected, almost by default, house leader. Sid had briefly and rather forcefully put himself forward, before being told by one of the Biff Boys that Eric was a big man in the Union and worth ten of him. To keep him happy he was unanimously appointed house cook, a role he took to with puppy-like enthusiasm. It meant he could accompany Eric to the camp store on the promenade every morning at 10 o'clock to pick up their daily food rations and carry them back up the hill.

The idyllic weather during their first weeks in the camp – cloudless azure skies, air crystal clear to the horizon, only hazing over in the late afternoon as the sun began its descent, the radiant heat mitigated by sinuous salty breezes wafting onshore – tempered the frustration of the prisoners still smarting over the injustice of their detention. The beauty of the place trumped the banal daily repetition for Tony. He found himself moving towards an understanding of a different existence that, when fully realized, would intellectually stun him, as much for being unexpected as for its implications for his future. The stultifying periods of inactivity that marked life in the camp nurtured activities – physical, sexual and cerebral – all aimed in their different ways at subverting the rationale behind their internment. For Tony the empty time was an opportunity to seek solitude away from the men who had, until then, been his fellow travellers, and to think anew. Solace increasingly lay, he found, in a burgeoning belief in the broader picture – the profundity of an all-encompassing nature that demanded he address his place within it. He had a growing feeling that there was meaning behind what was happening to him, that he was being tested, for some purpose as yet unspecified, but there was definitely a contribution to be made by him towards creating something better. Untested, the logic of his argument was alluring and he was drawn in, increasingly shying away in embarrassment from his old self and its fascination with power and violence.

Tony kept these thoughts to himself, the barrack-room camaraderie of his associates, that he still paid token obeisance to, was unsympathetic to any sign of sensitivity or questioning of the certainties they had all signed up for. For that reason Tony shouldn't have been taken aback at the ease at which he was able to exchange one set of verities for another. When the parallels did finally dawn on him one evening, as he sat bored in their drab living room listening to the swirling of well-worn arguments based on rigid adherence to the familiar dogmas of the Party, he was able to smile wryly to himself, as unbeknown to his friends, he parted company with them.

Every morning, bright sunlight raked the moth-ravaged curtains of the front bedroom, where Eric and Tony slept, motes of dust wavering in the golden spots that slanted diagonally across the space. In the hinterland of their waking a reveille bugle blew marking seven o'clock and the opening of another day. Half an hour later it was already muggy as they drowsily lined up on the makeshift parade ground for roll call. The names listlessly recited: "Matlock? Sir. Morrisson? Sir. Mortisson? Here Sir. Can't hear you. Sir," became a familiar litany. Tony tested himself by attempting to memorize the list, but new names would appear almost every day, and very occasionally one would be absent, and he never managed to get it off by rote. Incensed at the futility of it all he would work out his anger during the compulsory physical exercises that followed the parade. Half an hour of running on the spot, press-ups, stretching, sit-ups under the watchful eye of Sergeant-Major Steele, barking his orders in a broad Scots accent that in the still morning air echoed loudly round the camp.

"Jump, you fascist bastards, jump. Nobody leaves here until I've finished with you, jump."

Red-faced, sweat slicking their hair and soaking their clothes, the prisoners jumped, noisily gasping for breath, silently cursing.

"Faster. You at the front, I said jump. Are your shoes full of lead? Jump or its twenty times round the grounds. Remember I hate you all, there's no way you can escape me."

"This'll be the death of me," hissed the plump middle-aged man next to Tony, his complexion a sickly pallid green, the fug of his ailing body heavy in the still air. He was bent-double, saliva rattling in his throat.

"My chest, oh my God it hurts."

His name was Croydon and he had stood alongside Tony on parade since their arrival at the camp. Next day he didn't appear and Tony heard later that he had been sent to hospital on the mainland after a suspected heart attack.

"So it's true then, the only way out of here is on your back," said Tony wearily. The man who had passed on the news about Croydon shrugged.

"Yes, but in the company of the Lord, my son, in the company of the Lord. What more can you ask."

"My father-in-law would agree with you there."

"He's a man of the cloth?"

"A vicar in the C of E and a good Party member to boot."

"What's his name, I might know him?"

"The Right Reverend Carstairs."

"The one who wrote for Blackshirt?"

"The very same."

"I liked his column, always read it. It was a real inspiration to me. Was he picked up?"

"I don't think so. My wife's never mentioned it in her letters, mind you there's not been many of those."

"We should talk some more. I mustn't keep my flock waiting any longer. What's your name?"

"Tony Cox."

"Tony, very pleased to meet you. I'm glad you enjoy my little gatherings. The word of the Lord is not something that can be ignored in trying times like these, in ghastly places like this. Bless you my son."

The Reverend Captain Thomas G. St Barbe Baker MC had been holding prayer meetings every afternoon on the promenade as part of his mission, unsanctioned by the Anglican Church, Party or military authorities, to administer to the spiritual needs of the inmates. The fine weather, his charismatic speaking-style and his outlandish, often amusing ideas, coupled with the fact there was nothing else to do, meant that large numbers would come to sit in the sunshine and listen. He had built a small altar out of a bedside table he had found in one of the houses, covered it with a sheet on which he had painted a series of symbols – Egyptian hieroglyphics, the fascist flash and circle and the swastika. The crucifix was made out of two pieces of wooden flotsam nailed together, which he would prop up against the wire fence. When preaching he wore his army uniform and medals, including the Military Cross he had won at Passchendaele in the First War, a white sheet would be draped over his shoulders, fastened at the neck with a large silver scarab brooch.

"Brethren, thank you for joining me on this fine day. How I wish we could have met in happier times, but let me assure you the Lord is looking down on us. He is taking care of those who believe and let me assure you, if you listen to my words, if you rise up and follow my teachings, then he will take care of you. For we are the chosen people. Amen."

The tall gaunt figure then turned to face the altar, raised his hands in supplication and cried out.

"Bless us Lord for we are sinners. We come to you to beg forgiveness. Listen to our prayers. Do not leave us to rot unloved in this God-forsaken place. This construction of the Devil, this vile camp, built to test us by our oppressors. O Lord, bless us and redeem us. Amen."

The cries of distant gulls swooping over the laden fishing boats labouring into Peel harbour declaimed over the throb of engines and the hissing waves breaking across the sand. A member of the congregation coughed and St Barbe Baker took a step back from the altar, turned, clasped his hands in front of him and began to speak.

"Brethren, these are strange, but wonderful, times we live in. We are at war, a war that will end all wars. It is a device wrought by God to achieve his blessed ends and we, and by we, I mean all those held in this camp, are fighting on the side of righteousness. Our oppressors – the guards, the commandant, Mr Churchill, even His Royal Highness the King himself – are fighting on the side of evil."

The congregation gasped.

"You may question, you may not believe, you may think me mad, but it's true. They are doing the Devil's work. They are standing in the way of God's progress, God's plan for the world. For these are the last dying days of the Mammon world before God will overthrow the old order and establish his Kingdom on earth. War is his weapon in this last great crusade and those who do not join him on this campaign path to righteousness will be damned. Doomed forever to burn in the fires of hell, cast out for eternity from paradise."

St Barbe Baker clutched his head with his hands and leant towards his audience, who sat transfixed by his performance.

"Do you know how He plans to carry out his grand scheme? Do you know who will lead us into this new golden territory?"

He scanned the front row of the gathering, interrogating each upturned face with his piercing blue eyes.

"No? Then I will tell you. He has sent his only son back to earth to help us in our time of need. Believe me brethren, Jesus Christ has been reborn, resurrected for a second time. You may ask why have we not heard of him, why have we not seen him. Well, I will tell you. Your ears have been blocked and you've been listening to false prophets, your eyes have been blinkered. You, my poor sinners, have not stood a chance, but believe me you have taken steps others have not, you may not feel it, you may not know it, but you have. For that I rejoice, you must rejoice, for all is not lost."

With those words he flung his hands into the air and stared rapturously at the sky.

"Rejoice, I tell you, you have so much to be glad about. For you are the true believers. Let me tell you, you will soon see the Lord in all his glory, for it will not be long before his victory will be won. Already his armies, his air force, his navy, the forces of light, are driving all before them. Any day now the Kingdom of the Lord will be established here on earth. Our cursed chains will be cast off, barriers split asunder, the encircling barbed wire fall aside and we will walk free to take up our rightful place in the new Jerusalem. I cannot wait, dear brethren, I cannot wait. Let me tell you, I pray every night to let me live to see it. And my prayers have been answered, I know they have been answered."

Dabbing his mouth with a handkerchief he paused and raised his hand.

"Bear with me, dear brethren."

Turning his back on the congregation, he reached into his pocket and drew out a small metallic object. Slowly, dramatically he faced them again, holding high in the air a silver swastika. Those at the back craned forward to see what it was, a man near the front put on his glasses.

"This is the sign by which our Lord is now recognized. This is the sign under which he now labours. For his son has come back to earth not in Palestine as before, but in Germany. He has returned as Chancellor Hitler, yes, Adolf Hitler, the Führer of the Third Reich. I can tell by your faces that you are surprised, some of you even unsure, but listen to me then reflect on it, for it is true. Adolf Hitler is Jesus Christ reborn. Returned to this world to create heaven on earth. If you do not believe me, then look in the Bible, for there it is written clearly for all to see. In the book of Isaiah, chapter two, verse two, it says,

"And it shall come to pass in the last days, that the mountain of the Lord's house shall be established in the top of the mountains, and shall be exalted above the hills; and all nations shall flow unto it."

There it is. Adolf Hitler lives at Berchtesgaden high in the Alps. Ambassadors, prime ministers, kings all come to pay court to him there. Isaiah chapter eighteen, verse three, shows us how to recognize his coming,

"All ye inhabitants of the world, and dwellers on the earth, see, when he lifteth up an ensign on the mountains; and when he bloweth a trumpet, hear. And when he cometh among us, joybells will be rung".

It's so obvious to me brethren, that when his armies reach Britain, as they must, bells will be rung across the nation. A warning, so they think, but to us, the chosen few, a celebration, an exhortation, that the end is near, that our time has come."

Exultant, St Barbe Baker stopped speaking to mop his brow again, joy in his eyes.

"Then, my brethren, the great reckoning will be upon us and we will take our rightful place as soldiers for the Lord. I am tired. I thank God I can see my message, his message, has struck home. Let Isaiah, that great prophet, once again point the way forward for you. Chapter sixty-six, verse twenty-four,

"And they shall go forth, and look upon the carcasses of the men that have transgressed against me; for their worm shall not die, neither shall their fire be quenched; and they shall be an abhorrence unto all flesh, Amen."

I need say no more. Thank you for attending my modest gathering, my church by the sea. Have faith your enemies will perish and you will arise reborn anew in the kingdom of heaven."

There was silence, then scattered applause, which St Barbe Baker stilled with a wave of his hand.

"Friends, please no. If this was the house of the Lord you wouldn't clap. Please, I do not want such acclamation. I expect no reward on this earth, save that you listen, inwardly digest God's word and pass it on."

Prisoners began to get up and walk away quietly, stretching their stiff limbs, brushing grass from their clothing. Tony didn't move, he closed his eyes, felt the warmth of the sun seeping into his skin and was lifted on a wave of contentment and infantile well-being. It was a brief passing moment. His head lolled heavily to one side and he awoke with a start. Captain St Barbe Baker was still there, whistling to himself as he packed away the altar, his wooden crucifix hanging lopsidedly from the wire. Tony stood up, waved vaguely in his direction and wearily began to climb the hill back to the house. He wondered what time it was. Not having a watch was one of the things he hated most about being locked up.

"Watching time pass," he thought, "beats feeling it pass and it may even be quicker. Bugger it all. Adolf Hitler is Jesus Christ, do I believe that?"

"Tony, hold on, Tony."

Eric ran up the hill behind him, sweating, damp hair plastered to his head.

"You haven't been listening to that old fraud, have you?" he gasped as he came alongside, breathing rapidly. "He's completely mad you know. Gassed in the last war, buried a couple of times by bomb blasts in the trenches, it all turned his mind. Used to come to the "Black House" all the time, pestering Mosley, saying he worked for British Intelligence and could act as a double agent passing on information about what they were plotting against us. Oswald used to humour him, you know, old soldier and all that, but he never came up with anything worthwhile as far as I know. Mad having him locked up here, in my opinion. He's totally harmless. Should be in a mental hospital."

"Oh, I don't know."

Eric flung himself onto the grass, flicking back his greasy fringe with his hand.

"I'm bloody exhausted. I've just been swimming in the sea. It was wonderful. So refreshing. They've started letting us onto the beach in small groups. Every afternoon, around three. You should do it. Damn sight healthier than listening to that old crackpot."

Tony sat down beside him and stared out to sea, the shimmering light was dazzling and he looked away.

"I don't know," he said distractedly, "it's all very reassuring."

"What is? Old St Barbed Bacon?"

"Being told what to believe, you know, certainties."

"It certainly is."

Eric struggled to keep a straight face.

"Some of it was odd, but he has such a lovely speaking voice. I could listen to it for hours."

"Oh my God, but then he probably said that, didn't he?"

Tony looked at him strangely as if only just becoming aware that he was there.

"Looks like a touch of the sun to me, but it could be the touch of God, eh? What do you think Tony?"

"What?"

"Tony, I wonder about you sometimes. Anyway, I've something very important I want to talk to you and the others about. Exciting news. I'll tell you over dinner. Make sure you're there won't you?"

"Yeh, yeh I'll be there."

"Good, see you later."

"Where is Eric? He tells us to be here and then he's late, bloody typical."

"He'll be here Ray, give him a bit more time, it's not as if we're going anywhere or got anything better to do."

"I could be digging the garden, lovely evening like this. Takes my mind off things, instead I'm stuck inside waiting for Eric."

"Come on, it's not that bad and we'll be eating soon. Sid'll surprise us with another culinary masterpiece. We'll have a beer and Eric will tell us his story and all will be fine with the world."

"Well Tony, if you're so bothered about my welfare give us a fag."

"Sorry, I'm a bit short myself, almost used up this week's ration."

"No, I thought not. What are we having Sid?"

"Fish bloody stew, what do you bloody well think. It's stinking the house out, you can't bloody miss it."

Sid yelled from the kitchen at the rear of house. The others were sitting in the back room watching the orange orb of the sun sink slowly though a blood-red sky.

"Spuds, any spuds?"

"Yes, bloody mashed spuds. Soddin' different ain't it. A right royal bloody treat."

Sid appeared at the door wreathed in steam.

"There's no need to bloody shout, I'm not deaf. Ray you can bloody do this tomorrow."

He ducked back into the kitchen as a cushion missed his head by inches.

"Not bloody likely mate, you're getting too good."

"Sod off."

Eric appeared at the back door.

"Children, children, leave you alone for a few minutes and…"

"Where've you been? We've all been waiting."

"Ray, Ray, patience. I've been checking a few details, wait and see. Is everyone here, right. How long till grub's up Sid?"

"Twenty minutes or so."

"Fine, let's go through to the front. Should all be a bit clearer in there."

The curtains were drawn and the room was in semi-darkness. The two Biff Boys slept there and bed-sheets and blankets were strewn everywhere, two old battered leather chairs piled high with dirty clothes.

"God it stinks in here, don't you ever let in any fresh air? It's worst than my dog's kennel."

"Leave it," snapped Eric, as Sid moved towards the window, "we don't want any nosy neighbours listening in. Grab a seat and pay attention."

Sid angrily flung himself into one of the armchairs and glared at Eric who sat down opposite him in the other chair. Eric waited for the rest to find a space on the floor, then began to speak in a half-whisper.

"Now you all know that they've been bringing more and more detainees in here since we arrived, and not all good fascists like us. Italians, Germans, Irish, you name it, they're shipping them in. Well, I met one of them, an Irishman name of Ed Flaherty, well, it was more he introduced himself to me. He has an interesting…"

"What's he here for?"

"Didn't ask him, but there's three or four of them. I'm sure they must be IRA. They're dead keen to get out of here and return home. Well you can almost see Ireland on a clear day, it's that close."

"What do you mean get home? How?"

"That's what's interesting. They've checked out the camp and reckon they can escape."

Sid whistled and shook his head.

"Escape? If you get out of the camp, you've still got to get off the island, they're mad."

"No, Ray listen. Our house is one of the closest to the wire, it's also opposite that path that runs through to the fields at the back. And you all know its dead quiet up here most of the time. We hardly ever see a guard, even with the sodding guardhouse opposite. I've been watching it, they come and go at the back, never the front."

"So what are they talking about? Going over the wire? It'd be bloody dangerous."

"No, a tunnel."

"Whaaaat, they're not serious?"

They all looked aghast at Eric.

"They are and they want us in. They've been checking us out."

"But a tunnel?"

"Look, Ray, you'll know better than the rest that the soil round here is easy to dig. It's clayey but well drained…"

Ray nodded.

"…and it's not that far from this room to the other side of the road, the other side of the fence. What, thirty odd feet at the most?"

They all began looking around the room, seeing it for the first time in a different light.

"There's plenty of wood around to shore up the tunnel and we get rid of the soil in the garden, Ray's always out there pottering around."

"How many would be digging?"

"The six of us and three or four of them."

"And what happens when we get out of the camp? We swim for it?"

"No, they can get a boat, then over to Ireland in a couple of hours and away. No more of this bloody drudgery. What do you think?"

There was silence.

"Do we all get to go?"

"Of course you do Tony, no problem."

"And if we don't want to?"

"You don't have to, but I wouldn't want to be around here when they discover we've gone and you were living in the same house and knew all about what was going on and didn't say anything."

They all laughed.

"Anyway Tony, I'd have thought you'd be dead keen. You said Emily was ill and wouldn't be able to make it over here to visit. This would be your chance to go and see her. You've nothing to lose. Are you in? 'cause I am."

Tony thought for a moment, leaning back rubbing his lower jaw with his hand, hoping his ambivalent feelings about the whole enterprise wouldn't be obvious.

It was true that the last he'd heard, Emily was having chest problems and didn't think she'd be moving around much in the next few months. But it was tempting to stick it out here, keep your head down and not get into trouble. They were already letting a steady stream of people go and he couldn't be far from top of the list to be released. But, and it was a big but, Eric was his friend – a friend who'd stitched him up, the bastard – there was no way he'd be allowed to not take part as, by the sound of it, there were some hard men involved. And if I get caught, I'll get sent back to Walton, which is closer to home. So I can't bloody lose can I?

"I'm in," he said grimly.

A smile flickered across Eric's face.

"Thanks matey, you won't regret it. Come on, you other dogs, how about some digging?"

The two Biff boys nodded their assent in unison. Sid called out, "I'll be happy to get out of this bloody place, sign me up

Eric," as he headed back to the kitchen. "Show these fucking swine. If they treat us like dogs, they get dogs, eh?"

Yelps could be heard amid the clatter of pots and pans, then maniacal barking.

"Keep it down Sid, we don't want them to lock you up early, do we?"

Ray had got up and was standing in front of the dusty fireplace, looking apprehensively at the others.

"Look, Eric, I'm not sure about this. I'm sorry, but I don't think I can do it. The thought of tunneling puts the wind up me. The whole idea, you know underground, closed in with all that earth up above you. I've never liked small rooms."

Wringing his hands, Ray looked from face to face, desperately seeking reassurance.

"You know, I can't bear it."

Eric got to his feet and placed an arm around Ray's shoulder.

"I know what you mean. I'm not so keen on it myself. But tell you what I'll do if you come in with us, you won't have to do the digging."

Ray looked relieved.

"You can be our logistics man, getting rid of the soil, collecting wood that sort of thing. How about…"

Ray eagerly cut Eric off.

"Yeah, I'll do it. Look, I'm sorry, you know?"

"Don't worry, this calls for a celebration. Sid?"

"What?"

"Any beers left?"

"Bloody hell, give us a minute. Two."

"Bring 'em in here will you old chap, time for a toast."

"Fetch 'em yourself. I'm up to my bloody eyeballs with your fucking dinner."

Eric turned away from Ray and began to squeeze himself past the armchair towards the door, hissing under his breath.

"God, that little runt really annoys me sometimes."

Tony touched him on the arm.

"Forget it Eric, I'll go."

Tony returned holding a tray with two brown bottles, open and frothing, and four chipped white enamel mugs.

"Watch it, you're spilling it, you stupid sod. Bloody precious stuff that is."

The mugs were passed round, Ray took his sheepishly and placed it on the mantelpiece, the others were grabbed eagerly.

"Hold on everyone, I want to make a toast."

Eric took one of the bottles and raised it above his head.

"To King, country and home by Christmas."

"Home by Christmas," echoed round the room. Bottles and mugs were drained. Ray looked marginally happier. Sid belched.

"God, delicious. Grub's up."

"Before we dine gents, I've something to show you."

Everyone stared at Eric, who moved over to the window.

"Here, give us a hand to shift this chair."

Underneath was a filthy frayed rug. Eric raised a corner and flung it to one side. A number of the floorboards were free from dust and edged in places by pale splintered wood, where they had been prized loose. Eric lifted each board in turn to reveal a pit about a yard square and a couple of feet deep dug into the hard packed earth that lay a foot below the floor. The air smelled stale and musty.

"Don't look so surprised. I had to check it was possible."

"But when did you do it?"

"When you were all out the other day. This ..., " he pointed triumphantly into the hole, "took me less than an hour. It's dead easy. It shouldn't take us long, then freedom."

Ray flinched, thinking of the cold damp earth closing in on him, and stepped back feeling hot and faint, but nobody noticed in the dim light. Over dinner Eric talked incessantly about digging rotas, hiding the tools, shoring up the tunnel, putting in electric lighting, spreading the soil in the garden.

"Eric's in his element," thought Tony, "he's loving every minute. Fooling the guards and other inmates, covering his tracks, subterfuge."

The tunnel imposed its own routine, independent of, yet integral to their life in the camp. The eight men involved directly in the digging divided themselves into four teams, each spending two hours a day underground tunneling. The original plan had been for each person to work an hour at the soil face and an hour shifting earth and keeping watch. But cleaning up afterwards was more of a problem than they had anticipated, due to the shortage of water in the houses along the Ballarat Road. So, to minimize the numbers needing to wash, one man would dig for two hours one day and then move earth for two hours the next. Digging started after early roll-call. At the outset, the Irish were keen to press on and excavating would continue after the evening meal, but exhaustion and the increased danger of being overheard by prisoners in the neighbouring houses, led to the extra shifts being dropped. Ray took his duties seriously, the newly dug earth was rapidly spread across the vegetable garden and there was a constant supply of planking, cut to the correct length, stored in the space under the floorboards at the entrance to the tunnel.

Security was a concern when they first began the dig and they posted look-outs at the front and back of the house, kept the curtains drawn and the rug covering the hole whenever they were getting rid of the soil in the garden. They even ran practice drills to see how quickly they could hide the tunnel entrance and replace the furniture and they rehearsed standard replies to any questions about noises people had heard or things they may have seen. But as the weeks went by they realized that the camp guards rarely patrolled inside the wire and when they did, they never went into any of the houses, unless there was trouble. And none of their fellow prisoners appeared to notice, so they became increasingly relaxed. Life settled down into a productive routine.

Tony paired up with Eric and they worked the late afternoon digging shift, which suited Tony perfectly. Early in his internment at Peveril, he had volunteered to fetch fresh milk for the camp every morning from Ballawattleworth Farm, a quarter of a mile or so inland from Peel. Immediately after reveille he and five other prisoners escorted by four guards would pull a cart loaded with empty milk churns along a dusty dirt track between high hedges to the dairy. It was an escape, a brief respite from the snagging restrictions of life behind the wire. Outside you could move freely, Tony convinced himself, bask in the expansive air beneath an unmarred sky, absorb the rich textures of the open countryside and breathe in the natural scent of the burgeoning fields and the warm fecundity of animals. But above all he looked forward to the rich creamy smell of warm milk and the pungent rancidity of the creamery, not to mention the fleeting presence of the dairy maid. Yvonne always stopped and smiled at the prisoners as they drew up in the yard, before slipping into the dairy to reappear seconds later carrying a brimming churn, her cheeks flushed with the exertion. The farmer would not allow the prisoners inside any of his farm buildings, so they had to wait for Yvonne before loading them on to the cart. Tony would stand with the others and admire her muscular arms, the moving folds of her skirt as she bent over to position the heavy churns in the doorway, the sweat glistening on her forehead, dampening the wisps of blond hair that escaped from under her white cap; and imagine himself in love. Nobody ever said a word and they would slowly return to the camp, loaded down with slopping churns. These trips to the dairy excused him from other more onerous camp duties and the rest of the morning was free for football, swimming and playing cards. In the early afternoon he was a look-out and spent the time reading a book with his feet up in a shady spot in the back garden. He raised the alarm only once and that was to put the wind up Sid, who had been annoying everyone all morning. It worked up to a point. Sid was trapped petrified in the tunnel for over half an hour, while Tony and Eric crashed around above his head, moving furniture and tapping the floor with a stick. He was quiet for days afterwards, but refused to do any cooking, until an extra bottle of beer and a word from Eric won him round.

Tony enjoyed the act of tunnelling. He liked the hard, physical effort, quickly acclimatized to the stifling heat and was exhilarated by the risks they were taking. He was not alone. "It's as hot as fucking Hades down there," Sid succinctly put it one day as he emerged from the shaft wreathed in smiles, his sweat-bathed body caked in a muddy brown paste, "we've got to do something about the fucking ventilation, the tunnel's getting too bloody long. Soon it'll only be me and Tony going down there." Ray hauled him up, quietly satisfied that he had avoided slithering into that hell. Later in the afternoon he chalked the word "Hades," together with an arrow pointing downwards, on a wooden board that he nailed at the entrance to the tunnel.

Preparations for the descent into "Hades" became a particular ritual. Tony always undressed in the living room, neatly folding his clothes and slipping them into the space under the floorboards. He then placed his boots beside them. Brushing the hair back from his forehead with one hand, he then pulled down an oversize cap over his head with the other, checking no hairs had escaped. Tony then reached into the tunnel and tugged on the string that was attached to the man digging at the soil face, signalling he was to come up. He would emerge, a minute or so later, at the bottom of the ladder that led to the surface, having backed down the tunnel on his hands and knees. It would take seconds for him to turn round in the confined space, he would then stare blinking up into the light, waiting for the signal to climb out. It was about ten feet to the surface, but it took a great effort to climb the ladder with tired, stiff muscles. Tony often had to drag Sid the last few feet.

"How's it going?"

"It's me bloody legs, it happens every piggin' time, the bastards. First it's pins and needles, then this fucking awful cramp. Help me for Christs' sake… thanks. It's not going badly. You'll need to shore up the sides and roof of the tunnel, before you do much more. I don't know how you can do it, working with that bastard Eric."

He laughed and limped off to try and climb the stairs to the bathroom.

The atmosphere in the tunnel was sweltering, a wave of heat breaking against Tony's face like the searing blast from the opening of a furnace door. It felt abrasive in the nostrils and sat uncomfortably in the lungs. He would gasp for air, taking short sharp breaths, until his body acclimatized to the lack of oxygen. The smell, a metallic earthiness, would envelop him as he moved further into the tunnel, becoming a part of him. In the middle of the night, he would often wake up gripped by a profound anxiety. Drenched he would sit bolt upright barely able to breathe in the stench of the catacombs.

The trepidation as he lunged head first into the tunnel and his mastery of this fear became part of the rite – he discovered he had no concern for his personal safety and was prepared to leave his fate, as he rationalized it, in the hands of a higher power – crawling myopically into the feeble glow of the electric light bulb shimmering ahead of him at the soil face. The mining tools, a small gardener's fork and trowel, lay cast aside on a pile of newly dug earth, the wicker basket beside it half empty. The tunnel was getting too long to push the basket back each time it was full and Tony was working on a pulley system to make life easier and more efficient. He enjoyed problem solving, it gave him something useful to think about when he was digging, diverting his mind from a recent preoccupation of his with the life he was wasting and the crassness of men he was forced to spend time with. Even Eric was moving beyond the pale. He had taken to boasting about the massive "hard-on" he would get as he was working. He claimed it was perfectly natural, it would happen to anyone exerting themselves in a warm, dark confined space and that Tony was the abnormal one. They joked that Eric had a permanent erection and it would have been a surprise if he hadn't had one. It became a familiar refrain, "Never go down there ahead of Eric, and if you do, be careful."

Tony looked forward to his hours of solitary digging, to the stipple of perspiration that broke out across his forehead as he burrowed deeper into the tunnel, to the sensation of skin that was slippery to the touch when he began digging and would be bathed in sweat by the time he finished. The heavy repetitive work honed his muscles and labouring naked enhanced his appreciation of the steady refinement in his body. He began to disparage physical weakness and eulogize his own fitness. Never before overly concerned about his appearance, Tony became in these summer months increasingly vain, often casting approving glances into the dusty mirror hanging on the wall above the fireplace in the living room as he limbered up before work. He had rarely, in all his campaign forays for the British Union, felt particularly confident about his street fighting skills, relying on a brute physical strength that did damage, but left him dissatisfied at its lack of grace. In his heart he knew he had been fortunate to escape physically unscathed. Tunnelling changed all that and he began sparring with Eric and the Biff Boys and, when alone, trading blows with a punch bag they had rigged up in the garden. Day in, day out, he worked out his frustrations bludgeoning his way to a kind of contentment. In these calmer moments he could appreciate the irony of an increasingly disillusioned fascist finally understanding the power implicit in the perfect male body, but it didn't give him cause to change his behaviour.

Letters from home, often heavily censored, arrived infrequently in the camp and always caused emotional disorder, fanned by the recipient's elation, anguish or anger. A phase of psychic disruption would consume the prison body, often for days. Whatever the sentiment of the message from a loved one, the bored mind cut off from all commonplace mitigations – a kind word, the fleeting caress, a smile – was only too capable of misconstruing even the most innocent of phrases, succumbing easily to a paranoia which only grew with time. Tony was not immune. He always felt uneasy when his name was called out and he recognized Emily's spidery script scrawled in distinctive royal blue ink across a brown envelope. On the surface all seemed well with his family. His eldest son, Stephen, was enjoying school, while the youngest, Freddie, was learning to ride a bike and talking "nineteen to the dozen." Emily was coping with the shortages and getting by without him, but as she said, "she was not the only one these days." Her health was suffering, but then she had always had problems with her chest. Every winter had seen her laid up in bed with flu, or something like it, for weeks on end. But it was none of these things that troubled him. Tony struggled to put his finger on it and the best he could come up with, was that there was nothing in the letters about the future, nothing about the life they were going to lead after all this was over. Eric said he was mad, just imagining it, and what could he expect; but Tony was not reassured. For God's sake, what did Eric know about women? Emily was an impressive, strong-willed woman and she had loved him at the time of his arrest, he knew that. He loved her and tried to put that in his letters, but somehow it was missing in hers. The words were there, the emotions weren't. But then it was probably nothing.

A letter from Emily, which arrived in mid-August, really did worry him and reignited concerns about the lack of influence he had over his life and family. There was something definitely wrong at home – an implicit threat, ill-defined but real – a feeling that bolstered his determination to escape from the camp. It wasn't the letter that concerned him, that was much like all the others, it was a clipping from his local newspaper, "The Blackpool Gazette and Herald," that had been folded many times and slipped into the envelope. He'd not received anything like it before, maybe the censors had taken them and they'd missed this one or, more likely, they didn't care if he read this particular cutting. It was the front page dated from a couple of weeks before and headlined, "This is the Isle of Man today – an Island and its secrets," by a special reporter. It began as a general travelogue describing places of interest for the visitor, it then turned its attention to Peel and to the prisoners behind the wire:

"One could not help thinking as we watched the British Fascists interned at Peel, how fortunate is their lot. These people, some of whom would doubtless sell out their country for a dish of spaghetti or a bratwurst, live off the fat of the land and their wives bring them food parcels, which the patriotic residents of the island deem just cause for violent protest.

Like the aliens, interned alongside them, they sea-bathe, and disport themselves, and altogether their lot is pleasant, if boring.

The power of money is used to the last halfpenny by these Mosleyites, some of whom are well blessed with this world's goods. They are the plutocrats Hitler talks about.

I wondered what were the feelings of the soldier guards tramping outside the barbed-wire for a pittance, plus army rations, when they surveyed the life of idleness and semi-luxury enjoyed by these creatures, who do not even have the excuse they are foreigners.

I wondered what the feelings would be of the people of Blackpool if they knew that a number of their fellow citizens are enjoying the fruits of their treachery and basking untroubled in the sunshine of this holiday island."

Tony lay on his bed, the only light a yellow line at the bottom of the door. He couldn't sleep, despite being exhausted. A summer cold muddled his thoughts as he struggled to conjure up an image of Emily. After many months of separation it was becoming increasingly difficult, he found, and this worried him. Recently, he had confused her with other men's wives, those he had watched that day, paying a visit, walking close to each other along the promenade. Emily had never come to any of the camps he'd been held in. He understood why, but he desperately needed to see her. There was a scuffling sound from the stairway and a board creaked.

"Eric," he smirked to himself, "now there's a man who doesn't have these problems, there's a bastard who knows how to enjoy himself."

Rolling over he turned his back to the door, as it swung slowly open. There was no way he wanted to talk endlessly into the night with Eric. His mouth open, he deliberately deepened his breathing and closed his eyes. Eric would usually stumble to his bed, cursing loudly under his breath, and fling himself down, the springs straining noisily, to fall asleep almost immediately. Tonight, he came over to Tony and began shaking him roughly.

"Tony are you awake," he whispered, his stale breath hot on Tony's cheek.

"Bugger me, Eric, what are you playing at?"

"Shhhhhh, keep your voice down."

"Leave me alone will you, I was asleep."

"Tony, Tony I need your help, please."

His voice was shaking, edgy.

"Please Tony, you're the only one I can trust. Get up, will you."

Tony sat up, confused about what was happening.

"For God's sake. If you're…"

"No, no, there's no time to lose. Get dressed."

"Is it the tunnel?"

"No, it's me, me. Please hurry."

There was a pleading tone in the way he spoke and an urgency to his movements – his agitated pacing back and forth in the gloom unsettling. Tony swung his legs onto the floor.

"This better be good, you know. I mean it."

A clawing hand grasped his arm.

"Thank-you, thank-you."

"Hey, let go for Christ's sake, that hurts. I've not done anything yet."

"I know, hurry."

"Eric, come on, what's so important? What've you done?"

"Later, later. Please be quiet, no one else must know."

"What?"

Eric stopped and grabbed Tony firmly round the shoulders.

"Tony," he pleaded, "trust me. You're my only friend. I'll tell you later, I will, please, no more. Just come with me, hurry."

"Alright."

Eric sighed heavily and resumed his pacing.

"I'm going as fast as I can."

"I need a cigarette, have you one?"

"Eric."

Tony pulled on his trousers and a jumper, then unable to find his socks in the dark, slipped on his boots, which felt cold and sticky on his bare skin.

"I'm ready."

Placing a finger to his lips Eric led him quietly down the stairs and out through the kitchen, without disturbing anyone in the house. He seemed relieved when they reached the garden and paused to take several breaths of cool night air. Tony noticed he was trembling, but said nothing.

"Follow me and be quiet," he said abruptly, then stooping slightly he set off rapidly down the incline towards the promenade. It was difficult for Tony to see where he was going, a sliver of moon cast a faint silvery pall across Peel Bay, but the land was in almost total darkness. Stumbling on the broken tufted ground, he stopped, Eric was nowhere to be seen and all he could hear was the sound of his own rapid breathing and the distant crash of the waves on the beach. He sat down.

"This is fucking ridiculous, I should be in bed."

Several minutes later he heard Eric whispering his name.

"Over here."

"Stay close to me, will you, or someone will hear us."

"Wait for me then, will you. I don't know where we're going, remember."

Moving more slowly they reached the bottom of the slope, skirted the open parade ground and fetched up behind the wall that ran along the end of the gardens of the terrace that fronted onto Walpole Road. Each garden had a gate and when they reached the third one, Eric stopped.

"This is the place. No noise, just do exactly as I do, no one must see us."

The wooden gate was warped and misshapen and it took Eric several attempts to force it open enough for them to slip through. He led the way across the overgrown garden to steps that led down to the cellar. Grasping the wooden handrail he lowered himself gingerly down the steep stairs, his boots grating noisily on the sand that had drifted in to the well. Tony followed him down and noticed a faint glimmer of light shining under the door to the cellar. Eric tapped lightly on the peeling wood and there was a faint scuffling and a grimy fretful face appeared in the doorway. Seeing Eric, he relaxed and swung the door open.

"Where've you been?" he gasped, "Eric I've been going crazy. Eric?"

"Let us in, will you."

The young man moved aside. Tony had never seen him before. He was tall with jet-black, heavily greased hair, which he wore swept back from his forehead. A furrowed brow and chapped lips framed a handsome boyish face that was pale and racked with anxiety. His white vest and dark trousers were covered in grey dust. Behind him, a candle guttered in the breeze from the open door. In the flickering light Tony caught sight of an unmade bed, a sheet lying crumpled beside it on the floor. Eric closed the door and placed an arm round the young man.

"Everything'll be alright now, Paolo. Tony's my friend, we'll sort this out."

"Sort what out?"

"I was so worried…"

For the first time Tony noticed his Italian accent.

"…I couldn't keep him quiet. He kept struggling, Oh God."

"Eric?"

Tony whirled round, eyes searching the gloomy room. There were cobwebs everywhere, bowing drapes heavy with grime, festooning the shadowy recesses, but nothing particular to see. He moved towards the back of the cellar. He made out a washbasin and a filthy towel hanging lopsidedly from a wooden roller.

"Tony, I can explain."

A flight of concrete steps led up to what looked like a trapdoor set in the ceiling. There was a large wooden barrel blocking the bottom of the stairs and a number of battered boxes and chests were piled haphazardly alongside it.

"Over here, Tony."

Eric was standing in a small alcove set in the far wall of the cellar, reached through a brick arch, crudely daubed with whitewash. At his feet lay a man, gagged and bound hand and foot with strips of torn sheet. He was struggling and staring up with wide fearful eyes. His body smelled of urine.

"Bloody hell, Eric, what's going on?"

"He was trying to blackmail us. Said he was going to tell the authorities, everyone. I couldn't let him."

"About what Eric? What was he going to tell them?"

Eric hesitated, uncertain.

"Oh Tony, my friend…"

"What? Oh my God, the tunnel. He knows about the tunnel?"

Eric slowly nodded his head, his face breaking into a relieved smile.

"Yes, that's right, the tunnel. He was going to tell Faulkner about the tunnel. That's right. He saw me come down here to see Paolo, followed me down and then made threats. We grabbed him, tied him up and I came to get you."

Turning he grasped Paolo by the arm and pulled him close.

"My friend here was a great help, but he has no stomach for violence and we have to deal with this."

He nudged the man with his foot.

"What do you mean deal with it?"

"Think straight Tony, we've got to teach him a lesson. We can't risk all the hard work we've put in. If we let him get away with this, we may be here for years. We could even be sent back to Walton or some other God-forsaken hole as punishment if it comes out."

The man on the floor began grunting loudly and thrashing around, his feet hitting the walls, chipping large flecks of plaster and whitewash from the brickwork.

"How did he find out? Who told him?"

"I don't know. Look we can't hang about."

"Didn't you ask him, Eric?"

"No, I was so angry I just took a swing at him."

"We should find out, it could be someone in our house. Let's ask him."

"No wait, don't."

Eric grabbed Tony by the arm.

"Tony, we can't risk it mate. The house is full of people. They're just above our heads. If he managed to call out we'd be done for."

"What does he want?"

"What do you mean?"

"What does he want for not telling about the tunnel?"

For a moment Eric seemed nonplussed, he coughed and looked away.

"Sorry mate, dust or something. No, he wanted to be in on it, to be part of the escape, him and several of his friends, though he wasn't prepared to do any digging."

Tony panicked.

"What if he's told others?"

"No, calm down."

Eric placed a hand on his shoulder and squeezed. Irritated Tony pulled himself free.

"I'm certain he hasn't. Think about it, it's not in his interest to spread it around yet, is it?" Before Tony could give it any thought, he went on, "Come on, let's sort him out, we haven't got that long, it'll soon be getting light."

"Hold on a minute."

Tony stepped away, rubbing his forehead.

"What are you suggesting here, not killing him?"

The bound man lay perfectly still, wide eyes staring at them. Paolo got up from the bed where he had been sitting and moved across the room towards Eric. He stood beside him, one side of his face in shadow the other illuminated by the quivering candle.

"I don't know," Eric said slowly and deliberately, "I just don't know."

The dripping of a tap was the only sound.

"Tony we can't be pushed around on this, it's too important. We've no choice, mate, no choice."

Clear-headed, but nervous, Tony desperately wanted fresh air. "Who is he? Do I know him?"

"I don't think so. I'd only seen him a few times."

"Is he one of us?"

"I think so, from somewhere in the Midlands."

"What's his name? I must know his name."

"Albert Chalmers, a right bastard."

It would be very different if he had a choice, Tony knew that, but he had to escape from the camp, without the tunnel life here would be unbearable.

"Tony, we can't hang around, come on, please?"

Eric's voice was insistent, pleading yet edged with an abrasiveness that Tony feared would end up being turned on him if he hesitated any longer. He didn't know the blackmailer, after all. What harm would a good beating do? If they let Albert Chalmers get away with it, where would it end? Too many people had worked long and hard on this escape plan for some cheating bastard to muscle in and take it from them. With the three of them his punishment would be swift and easy. Tony knew he was strong and capable enough to carry it out.

"Yes, yes, let's do it."

Eric, who had been looking increasingly agitated, instantly stiffened, smiled grimly then grabbed Albert Chalmers by the legs and dragged him into the centre of the cellar. His body left a slick trail on the dusty floor. The man struggled for a moment, then lay still, his eyes flicking wildly from side to side. His gag was sodden and the corners spotted with blood, where the sheet cut into the sides of his mouth.

"Paolo and Tony, you hold him up, I'll do the honours."

Paolo shrugged his shoulders, bent down and grabbed the trussed man's right arm, Tony got hold of the other and they lifted him to his feet. He began moaning, trying to speak. Tony and Paolo turned their heads away and tightened their grip. Eric stepped up to within inches of Albert Chalmers face and spat at him. Then he picked up the sheet from the floor and tore off two long strips. Slowly he wound the cloth around each of his hands, grasping the loose ends firmly in clenched fists.

"Ready?"

The body convulsed and twisted, almost breaking free. Tony nodded his head. The first punch to the stomach, bent all three of them double, Tony and Paolo straightened up for the second and the third. A hammer blow to the head and they were supporting a dead weight in their arms as the body sagged close to the floor.

"Haul the bastard up," hissed Eric, "I haven't finished."

With the next strike Albert Chalmer's head whipped backwards, the neck audibly cracking, and then came to rest lolling lifelessly on one shoulder. Blood began pouring from his nose and seeping from the saturated gag. Eric stood back, then kicked him hard in the genitals, the only sound the thud of boot on cloth. The force cut his legs from under him and the unconscious body slipped from Tony's grasp, falling heavily face down on the floor. A further kick to the side of the head, cracked the skull and blood began to pulse in tiny rivulets from his left ear. Eric was preparing to kick the prone figure again, when Tony grabbed him.

"Enough, you'll kill him. Stop it."

Eric struggled in his arms.

"Let me at him, I've not finished. The bastard, I'll teach him."

"Eric, Eric."

Tony managed to turn him away from the twitching body on the floor, but Eric lashed out with his boot and caught his victim again in the stomach.

"Eric, stop."

Reluctantly, Eric moved away and sat down on the bed.

"Stay there. Paolo, is he still alive?"

The young man bent over the bloody crumpled figure and placed a hand on the side of his neck. Shaking his head slightly he moved closer.

"Quiet. I'm listening to…" he coughed, clearing an obstruction in his throat, and wiping his hand across his forehead smearing it with blood, "…to hear if he is breathing." The agitation of his body could be heard resonating in the quaver of his voice.

Tony didn't move, just stared at Paolo and the dark silent bulk of Albert Chalmers. His chest was gripped in a spasm of muscular pain that left him feeling nauseous. In a rising panic, he blinked and focused on the burning sensation, concentrating on the transitory, anything but what next. The only sound he could hear was the rhythmic creaking of springs as Eric rocked back and forth on the edge of the bed. Every so often he would break off, sniff heavily and clear his throat, then pick up again, his boots grating harshly on the gritty floor.

"Yesssss…," Paolo's relieved voice came from nowhere and Tony was barely listening, "… he's breathing. Yessss, yes, he's alive."

Paolo stood up, a look of profound relief sweeping across his blood-streaked face.

"Thank you, Jesus."

He crossed himself once, then, as if to underline his immense gratitude, a second time.

"Keep your voice down, will you."

Eric spoke in a matter of fact manner, the old authority

returning to his voice. He leapt to his feet, patted Tony on the back, then walked calmly over to Paolo, placed an arm around his shoulder and squeezed hard. Paolo smiled weakly.

"We'd better get him out of here, it'll be light soon. Untie him. I need to think."

Paolo palmed a flick-knife, deftly snapping out the blade, bent over and sliced through the bindings. Free of its restraints the body slumped, its limbs splaying across the concrete.

"Clean up in here, Tony and I will carry him up to the prom and leave him there. When it gets light, he'll soon be found."

Hearing the pronounced click of the knife as it closed brought Tony round and he listened alert to what was being said. He put up no resistance when Eric turned to him.

"Come on Tony, old mate, lend a hand. We can't hang around."

They wiped away as much of the blood and dirt from Albert Chalmer's face and neck as they could, then each taking an arm over their shoulders, they picked up his unconscious form – there was a moan at this first movement, then silence. They had no trouble hauling him up the steps, through the garden and out of the gate. Glancing back Eric noticed that dragging feet were leaving a distinctive double track in the sandy soil.

"Damn, we'll have to come back and cover that up. Can we lift him so he doesn't touch the ground?"

With effort they each took hold of a leg and carried the body out onto the promenade, where they dumped it, face down, away from the terrace, close to the wire. It was high tide and they could hear the rush of the surf over the sand just feet away. Tony stood and stared out to sea, it was still pitch dark, though it was close to dawn. For the first time he felt cold and shivered in an exaggerated manner, clutching his shirt collar tightly around his neck.

"Thanks mate, I couldn't have done this without you, you

know that. You get back. I'll go and brush over the tracks. See you later."

He was gone, swallowed up by the darkness. Tony vowed he'd talk to him as soon as he got back to the house, but he lay awake until way past dawn and Eric never returned.

"It's sixty-five feet long. There can't be more than ten feet to go."

Eric's smiling mud-streaked face appeared through the hole in the floorboards.

"What's that, a couple of weeks at the most? Then we dig up to the surface and away we go?"

Tony handed him a bottle of beer.

"Can't be too soon for me. This place is driving me round the bend. If it wasn't for this tunnel, I'd have gone out of my mind. Cheers."

"Cheers."

Eric drank with relish from the bottle, wiped the froth from his lips and hauled himself out of the hole. He reached down and grabbed his clothes before carefully replacing the wooden planks and treading them into place. As he flung himself into an armchair he flicked the rug back over the concealed entrance with his foot.

"We need to clean this place up a bit, the bloody mud's getting everywhere. A bit of a give away, eh?"

Tony stared at the ceiling and said nothing.

"What's the matter? You're not still angry with me over the other night are you?"

"Well …"

"Oh, come on Tony. The bastard can't have been out there for more than an hour. He was immediately taken to the sick bay at Ballaquane and I hear he's going to be sent to hospital on the mainland. He's fine. It was no worse a beating than I've dished out many times before. He'll have a few weeks taking it easy then he'll be as right as rain. Buck up, Tony, at least we've got rid of the sneak. Kept our little secret safe, didn't we? Cheers."

"No, it's not really that."

Eric scrutinized his friend carefully, he could usually guess what he was thinking, at least he used to be able to.

"You worrying about that letter?"

Tony looked away and shrugged his shoulders.

"I don't know what you expect. It doesn't necessarily mean anything's wrong. You can't seriously believe people love us, what with a war on and all that, but it doesn't mean they're having a go at Emily. Journalists are a bunch of Red sympathizers in the main, we've never had a fair hearing from them since Rothermere abandoned the good ship "Mosley" after Olympia back in 1934. Yellow's the word more than red."

Eric laughed to himself.

"The yellow press read by Reds."

He coughed violently, spraying beer across the room.

"Watch out, you bastard, what a waste."

Eric leaned forward in his chair and thumped himself on the chest.

"You're telling me. At least it brought a smile to your face."

Tony sat down in the other chair and raised his bottle.

"There's two more of these, let's get…tipsy."

"Good egg Tony, spiffing idea."

"Chin, chin."

They both drained their bottles and threw them on to the mattress in the corner. Sitting in silence, they could hear Ray whistling as he dug the garden.

"He never stops, does he?"

"He's a driven man."

"Aren't we all? Sit there, I'll get them."

Before Tony could move the back door slammed and Sid

rushed into the room. He was red-faced and could barely utter a word as he gasped for air.

"What ho, Sidney."

He raised his hand and looked pained as he struggled to speak.

"I'd say take your time, but I can see you're in a hurry," laughed Eric, "here take a seat."

Sid lowered himself gingerly into the chair, clutching his side.

"You're not going to bloody believe this."

Tony motioned with his hands.

"Believe what?"

"Stone me, you haven't a fag have you? I'm…"

"Gasping. No, get on with it."

"What's his name?"

Sid looked pleadingly at Tony and Eric, who stared back at him in blank incomprehension.

"Who?"

"Patrick, Pat, you know."

"What our Pat?"

"Yes, yes."

Sid was beginning to breathe normally again. He wiped his face with a sepia handkerchief and lay back with his eyes closed, his open mouth a gaping black hole in his flushed face. Eric shook his head in disbelief and looked over at Tony.

"Can you believe it, he's going to sleep? A bearer of important news and he nods off."

"Give me a bleeding chance. I've run all the way from the sodding prom, uphill an' all."

He opened his eyes and pulled himself upright.

"Did you know about this?"

He looked suspiciously at Eric.

"I wouldn't put it bloody past you."

"Know about what, for Christ's sake?"

Eric was becoming irritated.

"He's escaped."

"Pat?"

"Yes, Pat and two others."

Eric and Tony stared at Sid in astonishment.

"Are you sure?"

"Bloody positive mate, everybody's talking about it."

"When?"

"Today, after…"

"Who told you?"

"I heard it first from, what's his name, Bill Griffiths, but it's all over the camp."

There was silence as the news sank in. Sid was pleased that for once he had something over Eric, but it was not for long.

"Well, bugger me. He was here this morning and he said nothing. Who else?"

"No one we know – a Martin Quinn and Giles Halesoaken."

"How did they do it? Not another tunnel? They'll be all over the place if it was."

"Steady on, mate. No it wasn't. They were at that concert, you know, the one they have nearly every week at lunchtime in that little hall along the prom. After it finished the three of them had it away, 'cause they weren't there when they counted 'em back inside here."

Sid cackled to himself.

"Good on 'em I say, hope they make it."

"They'll have taken a boat, Pat always said he had one stashed away."

"Dunno about that, no one said nothing about a boat."

"Hold on, let me think. Where does this leave us?"

"With one less person digging…"

"Yeah, yeah. They'll step up security for sure and I'm a known associate of good old Pat. This is bloody awkward. Look we'd better stop all work till this blows over. I'm going to find out what the fuck's going on."

Eric angrily grabbed his clothes and began dressing.

"Tony, you come with me, Sid, you tidy things up here. Act as if nothing has happened. Oh, and tell Ray and the others when they get back, but keep it quiet, no arsing around on this one."

Grinning, Sid raised his hand in salute.

"Sir."

Eric lunged at Sid, then thought better of it, he was shaking and fumbled with the buttons on his shirt. He looked rattled.

"Sid, you get right up my nose sometimes."

"Oh ta very much, that's the last time I bloody make an effort for you."

"Eric, leave it. Come on, let's go. Here have a fag, it'll calm you down."

Glaring Eric took a cigarette from the battered tin Tony held out to him and thrust it into his mouth. Tony searched his pockets for a light, before noticing a box of matches sitting on the mantelpiece.

"One thing."

"Sid, don't push it."

"No, no wouldn't dream of it mate. No I was just going to say you should wash before you go out, mud 'n all that."

"Fuck, fuck, fuck."

Sid and Tony smiled at each other as Eric rushed out of the room. They heard him overhead seconds later, swearing and stamping around.

"Water pressure is low today, in fact it's fucking non-existent," said Sid with a wink.

Detainees thronged the camp entrance on the promenade opposite the Creg Malin hotel. A line of soldiers was keeping the gathering away from the gates, but was making no effort to disperse them. Tony and Eric could hear the excited babble of voices as they strolled down Walpole Road towards the sea front. They were smoking and trying to appear nonchalant, but both were agitated. Tony's heart was racing and he was unsure why. He couldn't see the problem; even if Pat was captured, he wasn't the type to say anything and Eric "associated" with a lot of people, so there was no particular reason to single him out. But his friend was worried and that was cause for concern. Eric's mood had darkened after they passed Pat's house. It was deserted, but a neighbour told them five or six guards had searched it thoroughly an hour or two before and taken away a suitcase. Eric had muttered, "So it's true then," and had not said a word since. They reached the edge of the crowd. Everybody was looking in the direction of the hotel. Tony tapped a spectator he vaguely recognized on the shoulder.

"Any news?"

The man turned round startled.

"Tony, you old…, you surprised me. He's in the hotel talking to Faulkner and the others. Supposed to be coming out any time now."

"Who is, Pat?"

"Pat? What are you talking about? No, that MP fellow, under-something at the Home Office."

"Osbert Peake," Eric cut in wearily.

"Yeah, that's the man. Here to see how we're all being treated."

"I'd completely forgotten he was coming. Not that many of us here though."

"Not surprising if people like you forget, is it? They've sent some lads off to see if they can drum up a few more."

"Other things on my mind, matey, here now though."

His eyes widened and he smiled maliciously, the man edged away. There was a cry and the company surged forward, pushing against the guards who held their ground. With a whoop Eric plunged ahead, elbowing his way to the front. On the other side of the wire, the doors of the Creg Malin had opened and a small group of smartly dressed men were standing on the steps looking across at the demonstration. A Brigadier was pointing something out to a small bespectacled man wearing a dark suit and a bowler hat. He was nodding his head, another man with a briefcase at his feet appeared to be taking notes.

"A bottle of C and S for anybody who knocks that bastard's hat off."

There was a loud cheer. The ministerial delegation moved towards the gate. A banner was unfurled at the back of the demonstration, a large white sheet with the words, "Mosley give us justice," daubed across it in black paint. As the gate swung open, prisoners screamed abuse and jostled with the soldiers.

"Jew, Jew, we don't want you here."

"Go home, we want justice, not visitors."

Tony hung back, wary of getting involved. His concerns, all-consuming only moments before, now seemed of no consequence, leaving only a sense of detachment.

"We want justice, we want fair treatment."

The chanting grew louder and the official party hesitated. Hurried words were exchanged between the Brigadier and the young Lieutenant in charge of the guards, the detainees sensed opportunity and rushed forward to the fence. Stones were thrown, and the Member of Parliament ducked behind the soldiers. Surrounded by the pushing and shoving rabble, Tony found himself drawn in. He began chanting.

"Justice, justice, justice."

The gates closed and were padlocked. The emissaries hurriedly retreated across the road to the sanctuary of the Creg Malin hotel. As they disappeared inside the large picture window in the front bay smashed sending a cascade of shattered glass showering onto the pavement. The prisoners were triumphant at their modest victory, jeering, shouting and shaking the wire.

Their quarry gone the line of demonstrators hard on the wire relaxed and broke away, splintering into small groups, heads turning, looking around, talking excitedly amongst themselves. The banner was hastily folded up and hidden, but the guards just gazed impassively from the other side of fence. Tony spotted Eric, his face flushed and hair disheveled, deep in conversation with Bill Griffiths. He held back. He would learn soon enough what was going on. The disturbance had alerted the whole camp and prisoners alone and in groups were moving down the hill towards the promenade. Others were hanging out of the windows of the houses on the front or gathering on the steps of the terrace. Tony sat down and leaned back against the fence, the soft sand drifting around his boots. It was another beautiful evening, outside the camp everything was tranquil. The sun, still high in the pale azure sky, was slowly sinking behind the hazy aqueous veil masking the horizon. The placid sea looked unnaturally green.

"This is the stuff of artists," mused Tony, "our struggle here in this tawdry world seems to amount to nothing more than swirling flecks of dust marring a masterpiece."

An urgent shout from near the gate silenced the mob. It was a rallying cry – in the lull a soaring raven cawed, harried by a flock of gulls. Men leapt to their feet, moved forward, pressing again along the barbed wire. There was a babble of expectation and prisoners craned their necks for a better view. Tony was caught up in the flow. The Creg Malin appeared deserted, the tall stained-glass entrance doors were barred, and nobody was visible at any of the windows. Glinting shards of jagged glass protruded from the flaking frame of the vandalized bay, a snagged curtain fluttering in the rising breeze. Tony jumped up, straining to see, his hands on the shoulders of the man in front of him.

"Hey, leave it out mate, will you."

An armed patrol could be seen in the distance marching towards the camp along Shore Road, there may have been civilians with them, Tony wasn't sure.

"What did you see? What's 'appening?"

"I don't know. I couldn't get a clear view. Saw some soldiers."

"What, reinforcements? They're looking for a bloody fight."

"No, there weren't enough of them to make any difference."

"Here do you mind mate, give me a leg up an' I'll see what I can see."

Tony bent down, cupping his hands together.

"There you go, put some of your weight on those in front."

The man peered keenly through the wire.

"It's them, it's the ones that escaped, they've been caught."

"Have they got all of them?"

"Looks like it. They weren't free for long were they?"

"Lucky old Faulkner, this gets his chestnuts out of the fire."

"How do they look? Can you see them?"

The clamour grew louder as the escapees and their captors drew nearer. The three prisoners, shuffling together in the centre of the party, had their hands tied behind their backs. All were dirty, their faces muddy and clothes torn, but demonstrators at the front, clinging to the wire, yelled out that they could see cuts and bruises.

"They ain't all there, there's only three of them. They've been done over right and proper by the looks of it, poor bastards."

Martin Quinn was limping, his body bent double. Giles Halesoken had a vivid scratch that was clearly visible across his right cheek and one of the arms of his jacket was missing. Pat Kenneally appeared unbowed by the ordeal, holding his head high and grinning. Their escort, on patrol all night, was tired and on edge. They had discovered the three men hiding among rocks on a remote beach five miles from the camp and it had taken them several hours to force-march their reluctant prisoners back to Peel. Disconcerted by the rowdy reception they were uncertain what to do next. The nervous soldiers taunted and gestured at the demonstrators while their Sergeant reported to the Creg Malin for orders.

"There's no escape for you bastards, you know that don't you? No escape."

"You dumb animals, you'll all pay."

"No escape, no escape."

The protestors' mood was hostile, goaded into a fury by the insults. The mood darkened further as another detachment of soldiers approached from the town at double-time, their boots drumming on the asphalt, they un-shouldered their rifles and formed up outside the gates. Captain Faulkner and Osbert Peake MP appeared on the steps of the Creg Malin to renewed abuse.

"Dispersing this bunch is going to be a problem, without using force. As I told you inside at this time in the evening, I have very few men in the camp, and those that are within the wire are heavily outnumbered and will keep well away from that crowd."

"Do what you have to man. This can't go on for much longer. Remember it's your responsibility to get things under control."

"Yes, Sir."

Anxious to reassert his authority, Faulkner barked out an order, the Sergeant ran back to his squad and the three captured men were dragged from the gate along Walpole Road. As they were about to disappear from view around the corner of the hotel, Pat Kenneally struggled free of his restraints, turned and shouted out in a broad Irish accent.

"We were done over lads, we were all beaten up."

His escort pulled him away, but his words did their damage. There was an answering roar from the crowd and missiles soared over the wire and ricocheted off the walls of the Creg Malin. A small determined band surged through the narrow gap between the fence and the end of the terrace and chased the prisoner escort, taunting them through the mesh. Shouted appeals for the demonstrators to calm down and disperse, that nothing had happened to the three escapees, were drowned out by whistles and catcalls. Swept forward, Tony was helpless in the crush, discomfort stoking his anger and he screamed in frustration.

Dusk was falling and the air shimmered in the dying light. The sky was stained with the cadaverous pinks and reds bleeding from a gash torn by the dipping sun. The sea mirror-calm flared yellow, magenta, and purple, the infernal glow mirrored in the windows of the Creg Malin and glinting off the newly laid barbed wire, un-ravaged by salt water.

"Get more stones will you, organize some of the lads."

Eric was yelling in Tony's ear. His face flushed and animated, he pointed up the hill.

"There's that wall at the back, that's half fallen down. Bring everything here that you can carry an' we'll give them something to think about."

Forcing his way out of the fray, Eric ran off, leaping the steps into the nearest house three at a time. He reappeared in the doorway before Tony had a chance to move, a dustbin lid in his hand. With a rapid flick of his arm he sent it spinning through the air, over the wire, above the heads of the guards, to land clattering on the cobbles in front of the hotel. He watched it settle and then with a whoop vanished inside the house.

"Yes sir," hissed Tony as he gestured at a couple of men who were standing next to him. "Let's get some ammunition. Grab that dustbin."

The ancient wall, its mortar perished, crumbled easily. The rough-edged lichen-covered bricks abraded scrabbling hands, choking dust lifting into the air. Below them in the gathering gloom they could just make out the convulsions of the excitable crowd and hear the shrill shouts and cries punctuating the hubbub of battle. The mayhem masked their approach as they dragged the half-filled bin back down the hill, then the perimeter lights flared into life, harshly illuminating the scene. Exposed they could see the prisoners massing on the front and others like them heading that way armed with makeshift weapons.

"Bugger me, this is getting out of hand," gasped one of the men hauling the bin as they stopped to catch their breath, "we'd better get a bloody move on."

Reaching the promenade they were engulfed in the mêlée, the bin dragged out of their hands and positioned close to the wire. A barrage of stones raked the Creg Malin. Every window on the floors facing the camp was smashed, shattered glass carpeting the road. A wooden lavatory seat sailed over the wire, hitting a soldier as he ran for the shelter of the hotel. He fell to his knees clutching his back, then scrambled unsteadily to his feet, skidding on the shards of glass, as he limped away. There were cheers. The other guards retreated out of range of the missiles to watch in safety, shielded by the falling darkness. Occasionally one would break ranks and retaliate, a stone arcing back over the wire, appearing from nowhere out of the black sky, sometimes harmlessly shattering into pieces on the cobbles, sometimes felling a protester. The screams of the injured, with bloodied heads and fractured limbs, were drowned out by the howling of the crowd and their broken bodies lay unremarked among the seething horde. The walking wounded meandered back from the wire to be treated on the open space behind the sea-front terrace where a bonfire had been set.

Havoc teased a pattern out of disorder and as the night deepened a routine settled upon the chaos. Scavenging parties, intent on destruction, swept across the camp, dismantling gardens, walls, buildings, returning with stones, bricks, and bottles to feed the mutual desire of the crowd for violence. Sated the rioters would surge along the wire, unleash a furious barrage, then fall back out of range, to mill around in the shadows, waiting, their hunger growing.

The commotion, raw and sustained, drew a vocal group of townspeople who gathered on the promenade beyond the Creg Malin. Soldiers tried to keep them away, but their anger spurred them forward.

"Fascists out. Traitors out. You are not wanted here."

Two figures, flat caps pulled tight shielding their eyes, scarves covering their mouths, leapt on to the wire, clinging there screaming insults at the detainees, before darting away. Their mock bravado saddened Tony. They were boys, fearless until someone snarled back, then they scurried away into the darkness. Not like the men he was locked up with, hard brutal thugs, who would have beaten their abusers to pulp given the opportunity.

Tony felt weary, disillusioned, he had to escape this misery – dig and dig and dig – was the only way. He stared through the wire, there was a lull, the demonstrators had temporarily dispersed and no one was close to him. He frowned and rubbed his eyes. In the shifting darkness at the extreme range of the perimeter lamps' sickly light, armed soldiers were lining up. Transfixed, he watched as they raised their rifles.

"Good God, they're going to fire."

Tony didn't cry out or dive for cover, but stood immobile. A small party of detainees was dragging a full dustbin towards the wire, shadowed by a grim-faced mob unaware guns were trained on them. Tony stepped back from the wire. He heard the order to fire, then the massive reverberations as one volley, then another, was loosed in rapid succession. Deaf to the shouts and screams Tony stood stock-still, hands covering his ears. Men fell to the ground around him and scrabbled panic-stricken in the dirt. Shocked to be uninjured, Tony believed everyone must be dead or seriously wounded, but as gun smoke wafted through the wire and the acrid smell of cordite pinched his nostrils, he watched dusty figures rise to their feet and run for cover.

"Attention, attention…"

Tony flinched. The disembodied, distorted voice continued.

"… in exchange for an end to the rioting the minister has agreed to meet a delegation of detainees to hear your grievances. You have ten minutes to consider this offer, before it is withdrawn. I repeat you have ten minutes then all disturbances must cease. Then, and only then, can discussions take place."

The announcement was repeated in the same rounded tones, before ending with an audible click. Silence settled over the camp.

"Tony, Tony."

He looked up, surprised, only vaguely aware of where he was. Eric and two others were crouched at the gates about thirty yards away and beckoning to him. It was clear what they wanted and Tony felt reluctant to get involved. He waved back at them, but didn't move. Eric's exasperated voice drifted over to him.

"Get over here Tony, will you, for Christ's sake."

Bill Griffiths he knew, the other man, Des Page, was someone he had seen around the camp but had never been introduced to. He shook their hands.

"The bloody delegation?"

"You've been co-opted mate, consider it an honour."

"Oh, I do, believe me."

"Could be history in the making here."

"Dafter things have happened I suppose. What next? Do we wave?"

"Here they come, they've seen us."

The Lieutenant was approaching from the Creg Malin,

escorted by three armed soldiers. His uniform was freshly ironed and his scrubbed face glowed in the artificial light.

"Are you the prisoner delegation?"

Eric pushed his face against the wire and brusquely asked who wanted to know. Taken aback the Lieutenant blurted out his name.

"Yes Davis, we are the official representatives of the British Union of Fascists' Peveril Camp branch. Interned illegally at His Majesty's pleasure. Take us to your boss."

"Hold on, I've been asked for your guarantees that there will be no more trouble. Do I have them?"

Eric looked at Bill Griffiths and gestured with his hand.

"You have our word…"

Lieutenant Davis stared quizzically at them through the wire.

"…that there will be no more trouble, while we're talking to the minister."

"Thank-you. Unlock the gate."

Muttering Bill turned away from the wire and raised his eyebrows.

"This must be how they behave in fucking public school."

A soldier stepped forward to unlock the heavy padlock and remove the chains. One slipped from his hands and rattled to the ground, he kicked it aside and opened the gate to allow the four men to pass through.

Tony felt self-conscious, sensing the many eyes watching them as they crossed the rubble-strewn street and climbed the steps of the Creg Malin Hotel. The black and white chequered tiles in the entrance hall were littered with multi-coloured shards from the damaged stained glass windows in the doors. The fragments splintered underfoot as the delegates entered the empty hotel lobby. They waited in silence before a small obsequious man in a dark blue smoking jacket appeared from a side door and with a few hushed words directed them up a short flight of stairs. The dining room had a high ceiling with ornate stucco cornices and three elaborate plaster roses each supporting a crystal chandelier, only one of which was illuminated.

During the day, the "Sunset Lounge" had clear views out over the bay, but the heavy velvet curtains drawn roughly across the windows suffused the space with a wan purple quality, oppressive after the airiness of the camp. There was a pungent smell of cooked cabbage and some of the tables were covered with dirty glasses, cutlery and dinner plates. Osbert Peake MP and Captain Faulkner were standing in the middle of the room, deep in conversation, when the Fascists were shown in. Eric and Bill stepped forward and were, without ceremony, ushered over to a table covered in a large white starched tablecloth. They sat down on the two chairs positioned on one side of the table.

"Gentlemen," the member of parliament gestured to Tony and Des, "find a chair and please be seated, we weren't expecting so many of you."

Pale blue eyes blinked myopically, his thick lenses gave the politician an expression of permanent astonishment. His thin angular face glistened under the refracted light from the chandelier directly above his head. He was immaculately dressed in a pin-stripe suit, a waistcoat with a gold watch and chain, paisley tie and wing collar and spoke with the assured clipped accent of the southern gentry. Tony had expected nothing less, but was exasperated at the boring inevitability of it all. As he sat down he could see Eric and Bill were feeling the same way. They were leaning back in their chairs and staring grimly ahead, their hands resting uneasily in their laps. Captain Faulkner, seated on the opposite side of the table, was rolling his swagger stick back and forth across the cloth and glowering at them. A vein pulsed rhythmically on his left temple and his upper lip would occasionally twitch. As Osbert Peake sat down beside him he shifted uneasily in his seat.

"Introductions, I think, would be appropriate before we get started. You know Captain Faulkner, Mr Prentice here…"

He motioned towards a tall thin, balding man standing beside him.

"… will take the minutes of the meeting. I'm Osbert Peake MP, Minister at the Home Office and representative of His Majesty's government. Now, who is your spokesman?"

Bill Griffiths glanced at Eric.

"I am."

He spoke with a broad Birmingham accent.

"Bill Griffiths, BUF National Inspector, this is Eric Baines, BUF District leader for West Ham, Tony Cox, the Party's District Leader for Blackpool and Des Page, District Leader for Derby."

As Bill Griffiths gestured at each man in turn he exposed damp stains under his arms and he wheezed when he spoke. He had lost weight in the camp and his clothes hung loosely on his body. Suffering from a permanent head cold, he felt feverish and light-headed, his confident nature depressed.

"Tea anybody before we get down to the serious business?"

Captain Faulkner snorted contemptuously, but said nothing. The others nodded.

"Fine. Now what exactly is the problem? I am here to listen and do what I can for you. But you must understand my position. There is a war on, so there is a limit to what is possible."

"There are three areas of concern. The first and most immediate is the condition and treatment of the three escapees. They've been beaten up and not given any food."

Captain Faulkner could barely contain himself.

"Now listen here, my soldiers have mistreated no one. I'll not have this from you lot. If people escape they have to face the consequences. It's just not good enough."

"Thank you Faulkner. Let's deal with this one here and now. I do not believe you gentlemen are correct."

Eric hit the table with his fist.

"We saw them with our own eyes. They looked in a bad way. How can you…"

Osbert Peake raised his hand.

"But, let me finish. I will interview the prisoners myself first thing tomorrow morning to ensure they are in a good state of health. As to food, Faulkner here will arrange for something to be sent to them now. Do it Captain."

Faulkner got rapidly to his feet, his chair almost toppling over and left the room. He could be heard angrily barking orders in the next room.

"Go on."

"Our main concern is the legal basis of our detention. When we were arrested we were promised reviews of our legal position, some sort of appeal procedure. This hasn't happened for most of us. It's just not bloody fair."

Osbert Peake sat back in his chair, twisting one of his cufflinks and smiled.

"This Gentlemen is, I sense, the nub of the issue."

He was about to go on when a waiter in an immaculately starched white jacket appeared at the door to the kitchen and coughed loudly.

"Ah tea, bring it here, please."

Nobody said a word as the waiter approached the table with his rattling tray of teacups.

"Put it down over there. Prentice will be mother. I hope there's plenty of hot water?"

The waiter nodded and lifted the lid on a large silver jug, releasing a cloud of steam.

"Thank-you."

Prentice got disconsolately to his feet.

"Milk everyone?"

The waiter backed away, almost colliding with Captain

Faulkner who had returned to the room. Apologizing profusely he turned and scurried through the swing doors into the kitchen. Sipping at his tea, Osbert Peake looked across the table at each member of the BU delegation.

"Gentlemen, I'm sure I don't need to remind you of the conditions of your internment. We are at war. You have been legally detained under Defence Regulation 18B."

Eric moved to object but was silenced by Bill Griffiths, who placed a hand on his arm. This was acknowledged by a nod from the minister, who went on.

"We have a perfect legal right to hold you here until we see fit to release you. Indeed, I feel I can be frank with you. For some, not necessarily those in this room, although I don't know your cases well enough, that will mean until the end of hostilities and maybe beyond. Mr Page you look shocked, but face facts, you are all members of an illegal organization deemed a threat to the state."

"Hold on here, that's surely up for debate?"

"No, Mr Baines, I'm afraid it's not. What is up for debate is the culpability of individuals, how involved they were. How much of a security risk would they be if released. That is the only area for discussion, not the nature of the British Union, which is a traitorous political party, pure and … "

Eric stood up and leaned across the table, desperately searching for the words to articulate his rage, without appearing to lose his temper. Captain Faulkner leapt up and began poking him on the shoulder with his swagger stick.

"Sit down both of you."

The MP's voice echoed round the room. He stared at Eric until he reluctantly returned to his seat.

"I can see you would benefit from a few basic facts before we go on."

He delicately took another sip of tea and wiped his mouth with his pocket-handkerchief.

"You have all been interned for over a year. You'll be somewhat out of touch with life in the rest of the country. I'm not going to make any bones about this. You are traitors and that is not something you can argue away, try as you might. That is how you are seen and I suspect that time will only confirm this impression. If you get letters from your families you will probably have gathered that life is not easy for them."

Tony winced and closed his eyes.

"Mr Cox obviously understands what I'm talking about. Government is of the people, for the people and in wartime morale is everything, even more important than justice, to be brutally frank."

As he was speaking he took off his glasses and wiped them with his handkerchief. He hesitated to breathe on the lenses, then looked up blindly and went on.

"Irrespective of any intelligence reports on the threats posed by the British Union and Mr Mosley, something I won't be going into here. One of the main reasons you were all locked up was to satisfy a public hunger for action. It was a tense period for us, some sort of action was needed. It was believed morale would suffer if nothing was done. And again to be brutal, nothing much has changed. There have been rumblings from the odd politician, invariably on the left, and from a few legal minds on the right but generally there isn't a great deal of pressure to move rapidly on this one. To sum up, to let you all out en masse would not be politically acceptable to most people at this particular time. And you should be aware that reckless actions like we've seen this evening also doesn't help, you saw how the good people of Peel reacted. They are not alone."

"But what are we supposed to do? Your attitude is just typical. I can't believe what I've been hearing."

Bill's face was flushed and blotchy.

"You've said nothing to make us stop."

Captain Faulkner laughed out loud, but then spoke in a voice that was low and calm.

"I'll stop you. Understand that. There's been enough pussy-footing around on this one, in my humble opinion."

"Bastard," muttered Eric gazing through half-hooded eyes across the table at the officer.

"More tea anyone? Prentice do the honours will you, there's a good chap."

Osbert Peake put his hands together and leaned forward in his chair. Bill Griffiths was forced to do the same to catch what he was saying.

"There's something I can do. But you have to do something for me. There's absolutely no excuse for this riot and it must cease or it will be stopped by force. Is that clear? If it's not, then we can go no further."

Bill nodded.

"Good. You are perfectly right there is an appeals procedure. My good friend Mr Norman Birkett chairs an Advisory Committee, which has been meeting every week for the last year looking into this very issue. I know for a fact that a number of detainees from here have appeared before the Committee."

"Yes, but none of them got off."

"That, Mr Page, is the nature of an appeals procedure."

"It's a bloody fix. There's no legal representation or nothing."

"That is true, but Mr Birkett and his committee are all distinguished barristers with a vast experience of dealing with such cases. Let me assure you a good many people who have appeared before them have subsequently been released. It is far from being the fix that you claim it is."

"But …"

"The Advisory Committee is all there is. I am not here to negotiate about the legal procedures. What I am prepared to do is this. I will ensure that the cases of all BU members at Peel are brought to the attention of the Committee and I will recommend that all those deemed suitable for review are dealt with as quickly as possible. It also goes without saying that your individual cases will be sympathetically reviewed as soon as I return to London next week. Believe me Gentlemen, I have no desire to see men detained any longer than is absolutely necessary."

"Why should we believe you?"

"Well Gentlemen…I give you my word. Do you need time to discuss this amongst yourselves?"

"No, I don't think so."

Bill Griffiths looked first at Eric, who nodded, and then at his other two colleagues. Tony thought he looked worn out, defeated, but said nothing.

"Fine, your little demonstration ends and after an appropriate period privileges will be restored. Captain Faulkner, I recommend that period is not of too long a duration. I, in turn, will interview the escapees within the next few hours and secondly, instigate a review of the cases of BU detainees here at Peel. You said when you arrived there were three issues you wanted to discuss."

"No, no that's all."

"Well, Gentlemen, I won't say it's been a pleasure, but I'm glad to have resolved this so amicably."

He got to his feet and reached across the table, shaking hands rapidly with each of the detainees. His hand felt cool and clammy and Tony sensed that they'd been cheated in some indeterminate way.

"It's him isn't it," he thought, "we've put our trust in that balding bureaucrat. God, I've got to keep digging."

"Gentlemen, your escort awaits."

The minister gestured towards the door, a smile of smug self-satisfaction creasing his face. There was the sound of boots rasping across the tile floor and seconds later the door opened to reveal a squad of soldiers standing to attention at the top of stairs leading to the hotel lobby. Tony dejectedly got to his feet and out of habit pushed his chair under the table.

"Delegates of the British Union…"

Surprised he looked up. Eric and Bill Griffiths were standing to attention a foot away from the table, their arms rigid by their sides, facing Osbert Peake and Captain Faulkner, who looked on quizzically.

"Attention…"

Tony snapped smartly into line with the others and then watched with immense satisfaction as the expression on the Minister's face changed to one of open distaste as they raised their arms in the fascist salute. Seconds passed in stunned silence, Tony's spirits soared, he felt exultant.

"About turn…"

Eric's voice boomed around the dining room.

"Quick march."

Chapter 9
PIECE OF ETERNITY
8th September 1995

It was a beautiful evening. A sheen hung over the city blunting the sharp edges of buildings and obscuring their detail. Shapes were smeared and the atmosphere benign. Pine scented the air, its piquancy tempered by the faint lingering aroma of coal dust. The distant age of steam, its tracks long abandoned, indelibly imprinted on the landscape.

The raised embankment, clinker-strewn, was now a public footpath. It ran wild and untended for several miles through a maze of north London Victorian terraces and thirties semis before coming to an abrupt end at a boarded up tunnel, its crumbling length and treacherous drainage too hazardous for walkers to explore. Where trains used to run three times an hour each way, people now exercised their dogs and themselves, couples walked hand in hand, occasionally passing from sight down the overgrown banks, joggers would run from the park to the tunnel and back in the early morning and early evening. A constant traffic, but one could nonetheless find solitude, appreciate the urban panorama laid out before you and listen to the birds and the rustling in the undergrowth.

David had been a regular visitor in recent weeks. He had found a place that suited him, sitting on a cushion of pine needles at the foot of a tall conifer. It was well away from the path, about halfway down the slope on one of the steepest sections of the embankment. Completely hidden by burgeoning hawthorn and elder bushes he would stare through the gently shifting leaves at the back of a tall four-storied terraced house. He had a clear view into all the windows at the rear of the building, except the two on the top floor – one of the kid's bedrooms most likely. He watched the family eat their evening meal in the kitchen on the ground floor, which opened through a pair of large patio doors onto the well-tended garden. He followed them up the stairs to the living room, where they watched television. Up another flight to the master bedroom where the wife would change out of her work clothes, before returning to the kitchen to load the dishwasher and read the paper, listening to the radio. She appeared to say very little to her husband. The couple went to bed before eleven most weekdays, more often than not at different times. David was sure they made love infrequently. He wasn't there all the time of course, but he was confident he had their measure. The routine nature of their lives surprised David at first but then became reassuring. He noted every significant activity on a little pad in neat block letters and after a few weeks felt he could predict what they were going to do next, most of the time.

Tonight was Friday. The two teenage children would be going out very soon. One of them was in the bathroom, the other had been hammering on the door and yelling for her to hurry up – he could hear everything clearly through the open windows. They would be away from the house until the early hours of the morning. The wife had already left for her evening class, probably aerobics or something like that, judging by the colourful leggings she wore and the sports bag she slung jauntily over her shoulder in the bedroom before leaving. She never returned before 10 o'clock. David thought that most likely she had a drink after the class with friends, but secretly hoped she was having an affair. That left Larry Beckinsale. He would be in all evening, probably open a bottle of wine and carry it up to the living room, where he would sit in a large armchair close to the picture window overlooking the garden and watch television or read until his wife came home.

There was exactly three weeks to go until David was formally made redundant. All the appeals procedures had been exhausted. One of his colleagues from the department had been relocated elsewhere in the company, the rest were out. Some were receiving redundancy pay, but he was getting nothing. His case had been taken up by the Union, but they hadn't achieved anything.

David hated the person he could see sitting relaxed and untroubled less than one hundred and fifty feet away from him. He loathed Larry Beckinsale with a passion he found difficult to articulate. To think about him, which he did most of the time, left him enraged. He was frightened at the prospect of violence, doing damage, but could barely contain his feelings, unable to suppress the urge to do the man harm. Spying on the Beckinsales helped calm his nerves and focus his thoughts. He had tried to threaten them, shake their complacency with anonymous phone calls, but they hadn't had the desired effect on the smug family, hadn't impinged on their safe little world. The daughter had told him in no uncertain terms, the second time he had rung at one-thirty in the morning, "to fuck off and die, you pathetic wanker." David's wife, Susan, had overheard him phoning, and asked who the hell he was calling at that time of night. She had not believed David when he had said the talking clock and had accused him of seeing someone. It was the first time, but not the last, that she had slept in the spare bedroom. So David had stopped the silent phone calls. Heavy breathing in his own hallway was not, he had discovered, the cure for his particular malaise.

The idea of stalking his foe had come to David by chance. He was late leaving the office one evening, having stayed on to print out a few extra copies of his curriculum vitae, when he saw Larry Beckinsale in front of him as he came out of the lift. David's first thought, that "the bastard will be waiting for his limo to take him home," proved to be wrong and Larry had set off up the hill towards the underground station on foot. David was going that way anyway and pausing briefly to let some distance open up between them, followed him. For a vague reason, that he didn't fully understand, he decided to keep him in his sights. It dawned on David as he followed Larry slowly through the milling rush-hour crowds that he ought to, at the very least, know where he lived. It seemed a useful piece of intelligence to have at the time and the thought of shadowing him was appealing. Deliberately, he sought out the shaded anonymity of the shop fronts and flitted from doorway to doorway, but the subterfuge was unnecessary as Larry never looked round. David had to speed up as his mark disappeared into the underground station and he only just caught sight of him as he walked down the escalator to the Victoria line. Running to catch up he collided with a commuter, causing the woman to drop her briefcase, and stopped to apologize.

He burst onto the crowded platform and realized he was standing directly behind his target. Slowly, scarcely breathing, he drew back, sidling away until he was masked by a group of schoolboys, arguing about football. The exhilaration of the chase was strangely compulsive – his heart raced as he waited for the next tube to arrive and he rocked back and forth on the balls of his feet. He felt alive.

The train was packed, perfect cover for David, who, concealed by the crowd, made sure that Larry was always in view. The man was holding onto the vertical handrail in the middle of the carriage and staring at the legs of a young women sitting below him. His gaze was lascivious and relentless. She shifted uneasily in her seat, sensing the violation, but did not look up. David, watching as the object of his hatred openly demeaned himself, was filled with voyeuristic pleasure.

The crowd thinned out at each stop as they headed north. David was constantly forced to subtly shift position in order to hide behind the remaining passengers. Suddenly, Larry Beckinsale was gone. David lunged forward, elbowing a young man out of the way, and caught the door as it began to close. Pushing himself on to the platform, he shouted out an apology and set off after his quarry whose head and shoulders he could clearly make out above the threading crowd heading for the exit.

The run down, litter-strewn, streets around the station soon gave way to wider, cleaner, leafier avenues lined with newer, more expensive cars. The large Victorian houses were nearly all well kept and the odd skip full of building rubble pointed to the upward mobility of the area.

"No net curtains round here. Should be easy to spy on what everyone gets up to," thought David as he closed in on Larry Beckinsale. His prey appeared oblivious to everything going on around him and David was feeling more confident. He vaguely knew where he was, he'd lived nearby in a small flat with Susan before they'd got married and they'd used to walk around this neighbourhood fantasizing about the houses they would own when they were rich and successful. Fat chance of that now.

Larry went up to the front door of a tall Edwardian house – black and white chequer-board tiled pathway, grey front door with stained glass surrounds, double bay windows – that David and his wife would have been only too happy to have owned, and let himself in. David walked past and then backtracked on the opposite side of the road, peered briefly through the hedge in front of the house, noted the number – 77 – and then moved on, satisfied. He had discovered that the house backed on to the old railway line on his second visit, having found it impossible to stay away from the area once he knew where his adversary lived. He felt driven to uncover as much information as he could about the man, with initially only an indeterminante feeling about how it might be useful.

The houses all looked the same from the embankment at the rear and it had taken him a while to establish which was number 77. He had a clear view into the back gardens from the footpath and he deliberately counted off the houses one by one. He had been careful, as he didn't want to draw undue attention to himself, in what was a "neighbourhood watch" area. On his second attempt he was confident he'd worked it out, when to his surprise Larry appeared in the next-door garden in a pair of cutoff shorts and an Hawaiian shirt and began setting up a barbecue. David ducked behind a bush, then slithered down the bank. He had discovered his vantage point in the shadow of the pine tree and immediately felt at ease. Time had slipped by as he watched fascinated as his enemy relaxed in full view, unaware that he was being observed. For the first time since the trouble at work had begun, David felt the scales tip in his favour. Knowledge was power after all. His resolve had never wavered after that and he returned to spy on Larry Beckinsale and his family, at every opportunity.

His wife queried where he was at first, but seemed to accept his excuses that he was working late trying to find a new job, meeting with prospective employers, drinking with old friends working elsewhere in the business, networking, and never asked again. She was often in bed when he came home and he would sit downstairs in the dark with a bottle of beer, brooding about what he should do, his dark mood calling for a cathartic act of retribution, an explosion of outrage. So absorbed was he in this violent fantasy world, cast free of any rational restraint, that he found to his puzzlement, as he awoke with a start at dawn one morning, that the boundaries between sleeping and waking were becoming blurred, that he could no longer differentiate between invention and truth. Larry Beckinsale was an obsession, haunting his dreams and dogging every conscious moment. No firm decision was ever made, no strategy actively formulated, a plan just slowly took shape, coagulating in the rich broth of his boiling imagination. David knew he would take measures to right the injustice that had been done to him, that was a self-evident truth. He had the template for action, it was there documented in black and white, the folly of the man, trapped by the foolish routine of his life. They were both incapable of escape.

The pine bark felt harsh, unyielding to his hesitant, probing fingers. A sudden sharp pain made him gasp. There was blood on his hands and he tentatively tasted it, his tongue flicking between dry chapped lips. He looked up. The sky, dimly visible through the dense mixed tree canopy, appeared to be darkening, light draining away. A couple talking loudly, arguing, passed along the path above him.

"I don't care if you say you never slept with the guy, he acts as if you did and that's what bug…"

"For Christ's sake, he's an arsehole, how many more times. He's just playing on your insecurity."

"Yes, but that doesn't get away from the fact that you really want to fuck…"

Their voices ebbed, drowned out by the distant sound of a police siren.

"Time to go."

David stood up and brushed the seat of his trousers. The material felt damp. For an instant he was distracted, peering round to see the extent of the problem, but immediately lost interest and stared intensely down the slope. The bank fell away sharply and towering clumps of verdant vegetation blocked his way. Thickets of sycamore saplings, strained towards the light, while contorted tangled bursts of brambles clung to the steepest sections of the embankment, claiming space with their long barbed tendrils. There was a rickety fence at the bottom of the bank that marked the boundary with the Beckinsale's garden and David could make out the darker green stands of nettles growing profusely in the damp ground. He would have to be careful and tread warily.

A thin trunk bent dramatically under his weight as his feet slipped in the slack shifting soil. He grabbed another to steady himself and then another to lower himself down the slope until he stood waist high in nettles, peering through a crack in the old wooden fence, where a slat had come loose. Nobody had noticed him, the air was unchanged, he could hear the drone of the television and see Larry sitting in his armchair through the large open picture window. Suddenly aware of a stinging pain across his lower legs – the lightweight linen of his summer suit no protection against the nettles – he bent down to rub his burning skin.

"Shit, that hurts."

The air was clammy in the overshadowed hollow behind the fence and smelled of dank decay. Clouds of midges, attracted by the heat of his body, swarmed across David's face, catching in his hair and swirling around his nose and mouth.

"Oh God."

Flailing his arms brought only temporary relief, the insects rising above his head, before descending in growing numbers, assaulting ears, eyes and nostrils. He looked up at the house. Larry Beckinsale had not moved. About ten feet away from where he was standing, right in the corner of the garden, David saw that one of the fence panels had come loose and was propped up against a concrete post. There was a space at the bottom large enough for him to squeeze through, and he would be hidden from the house by a large flowering shrub. He knew he could turn back, but he had no reason to, he didn't have a definite plan.

The rest was easy. Keeping constant watch on the back of Larry's blond head silhouetted against the window, David crawled into the garden, crossed the lawn, hesitated for a moment before silently sliding open the kitchen doors and stepping inside.

Chapter 10

RIGHT REVEREND

3rd December 1972

"Good morning, Mrs. Owen I'm glad you could make it to the service. You're obviously feeling better?"

"Yes vicar, thank you very much. I hope I'll see you next Sunday."

"If not I'll come to see you the following week, Mrs. Owen, goodbye to you."

The old lady slowly made her way down the brick path towards the church gate, clutching a knobbed walking stick in one hand and the arm of her young niece in the other. As the Reverend Anthony Coxon-Dyet was about to turn away, she raised the stick and waved farewell.

"Game old bird," thought Anthony, "If I'm like her when I reach that age I'll be doing well."

The service had passed off without any interruptions. Things appeared to be returning to normal. "Thank God," mused the vicar as he turned to head back into the church. Suddenly he changed his mind and stood staring out across the churchyard, where the last of the previous night's harsh frost was melting in the bright winter sun.

"It really has been a nightmare," Anthony mused to himself. "If I was younger I'd have been more careful, and I still haven't heard from the Bishop. He won't be pleased, not after the last time."

The previous Sunday the church had been filled with reporters and photographers – the best congregation St Botolph's had seen in years – and after matins he had been pestered for interviews, statements, photographs, in the church, outside in the graveyard, clutching the parish magazine, sitting on a gravestone. It had become very undignified, much as he enjoyed the controversy.

"A little too much spice is not good for anybody, so sayeth the Right Reverend Archibald Jenkins, Bishop of said diocese. What a prig. I can hardly wait to go and see him."

He could clearly hear the senior clergyman's pompous over-modulated voice.

"I fought in the last war to defend freedom of speech Anthony, but there are responsibilities that go with it, particularly for someone in your position. Please, old boy, let's have no more trouble. A little local difficulty is not a problem but the nationals. Come now, see it from my point of view. Dickie won't be pleased and you know things are, how shall we put it, a little tricky for me with Lambeth Palace at the moment. Team players are what I'm looking for. A few years of calm that'll see you and me to retirement are what I want. Come on humour me, Anthony ... Tony? Good man. What are you having?"

A magpie settled on a headstone, its tail bobbing urgently, then sailed into the air with a harsh shriek. Anthony smiled, life really was playing tricks on him. He fondly believed that every Sunday, at this time, after Morning Prayers were over, he would stroll round the churchyard and visit the grave of his late wife, Emily. He knew, however, and this was what was amusing him, that this happened less and less often these days. "Why?" was a good question, one a vicar should address, guilt or the lack of it being one of his areas of expertise. But not now, today he would make amends and pay her a call.

Emily was buried on the edge of the cemetery, in one of the furthest points from the church. Her resting place was overshadowed by a line of tall lime trees, which in the summer dappled the area in a bright green and yellow light and showered the gravestone with a sticky resin, that, over the years, had all but obliterated the rough-hewn inscription: Emi…Cox…Dy..t, Born 191…, …ed 196…, ..oving w… of th.. …end Anthony … …t.

Parishioners in the past had tried to scrub the stone clean, but it had achieved very little, and he'd told them not to bother. It appealed to his sense of the order of things to let her memorial on earth fade away as his own memory of her dimmed. Now, if he forgot his glasses he could read very little of her epitaph. At this time of year, the trees were bare and there were views from her grave across an open expanse of undulating pasture that stretched from the churchyard to a wooded ridge about a mile or so in the distance. A low brick wall marked the boundary of the graveyard and it was possible to get into the field through a small wooden gate, built with massive black iron hinges and a spring, far too powerful for its size, that would slam the gate shut if it was released too soon. Summertime in the church grounds was marked by the irregular sound of the banging of the back gate as visitors were caught unawares. On fine days, Anthony used to lean on the gate and stare out at the cows and sheep grazing on the lush grass, the rooks roosting noisily around their nests in the tall trees and think about nothing specific. The past would frequently occupy him, things that he had done, people he had known, rehashing decisions made, reappraising relationships, reordering events. Such reflections involved convoluted lines of argument, with connections and assumptions constantly shifting, but he managed, most of the time, to usher himself into a realm of contentment with the life he had led, tinged inevitably with a feeling of having got away with it, of surprise. And the Reverend Coxon-Dyet was sensitive enough to appreciate that self-satisfaction was dangerous territory for a priest to stray into. If disturbed, he would turn with a pained, distracted look on his face, the front of his clothes smudged with the powdery green algae that covered the leeward side of the old gate.

Today he went to sit on the wall, the chill of the bricks seeping rapidly through his thin overcoat and trousers. He had a direct line of sight from there to his church, where he had been the vicar for over twenty years, and he wanted to check the state of repair of the roof. There had been a number of leaks recently in the sacristy and transept and the Parochial Council was to meet that week to discuss the options. It was not as clear a vantage point as he remembered – much of the roof of the nave was obscured by the dark sullen bulk of two ancient yews, their branches saturated in gold from the late morning sun and shimmering in the light breeze. Looming above these evergreen crowns was the flint tower of St Botolph's, glinting in the glorious brightness. A flock of pigeons swept out of the black louvers of the belfry and banked steeply upwards across the pale blue face of the clock, its crimson hands halted permanently at five to twelve.

"Only a few minutes slow."

Anthony smiled, glancing at his watch.

"Emily would have found that funny."

He absentmindedly kicked at the ground in front of him rubbing his hands as he watched a small cloud of dust rise up then settle gently on the toe of his brown suede shoes. Distant voices made him look up.

On the paved path that ran round the churchyard a man in a dark overcoat was leaning over a hunched figure in a wheelchair and tucking a red and black check blanket around his legs.

Anthony smiled at them and waved, then looked again at the church. He hoped it wasn't the copper cladding on the north aisle that was letting in water, that would cost a fortune to mend and any patch would take years to weather back to match the stained turquoise wonder of the present roof. The aesthetics would be ruined. If there was one thing he truly loved about the church it was the vibrant blue flashes that ran the length of the nave and could be seen from miles around in clear weather. Frustration with the deteriorating fabric of the building and what he considered a dereliction of duty on the part of the Parochial Council was a recent grievance of his. It was closely associated in his mind with a deepening appreciation, as he aged, of his fortunate position. In the past, when he had been less settled, he had been more phlegmatic. But not now.

"The philistines on the council probably won't even stump up for copper to do the repairs, the bastards."

He relished the intensity of his feelings, burnishing his anger at every perceived slight and material failing, collating a mental compendium of wrongs that formed the substrate for his subsequent actions. Lately, he feared he might be overwhelmed by the parish and its many demands and was determined not to let that happen, but he was getting old and he needed that core set of justifications from which to draw strength. His last escapade with the parish magazine had been effective publicity for St Botolphs, perhaps a little less good for him personally. Thinking first rather than doing was now the order of the day, for the time being at least. Emily had been right, he should have kept a diary, it would have helped. If he'd written things down, everything, not just what had happened to him, the events of his life, but what he had really thought. If he'd kept nothing back, perhaps he could have forgotten more, safe in the knowledge it wasn't lost. Emily had been right about a lot of things, thinking back.

Smiling vacantly, he looked around as the young man approached, pushing the creaking wheelchair with difficulty along the narrow gravel track.

"It's easier if you stick to the main path, the graveyard can be a bit rough I'm afraid. Not ideal for anything on wheels. Shall I give you a hand to turn around?"

Anthony eased himself off the wall, dusted his hands, and nodded at the elderly man slumped in the wheelchair.

"Lovely day isn't it, although a bit on the nippy side."

The man's head lolled loosely to one side, and saliva dribbled from the corner of his mouth, yet he stared fixedly at Anthony with unblinking blue eyes. A gloved hand tapped repeatedly on the arm of the wheelchair and his legs moved restlessly beneath the blanket.

"Here let me."

Anthony bent down to grab hold of the chair.

"Leave it alone," the younger man said curtly. Anthony withdrew, taken aback at the tone of his voice, "There's no need to bother."

Anthony straightened up, surprised. The older man in the wheelchair was nodding his head vigorously and trying to speak, but as he grew increasingly agitated was having difficulty enunciating his words. Placing a hand gently on his shoulder, the young man spoke softly,

"Easy Grandad, I understand, calm down, there's plenty of time."

Taking a tissue from his pocket he wiped his grandfather's mouth and looked at Anthony.

"It's you we've come to see. You are the Reverend Anthony Coxon-Dyet?"

Anthony nodded.

"They told us we'd find you out here. This your wife?"

He spoke with a mild Birmingham accent. He was rather

a good-looking boy, Anthony thought, tall with brown, wavy, shoulder length hair, parted in the middle, piercing blue eyes like his elderly relative and long pale fingers that clutched the handle of the wheelchair. The pair of them looked very similar, long thin faces, with fine features, the only real differences were the wrinkles and receding grey hair of the invalid.

"Yes, yes it is."

Anthony couldn't stifle his annoyance, the last thing he needed was some convoluted sob story that would take up most of the afternoon. He was already dreaming up an excuse that would allow him to get away. It was uncharitable, he knew, but he felt he could justify it on the grounds that they had not got off to a good start, and he wasn't inclined to give them a second chance.

"Look, I'm very sorry, I have to dash, a parishioner has invited me to lunch and then I have to prepare for Evensong. Nice to have met you, goodbye."

"Wait, you can't treat us like this, we've come a long way and my Grandfather's a sick man."

"Look, I've said I'm sorry. There really is no need to take that tone with me. I'll be only too willing to see you if you make an appointment, even though you're not one of my flock. By the way have you tried your own priest? I can't drop everything just to suit you. I really have got to dash."

A car passed the church and blew its horn, sending the flock of pigeons circling the belfry once again. There was silence. The young man stared morosely at Anthony while patting his Grandfather on the shoulder.

"Fine? Goodbye."

Anthony moved to edge past the wheelchair, when he was grabbed firmly by the arm.

"Excuse me, that hurt."

"You haven't even asked who we are or what we want."

"Let go of my arm, now."

Reluctantly the man loosened his grip, but didn't let go.

"No bloody manners, that's the trouble with you. Must be a real comfort to your flock, as you call them, Baaaaaa."

Anthony angrily shook his arm free.

"Young man, that's absolutely no way to speak to me. If you think you're being clever then you're mistaken. I feel sorry for your Grandfather."

"So you bloody should. That's why we're here."

"Whatever you want I've no time for this. I can see your Grandfather is very sick, but …"

"Shut up."

"That was uncalled for."

"Shut up and listen, you're upsetting him."

Anthony turned and began to walk back towards the church, the gravel crunching beneath his feet. High above he noticed the fraying white slipstream of an aircraft. His chest was aching and he had an unpleasant taste in his mouth, but he was feeling calmer as he congratulated himself on not losing his temper. Suddenly there was an animal sound, a roar, of commanding intensity that spun him round. The two men hadn't moved and were staring at him. He almost ran back towards them.

"What's going on? What are you playing at? You can't carry on like this."

The young man smiled malevolently.

"My Grandfather's name is Albert Chalmers."

The name meant nothing to Anthony and he stared quizzically at the men.

"You don't remember him. Typical isn't it, Grandad, must piss you off, eh?"

He looked away, shook his head and then with a look of utter contempt he screamed at Anthony.

"You bloody well should, you fucker. You did this to him. You made him like he is."

Anthony stared open-mouthed, shocked. It was there in an instant, the sweat, the sandy concrete floor, the crunching, sickening blows, Eric's dead eyes.

"You a priest, I can't fucking believe it. How could you? Standing face to face with you, it's no easier to understand. I still don't bloody get it."

His words spilled out in a confusion of anger and hatred, and he turned and hugged his Grandfather. Anthony lowered himself onto an old weathered timber bench – "In loving memory of Jocasta Evans, who loved this place, 1943" – which moved unsteadily beneath him. He stared at the man in the wheelchair, but recognized nothing, the eyes, nose, hair, were totally unfamiliar. Even after all these years surely there would be something. He began to feel there might be some mistake, that this was not true. It was a misunderstanding. He smiled, tried to move and say something. Then his optimism faded, overwhelmed, he gasped out loud. The young man turned to look at him. Anthony realized he had never known Albert Chalmers, had never met him, never spoken to him, never seen his un-bloodied face, would never, ever recognize him. Yet he knew this was the man he had held in his arms in that basement. He knew it was true.

"What are you talking about? This is ridiculous. I don't know where you get such terrible ideas from."

He leaned back, throwing his arm over the side of the bench, and looked straight past the crippled man in the wheelchair. He didn't want to have to deal with this, he had buried it too deep. He believed in the Resurrection, or at least he told himself he did. That was the glorious day he would face up to his past deeds, not now, this was like digging someone up – Emily on her deathbed flashed before his eyes – disinterring them before their time. His faith would see him through. The belief that he could hide from anything, lie, dissemble, cheat, fight the good fight and vanquish the bloodied foe. Anthony winced.

"What a load of fucking bullshit. I can't believe you're a man of the cloth."

The words hung in the air. Anthony couldn't be sure he hadn't spoken his thoughts out loud and smiled grimly. The young man sneered at the priest.

"You can tell by your bloody face you know what I'm talking about. Look at that Grandad, a guilty man if you ever saw one."

Albert Chalmers grunted in acknowledgement as his agitated body slumped forward, his head almost touching his knees.

"Take a good look, you did this. He's been in a wheelchair ever since the war. His condition has got worse if anything. You bastards. And he was one of your lot as well."

"I had no … What makes you think it was me?" Anthony said weakly.

"Oh my God, he fucking recognized you. He's been searching all his life for the men that did this. Him, his daughter, my mother and me, the whole family have been involved. He's not always like this you know, he can be quite lucid at times, talks a lot and is quite easy to understand if you're tuned in."

"What do you mean recognized me?"

"The bloody newspapers, you've been all over them with your "Mosley had the right idea on Europe" comments. Bloody clever, if you ask me. Couldn't resist it after all these years could you? Suits me, you breaking cover like that. I was beginning to believe we'd lost you. Gone to ground, deep cover somewhere. Well fuck me I can tell you. It was bloody deep. A fucking vicar and one living and working not too far away from where we live. You could have knocked me down, but we've got you now. Revenge will be sweet I can tell you."

"Hold on a minute…"

"There'll be no holding on to anything mate, believe me."

The bench moved unsettlingly as the young man sat down close to Anthony.

"You don't mind do you? Fucking tough if you do."

Anthony was speechless, unable to think through the sick pain pulsing between his temples. He was suddenly afraid of the sunshine, open spaces, the fresh air he was breathing and craved the closeness of his snug office in the vestry. The bottle of cognac, normally hidden in the middle drawer of the filing cabinet, open on the sideboard, his feet up on the desk, the ancient iron stove belching delicious wood smoke into the chill air.

"Look, we obviously have a few things to talk about. Can we go inside? It's much warmer there and I can, we can have a drink. I'm sure this can be sorted out."

"Think on mate, we believe in the Old Testament code of justice, know what I mean?"

The young man smiled.

"But of course you do. I assume you've got some qualifications for the job?"

Anthony stared at him, expressionless.

"That blank look suggests maybe you haven't."

"You can rant on all you like, I'm going inside. Your Grandfather looks cold to me."

"Makes no difference to me, we'll come in if you push him."

Grasping the greasy handles of the wheelchair, Anthony noticed a finger on his right hand was bleeding. A splinter of wood from the rickety bench had worked its way deep beneath one of his nails. At the moment of horrified revelation, he had felt nothing, clutching at the rotten frame for support. Now suddenly, it was painful and he hesitated, staring at the ruby flow as it welled upwards, beading briefly in the bright light before trickling down his bent finger to pool in the palm of his hand.

"I've hurt myself," he blurted out, but they weren't listening.

The young man was up ahead, staring at the inscription on a white marble gravestone. Albert Chalmers' eyes were closed. He looked to be asleep, but Anthony, ever the opportunist, thought maybe the excitement had killed him. For a moment he contemplated sneaking quickly away, through the gate, which he would close quietly, and across the park. Exhilarated at the thought of escape, he glanced over his shoulder, before the grim reality wrenched him to his senses. He violently pushed the wheelchair. It edged forward slightly before its front wheels sunk into the soft gravel of the path and brought it to an abrupt halt. Albert Chalmers jerked forward, grunted and opened his eyes.

"Sorry," hissed Anthony guiltily.

The young man looked up.

"I realize," Anthony continued in a voice heavily tinged with false bonhomie, "I don't know your name."

"Cedric Burrows."

"Oh, Cedric. That's not common these days."

The young man shook his head in amazement and laughed.

"You're obviously a stranger in your own bloody graveyard. I'm standing on dear old Cedric. Before your time, I suppose is the charitable explanation. I'm Peter, Peter Erskine. And don't say the pleasure's all yours, because believe me it's all mine."

Grim-faced he turned away and strode purposefully towards the church. Anthony pulled the wheelchair backwards out of the rutted gravel, then manoeuvred it up the slight bank onto level ground. Breathing heavily and with his heart pounding he pushed the heavy load through the long grass. As he laboured, he was assailed by a memory of the bittersweet smell of the terrified man in the Isle of Man basement and he leant forward and sniffed the thinning crown of grey hair in front of him. There was nothing there to orientate him, just the faint hint of sickness – an institutional smell he was familiar with – and hair tonic, nothing of the acrid pungency of a heaving body in mortal terror. Anthony, in growing panic, felt the dam he had carefully constructed over the years creaking under pressure from a rising flood of memories. The colours of his past – the blacks and reds – were there as vivid as ever, as were the sights and sounds: shirts, boots, banners, the songs, screams, curses, the grazed knuckles, the violent body-shaking jolt of the fist striking home, the glazed eyes, the scrabbling, blood gushing, spurting, trickling, solid and glutinous wrenched from the ravaged lungs of his wife and coughed onto crumpled bed sheets. It had always been there. Red and black on white, the script of his life that years of administering the sacraments of the Church had done nothing to erase.

"Vain hope, vain hope," he muttered.

He had believed he was getting away with it, making amends. He had thought that his good works and charitable deeds would in some way counterbalance his other life when the scales came to be weighted on that final day of judgment.

"Stupid bugger, stupid bugger, stupid bugger."

He was certain Albert Chalmers looked up at him then and smiled, even agreed with him.

"You are Tony, always have been and always will be."

"Albert believe me, I thought it was possible to put things right, you know, do a little good."

"But you're a fraud Tony, that's the problem my old mate."

"Maybe at the beginning, but I got better, even came to believe in much of it. That must count for something, surely?"

"Tony, a fraud is a fraud is a fraud and that's being kind. Face it, if I was a harder man, words like liar, hypocrite, dishonest, violent, crook, would spring to mind, but I'm not, so fraud will have to do."

"You're a cruel man Albert, there's good in every one."

"Not in your case Tony, you've never owned up to anything in your life. Even to your precious wife, your so-called confessor, I bet you didn't even tell her about us did you? No, I can tell by your expression you didn't."

"No, but…"

"No buts, Tony. You and I were the most important thing that ever happened to you. The rest, well, was just flim-flam, the excesses of youth, boyish exuberance. You were not the only one to end up on the wrong side of history, I was a follower like you remember. We made our choices. But some of us paid a heavier price than others for our mistakes. You'll have thought of them all I know Tony, all the excuses, but face it it's all bollocks and you know it."

"Albert, Albert, so it's down to you?"

The jolt of the wheelchair as it passed onto the smooth tar macadam surface of the path that circled the church forced him to look up. Peter was waiting for them.

"It's no good talking to him, he's virtually stone deaf without his hearing aid and it's switched off. Thought we'd save the battery so he could hear your side of the story."

Nauseous, Anthony gazed at his church, the gold weathervane moving in the chill north-westerly breeze, the weathered stone heads of a man and a women on either side of the thatched porch, the ornate rusty ironwork on the medieval door into the nave, all reassuringly familiar, yet everything was different. His universe had changed.

"After you, lead on, as you seem to have forgotten about your lunch."

Anthony smiled weakly. As they approached the shadowy covered entrance to St Botolph's they could hear and feel the rumble of the organ, the deep resonant bass notes vibrating through the ancient stone flags and rattling the ancient wooden portal. Smooth and cool to the touch, Anthony turned the worn iron handle and heard the familiar metallic clunk as the catch disengaged, the heavy door then swung silently open. He breathed in the redolence of his ministry, dusty old papers, wilting flowers, polish and paraffin, a delectable concoction, which had scented his life for so long. It almost choked him today. Together Anthony and Peter lifted the wheelchair over the abraded stone sill and through the doorway. Albert's feet knocked against a pile of hymn books stacked along the back of a pew and sent them crashing to the floor. The music stopped and a grey-haired woman turned and peered over the top of the carved wooden organ screen. Catching sight of the Reverend Anthony Coxon-Dyet, she waved and called out.

"Ah, It's only you vicar. That noise gave me quite a shock, I can tell you. I'll soon be finished here. If you've got a moment later I'd like to talk to you about the flowers for next week. A problem with the suppliers putting up their prices or something."

Anthony limply waved, then smiled and bent down to straighten the books. The organ boomed out in a triumphal flourish that drowned Peter's words. Forced to repeat himself, he leant over to shout angrily in Anthony's ear.

"Which way?"

"We can talk in the vestry, it's over there."

"Can't you stop her? It's giving me a headache and Grandad won't be able to hear a thing, even with his hearing aid."

"You heard her, it'll be ending in a minute or so. Suits the mood don't you think?"

"You can bloody joke about things. A vicar who's a right bastard, I'd never have believed it."

His face flushed a furious red and he clenched his fists.

"I want to get this over with. Hang on, it's not that warm in here. What's wrong with the vicarage? Are you hiding someone away in there?"

"No, there isn't one, it was demolished," Anthony added as an afterthought, "it was in a bad condition."

Peter looked at him in disbelief.

"I have a flat. A small one, a mile or so away. It suits me. We can go there if you want, but there are rather a lot of stairs."

Peter shrugged and nodded towards the vestry.

Anthony's desk was as cluttered as always. His pencil notes for that day's sermon lay where he'd left them, scattered across the shiny green surface. Copies of the latest edition of the parish magazine were piled on one corner of the table and on the floor in neat bound bundles of one hundred. An overflowing ashtray spilled cigarette ends on to a yellowing copy of the Daily Telegraph and a half-filled mug of scummy coffee stood in the middle of an array of brown-tinged circular stains. Natural light, filtered through white-tinted glass, flooded the small room creating the illusion, at certain times of the day, of being underwater. Anthony found the effect strangely unsettling and always switched on the battered black spring-loaded table lamp whenever he was working in the room. Sitting beneath its harsh artificial yellow light he cut himself off from his dusty, shabby surroundings and could write and read for hours. Today the magic was gone and, suddenly frightened, he switched the lamp off.

"Come in. Drink anyone? Afraid it's only a rather inferior brandy."

Peter drew the heavy threadbare curtain across the doorway, cutting them off from the nave and sniffed noisily as he looked disparagingly round the room. "This the offending mag?" he asked as he tipped a bundle of parish magazines off the only other chair. Anthony looked up as they thudded to the floor, broke loose from their string binding and scattered under the desk.

"No, next weeks."

"What you on about this week, Jesus was a Fascist? Mosley was a prophet?"

"No, immigration if you must know."

"You've probably been doing this for years, haven't you? Nobody really paid any attention. Just seen as a local character, I suppose, a bit of an eccentric. Met them all down the local pub: "Good fellow that Coxon-Dyet, sometimes a bit rich for my tastes, but generally sound, eh what?" God I hate you."

Peter placed a hand on his Grandfather's shoulder, switched on his hearing aid, and then sat down. Anthony reached over and with effort pulled open the middle drawer of a battered military green metal filing cabinet standing to one side of the window. He lifted out a three-quarters empty brandy bottle and two stained tumblers.

"Your Grandfather, will he have any?"

"I don't think he'd like to drink with you. Me? I'm not so particular. Give me a large one."

Sipping at his glass and letting the raw burning taste of the brandy trickle slowly down his throat Anthony came to the decision to deny everything. Thinking clearly for the first time he realized that they could prove nothing, it would be his word against Albert Chalmer's and it was far from clear whether Albert could say a sensible word.

"Look, I think there's been some sort of mistake."

Peter stared at him aghast.

"You're bloody unbelievable, you really are. There's been no mistake."

He spoke with such vehemence that Anthony's new found resolve immediately began to crumble – the knot in his stomach tightened and he felt palpitations in his hands and forearms. Clutching the desk firmly with his left hand he shifted forward in his chair, swallowed hard, then looked directly at Peter.

"What do you mean, no mistake? I should know what I got up to…"

"Aaaaagh, this is pathetic. You really are beyond fucking belief."

Albert moved agitatedly in his wheelchair, a series of jerking motions of the upper body that brought his grandson to his feet, he began to moan. Gently restraining his Grandfather, Peter turned to Anthony.

"See what you're doing, he deserves better than this from you. You bloody owe him."

He then reached into the inside pocket of his heavy blue overcoat and took out a buff envelope. Sitting down he opened it and watching the priest intently, slowly withdrew several neatly folded sheets of paper. Deliberately smoothing out each one in turn and glancing at the text he selected one from the bottom of the pile and handed it to Anthony. It was closely typed in single spacing and for several seconds Anthony saw nothing but a black blur of letters moving jarringly before his eyes.

"It's Grandad's statement to the military police in Liverpool, when he'd recovered enough from his assault to talk. That was several months after he was beaten up I believe, but it points the finger firmly at you Tony Cox and your friends, Eric Baines and Paolo X. He didn't know the Italian's surname, but you and Mr. Baines were well known. Oh, by the way, it's only a copy."

Anthony could see clearly now.

"This is the sworn statement of Albert Bertram Chalmers – internee no. 247586, formerly of Peveril Camp, Peel, Isle of Man. Currently residing Walton Prison infirmary. Dated the 23rd September 1941. Those present Inspector Ernest Rothman and Constable Dick Mason."

Anthony read on, the events of that fateful evening running through his mind with an unerring clarity.

"...Eric Baines returned with his friend Tony Cox. They were often together and were billeted in the same house in the camp. (Witness believed it was number 13, Ballarat Road). I clearly saw his face in the candlelight and I recognized his voice. They talked briefly and then came over towards me..."

He dropped the paper on to his lap and looked away, his eyes filling with tears.

"There's much more, Grandad was very detailed."

Anthony raised his hand.

"Had enough?"

"Where did you get it from?"

"None of your bloody business. Let's just say Grandma was very determined and very persuasive. Also Grandad could talk more after it happened, he told the family his story many times. I don't know what you expected."

Anthony shook his head, but said nothing.

"What pisses me off is how you got away with it. I bet you were never even questioned about the assault?"

Shaking his head weakly, Anthony drained his glass and covered his mouth as he coughed. His eyes were stinging.

"What was it, bloody fascist sympathizers in the police force? Or weren't they bothered about fascists beating up each other? Good luck to them, I suppose?"

"It was wartime."

"Oh God, that old chestnut, for fuck's sake. You know what gets me about all this is that I hate the whole fucking lot of you. Here I am chasing round the country tracking down one filthy fascist for kicking another one half to death. I shouldn't care should I? It was a long time ago, you're all fucking spent anyway and today we've got blackshirts of our own out on the streets. I should be going after them."

He wiped a fleck of saliva from the corner of his mouth.

"But you know what kept me on your tail? It wasn't just a family thing, it was the unbearable thought that you were out there, thinking you'd got away with it, living a life. Your own family oblivious to your rotten past. There was no way I could let you get away with it. Grandad here's paid for his mistakes. He's paid far too high a price, mind you. Now it's your turn."

Anthony thought the young man was about to lunge at him across the desk and momentarily clenched his fists, but Peter relaxed into his chair. There was silence. Anthony held back, he felt he wanted to talk about it, to confess, he had never put it all together even for Emily, but there was still a key element missing. The final nail that would seal him firmly into his coffin had not yet been driven home, something was bubbling through the queasiness, the hot and cold flushes, an instinct that had served him well all his life, told him it may not even be coming. Hold on. The church door thudded shut and the metal latch clicked comfortably into place.

"Oh God, Miss Vestey. How much had she heard? Everything, knowing her, oh hell."

Rustling papers, the creak of the old chair, Peter was leaning towards him.

"Here, you should read this."

The piece of paper he was holding was folded and it was unclear what it was. Then the hammer blow came, as it was opened out to reveal a page from the British Union party newspaper, "Action". He'd not seen a copy in years, but it was instantly recognizable, and this one was particularly familiar. There he was in black and white, younger of course, but unmistakably him. He glanced at the masthead, January 23rd, 1937, they had kept a copy of this at home. The headline read, "More British Union candidates, Eight more prospective parliamentary candidates – Further announcements will appear in "Action." There he was seventh in the list.

"Liverpool (Walton), T. Cox. Mr. Cox was born in Blackpool, where his family has long associations. After leaving school he assisted in his uncle's wholesale grocery company, gaining great knowledge of the commercial side of the business. Mr Cox had no political interests before joining the British Union in March 1933. Since then he has become well known as a capable and energetic propagandist. He has thoroughly mastered the policy and spirit of British Fascism, and speaks in a thoughtful and convincing manner on the platform. He is now 26 years of age."

Tony Cox stared unsmilingly out at the Reverend Anthony Coxon-Dyet. Nothing had changed, he was the same person, there was nowhere to hide. He smiled, the write-up had all seemed overblown at the time, if he was honest. He and Emily had had a good laugh about it, but ambition and vanity had banished any concern for the truth. Now it seemed appropriate that he was finally being nailed down by that earlier lie. A lingering glance at a figure that seemed more real to him than anything that had come afterwards, sandwiched between other familiar figures. He could hear their voices, smell the hair oil, the sweat, see the black shirts, the glinting brass buttons and shiny black boots. He handed the sheet of newspaper back to Peter with a sigh.

"My Grandma kept them all. I've even got your wife here somewhere."

He began sorting through the papers on his lap.

"No, that would be too much, please."

"All I want is my Grandfather to hear your side before he dies."

Through his sudden tears, Tony saw the faces of smiling young men and women marching past him, waving, calling out, beckoning him to follow. The songs, he had never paid much attention to them at the time, but the words were as fresh as ever and he knew he could recite every verse and hum all the tunes. Then there was Eric standing before him with the old enticing grin and arms outstretched. Softly he began to speak.

"There was a riot and privileges were suspended; there were no visits, everyone was confined to the camp and all organized games, lessons, meetings were cancelled. Security was stepped up, but only along the wire, none of the houses where we lived were searched. Work parties were sent out to clear up the debris and repair the damage to the seafront terrace. None of this impinged on us in house number 13 though. We were doubtful that anything would come of the meeting we had with that politician – he had a funny name, which completely escapes me now – and we were scared that they would break their promise and get back at those they saw as responsible for the riot. So we were spurred on to greater efforts with our precious tunnel. We were trying to dig ourselves out, you see. Escape. I believed at the time that it was the only way I was going to get away from there. You'll be pleased to hear I paid the price for all the rushing, the cutting of corners. The tunnel caved in on me when I was digging and I almost died, smothered by tons of earth, it was horrible. It terrifies me even now, although at the time I was much braver … funny."

Tony closed his eyes for a moment – the oppressive compression as vivid as ever, the air hot, particulate, the slipping away – before continuing in a whisper.

"Anyway, Eric pulled me out just in time. I had stopped breathing. I was completely buried, only my feet were visible in the rubble. He saved me. That was the sort of person he was. Albert, you've got to understand, I owed everything to Eric, my career, meeting my wife, the innumerable times he saved me in fights, the nights of drinking, the endless debates about everything under the sun. He was my dearest friend and he asked for my help, I couldn't refuse. He was begging me, what could I do? I had never seen him so distraught. He was a very angry man, but I stopped him going too far. He would have killed you, I could see it in his eyes. We moved you out of the basement and left you somewhere where you'd be found quickly. I kept my ears open, I knew you were picked up and taken to the infirmary at Ballaquane. You were still alive. Then I was told that you were shipped out to hospital on the mainland. That was the last I heard of you. I assumed everything was fine. That was why I didn't say anything. There were always fights between inmates and nobody thought anything of it. You certainly never spoke to the authorities about who was responsible. That was the unwritten rule. God, you've got to believe me I had no idea that we'd beaten you so badly, I swear. There was no way I could have known and even if I had learnt of it somehow, there was no way I could have said anything after Eric later saved my life in the tunnel. I was not going to rat on him after that, you have to understand. Life went on. We had the tunnel and we'd had our riot, we just had to escape, that was my only priority."

He searched their faces for a sign of acknowledgement, some indication that they understood. But there was nothing. Albert sat impassively in his wheelchair, totally still for the first time, while Peter stared morosely at the floor. After several seconds of silence he looked up.

"My ribs were badly crushed by the falling earth. We bound them up and tried to go on as usual, but I could hardly move. I couldn't make it down to roll call. So we cooked up a cock-and-bull story about me and Eric colliding on the stairs in the dark and both of us falling down and him landing on top of me and they bought it. I ended up in Ballaquane, like you, Albert. The others went on with the tunnel, cleared up the mess and made it through to the other side of the wire, coming up exactly where we had planned. They even built a trapdoor, covered with turf and everything to disguise the exit. But the tunnel was discovered completely by chance, the neighbour's dog sniffing around, I believe, before anyone managed to escape. It was a catastrophe for the poor bastards left behind, after all that hard work. They were shipped off to prisons in Manchester and Liverpool and the tunnel was filled in. It didn't affect me, as I never returned to House 13 and barely made it back to the camp.

They must have been considering me for release, though I had no idea about that at the time, and my "accident" took me to the top of the list. As soon as I could walk on my own, they sent me to the camp and released me. I can still recall that moment when the army major came up to me and said I was to report to the guardroom at 0700 sharp next morning to collect my belongings. They gave me my papers with internee stamped across them and a travel voucher to Blackpool. I've still got them, they're the only things I held on to after I began my new life, the rest had to go. Emily was afraid someone would find something and expose me. She was always the more practical one. Even had to keep it from the children, told them some tale about me having been away fighting in the Army. They believed me and after a while I began to convince myself. But it was always lies, a great tissue of lies. It's even harder to disentangle fact from fiction now. Ah well, more brandy?"

Peter nodded and held out his glass. Tony half-filled it then drained the rest of the bottle into his tumbler. He fumbled around in the desk drawer and pulled out a crushed packet of ten Wills Whiffs and a box of matches.

"I've been trying to give them up, though without much success I'm afraid," he nodded at the full ashtray, "Do you mind if I do?"

"No, kill yourself."

His hand was shaking as he brought the burning match up to his face. The glaring flame hurt his eyes and it was with relief that he extinguished the match and drew the smoke deep into his lungs. Light-headed, feeling disengaged, he sat there mournfully allowing the smoke to seep out of his mouth, only to suck it greedily back up his nose moments later.

"Sorry, would you like one?"

"No."

"Now, where was I? The camp gate always opened promptly at 0715 in the morning. There I was, one second a prisoner, the next a free man. I stepped out on to the promenade opposite that hotel – the Creg Malin – I was euphoric, never been so happy before or since. I felt I had everything to look forward to. In less than a day I would be back with my family. l could hardly wait. I tell you, I walked along the front in a state of utter joy. It was an overcast day and the sea was rough. I remember, because the tide was in and waves were breaking over the sea wall. For me, the sun was shining and everything was perfect. I raced along trying to catch the spray on my face – the delicious chill – I can feel it to this day."

He closed his eyes again and the salt water whipped his glowing cheeks and the wind ruffled his long greasy hair. He cried and screamed and shouted at the top of his voice. He spun round and round, his shoulder bag flying faster and faster. He stumbled, unsteady on his feet, dizzy, and sat down on the stonewall, laughing like he'd never laughed before.

"Thinking back, I got a few funny looks, but no one did anything to stop me. Everybody must have known where I came from and who I was, but the camp's reputation had spread far and wide – they are hard men, leave well alone. I relished that at the time, but now I see it as pathetic. You probably won't believe me, all a bit too convenient you'll be thinking, but sod it, this confession isn't just for you anymore."

A column of grey ash had dropped onto his trouser leg and he brushed it off.

"I spent some of the money they gave me on a couple of cigarettes from a small shop on the front and smoked them with relish on the train to Douglas. It was a stopping train and the carriage slowly filled up as we went along. I had grabbed a window seat and the one next to me was the last one to be filled. Everyone stared at me, but I didn't care, they nudged each other and whispered. A young woman even giggled. She was plain enough, but to me she looked gorgeous, brown hair held back in a headscarf, blue floral dress, black shoes. I remember bright red lipstick, but I can't believe that. It was in such short supply. Anyway, I got my own back by staring at her, which so embarrassed her she eventually left the carriage. Talk about cutting off your nose to spite your face, as her seat was taken by a fat and disagreeable farm labourer, who smelled. A couple of stations from Douglas a young schoolgirl finally took the seat next to me. She had curly blond hair and looked at me through ice-blue unblinking eyes for the rest of the journey. I gave her a penny as we were leaving the station and her good upbringing got the better of her and she murmured thank-you, before running away. She was the first real person outside the camp to speak to me for oh so long, it did me the power of good, I can tell you. It meant I could shrug off the behaviour of the officious bastards who I had to report to at the harbour. I think they were from the Met police over on the Island to bump up security after the riot – you know that old buffer who ran the camp, Captain Faulkner, was kicked out after the trouble, brought in a Superintendent somebody and a few constables – one in the eye for the army that was, it was the only good thing that came from all that nonsense. I thought they were a bunch of complete tossers. Anyway they checked my papers, searched my bags and hustled me up the gangplank and that was it, goodbye to the Isle of Man. I've never been back. I was tempted, but could never quite bring myself to do it."

The memories were painful and Tony frowned deeply, stroking his glass nervously. Touching his brow with his fingertips, he purposefully sat up, opened his eyes wide and stretched his face muscles.

"The sea crossing was very rough. People were being sick everywhere. I've never seen it so bad in my life. I felt terrible, but there were others far worse. Even members of the crew were throwing up as it was unbelievably stormy."

Tony shook his head.

"I think I passed out for a while, I was very weak. Woke up as we sailed into Fleetwood. Knott End-on-Sea, the lighthouse at the end of the pier, I was coming home. There was nothing to compare with that. I felt elated, in spite of the physical battering of the voyage. I still had miles to go, but it was my old stamping ground. South along the sea front – Cleveleys, Norbreck – I had my first pint at the Castle Hotel, I can taste it now – Bispham, my first sight of the Tower, North Shore. It was strange, dusk was falling yet there were no lights. It was completely different from how I had it fixed in my mind. There were couples out hand in hand taking the air, it was the first time I thought of Emily. What being back would be like, what I'd been missing. It was painful, like your first kisses, you know what I mean? Then maybe the young of today don't know, it all comes too soon, too fast."

"Oh God," Peter sighed, "this is pathetic. Get on with it and cut the sermonizing crap."

"The North Pier, the Tower, the swimming baths, South Shore, the Pleasure Beach, although it seemed to be closed, then Squire's Gate and home."

Clutching his head in his hands Tony paused. He felt tired. This was not something he wanted to be doing, dredging up disquieting recollections of the past. Angry, he snatched at the packet of cigarettes lying in front of him on the desk, instantly registered it was empty and tossed it in the direction of the wastepaper bin in the corner. The crushed cardboard box bounced off the chipped green rim and skittered across the floor to lodge under the rear wheel of Albert's chair.

"Sorry."

Tony's head ached and he massaged his temples, with eyes closed, tasting salt in the corners of his mouth. In that moment he recalled his wedding ring, a flash of gold on a fattening finger. He hadn't worn it for years, had taken it off one day to relieve the pressure, meaning to clean it and put it back on and never had. "Where was it now? So much had been lost. Some light-fingered boy had stolen it most likely."

"It was how I pictured it, the house. Garden a little overgrown perhaps, paintwork peeling, a neglected look, but then many of the houses were, with the war and everything. The downstairs windows were boarded up, that should have tipped me off that all was not right, but I put it down to the air-raids. What did I know? I was a young man full of himself. It's hard to believe now but I saw myself as some sort of returning hero, hardened by the flame of adversity, burnished by hardship. It was too dark for me to register the graffiti which had been scrawled on the front door and then roughly painted over, I just joyously hammered away."

Tony smiled as he remembered Emily's shocked expression – her face pale and shrunken, with bloodshot eyes and hair, already greying, pulled severely back from her forehead in a tight bun – the yell of recognition, the embrace. She felt light to him, thin and insubstantial, smelling of stale cooking. The cries of his two boys, their running feet, stopping suddenly in the hall, surprised, uncertain, shy.

"It's your father," Emily had said, "back from his war. Now maybe it'll end boys. Give him a hug."

The formal handshake with his eldest son, pulling away embarrassed from any further contact, the small arms briefly round his leg.

"My wife was overwrought to see me and my sons were distant. For the first time it really dawned on me that others had been affected by what had happened to me. What I had done. It was a fleeting thought though."

Tony sighed to himself and sipped his brandy.

"I'd had my fill of violence, even death. Illness had been a part of life in the camps, but to see Emily changed was a shock. It was the lines on her face that got me most. She had aged and looked unwell. The terrible thing, and I feel guilty now thinking about it, admitting it, but she was no longer beautiful to me. It had gone, slipped away and I had had no time to come to terms with the loss as I should have done. Emily noticed I noticed, and in that moment the resentment was born. Try as hard as I could, I never recovered the ground, never made it up to her. Equality of suffering was nothing, the dimming of the light in my eyes as we first looked at each other marked the full stop in our relationship, the rest was just … a footnote."

Peter shifted in his chair, he had barely moved, and he was getting cramp in his right leg. The soft rounded tones of the vicar's voice, still tinged after all those years in the South with a faint trace of a Lancashire accent, were insinuatiing their way into his consciousness. Soothing the sharp edges of his anger, sapping his determination to hate him, dampening any thoughts of revenge. The pain in his calf was his saviour, waking him up and hauling him back, rekindling his hatred. Almost to himself he muttered the words, "I can see how you got away with being a bloody vicar for so long." He then leant over and whispered in his Grandfather's ear, "can't you Grandad? He's got a very smooth voice, addictive, nothing more than a drug."

Tony didn't appear to notice.

"Physically it came back, we were affectionate with each other, at least for a while. Her pent-up frustrations only filtered out slowly over the weeks. How bad things had been for her, for them. I had been right to worry in the camp. She had sent me a cutting from the local paper hinting at how people disliked the fascists, well that was nothing to the reality of it. There was physical and verbal abuse, the windows in the house were regularly broken, the door and footpath were daubed with the word "Traitor" mostly, it was a respectable neighbourhood after all."

He snorted dismissively.

"It still angers me today. These were friends, neighbours, people I had grown up with, ostracizing Emily and the boys. God they had a terrible time at school, with the other children. The whole town seemed to know about my internment, people pushing in front of them in queues, barely speaking. Shopkeepers would claim they had run out of food when Emily finally got to the counter after queuing for hours. Even my bloody family, who were in the grocery business, can you believe it, refused to lend her a hand. I haven't spoken to most of that side of the family since. The Council was useless, they made no special arrangements to help and Emily eventually had to apply to the Local Assistance Board. She was a proud woman, she felt so humiliated and then they turned her down on the grounds that she had relatives in town and we owned the house, which wasn't strictly true. They told her that her husband was disloyal and should be shot and that she had to get out to work or starve. Bastards, I couldn't believe it when I heard. I almost went round there. Emily and I had our first serious row over that. She told me that violence was my response to everything, brawn before brains, and she was sick of it. It achieved nothing. So I didn't go. I felt so angry I didn't speak to her for days. Seems stupid now. They were different times and we were different people. It was all very well saying find work, but nobody would employ her if they knew about me, and they all did. The local ammunition factories, employing women by the score turned her away saying they couldn't take on a security risk. A bakery in Poulton gave her a job, but then the other workers found out somehow and she was blacked, if you pardon the pun."

A fleeting smile crossed Peter's face.

"There was no way she could grow anything in the garden like everyone else, as it kept being dug up and vandalized. Her family helped out a bit, but her parents were getting on and lived a fair way away. Emily had always had a weak chest and she was seriously ill over the winter, almost died I was told. She got better but was never quite the same, any heavy work had her gasping for breath, poor woman, it eventually killed her you know. December 15th 1961, coughed her life away. I was with her. I felt so guilty. I know my sons blamed me. They've been distant ever since, dutiful, but remote. I hardly ever see them. Things have been better with one of my grandsons though, David, he stays with me a lot, but I'm not sure he knows anything about my background, in fact I know he doesn't."

Taking a handkerchief from his pocket Tony noisily blew his nose. His voice was hoarse when he began speaking again and he wiped away a tear, hiding behind the pretence that he had something in his eye.

"What a house of cards, eh?"

He dabbed at his nose and mouth, then looked across at Peter, expecting a sign of reciprocity, some evidence of comprehension. Nothing. Wincing slightly, Tony remembered where he was and what was happening. He was confessing his crimes without any hope of absolution. "Redemption, what's that?" he thought and smiled wanly.

"You know the irony of it all? What kept Emily and the children going? It was the bloody fascists. The party paid most of the bills and kept the wolves from the door. An old friend of Emily's from her days at the British Union headquarters in London set up a charity, an official one, the 18B Detainees Aid

Fund. As soon as they found out about her predicament they helped as much as they could, but there were a lot worse off than Emily, homeless and that. She survived, all credit to her, but at the time I couldn't see the price she had paid and what she wanted from me.

All I did was rage, take people on in the streets, argue back, get into fights. I was lucky I didn't have any trouble with the police, as I had to report to them regularly. Emily couldn't stand my nonsense, she just wanted support and most of all calm. But I didn't see it. I genuinely believe now, although it sounds very naive, that I didn't understand why everyone was so antagonistic. After all these were people I'd grown up with, many had come along to my meetings before the war, heard me speak, given me encouragement, expressions of support, bought copies of "Action" from me, some had even been members of the Party. And now they were abusing me and my family, it was too much. The upshot was that there was no way I could find work, or to put it the other way, there was no way anybody would give me work. I was just another mouth to feed at home, adding to the pressure on Emily. None of it was helped by the restrictions placed on me when I was released. I had a bloody red stamp on my identity papers, singling me out as a detainee. Never found guilty of anything and there I was marked for life, or so it seemed at the time. As I said I had to report to the police every month, wasn't supposed to meet any of my old mates in the Party, although I didn't take much notice of that, they were the only ones who would talk to me and the final thing was, I wasn't supposed to travel more than seven miles from home – made finding bloody work even harder, I can tell you."

"My heart bleeds for you."

Peter was standing and stretching his arms.

"Any chance of something hot? I see you've got a kettle down there on the floor. I'm sure Grandad would like a cuppa."

Wrenched from the brutal dream world of his past into the challenging present, Tony was several seconds in replying. It then took him an age to make three cups of coffee. He moved slowly, his stooped body shuffling round the crowded room, squeezing with difficulty past the desk, the chairs, the piles of papers. For the first time in his life he felt his age.

"So what did you do then? I can't wait."

Peter was sitting closer to the desk than before, he was cradling the hot steaming mug in hands protected by the rolled down sleeves of his grey sweater. His voice had a cruel edge to it and Tony realized he was enjoying himself, feeding on his own growing misery, feeling stronger and more powerful by the minute.

"I didn't have a lot of choice with a war on. Many British Union members joined the army or whatever as soon as they were let out. They had been stung by the traitor tag and wanted to prove themselves, I suppose. It was all completely untrue – none of us were traitors…"

"Oh come on."

"…no, look we were British patriots. We just believed in a different way of running things. Fighting Germany was not in our interests. We should never have gone to war in the first place, we should have done a deal with Hitler. Negotiated on the basis of mutual spheres of interest. That was what it was all about – we had the Empire, he could have Europe. Look at us now the victors, we've lost the Empire, our position in the world and are part of some United States of Europe. Who was right?"

"That's all bollocks."

"It most definitely is not. Two world wars Britain has won this century – ostensibly to save Europe and where are we? Going cap in hand to country's we either defeated or bailed out, things could have been so different."

"…and you're full of shit."

"Like your Grandfather then. At one time he must have believed in all this, probably still does. Have you asked him?"

"Leave him out of this, you've no bloody right to side with him. He's paid a fucking awful price for any mistakes he's made. How dare you? Feeling better are we? Airing the old familiar arguments again, reassuring yourself that what you did has some intellectual justification. Well let's get something straight. To everyone else, that is who has a streak of decency in them, you're a fascist, a blackshirt and one who helped cripple another man and laughed it off. Then hid his dark past behind a facade of decency that has successfully taken in generations of people. They'll not be too pleased when they find out the truth believe me. Now tell us how you did it, that's what we came for."

"We were not traitors," Tony said meekly, "I would never have done anything to undermine Britain. I supported the King."

His voice trailed off and he wiped his eyes again with his handkerchief.

"I joined the Auxiliary Fire Service. They were desperate for volunteers, what with all the raids on Liverpool. Spent much of the rest of the war down there in the docks, that absence and the money coming in helped out at home. I hardly saw the kids for weeks on end, and then you only got a couple of rest days and you went back. But I think that made me more acceptable, more like everybody else who had men away in the forces or whatever. People were still having a go at them, particularly the boys at school – you know what children are like – but it was getting more routine. Emily seemed to be coping better and we were very friendly whenever I was around. From my point of view much of the work was at night so you didn't meet a lot of civilians, no need for explanations. Also, it was so hard going that you slept for most of the time you weren't on duty. Fire-fighting was seen as honourable war work so the police took a more lenient view of me."

"It all finished at the end of the war though. It was a shame, I had got used to the routine, and being unemployed again raised a new set of problems. Back in Blackpool the neighbours seemed more antagonistic towards me, rather than less. I suppose with the threat and anxiety of the war gone, they were looking for someone to blame for all the hardship. I was sent to Coventry by our whole street, my local barred me – "no traitors allowed in here", the pompous ass – the ban quickly spread so that I had to walk up to the busy pubs on the prom that were full of holidaymakers, to get a drink. Initially I was angry and defiant. I considered I'd paid my dues, but no one else did. I became depressed and increasingly taciturn. I started taking long solitary walks, occasionally staying out overnight, sleeping in haystacks, barns that sort of thing. But was I believed? No. Not the recipe for a happy marriage I knew, but I didn't have the emotional maturity to cope. We were drifting along. Largely out of a lack of anything better to do, rather than any burning commitment, I got back in touch with old members of the British Union. There was quite a network I discovered. It helped for a while. Most were in the same boat and it was some sort of comfort, but the fire had gone out of most of them and people slowly slipped away as they got themselves sorted out. There were a few, mind, who believed in it still, their views hardened by the reality of defeat. They were full of all that "out of the ashes" crap. But I hung around and even went down to London for a reunion dinner. It was Christmas 1946 – pretty austere times as you can imagine, but infinitely more exotic than Blackpool. I hadn't been to London for years and it was a real escape for me. I was a bit out of my depth as the get-together was at the Royal Hotel in Woburn Place, very up-market. That was the last time I saw Eric, he'd invited me. Dragging me along as usual. He was drunk for the whole time I was with him, talking non-stop about starting afresh. He seemed to have run into money. With all that had happened, I wish I could honestly say I saw through him. But I didn't, he just seemed to have left me behind. I've no idea what happened to him, but knowing him he'll have done alright for himself."

"Well he hasn't."

"What?" Tony was taken aback, "How do you know?"

Peter smiled.

"You really haven't twigged how serious we are, have you? We left no stone unturned to track you lot down. It obviously never occurred to you we'd have gone after him first, as he was the one who did most of the damage to Grandad. He was hard to find, but nothing like you. It was difficult because he's sunk so low, but at least he still uses his real name."

"What's he doing?"

"He's working on and off as a barman in a pub in Birmingham. I think his hours depend on when he's sober, which means he doesn't work much. He's a bloated, drunken pig and we got very little that was coherent out of him. He was pitifully abject when he realized who Grandad was, crying and grovelling at his feet. But it was obviously only the drink talking as nothing else touches him now. Not totally satisfying from my point of view. To make matters worse his boss, the landlord of the pub, couldn't give a toss when we told him who he was and what he had done. He just laughed and said if he refused to employ people with a dodgy past he'd never have anybody behind the bar, himself included."

"Did he mention me?"

"Ooo, it wouldn't do to leave you out, would it. As a matter of fact through his tears Eric did speak well of you. Said you were the best friend he'd ever had, but had no idea where you were. I didn't believe him, and I think I broke his nose trying to get it out of him. It was very unpleasant as he cried easily, his whole face was damp and bloody. I intended to hurt him, but when it came to it we're not all like some we could mention. We left him blubbing away and continued our search for you, who really had hidden himself away, hadn't you?"

"It was my father-in-law who finally sorted me out. He turned up in Blackpool out of the blue one week-end, he'd obviously been talking to Emily, and invited me out for a meal. God that was a treat, just after the war, rationing at its height, to go to a restaurant was really something. Hard to imagine now. I was surprised and on my guard, edgy even. Looking back I was extremely boorish and probably rather rude. It wasn't that I disliked him, in fact quite the opposite. He looked a lot like Emily and had an easy natural charm that he had refined over the years in his dealings with generations of reluctant church goers."

"He was a vicar?"

"Didn't I say? Yes. A beautiful parish in rural Cheshire. He would have gone far in the Church but for his mid-life indiscretions."

Peter looked genuinely surprised for the first time that afternoon, his interest piqued.

"Not choirboys, don't tell me it was choirboys?"

Tony shrugged, no longer offended by the man's base view of his profession.

"He wouldn't have stood for that. He'd have given you a good hiding just for suggesting such a thing, he was a tall fit man. No, nothing like that. He was in the British Union."

"A fascist? I don't believe it."

"Yes, he was one of a number of black-shirted vicars dotted around the country. He was also one of the first members of the Party, an early enthusiast. But that wasn't really what held him back. It was the fact that he wrote a regular column for our paper," The Blackshirt". Week in week out he tackled the moral and political issues of the day from a Christian fascist perspective."

"You're joking aren't you? This is hard to believe."

"No, he was very good at it. One of the few intellectuals in the Party. The powers that be in the Church didn't mind at all before the war, maybe some of them even agreed with a lot of it. But the war and the internment of party members changed that. He must have come close to being locked up himself, but he somehow managed to avoid that. Pulled a few strings I expect. Anyway, he was told to stop his writing activities, lie low and as far as possible draw a veil over his past activities. And that's exactly what he did for the duration of the war. He actually recanted his fascist past in print sometime later, in 1948 or 49 I think. Tore up his party card. But when he spoke to me over our steak and potato pie – heavens it was delicious – he was still a member. l respected him and he threw me a lifeline."

"He got you into the church. I don't believe I'm hearing this."

Peter was aghast. He sat there looking wide-eyed at Tony, shaking his head.

"It's a bloody conspiracy, that's what it is. The whole thing stinks to high heaven."

"It wasn't like that."

"It wasn't like that. Grandad can you fathom this?"

The damaged man shifted in his wheelchair, his gaze fixed on Tony.

"My father-in-law pointed a way forward for me, that's all. Suggested I consider it. Give some thought to whether I had any sort of vocation. He was a perceptive man and thinking about it now, yes, he flattered me. He said he had always seen a spiritual side to me. One he felt sure events had forced me to neglect. But it was never too late."

Peter laughed out loud, his whole body shaking, his right hand beating time on his thigh.

"What's so funny?"

"I know what's coming," he struggled to find the words, "you had a …damn it, it's on the tip of my tongue. What is it?…that's right. It was like Paul on the road to Damascus, a blinding light."

"You're thinking of an epiphany."

Tony couldn't help himself, Peter shrugged.

"No, not exactly. He had planted a seed and the idea grew on me. To my surprise I wasn't put off by the thought of becoming a priest and on reflection I did discover I had another more contemplative, compassionate side. It was a little bit like a revelation, a dropping away of the scales, but nothing dramatic. I just felt an intellectual opening up, an appreciation of some inner worth hidden deep within myself. It gave me hope for the future, where before I'd had none. On the practical side, I'd have described myself as a lapsed churchgoer, particularly since leaving home. As an adult I never ever went to services, but before that I was there every Sunday, regular as clockwork with my mother. So you could say I knew the basics. And I'd had lots of practice speaking in public during my time with the Party. People said I had a good voice, persuasive even. It was also a challenge. William, that's my father-in-law, said he could smooth the way if I was interested and he left it at that, no hard sell."

"You obviously leapt at the chance, you fraud."

"It probably looks like that. I can understand why you see it that way. It certainly helped me out of the hole I'd dug myself into. But, please believe me, l did have faith when I decided to have a go and its grown over the years. I am a Christian. Forgiveness is important and I forgave myself for my past. It was the vital first step and I took it. I genuinely believed that every prayer I offered up, every service I held, every damaged soul I comforted over the years gradually helped tip the balance back in my favour. Until you turned up, I thought I had made real progress in making amends for my youthful sins, that the scales were balancing up, but it turns out I was very wrong. I'm sorry, so sorry."

Sighing quietly to himself he rested his forehead on the edge of the desk and stared down between his legs at his scuffed brown shoes. It was painful sitting like that with the wooden rim of the table cutting into his skin. He was tired and miserable and it did all seem such a long time ago.

The bishop was coming towards him with an outstretched hand.

"Mr Coxon-Dyet very pleased to meet you. William has told me so much about you. Do take a seat."

His fingers were short and chubby, two large rings nestled in the rolls of skin and his hand felt moist. The bishop's palace, a stately Georgian mansion hidden away in a cobbled close near to the Cathedral, was more or less what Tony had been expecting, a forbidding exterior to a world that was daunting in being so far outside his experience. In that instant it did not seem the right path for him to follow and he had hesitated outside in the narrow courtyard, had been about to slip away when he was seen through a window by a young cleric who opened the door.

"We're expecting you. Please follow me."

The book-lined office smelled of mothballs and was stuffy, the viscid air resistant to movement. Tony, obliged to enter, felt the medium stretch then part around his body, sucking him in. He was conscious of stumbling onto a lit stage, illumination streaming from his right. The afternoon sun was glinting through the leaves of an immense horse-chestnut tree, whose branches shifting in the slight breeze scratched gently on the glass of a large floor to ceiling casement, its windows firmly closed. The Bishop waving his hands expansively round the room directed Tony to sit wherever he liked. He chose a capacious red-leather armchair in front of the ornate marble fireplace, only realizing his mistake as he sank down between its ample arms, the plumped velvet cushions offering little resistance or support. His discomfort was acute wedged, as he was, in a confined space close to the floor, embarrassment flushing his face and his temperature rising. He fought the urge to loosen his new starched collar. From above and behind him he heard the Bishop's mellifluous voice, his words floating on the heavy dust laden air, making little sense.

"Sherry or would you like something stronger?"

"Yes, thank you."

Tony noticed for the first time the ticking of the large clock on the mantelpiece and looked up. One minute past three. He had been in the room less than sixty seconds and it felt like an age. Flustered he dusted his face with his right hand, then discreetly wiped his sodden palm on his jacket.

"Mr Coxon-Dyet, what would you like?"

"Oh God, what was he asking me? This is stupid, what am I doing? I'll never pull this off."

A stupefying blankness settled over Tony and his temples throbbed. The woollen trousers of his black suit adhered to the back of his legs as he tried to get up. Then thinking better of it he shifted uneasily in his seat and sat there blinking, staring at the empty chair opposite with its halo of green and yellow.

"I'm having a sherry, a very fine amontillado."

"Ah yes," said Tony, his relieved voice booming round the room, "I'll have one as well, thank you."

A giggle, faint like a rustle in a hedgerow, then the squeal of a cork being pulled, the glugging of liquid and the chink of glasses.

"No need to shout. Has someone been telling you I'm going deaf? Don't believe a word of it."

Laughter again, this time drawing closer. Two sherry glasses appeared on a silver tray. He took one. The heavy bulk of the Bishop lowered himself into the other armchair with a sigh. Tony could see nothing clearly, the sun was blinding, having sunk below the leafy branches of the horse chestnut, it was now shining directly through the window. A voice, kindly this time, some barrier having been lowered, floated on the warm drenched air.

"Good health Anthony, I may call you Anthony?"

Tony nodded.

"I'm very glad you came to see me. William had nothing but good things to say about you and, as you probably know, William and I go back a long way. I'm always on the lookout for serious young men to join the church. Particularly now, of course, when the need is even more urgent."

The mature, well-rounded voice, obviously used to pronouncing and brooking no interruption, soothed Tony fears and lifted his fading confidence. The words of his father-in-law came to him, "Basil loves the sound of his own voice, so say very little, agree with everything he says, laugh at his jokes and if he likes you, you'll be fine. And he'll like you, believe me."

Tony found it hard to believe the two men who were so completely different in appearance were, according to Emily, almost exactly the same age. She'd sat on Uncle Basil's knee many times and wondered how anybody could get so fat. All the men she had known, apart from him, had been tall and thin, with a full head of hair like her father. Tony, relaxing and focusing, could now see where his nickname of "Piggy" came from. The bishop had a slightly upturned nose and his almost complete lack of hair accentuated his large protruding ears. Emily had spoken affectionately of "Piggy" and Tony was now reassured to have his fate resting in the hands of such a kindly, undemanding individual. His glass was empty and still there had been no questions. When one finally arrived he was well prepared.

"Anthony, I must ask you this. Do you have a faith strong enough to administer to a flock of what are often virtual non-believers? Are you prepared to work hard in often difficult circumstances to advance the word of God?"

"I am my Lord."

"Oh come now, Anthony, no need for such formality, call me Basil, at least in the confines of my office, you know what I mean? Your wife stands on no such ceremony with me. I know full well what she calls me behind my back, the little rascal. How is darling Emily by the way?"

"She is very well, Basil. She sends her love and hopes to see you soon."

"I'm glad to hear that, she was seriously ill I heard?"

"Yes, but she seems to have got over it. If I can find some work that will help of course. Things have been very difficult for her."

"I'm sure, I'm sure, difficult times for all of us. Let me top that up for you?"

"Thanks, but let me."

"Would you dear boy, thank you. Anything that saves my poor legs these days is very welcome."

Light-headed, his equilibrium somewhat restored, Tony handed back a full sherry glass. His grip was steady and his mind clear. For the first time in months he sensed a realistic way forward, an escape, and he was determined to pursue it.

"Thank-you. You've had one yourself, oh good. Bottoms up. Now where were we? Ah yes, you were telling me about the strength of your beliefs and your commitment to the Church."

"That's right. I've always been a regular churchgoer, for that I thank my mother, God rest her soul."

"Remind me where you're from?"

"Blackpool."

"Know it well. I've fond memories of many a happy holiday spent there, though I haven't been back in years. I expect it's changed?"

"It's getting bigger but the prom is much the same, though you won't recognize the Pleasure Beach, some great rides there now."

"Mmmm memories. Sorry, you were saying."

"I had strong beliefs as a boy, which, through a variety of circumstances largely outside my control, lapsed as a young man. But it was during my war service…"

"Good, good."

"… that I re-discovered my true faith. For the first time I felt I might have a calling and it was here that William played a huge part in helping me understand the way forward. He put my faith to the test and I believe I can say found it not to be wanting. He then suggested I come and see you, Basil."

The Bishop smiled.

"So you believe in the redeeming power of our Lord Jesus Christ?"

"I do, I believe in nothing more strongly."

"That's more than enough for me. I'll set everything in motion. There'll be no problems at our end. You'll be hearing from us soon. Good luck young man. I'll follow your career with interest. Very pleased to have met you."

He held out his hand.

"It was so easy, so very easy."

Peter was staring impatiently at him.

"What was?"

Tony lifted his head slowly from the desk. He had forgotten for a moment that he was not alone.

"Getting into the Church."

"Nothing bloody surprises me any more. When you've finished feeling sorry for yourself maybe you'll tell us?"

"With the Bishop's blessing I …"

"Hang on what Bishop?"

"Bishop Basil Smedley, old college room-mate of my father-in-law and long-time friend of their family. I went to see him and he liked me…"

"Surprise, surprise."

"He gave me the go ahead to apply to Bladen College. He effectively sponsored me, wrote a glowing testimonial."

"Pulled a few strings you mean."

Peter placed a hand on his Grandfather's shoulder and shook his head in an exaggerated manner, his face expressing total disgust.

"It's not who you are but who you know, it makes me sick."

"I understand, I really do," Tony leant forward earnestly, "It's the one and only time it's ever happened to me. With my background such things didn't happen. Not as a rule. But believe me I wasn't in a position to say no. I was desperate and I leapt at the chance. William, my father-in-law, knew people at the college, he used to teach there part-time, and they drew a veil over my checkered past and rather shaky qualifications. They were never ever mentioned. I think it helped I turned out to be quite a good student, hard-working and industrious. I found I really enjoyed the course, it was totally different to anything I'd done before. I suppose I rose to the challenge."

"Bully for you, I'm so pleased, finding fulfillment at last."

"It was, looking back, the happiest time of my life, as a student then in my first parish near the docks in Liverpool. I was worried someone might recognize me from my Party days as I had been active in that area at one time, so I grew a beard, which was quite the trendy thing in young religious circles at the time, and no one ever did. From a black shirt to a black habit was too big a leap for most people."

Tony smiled self-consciously to himself and looked guiltily over at Peter, who stared icily back at him.

"Pathetic, really pathetic."

"I was lucky and it saved my life and my marriage. It was like coming home for Emily. She intuitively took to the role of vicar's wife. As she used to say she drank the life in with her mother's milk, and she became increasingly like her, in fact, as the years went by. It was particularly the case when we moved here to Dumpton Gap in the early fifties. It had everything I could have asked for. It's a beautiful part of the world, with a docile set of parishioners and not too many challenges for a lazy vicar. Perfect. She took to the yearly round of fete's, tea parties, committees, visits, that is the lot of the vicar's wife and our relationship got back on an even keel again for a while. I was busy, we were both pulling the same way. It was as close to perfect as one can hope for, I think."

"I'm so glad for you. It warms my heart to hear that things worked out. I have to admit I was getting concerned earlier and I'm sure there's a simple explanation for the name change. From what you've told me it can't have had anything to do with covering your tracks and making you that much harder to find. That would be underhand and not something a man of the cloth would do?"

Tony was at a loss for words. He looked around uneasily as if searching for something, then when he couldn't find whatever he was looking for stammered out an answer.

"It was, sort of like that. I mean not exactly deliberate. It just sounded more the part. Dyet is my mother's maiden name. So it's not stretching it that far …"

"Noooo."

"… went better with Coxon than Cox. Rolls off the tongue, don't you think?"

"If you say so."

"… in fact it's increasingly common these days to have a double-barrelled name, calling yourself after both your mother and your father. I should know I've christened enough of them in this very church."

"Oh, so that's alright then."

"My friend's still call me Tony."

"Well, Tony, may I call you Tony, Anthony? You won't have

many of those left, I suspect, when this comes out. They won't be too impressed and they may not be as understanding as me and Grandad here."

With a gloating sneer he laughed out loud, to Tony the sound was chilling.

"I've been alone so long now I hardly know what the truth is any more. So many stories, so many tales told to myself and others. Where does it all leave me?"

Tony wasn't sure if they could see he was crying or not. His eyes were drenched and heavy, but tears were not flowing, his skin hot and damp. The heat issuing from his body, trapped by his heavy clothing, was a palpable ordeal. It was stifling. He shifted uneasily, loosened his dog-collar and pumped his shirt like a bellows drawing cool air over his chest. There was momentary relief, nothing more, a fleeting distraction from his pain. All he could hope for was that his final question would yield an answer that would help him, maybe even excuse him. He paused and clutched his aching head. He silently prayed – with a fervour unfamiliar to him during the myriad services over an eternity of Wednesdays and Sundays that he had appealed to his congregation to have faith – that this was the case, that he would be delivered a last-minute reprieve. Pardoned. His torment was physical – his soul, brittle at the best of times, appeared incompatible with his body, a transplant rejected. Quaking, he turned to face his accusers. They had not moved.

"Albert, why were you going to tell the authorities about our tunnel? Why were you going to rat on us?"

Tony paused, expecting a reaction but there was none.

"That's why we did it. That's why we gave you a beating. We had to keep you quiet. How could you? We were all in the same boat after all, all members of the Party, for God's sake. Why? We could have come to some arrangement. We could have cut you in, if that was what you wanted. That wouldn't have been a problem. Why, just tell me why?"

His voice was high-pitched, close to hysterical. He wanted to shake the crippled man sitting in front of him, force him to shoulder some of the blame for what happened. He wanted him to admit that it had been his foolishness, his arrogance that had brought them to this pass.

"Why?" he asked despairingly.

Peter looked on open-mouthed, incredulous. Albert stirred in his wheelchair, his expression, which had flickered from worried concern to blank detachment while Tony had been talking, now broke into a distorted grimace, uneven yellowing teeth bared between cracked bloodless lips, his lined brow relaxed and almost clear, his watery eyes focused intently on Tony's face. Surprised and embarrassed, Tony glanced away only to be drawn back by Albert's startling laugh. Mute and helpless until now the sound he made was one of such crazed amusement and volume that Tony winced. He smiled feebly, eager to understand the joke, then quickly became serious. He looked at Peter, but he was also laughing. The Saxon walls and high ceilings of the nave echoed with these human sounds, amplifying their pitch until they rang in the vicar's ears like the tolling of an executioner's bell. Everything he had ever achieved in this holy building of his was, as of now, worse than nothing – the joyous sermons he crafted each week, at christenings, weddings, Christmastime, the prayers he had offered up, the hymns he had sung, the uplifting words at Easter, at funerals – they were all one big lie. He looked on in horror listening.

Peter's voice was calm and still when the answer to Tony's question finally came.

"The tunnel, your tunnel? That was nothing at all to do with it. Grandad knew nothing about that."

His grandfather, alert and attentive, nodded his head in agreement.

"You mentioning it now is the first time we've heard about any tunnel. No, what happened was Grandad stumbled upon your friend Eric in bed with a young Italian man, what was his name, Paulo. Nothing more, nothing less than that. Grandad swears he was never going to breathe a word to anyone about it. He says he told Eric that at the time and I believe him."

Chapter 11
BOO TO A GOOSE

David glanced behind him, feeling nervous for the first time since he'd entered the house, but nothing had materially altered. The orange glow of a resplendent sunset hung over the garden, the kitchen doors were open, as he had left them, and the sound of the television buzzed above his head. A large stripped pine table was strewn with the remnants of a meal and the sink was full of dirty pans. David walked over and stared at the dishes.

"Bloody typical," he thought, "they'll be leaving all this for the au-pair to wash up, no doubt."

He drained a half-full glass of red wine that was sitting on the draining board and nodded with satisfaction. Then he froze, a look of panic crossing his face, as he remembered where he was.

"Fingerprints, fucking fingerprints."

Calmly he wiped the glass clean with his handkerchief, replaced it carefully and then turned and surveyed the kitchen.

"Just the door handle," he muttered, "that's all."

He took care as he approached the back door to check that no one was passing along the railway embankment. All was clear and he quickly rubbed the handle to a bright shine.

"Dead give-away or what?"

He smiled. It was warm in the kitchen, he noticed a battered green Aga in the corner that was radiating heat into the room. Its presence was reassuring for David, so much was conforming to his preconceptions about the Beckinsale's lifestyle that it boosted his confidence. He felt to be on familiar territory. Taking a deep breath he slipped his suit jacket over the back of a Shaker-style wooden chair, took off his tie and watch and placed them in one of the pockets. He then rolled up the sleeves of his shirt. Handkerchief in hand he carefully inspected the kitchen knives in a polished wooden block that was standing on one of the black granite work surfaces, doubling up as a book-end for a long line of cookery books, before picking one – an eight-inch cook's knife – that felt comfortable and balanced to hold. David's thumb scraped satisfyingly across the edge of the stainless steel blade, he sighed and headed through the arch into the corridor.

St Botolph's church was in darkness when Tony returned. The sky was clear and intensely grey, the graveyard hollows brimmed with mist and the black bulk of the nave loomed ahead of him, its presence familiar, yet now vaguely mocking. He walked slowly but resolutely along the path towards the porch. He was aware of the gravel crunching under his feet and when he stopped to stare at the smattering of stars that were visible overhead he noticed his heavy breathing and the pneumatic beating of his heart. Such feverish exertion was starkly at odds with the scouring cold at his core, a chill too vital to ever again be dispelled by a warm hearth or an intimate embrace. He shivered. His immediate fate lay in the hands of his verger of many years, Raymond Sturgis, a man as old as the century and as worn out. Had he returned and locked up the church after organ practice? He often didn't bother, being either too trusting of people or too absent-minded, which one, Tony had never been able to ascertain. Over the years the parish had been fortunate that there had been no thefts or vandalism so

Tony had never had the heart to challenge the verger about his lack of rigour. This evening he hoped to be grateful for his own acts of benevolence; he had mislaid his church key and had not had time to look for it after Albert Chalmers and his grandson left. They had promised to return, after thinking through their next steps, and had reiterated that he was not to think this was the end of the affair. Tony had not thought that for one minute and had gone to see his solicitor.

A dog fox coughed in the limes close to Emily's grave. An eerie, plangent sound that made him peer over his shoulder into the gloom. Through the gathering mist he could just make out the glow of the streetlight that feebly illuminated the old covered gate on Church Lane. There were shadows everywhere, manifestations seemingly tangible, the next instant elusive. Beguiled by ephemera, he stumbled.

The air was heavy with wood smoke and the powdery aroma evoked a memory submerged until now beneath a turbid wash of remembering – the cold silvery-white ashes of a freezing morning, the ashes his Grandmother would sweep from the frigid hearth onto a crumpled newspaper as he stood beside her shivering in his dressing gown, the ashes she would take out to spread on her frozen vegetable beds, her footprints darkly tracked in the frosty grass – it was such a long time ago and he had been happy. Those days alone with his Grandmother stood out like islands in a murky race of misplaced commitments and unhappy connections. Though he had long since given up harking back to find anything meaningful or significant in his past. What he had not bargained for, which was a surprise for someone like him who had been a gambler all his life and knew the score, was that when his view of the past achieved some clarity, as it had today, it should be of a landscape he didn't recognize. Travelling across this terrain as he was now destined to do was uncomfortable, the scenery ugly, the climate foul. There was to be no respite from this expedition that he understood, his route was fixed, his destination immutable. He could take his time though, there were no stewards along this course hurrying him forward. He had a moment to reflect on the time he had wasted waiting for a stroke of fortune that would redirect him, galvanizing his efforts to search for a higher place. He had believed for a while that it was his ordination into the church but that, he now knew, had been an opportunistic detour, not the action of someone with a clear direction. All he had been doing as a vicar was peddling a line, to those who would listen, about gambling everything – your life, fortune and immortal soul – on faith in an unknowable outcome. If challenged, he would have insisted that the Holy Spirit was his only mentor. But honesty had never been his strong suit and he was fooling himself, even after decades as a priest. The bet he had personally made had finally come in. The odds had been struck that afternoon and the scenery had changed revealing his true journey's end – it had been the most shocking outcome imaginable. The best he could hope for was that the map of the region he had now would be simple to follow on foot.

He steadied himself before moving on.

He reached for the iron handle. It was icy to the touch. He turned it clockwise and heard the clunk of metal on the far side of the heavy wooden door, as he had many times before, felt the heavy iron bar lift and disengage. He pushed. It moved, swinging open. The ancient air rushed over him. Good old Raymond, he thought, you could rely on him. We are all chancers. His fate was sealed.

The stairwell smelled of potpourri – a sickly sweet fragrance that reminded David of his parent's house, an association that left him unmoved. His father and mother were peripheral to him now. Throughout the recent drama in his life – the revelations about his grandfather and his redundancy – he had never thought to approach them for help, never would have dreamt of it, despite his wife's constant urging, never asked them what they knew or what they thought. He had resolved only one thing in his mind – an inexorable line of logic – and that was that they must have known everything about his Grandfather. If they knew then why didn't they tell him? It was a betrayal that was impossible to forgive and he never would, but it was not a surprise. Dad obviously hated his father, he didn't have a single good word to say about him and he never visited him from one year to the next. The whole affair was dead and buried as far as he was concerned, so dead and buried is how it would stay. His son's ignorance of the family's sordid past was no bad thing. It would do nobody any good to reopen that particular can of worms. There was nothing to be discussed.

Silently David moved across the multi-coloured tiles of the basement passage to the foot of the stairs. The television was louder now. Deliberately, he climbed one step at a time up the steep staircase past a wall crowded with a series of framed theatre posters. A large potted Swiss cheese plant sat in the corner of the small landing and as he turned he glanced out into the garden through the high window. He could clearly see the tall pine tree and guessed where in the mass of vegetation that obscured the bottom of its trunk he had sat observing and plotting. It seemed an age away.

The front door of the house was ahead of him, more or less at eye level, it was old, ill-fitting and daylight streamed through a large gap at the bottom. A shadow appeared, then a pair of black shoes, causing a momentary panic, before a local newspaper crashed noisily through the letterbox and thudded onto the mat. The feet disappeared. Nothing stirred in the living room. David, his heart thumping, climbed the last few stairs into the hall. The door to the living room was open and tinted images danced and flickered across its highly varnished surface. Peering through the crack between the door and the jamb David saw his quarry slumped in a large off-yellow armchair, a glass of red wine teetering precariously in one hand. He was bare-footed and wearing black jeans and a dark blue "Boston Red Sox" T-shirt. Most important of all, he appeared to be asleep.

It was pitch dark in the church. A black intensity he had known once before in a tunnel in a distant time and remote place. It wasn't simply the loss of vision, the blinding, but the emptiness that made these moments unique, binding them together across the years. Humanity had been banished and Tony was alone. The old church door thudded shut behind him. He stood for a moment. Silence, a solid presence, weighed him down. St Botolph, the patron saint of wayfarers – they had only just celebrated his feast day – had deserted him but he ceased to care. His journey was almost over. He sank to his knees. Reaching out with his hands.

"It's here somewhere," he whispered.

The small brass handle felt surprisingly warm to the touch, he reached for the key hanging down the back of the cabinet, felt the thick dust, repellent to his searching fingertips, and the courseness of the string. The key slid easily into the lock, but refused to turn – back and forth – it required careful positioning before it would yield. Inside was the greasy bulk of a candle and, sitting on the shelf below, a full box of matches. His life proceeded in finite stages until the flowering of a flickering intimate light – molten wax hissing onto the stone flags – shut out the rest of the world more completely than the darkness had done, obliterating time.

He felt the smooth knife handle in his right hand and looked down at the dull sharp-pointed blade. Hiding the weapon behind his back he stepped out into the room. Larry Beckinsale didn't stir. A high corniced ceiling, wide sash-windows, off-white walls and varnished floorboards filled the space with a vacant airiness that David found pleasing. He admired the ornate grey marble fireplace, the tasteful abstract prints – or maybe they were originals, he wasn't sure – that dotted the walls, the fine Persian rug, the towering shelves of books, the bank of black hi-fi equipment. Suddenly edgily aware he turned. Larry Beckinsale's eyes were open.

He made his way cautiously towards the belfry, holding the candle ahead of him. The flame quivered, then almost died in the maelstrom of chill drafts whipping around the nave, before flaring back into fiery life when he shielded the guttering wick with his hand. Crazed shadows dipped around the stone pillars, skimmed across the wooden arches of the high vaulted ceiling, flitted past Tony and tripped out along the backs of pews before diffusing in the gloom. Eyes, red, blue and green blinked at him as he glided past the stained glass windows and their wrenching parables of saints and sinners. He had always enjoyed conducting the candlelit services, the coming together, the sense of wellbeing, the community feeling of the procession. This passage however was different, for the first time in his church Tony felt abandoned. He was frightened, sensing again the knot in his stomach, the muscular tightening of his frame, the gut terror, familiar from his street-fighting days. This was a mockery of parades past, present and future. This was hell on earth.

"What the …who are you?"
Rubbing his eyes, Larry Beckinsale sat rigidly in his chair, and peered at David in astonishment.
"What do you want? Who let you in? Is my wife back already? Dawn?"

He got to his feet and confronted David, his surprise turning to anger.

"Get out. I'm calling the police. You?"

He pulled himself up as he recognized the person standing in front of him.

"You're..."

David smiled faintly but said nothing.

"... from work. Um, what do you want? This is bloody irregular you know. I never see colleagues at home. You better have a damn good reason for coming here unannounced. How did you find out where I live by the way? I don't give out my address to just anybody. What's going on? You haven't said how you got in."

As he spoke his face assumed an expression of righteous anger tinged with contempt. It was a look familiar to David and many of his colleagues too, it was the look of a man who believed he was in control, the look of a man used to authority and wielding it. It was a look that collapsed into one of sheer terror as David stepped forward, knife in hand.

Three thick ropes looped out of the darkness above. Their yellow and blue striped towelling handles dangling hypnotically before his eyes, swaying in the demonic blasts of air. In the corner behind a curtain lay a pile of new bell ropes, bought with money collected at the summer fete – it had been the most successful for many years. A coil was heavier than he remembered and it was with difficulty that he hoisted one on to his shoulder, and staggered back into the nave. The rope was oily to the touch and smelled strongly – of linseed, cricket bats, warm summers, of women in light floral dresses, laughing as a gust of wind lifted the flimsy material briefly exposing white thighs to his eager adolescent gaze – his neck chaffed against the roughness of the rope and in his rush to reach the centre of the nave he almost extinguished the candle.

"More haste less speed," he found himself saying out loud. Then laughed. It was something his mother would have said and it was so banal, so inappropriate. Dumping the rope on the flags he hurried to his office in the vestry, placed the sputtering candle on top of the filing cabinet, watched as it settled then dimmed before flaming into life. He sat down at his desk and with trembling hands unwrapped the cellophane from a new packet of cigarettes, removed the silver paper and took out a single cigarette, placed it on the desk and then threw the box into the waste-paper basket.

"Yeessssss."

With difficulty he opened the box of matches that had lain there undisturbed since Albert had manoeuvred himself out of the church that afternoon, aided by a disdainful Peter, the squeal of his wheelchair, which he hadn't noticed earlier, piercing his ears like a needle, setting his teeth on edge. Picking up the cigarette he ran it between his fingers before bringing it slowly up to his nose. The seductive smell infused his unfamiliar body – aching arms and back, itching face, a sensitive scalp and a bloated stomach bulging uncomfortably over his belt – with yearning. When lit the rush of smoke lifted him temporarily, an all too brief high, before depositing him gently back into a freezing cold church in the middle of the night.

The blade passed easily through the thin cotton of Larry's designer T-shirt, assertively through the muscle wall of his stomach and into his intestines, meeting no resistance until it came to a jarring halt as the tip of the knife pierced one of his vertebrae. David was surprised and pulled out the knife. Larry stood there offering no resistance, just clutching his stomach with blood-stained hands, staring through bulging eyes and groaning in a strange constipated way, his cartoon mouth circular with surprise. Uncertain what to do next, David stared back, watching the stain spread rapidly across Larry's chest, obliterating the red lettering on the shirt. He could have stood there forever, but Larry lunged at him with a wild cry, his last act.

Opening his eyes, he stood up, slightly dizzy, stubbed out the cigarette in the overflowing ashtray, which he then carried carefully to the basket where he emptied it. The office was a mess and he tentatively began tidying the piles of papers and magazines that were strewn around the room. Then as quickly as he had begun he lost interest and wandered over to the curtains that divided his office from the nave. Parting the faded drapes he stared for an instant into the darkened body of the church, then returned for the candle and his chair.

David stabbed Larry over and over again, piercing his stomach, chest, arms, thighs, before dispatching him with one final thrust to the neck as his body collapsed to the floor. His Grandfather marched before him, a grey haired old man in a black shirt and shiny leather boots, his raised right arm outstretched in a salute. There were unfurled banners and the serried ranks of his fellow fascists were singing a marching song, the words indistinct, the melody dissonant but everyone was happy. They were cheering and clapping. David swore his Grandfather winked at him as he strode past. He hesitated then ran after him, slipping his hand into his. Other children were doing the same, joining the parade. The sun was shining.

Standing beneath an old age-blackened oak beam that ran the width of the nave, and from which traditionally every Easter was hung a wooden sculpture of the crucified Jesus on a cross, Tony carefully positioned his chair. The seat was covered in an ancient cane latticework and he worried that it would not support his weight. He'd sat on it for years at his desk and it had creaked and strained deliciously under his bulk, but he always used a red, purple and black floral patchwork cushion made by one of his parishioners, to spread the load. The cushion now lay discarded on the floor of the vestry. He was obsessed with this problem for a moment before abruptly deciding it was too late to go back for the cushion or another more robust chair.

Carefully grasping one end of the rope he uncoiled about half its length, looping it casually over his left forearm. He then climbed rather unsteadily onto the chair, which shifted position but held his weight. With a calm sense of deliberation, he looked up and began slowly to rotate the end of the rope, letting a length of it gradually slip through his hand as he did so. Judging everything to be as it should be he let go of the rope and it snaked upwards into the darkness. To his surprise it passed first time over the beam and slithered back down towards him. Perfect. In his eagerness to grab the running end he almost unbalanced and wobbled precariously on the chair.

"Bugger me," he gasped, "that was close."

A school playground far away and Tony and his best friends, Leonard and Frank, were tying knots in girls skipping ropes in the stinking boys' urinals, safe in a sanctuary where nobody would dare come looking for them. Reef knots, slip-knots and Frank's speciality, a sheepshank, Leonard pointed out that it sounded rude and everyone laughed. Tony's party-piece was a hangman's halter, which as he said "you never know when such a knot might come in handy." They had pulled a face at that one, then the bell had rung and they draped the noose over the water cistern above the leaking brass pipes and stained porcelain and run giggling back into Miss Govern's class. They were never caught, no one ever told on them.

The rope moved effortlessly through his hands, the memories were so vivid it could have been yesterday, a tear ran down his cheek. He wiped it away angrily and tested the knot. It was close to perfect, tight and compact, and the rope ran smoothly. He let it hang.

Measuring by eye he adjusted the length of the rope and then tied the bitter end tightly to a pew. Breathing heavily he stared at the noose in the flickering candlelight. He felt nothing but the thumping of his heart.

"Time to go. Fuck you, Anthony."

He folded his jacket and placed it on the ground, blew out the candle and in the pitch dark climbed on to the chair. Standing on the tips of his toes he placed the noose round his neck, carefully positioned the knot behind his left ear and tightened. Static everywhere, he wanted to hear, but there was nothing, only static, the hiss, the crashing of waves. He kicked the chair away. There was intense pain, a burning around his neck, building pressure behind his eyes, his tongue was swelling and the airway in his throat was crushed. He was unable to breathe.

"Oh God."

He reached up above his head with both hands, grabbed the rope and pulled with all his strength. Relief. He thought he saw a light, the faint flicker of an early dawn, heard a bird singing.

He could hold on no longer.

The drop.

Black.